THE

TÉUTA'S

CHILD

STUART G. ULLMAN

ISBN [eBook]: 979-8-9867610-0-8
ISBN [Paperback]: 979-8-9867610-1-5
ISBN [Hardcover]: 979-8-9867610-2-2
ISBN [Large Print]: 979-8-9867610-3-9

Library of Congress Control Number [LCCN]: 2022916338

Interior Design by Beth Martin.
Publishing Management by ⬤ BookWhisperer.ink

First Printing, 2022 – Stuart G. Ullman

This book is dedicated to Lola,
who lived 5700 years ago in what is now Denmark.
Although she lived distant from and long after
the characters in this story, her image,
as drawn by artist Tom Björklund and
published in the *National Geographic* magazine,
inspired my vision of Kaikos.

PROLOGUE:
WELO AND THE
NEOLITHIC EARTH

Long before Kaikos, before Chaisa or Sntejo, even before Prsedi—before any of the people in the new Téuta village—there was Welo the giant, and the curse of him lay miasmic across the whole of the Téuta. It lay across the village and across the people. It lay across the fields and across the mountains around them. Maybe it even lay across everything beyond.

And it lay with particular venom across the girl, the blind child; it wrapped thick around Kaikos. Twelve years old and small for her age, she looked harmless. But the curse contained her like a cocoon from which, even after all the tranquil years, an implacable anguish might still emerge.

Or so the Téuta people thought. So they felt, and the oldest among them had reason to feel it, although no one, not even Kaikos, could sense the curse. They couldn't taste it or touch it. They couldn't see it.

Kaikos, since it wasn't her nature to worry, ignored it most of the time and behaved as though it didn't exist. She played and hunted with Sntejo. She cared for her garden and did her chores without dwelling on the curse. Kaikos and her mother ate in their hut together in the evenings and bathed in the river together in the dark mornings without feeling the burden of it.

They swam hard in the mornings to warm themselves. The water they bathed in was cold because it was new from the mountains, and it was clean because the Téuta village was a half a morning's walk downstream from where they lived, so there was no one above them to soil it. In the autumn or the spring they ran back to their hut to stay warm in the cold morning air. Kaikos had reached the age when she could just outrun her mother, so now she had to slow from time to time to let Chaisa catch up.

The hunting, the running, the swimming all felt good. The air and the water felt good. Nearly everything felt good to her, so it was hard for Kaikos to remember the curse that the Téuta seemed to understand as a toxic mist seeping from Welo and flowing toward their village across time and distance. It was hard, since she was so young, to remember why they said so. To her, Welo seemed no more than an old story from a long-faded past.

And so he seems to us now. Both Welo and the events around him seem very far away, and the idea of curses seems to us like a social relic. We find it hard, in the modern world, to believe in things we can't calculate. An idea is real to us only if we can create mathematics to describe it. But there was a basis, a reason for their belief, that made sense to the Téuta so long ago.

The year that Welo was born, nearly 8300 years ago, a remnant of the Laurentide ice sheet collapsed in what is now North America, spilling trillions of tons of frigid fresh water into Hudson Bay, raising the level of the oceans by more than a meter, and causing abrupt and rapid global cooling. It's an interesting fact that the flow of water through the resulting gap was fifteen times greater than the flow of water from the Amazon River today. Still, it took more than a year to drain the meltwater sea that had been contained by the dam.

I want to be clear, since we have a very different experience with climate change in the modern world: this ancient event was no one's fault. We know now, in easy hindsight, that it was just one tiny episode in the long, turbulent way the earth works.

We can wonder, from eight millennia away, what impact the resulting dramatic climate change had on the lives of the people who lived on Earth then. We can wonder what Welo might have thought or done about it all, or what his descendants or any of the others around them did. I admit we can't truly know. Not in detail. Not at the level of the exact events of individual Neolithic lives. The archaeological record is not yet precise enough, not yet clear enough for that, and there's little reason to think it ever will be.

Because that's true we may still, to some extent, choose our own beliefs about this. We can create our stories.

The record does seem to show that life was troubled for people firmly fixed in stone age villages during that time. Seasons shifted; animals moved to warmer places; vegetation changed; rising seas and heavy rains created flooding and erosion—and all of this was piled on top of the more commonplace disasters, the volcanic eruptions and landslides and ordinary floods and all the rest, all the disruptions our restless, indifferent planet imposes on us. How did they react? It's easy to imagine that they searched hard for some reason for it, that they searched their history for something they had done to anger the various gods who, they thought, gave them the earth or the sky or the weather. This was the science of their time. They must have turned to it for answers.

For reasons that might be strange to us, but were clear enough to them, the people of the old Téuta village blamed Welo, and they fled from him and all the destruction around him. During the early time when chaos came to the old village, they thought it must have been him. It *must* have been: the cooling started when he was born, and he was different, a gangling, bony giant who stamped the earth, and who could see things that couldn't be seen. If he had been born in another year, before the cold, the rising water and the uneasy earth, or if he had seemed less odd, they might have thought of his abilities as a gift. His life, and Kaikos' life, might have been different.

But they couldn't explain what seemed to be constant misfortune. They needed someone or something they could blame for it, and Welo's odd, aloof boniness stood out like a fire in the night. His presence must have angered the gods, they thought. So they left him alone there to survive as best he could, and moved to lower, warmer ground where spelt and barley could grow across long fields and the game came down to the river to drink. They left Welo to become a bad memory, a frightening legend in Téuta history.

The cooling of the years slowed, a little. Life seemed steadier in the new village, and life seemed good. They grew complacent. Surely leaving Welo was enough, they thought. Surely moving the whole village, all the huts, the longhouse, the village wall, surely that was enough. They had come to a new place. They had dug deep structures into the ground near the river, built a temple there with many rooms, and each room decorated with the plastered skulls of auroch bulls that had been sacrificed for them. What more could the gods want?

When any new misfortune struck they felt shock. Welo, by then, was gone. When bad things happened, as they sometimes do, they needed something, or someone, nearer to the new village, the new Téuta, to blame. So they blamed Welo's granddaughter Chaisa, and Kaikos, his great-granddaughter. Kaikos was thought to be particularly cursed because she was small, because she was blind at birth, and because she, like Welo, seemed strange, seeming to sense things that couldn't be seen.

It wasn't fair. When did fair ever have anything to do with daily life? To us, looking at all this from such a great distance, knowing the modern science of the earth, it's obvious it wasn't *Welo* who caused the cooling, or Chaisa, or Kaikos. It was simply a natural result of an event far away, an event that was itself the natural result of the slow melting of massive ice sheets left over from this world's latest glaciation.

But when the gods seem angry—when the gods seem to be punishing the world and all that's in it—it isn't easy to be fair.

It didn't last forever, of course, or the world would still be frozen. After a little over seventy years the cooling stopped, and the earth—again abruptly and rapidly—began to warm, until it returned to its normal state and then continued the long, slow trajectory it had been following before the ice dam broke.

Welo would never get to see the warming time. He would have been seventy-three years old the year the warming began, which is a ponderous age for a Neolithic man. But after a long and difficult life Welo's health had withered. His life ended with an almost trivial illness early that spring.

But the death of Welo and the warming earth is a story for another time. Let's not run too far ahead. Let's slow down to let Kaikos, Chaisa and Sntejo, and even Prsedi, catch up to us.

PART I

Late Summer on the Plains
6192 BCE

CHAPTER ONE

ⅢⅢ

"Kaikos, slowly! Be careful," Chaisa called out after her daughter, but laughed even before she said it because she knew it was no use. Kaikos burned the joyful, eager energy of childhood. And Chaisa's shouted caution to her daughter was only habit; she didn't really worry about her blind child running hard across the earth. She knew that somehow Kaikos could sense everything around her.

So Kaikos ran, racing up the slope toward home. Chaisa ran too, but Kaikos ran faster, and Kaikos had cheated at the start. She had simply scooped up her belt and waistcloth from the ground and started off straight out of the water, fastening her clothing around her on the run, while Chaisa, laughing about Kaikos' boldness, took the time to quickly dress before she started. The distance between them had extended far enough that Chaisa had to call loudly for Kaikos to hear her. But there was no slowing her daughter now, refreshed in the dark by her swim in the river, and now running in the cool, clean morning with the sun already awake.

Chaisa watched her daughter's dark, late-summer back as she ran ahead, watched the small humps of muscle in it shift from side to side as her arms moved with running. Kaikos ran until she reached the hut, then she turned her face to the sun to catch its warmth and waited for her mother.

How could Raghe even think about killing something so wonderful? Chaisa thought, remembering how close that danger had come. Remembering how close it still could be if the issue had not been submerged by neglect, buried beneath the placid rhythm of daily life. But not gone. It was not gone. The layer of neglect that lay over it was not so thick that it couldn't be broken.

Some dream in the night had pushed this memory toward her, so as she ran her mind strayed back to the time of her daughter's birth, the time before Kaikos even had a name. The shaman had wanted to kill her, probably at her birth, but certainly a week later, and by then he had many who agreed with him. It had taken Chaisa only hours to know her baby was blind. After a week everyone knew.

A child born blind was a bad omen, a curse from the gods, Raghe had said, and as shaman he was an authority on gods and curses. And on death. He seemed to like it, Chaisa told herself bitterly as she ran.

Chaisa brushed Raghe from her mind and watched her daughter.

When she reached the hut Chaisa put an arm around Kaikos' shoulders, and they walked toward the doorway of the hut, both still laughing and warm from their run and still slightly damp from their river-bath.

"I'm hungry this morning," Kaikos said.

But it was late. The sun's lower edge was fully above the horizon when they reached the door.

"Get started on your work, Kaikos. I'll bring bread out to you when it's done. It won't take long; the stones are hot, and the dough is ready."

The hut seemed close and warm when she entered. Chaisa, coming in from the bright early sunlight, waited a moment for her eyes to adjust to the room where the only light was from the small door, the firepit and, dimly, the smoke hole in the roof. She had put some moss and dry dung on the fire and blown it to life when she woke, and she had added some wood just before they left for their bath. She had mixed water and wheat and barley flours, and a little salt, the night before; the dough was waiting in a crock. Now she only needed to form the flat loaves and put them on the stones.

While she worked her mind still watched the girl running ahead of her. The vision made her happy, so she added some walnuts to the dough to please Kaikos. Bathing and running were good, the first cold and the second warm, and she had the pleasure of both still with her. But her mind was restless. While she waited to turn the bread her mind returned to that danger time, twelve years ago. She didn't want the thought, but she couldn't stop it. She often remembered that single moment, in her mind the most important moment, the most important single act of her life.

Even then Raghe had seemed to love death. Bulls and babies, the strong and the weak: death, the shaman said, to prevent greater death. Death to preserve the living. So when the rumors came to her that Raghe was on his way to take her child, Chaisa had done the only thing that she could do: she lifted her naked baby up from the ground and ran hard toward Prsedi. Only Prsedi could stand against the shaman.

She came without warning into Prsedi's hut, hardly aware of the flagrant impertinence of approaching the woman without permission or any gestures of courtesy. Prsedi was honored and important among the Téuta, and even more so among those who lived outside the wall. Prsedi was old, even then more than forty years, and Chaisa was young; Prsedi spoke to gods and they spoke back to her, and Chaisa was just another Téuta woman with no distinction. She had always kept a respectful distance from Prsedi before that moment. But Chaisa had ducked through Prsedi's door on the run without thinking of any of that.

Prsedi had barley flour on her wrists and bread dough in her hands, and when she turned to see who had come there was that single moment that returned to Chaisa again and again: Chaisa simply put the baby in Prsedi's arms as she turned.

Of course Prsedi was startled, and of course she was charmed; how else could she respond to the surprise discovery that she was holding a baby? Prsedi couldn't keep from covering this sudden child with flour, and even a little sticky wet dough on the child's ribs. She had dropped the dough into Chaisa's waiting hands, and Chaisa flattened it and went to the firepit to put it on Prsedi's oven stones then, which was why making bread now reminded her of that moment. She had been embarrassed to keep Prsedi from her breakfast, but there was nothing else she could do.

When Raghe finally realized where the baby was and came through the door of Prsedi's hut, ready to demand that the baby be given over to him, Prsedi was sitting with the baby in her lap, smiling and stroking the baby's feet to watch her toes flare. She was absorbed in that diversion.

"It belongs to me."

The voice was abrupt and abrasive in the small room, and Raghe stood just inside the doorway looking entitled, looking imperious, and looking directly at Chaisa—and the room became very still. Prsedi's laughter stopped before her head rose to look at him. When she did raise her eyes, Raghe stepped back to press his shoulders against the wall above the doorway. Those who had gathered outside, crouching to look through the entrance, stepped back too. It was a shock to them. Prsedi was never angry, and no one in the village thought she could ever be fierce, but the fierce anger in her face when she looked at Raghe would have frightened a leopard.

Raghe recovered from that first fright, though, and stepped forward again to assert his rights. "The baby is mine," he insisted.

Prsedi had almost laughed at that, but her fierceness never left her.

"Stop staring at Chaisa, Raghe, as hard as that might be for you. Look at me." She waited for him to do that, to turn to her, so she could see his eyes when she continued.

"This baby is not yours, Raghe, in any sense, although I know you wish it were yours in every sense. Don't deny it; everyone has seen how you watch Chaisa whenever you walk outside the village wall. But resenting the mother is not a reason to kill the child."

"You know that's not what is happening, Prsedi. You were there. *We* were there. We know what the gods can do."

He paused, looking at the baby in Prsedi's arms, and continued, "The child is blind, Prsedi. It will be a burden to us as it grows, but even that is not the worst. It's a cursed child. Cursed. It's Welo's family, born blind; you know it's cursed. We don't want it among the Téuta, among the people, to curse the rest of us; we don't want Chaisa's curse to stay among us to make other women bear blind children. And we don't want to anger the gods again. You may regret the loss of a single child, but better the loss of one life than the lives of all the Téuta. You know that. You know it must come to me. I'll get Krepus to enforce this."

Prsedi had smiled at that and relaxed a little. Krepus, at least, was not a fanatic.

She knew Raghe watched Chaisa only partly because he found her attractive, but also because he was afraid of her. He was afraid of everything that raised his memory of the old Téuta, of what had happened there. So perhaps her accusation had been a little unfair to Raghe. But only a little, and he needed that. No one else could stand up to him except Krepus, and Krepus rarely did. Raghe needed to be brought to earth sometimes.

"Yes, good. Get him," Prsedi said, and Raghe left.

Krepus, when he came with his strong young friend Sntejo, darkened the doorway as he squeezed his shoulders to get through it. Sntejo, behind him, was also big, but not so big that he blocked all light; he was a smaller, younger and happier version of the Téuta leader. Krepus was irritable, as he often was, and stood with his usual frown looking over the scene. He had been pulled from other business, other demands of leadership, at the request of Raghe, his shaman, his speaker-to-gods. But he knew Raghe was not the only one who spoke to them. Prsedi spoke every day to Dhegm, the earth, the mother. It wasn't his purpose to anger Dhegm. It wouldn't help the Téuta to do that.

Krepus consulted briefly with Sntejo, who responded with some unexplained and whispered vehemence, then chose diplomacy rather than decision. He found a compromise between his god-speakers, between Prsedi and the shaman: Prsedi and Chaisa would keep the child; they would guarantee it would add no burden to the Téuta. But Chaisa must leave the village, so that this child didn't live among the Téuta, so that if there was a curse at least it was a curse far away. "Go a proper distance away", he said, "and take the blind child with you."

Krepus softened when he looked at the baby and had asked what her name was. Chaisa hadn't chosen a name yet. Krepus watched the baby for a moment and called her "kaikos" meaning only that she was blind, and Prsedi smiled at the word. And so Kaikos it was; a strange name, but one given by the king, and blessed by Prsedi.

Krepus asked Sntejo to walk with Chaisa and Kaikos when they left so Raghe's adherents wouldn't attack them on the way. Sntejo and Chaisa left without waiting, before Raghe could protest; she left her hut behind, with everything in it. Better to be far from the village while Krepus' decision was fresh. Sntejo said he would bring what he could from her hut over the next weeks. And after a long walk they found a place near the river but hidden behind some hills, so the Téuta didn't have to be reminded of her every day.

While they walked Chaisa talked with Sntejo, for no reason other than that he was there. It felt strange to speak so casually to him. He was close to Krepus, the king. He lived inside the wall, and she did not, so she only knew him a little. She was nervous talking to him. But she was also grateful.

"Thank you for saving my child," she said. "I know you spoke for her."

"She's beautiful," Sntejo replied.

Chaisa looked at him then, a little puzzled. "You're not afraid of her curse?"

"Prsedi wouldn't have held her or defended her like that if she were cursed."

"And Raghe? You're not afraid of him?"

"Maybe that. He has power. But I—I don't like Raghe."

"Why?"

But Sntejo simply walked ahead with a sour look. He didn't want to talk about why he didn't like the shaman. Chaisa had not asked him again then, and she had never asked in all the time since then. It seemed a long time. Twelve years.

And now Kaikos was nearing the end of childhood, bright and quick, and it made Chaisa happy just to watch her run. Still blind. Nothing would change that. But she ran without any concern about what might be in her way; she knew what was in her way and ran around it.

How she knew was a little mysterious. She sensed things. Chaisa knew the word Kaikos used to explain her sense. "Bholos" she said. Chaisa could never completely understand what that meant. It was something like fog settling into the landscape. But Kaikos couldn't see the landscape, so what she sensed was this fog with the landscape's shape under it. Chaisa couldn't really envision it, but she accepted it. She believed the words. She believed them because Kaikos proved them every day.

Kaikos sat on the far side of the hut and began her task for the day. After a time, Chaisa brought the barley bread with walnuts out for her, and a little honey to dip the bread in. She brought a woven grass shawl too, to keep Kaikos warm in the early morning. They sat and talked in the sun while they ate.

When they were finished Chaisa went in to begin her own work, and she sang to herself.

Inside again, tidying the area near the firepit, she thought again about Prsedi and Raghe. They were not friendly with each other before that encounter, the moment when Kaikos' life or death was decided. An old difference, a leftover grievance from the old Téuta, gnawed at them. But after that day there was animosity between them, because Raghe still wanted death for Kaikos, and Prsedi still wanted life for the baby she had covered with barley flour before it had a name.

Chaisa wasn't happy about the animosity. What was the good of it? What was ever the good of it? But she did not regret the action she took that created it. Prsedi's friendship, and Sntejo's, had come from that moment, and both had high value. Chaisa felt honored by them. But it was still true that Prsedi's goodness and Krepus' decency were all that stood in Raghe's way. Chaisa watched the balance of power between them carefully; a little change, a little carelessness, might give to Raghe what he had wanted for so long.

Again Chaisa shook her head to brush all the old memories from her mind. Prsedi was far away. Raghe was far away. But here—here there was Kaikos, alive and quick and young, quietly working just outside the hut.

CHAPTER TWO

Stone bed and black around him and his mind musty still from mushroom sleep, Raghe woke from a dream of his sister's last hard-running moment, watching her come as fast as she could toward him, toward safety, but too late. He closed his eyes tight, but she still ran toward him. He had been always her safe place. He watched, grieving her even before her death, grieving even as he ran fast and left her behind him, since he knew he couldn't save her.

When he was out from under it, he turned to look, to hope. But there was no hope. She ran, then and forever, toward him on her small legs; she ran until that huge rock smashed the ground and she was gone. Everything under it was unalterably gone. He had been too weak to save her—too weak and too afraid to stop a falling cliff.

Even in the thick stillness of his room, the only opening a crawl hole into another black room, he could tell it was night outside. He could feel the clean night breeze even though the air in this room was smoky and still. He could feel the whole sleeping town around him, and the river below him, and the cold in the mountains, and the high ice, and he wanted none of it. He wanted his sister. He wanted that last moment back. Maybe. Or maybe he didn't even want that.

No. He knew what he wanted, what he always wanted, what he had wanted every day since the cliffs fell. He wanted fear to go away. He wanted grief to go away.

He wanted remorse to go away.

What time was it? Darkest night, as it always was in this room, and darkest night outside, dawn still far away. He could feel it. But outside at least there was a moon to help light the world.

"A full moon," he said into the stillness, "bath day, and after bath I visit the dead."

He wanted to say he would see her there. He knew better. No matter how many times he went to the land of the dead, no matter how hard he searched, he never found her. She could have come to him if she had wanted to. She never did.

He crawled through to the next room to wake one of the young, one of his acolytes, to get the sap lamps ready and to help him prepare. It was too early, but he had nothing to do in the hours before the sun rose. So the boy came to watch for him. They started the fire in the outer room, steeped the mushrooms and had their tea.

Raghe didn't leave his body in the night, but he dozed, and he had great visions in his mushroom sleep. He had visions of Krepus and Sntejo, and of Chaisa, and of her daughter who had no shape in his mind, who still in his vision was an infant. He had visions of the past and of the future, and of safety, and of death which was safety's only other name.

Something was changing. Something was changing. He smiled at his dream of death, and of Chaisa, and the sense of change all around him.

He dozed until the boy woke him for the day.

CHAPTER THREE

It wasn't the wind over the peak that caused the tenuous snow to break apart in the night, that made part of it buckle and tumble down along the slope; that was caused by something else. The blameless air simply dropped over the remaining snow-crust, slipping down the mountain across the stretched ice, and settling into the steep-sided canyons where the river had cut the rock away. Through the wreck of the old Téuta the wind blew, through the few crumbling hut-walls that remained thirty years after the cliff fell over the whole of the town center and over two-thirds of the town's people. On and on it blew down the long, ruffled, rocky water.

When the river broadened at the mountain's base, the air rode over the foothills like a tide. It spilled out of the river channel and across the plains, and the ground, still warm from yesterday's sun, mellowed it. It moved on, past the hills, past the trees along the riverbanks, through the fields of grasses, and around the lonely hut a half morning's walk from the new Téuta village, until it arrived at the cursed girl, Kaikos, working in the bright early morning, quiet and happy at her chore.

The air cooled her and pestered her dark hair, but nothing in it told Kaikos about the fleeting snowslide in the mountains. None of her senses warned her that impalpable coils shaped by gods or fates had tightened just a little more firmly around her. She didn't feel them. She had never felt them, so she worked untroubled by them.

Summer was past, finally, so the wakening day was fresh and chill. In summer even the mornings were hot. Today Kaikos kept her shawl close around her shoulders. She thought about going in to get a heavier skin to keep herself warm; the shawl of woven grass was not enough, really. But she liked the cold after the long summer. Her eyes, startling green against the brown of her face, seemed to gaze into the distance. Kaikos saw nothing though, except the single thing she could see without eyes.

Kaikos was content listening to the sound of the wind weaving through the rocks that made a corner of the hut she lived in, and to her mother singing softly inside tending to whatever tasks she had there, and to the insects in the garden, and the grasses in the fields. She swayed very slightly back and forth hearing these things, even though that made her task a little more complicated. It was hard for her to keep completely still when she listened to all the music around her.

The years were good, Kaikos thought. This day was good. On days like this the world seemed safe, even though they lived so far outside the safety of the village wall. Kaikos tried to be alert for danger in this lonely place, but it was hard to stay vigilant when the wide eternal world was so sweet. On days like this she was glad they lived far outside the village. There were many smells in the village, some good but others not at all good, and there were many sounds. And even though there was danger here, Chaisa said that for them the dangers inside the village wall were even greater.

They were not allowed inside the wall, Kaikos remembered. That was something she had been told so often that she always remembered it, even when she didn't think about it. Raghe, the shaman, told the old story that just by living Kaikos and Chaisa brought trouble to the Téuta, and inside the wall there were many who believed whatever Raghe said. So Kaikos was glad to be far outside the wall. She was glad for the solitude and the quiet here, and for the smell of the fire from inside the hut, and for the clean earth, and for Chaisa singing to her alone.

The singing became louder as Chaisa stepped out of the hut. She turned and said, "I'll be working with the pots today, Kaikos."

That meant Chaisa would be on the other side of the hut at the big oven where she fired things she made from clay. She made them to trade for what they needed. Pots and salt that had collected around a spring of salty water hidden in the hills; those were the two things Chaisa had that she could trade. They were enough.

Chaisa was letting Kaikos know where she would be, but she didn't need to. Kaikos always knew where Chaisa was. It also meant that Chaisa might not hear if Kaikos called to her, and that Kaikos would be alone with her thoughts for a while.

"Okay," Kaikos said, her face still seeming to look toward something in the distance.

Her mother had set Kaikos to clean the grain today, and for the days ahead until the task was done, which was a good thing. She liked tossing the grain. The chaff made her sneeze sometimes, but it smelled delicious; she could smell the coming winter's bread in it.

There were many tasks Kaikos was not allowed to do because of her blindness. But she could thresh, which was fun, and she could winnow. Chaisa didn't let her grind the grain, though, on the great flat grinding stone near the fire-pit oven. She couldn't see the soft flour or hear it when it fell, so she spilled too much valuable flour off the edges. The whole grain kernels were bigger and easier. They sounded hard, they made a tacking sound in the bowl but sounded like a puff when they fell to the ground. Even blind she had learned to make the grain always fall back into the bowl, and that was all that mattered.

When the grain felt clean enough in her hands Kaikos took her bowl to show to Chaisa behind the hut and the grain was taken inside and poured into the great clay pot near the back of their hut for storage. Kaikos took her bowl outside and filled it again with new grain to clean.

By mid-morning the heat had come, and the sun was hot, so Kaikos folded the shawl and draped it over her lap under her bowl of grain. After the cold in the early day the sun felt good on the bare of her back and legs. From time to time Kaikos paused to brush the chaff off her face and shoulders, and all of her back that she could reach. On late summer days when she was sitting outdoors like this everything smelled musty-sweet, the world was clean, the sun was hot and the breeze from the mountains cooled her. Kaikos rolled the grain in her hand. It was rough against her palms, and that roughness seemed to match Chaisa's song behind the hut.

So, absorbed in the luxury of her senses, Kaikos barely noticed when a single dusty shaft of bholos sprang from the ground, as though a tall stalk of late summer grass grew to full height in an instant, and then dissolved in the gentle autumn breeze and blew away. But she turned toward it when another shaft sprouted up beside it and dissolved in the ceaseless drifting of the air.

Her eyes might be blind, but she could sense bholos, the gray dust that no one else saw, that others sometimes said was the stuff of spirits. Sometimes, when people near the village wanted to taunt her, they asked her to describe what she saw in it and to tell them whether what she saw was the spirit animals that lived in the shadows under the world or whether they were those that lived in the light above the world.

Kaikos told them that spirits had nothing to do with it, that bholos was just stuff like any other stuff. To her there was nothing mysterious about it. There was nothing important. It was just a dim gray sense of something that clustered near objects and blew through empty spaces. It helped her, a little, to get around, and to not run into things. It clustered all swirly around people or living things and helped her know who was near her. But no one else could see bholos, so to them, if there was any truth in it at all, it must be a view of a different world, a world of spirits, or of something more interesting than dust.

Because she had this, the other sense, the other sight, she could sense the two shafts of bholos that no one else in the Téuta could ever see. Two shafts. That was all for the whole morning.

She paused, briefly, when it happened, and wondered what would cause that. It wasn't much, two sprouts from the ground, but it was all that was needed to alert Kaikos that something unusual had happened. Bholos had never done this that she could remember. Still, she was young, and she knew she was young. Maybe it was nothing. Or something that just happened from time to time.

She waited. No more shafts came up just then, so she sat and did her work. She felt the sun on her skin and listened to her world.

Chaisa would sing through the morning. Chaisa's voice was like the flight of a hawk, Kaikos thought, although she had never really seen a hawk flying. Most of the time they flew too high for her to follow with her sense. To her they were solitary arcs of bholos in the sky, appearing from nothing and returning to nothing, but always alone. Kaikos thought her mother's voice, singing behind the hut, was like that.

In a few weeks, after all the grain had been cleaned and stored, the Téuta, the whole village, would have a party. She and Chaisa were allowed to go to that. Not deep into the village itself, never inside the village wall, since their presence there would be an offense to the gods. Raghe said so, and it was probably true because he spoke often to the gods, and sometimes to the dead. But Kaikos and Chaisa were allowed to go near the edge of the village for the party.

Perhaps they would venture in as far as Prsedi's hut. Sntejo would bring them roasted meat and bread and barley beer, and everyone would be happy for a day. Kaikos would eat a lot but drink very little except water from the river. Too much beer made her dizzy. Maybe for people who could see that felt good, but Kaikos couldn't see with her eyes so to her it just felt lost.

After twelve winters and twelve summers Kaikos had the years figured out. Winter was hard; spring was happy and there were celebrations then too; summer was work. But the end of summer felt the best. The spring celebrations were just relief after the winter, but all the year's work was still ahead of them. The autumn celebrations were because the work was done, the heat was done, and months of cool friendly weather lay ahead before the deep cold came again. There was still work—that they always had—but it was different work: making tools, repairing huts or firepits or replacing pots, and also hunting and drying meat and cleaning skins so they could keep warm when winter came, and other things that could be done in their own time. But Dhegm pushed the grain from the ground on her schedule, and the work of caring for it and harvesting it had to be done to suit her, not to suit the Téuta.

In the early afternoon three more bholos-weeds sprang up and scattered, then later another, and then they stopped for a while. Then five came up in a few seconds, and the bholos settled again.

But Kaikos didn't. After the day of sprouting bholos something hurt in her chest. Kaikos worked, but nothing felt as good anymore. Not the sun and not the wind. She put her grass shawl over her shoulders to shade her back in the afternoon and tossed the grain, but her mind wasn't on the work. She stretched her sense out to find the slightest oddness. There was none that she could feel. The bholos seemed quiet. It seemed ordinary, as it always felt.

Her mother was singing aloud now, singing like the smell of new rain in the hills, singing like a fox hunting.

Kaikos waited, and she watched everything around her with her othersight. Her hands moved without her, moving by habit through her bowl of grain.

Chaisa came out of the hut with a spear and walked toward the river to try to find a fish for their dinner. Kaikos meant to call to her, would have called to her, but she wasn't sure what she would say. She felt a tension that needed advice from an adult, but she couldn't explain why even to herself. Trying to tell Chaisa would be a long confusion. Chaisa would just be short with her in the end. "Work needs to be done," Chaisa would tell her, "and I need to fish or we will be hungry tonight."

Late in the cooling day a flurry of bholos shafts shot from the earth in the direction of the village, and another flurry on the other side of her hut, toward the river. Then strange quiet again, quiet, quiet, the unquiet bholos spread out across the ground, and Kaikos waited, tense and watchful—and suddenly there were sprouts of bholos everywhere. They spurted from the earth and blew away, and others spurted up to replace them, thousands of them all around her. The whole of the plain was thick with them.

Kaikos placed her bowl on the ground. Her shawl fell to the ground too when she stood. She turned a full circle, and again, and everywhere, in all directions, tall stalks of bholos bloomed and blew away and bloomed over again. The ground was covered with them as far as her othersight could reach.

She waited and watched, wishing Chaisa were there, wishing this storm would pass. It didn't. For as long as she stood to watch it the storm went on and on, a huge field of bholos gushing up from the ground. Her chest still felt tight, nervous, as though there were a thunderstorm, but there were no sounds at all except the soft sifting and purling of the breeze around the corners of the hut. Even the insects were quiet.

She was certain then that something was wrong. And she knew she alone could see this, the bholos jumping from the ground as high as her head. Kaikos watched, trying to understand what she was seeing, but she had never seen anything at all like this before, so she had nothing to guide her thoughts. Nothing about this storm made sense.

She wanted Chaisa. Or Sntejo. She wanted some adult to talk to.

But Sntejo was nowhere near, and Chaisa was still fishing.

Whatever the bholos was doing she knew the grain had to be cleaned now, before winter came and made it impossible. She retrieved her shawl and bowl, and she sat down to work again. She worked into the evening, but it was like working in a fog, or under an ocean, with bholos from the dissolving shafts drifting around her in the slow-moving air.

In the evening, when she finished her work for the day, she watched Chaisa return from the river. By then she could feel tension if she put the palm of her hand on the ground. She wanted to cry out to Chaisa, but her tension held her and made her silent. Chaisa entered the hut with two fish in a sack and began to rustle inside, adding dry dung to make the fire bigger for the night.

Kaikos thought in silence and felt the weight of blame about what only she could see. Had she done this? Were the spirit animals under the world so angry with her, after all this time? Was Dhegm so angry with her?

"Are you angry, Dhegm? Is that what this bholos-grass means?" she said out loud, although nothing but the wind heard her.

She couldn't think of anything she had done to anger them. But she had never known. She had done nothing. There was no reason for the gods to be angry except the old story of Welo, a giant she had never seen, who lived a very long time ago, very far from here, but who sired Chaisa's mother, her grandmother. For that crime, the village said, Dhegm had made Kaikos blind when she was born. Kaikos didn't know.

"If that is it, if blindness is a punishment for something Welo did, then why is Chaisa not blind?" she asked the wind, "And if my great grandfather was a giant why am I so small?"

The whole village would not be wrong about this, so it must be true. But Kaikos had always wondered about the story. She had never felt any anger from Dhegm. The opposite, really. If the gods even knew she existed it felt to Kaikos like they were glad of it, and Dhegm more so than any of the others. The earth, the soil, had always felt to Kaikos like a friend before this.

Yes. Before this. Before today. Now the ground really did feel angry when she touched it, and bholos gushed out of it toward the sky like a heavy rain falling up instead of down.

There was more. Now that she watched the ground instead of her grain, she saw the storm was not all there was to see. Bholos usually covered the ground like dust on water. That was how Kaikos knew where to put her feet when she walked. But now as she watched with her othersight the film of bholos over the ground began to craze. There were cracks forming along the surface, wandering along the ground around her. They were tiny cracks, cracks in the bholos only not in the ground. The ground felt whole when she put her hand on it. But Kaikos couldn't see the ground. She could only see the bholos. Now there were fissures where the bholos was not there. To Kaikos it looked as though the universe was breaking into pieces and leaving only emptiness behind.

She held her bowl tightly, pressed against her legs. What was happening? The evening around her was pleasant; the wind still rustled the grasses, the river splashed peacefully. It flowed sweetly in its bed.

And the world was breaking.

She went inside again, bringing the day's last bowl of clean grain, to tell Chaisa about the bholos, and to ask her what to do.

CHAPTER FOUR

𝍩

Morning was no more than a dark burnish on the eastern hills when Sntejo woke and rolled off his sleeping mat. Kaikos and Chaisa, he thought, were still bathing in the river; it had become habit after so many years to think of them first in the morning, and he knew their morning habits well.

The sun was still only a promise, but the wind was awake. The same long wind that blew past Chaisa's distant hut, past the two women and the river they bathed in, made a vortex along the Téuta village wall to lift itself over, dropping down on the other side where it eddied and tumbled along the ground between the huts. It found no people there at that hour. Only the early risers were awake, and none of those were in the streets yet. Most were at their breakfasts.

When Sntejo ducked through the door of his small hut the streets were empty, but the morning smelled already of bread and porridge, and, sharper but scarcer and more distant, of fish and mutton roasting in firepit ovens. The heat of the summer had waned, but rain had not come for many days so he also smelled dust in the air, and dried grass laying on the ground somewhere, a little damp this cool morning with dew. He looked to the east toward the lifting day,

toward the edge of morning, toward dawn, and waited to welcome
that goddess again to the world.

His sense of beauty didn't last beyond that single moment in the
thin light. Turning toward the longhouse ended it, not because of
the work he and Krepus would undertake that day, but because of
a sight that always disturbed him: the sight of Raghe, who had just
emerged from his temple and was walking toward the town wall,
toward the gate that opened to the world and to the river.

This must be the shaman's morning to bathe for this month, Sntejo
thought. In fact he should have remembered. He should have
expected to see Raghe, who bathed, always and only, and briefly
at best, on the morning after the full moon. The thick smell of old
sweat, burnt sap and boiled dung-mushroom preceded Raghe and
trailed after him as he passed.

Raghe was only a few steps away, though, when unexpectedly
he turned, with his strange eyes and oily hair, and spoke. He spoke
directly to Sntejo. Raghe rarely spoke, and when he did what he said
made little sense anymore, or at least he said little that made sense to
Sntejo. *After so much talk with the gods*, Sntejo thought, *Raghe finds
conversation with ordinary people to be too strenuous.*

"Remember you have no place there, Sntejo, no place in the dark
with all the gods, or with any gods," Raghe said as though this were
an important fact Sntejo might forget. Raghe stared with the huge
black centers of eyes that didn't blink, so long that Sntejo became
restless from watching them, before he continued, "When she comes
with Krepus in her hand you have no place there."

"What does that mean, Raghe?"

But the shaman only glared at him, half angry and half afraid.
Then Raghe turned and walked away toward his morning bath.

Sntejo watched him go until he walked through the gate, wondering what ugly fantasy the man was rambling on about. When
who came with Krepus? Was this the old dispute? Was this his old
obsession with Kaikos? Did the gods tell him Krepus would at

last bring Kaikos to him, after twelve years of waiting for her? Or twenty, or fifty? Was this a vision of some distant future?

Raghe usually didn't speak to Sntejo at all, so this was an extraordinary eloquence from him today, as though he sensed something new in the tumbling wind. Raghe was strange enough that anything was possible. Maybe he was talking about something else completely. The man was a shaman, so this could be real. But he was also a little crazy and filled with sap-smoke, and he had become crazier over the long years living in the smoky dark of his back rooms, so this could be babble.

Sntejo wanted to understand Raghe, but he didn't. He wanted to feel sympathy, with Raghe and with all the others who had been in the old Téuta on that day thirty years ago—not only there but old enough to really feel what had happened. Prsedi had been there, he thought, and she seemed normal, or at least she seemed at peace. Two or three times in his life, when someone she cared about was threatened, he had seen Prsedi rise to an anger that showed the pain of her loss that day. Then she could be harsh, not quiet with the world. Apart from those few times she was always tranquil, always glad of life.

But Prsedi was the rare exception. Of those who had been there some had simply become silent, with lips compressed. Some had found solace in too much beer. Some had become obsessed with work. All of them, he thought, had lost the sense of hertus, the sense that the universe was in balance. For them all balance was taken in a few minutes thirty years ago. Retrieving it seemed to be very hard.

Raghe, too, had his response to the loss of hertus, which was to become continually stranger, to let his mind leave this world. *A shaman without balance is dangerous*, Sntejo thought.

Raghe lived now in his world of sap smoke and mushrooms. He lived now only with the gods and the dead. He lived apart from the living Téuta.

Sntejo couldn't spend his life worrying about anything as tangled as Raghe's thoughts.

The old shaman walked on, and Sntejo watched him. So did the others who happened to be up and emerging from their doors at that time. Many did so kneeling and facing the ground, giving him honor.

This, too, disturbed Sntejo. As Raghe's reputation as a speaker to the gods rose among the Téuta, his power rose also, and it had been rising steadily over the same long years that had distilled his strangeness. Awe of Raghe challenged Krepus, who was still, for now, the leader among them. But even now the balance was uncertain; Krepus was stronger, and better known, and better liked, but Raghe spoke to gods and the dead. Sntejo was well aware of Raghe's small army of worshipers. If it came to a contest of wills between Raghe and Krepus it wasn't clear anymore whose side the Téuta would take.

For now the balance was determined by the physical: Raghe was much smaller than Krepus, and was afraid of him, so there would never really be a contest of wills between them that fell to the Téuta as a whole to resolve. For that, Sntejo was grateful. Raghe, trapped in the bewildered world of his gods, would do anything at all, no matter how terrible, to rid the Téuta of Welo's curse. Only Krepus and Sntejo, and most importantly, Prsedi, stood between the shaman and the sacrifices he wanted.

That was one reason Sntejo didn't like him. There were others. Deep in the packed ground beneath the doorway into Raghe's public space, a doorway so tall that even Krepus could walk through it standing, lay three infants, whose bodies guarded and sanctified the space. At least that was what Raghe said. One was dead at birth, one might have been dead either at birth or soon after—no one really knew; Raghe had the body before anyone else saw it. And one, Sntejo knew, was sacrificed alive there in the doorway. It was sacrificed to various gods as Raghe had asked. All three infants were wrapped tightly in woven flax cloth, even the one who was still living, and all were carefully placed deep in the hole over which the door was to be built. They were placed there so that anyone entering that space had to cross over them. And beneath the opening to the inner chambers, beneath the crawl area, were two more infants buried deep.

Sntejo was eight years old when that happened. He had been in the longhouse, close enough to hear the living child still crying loudly as dirt was piled onto her. Every time Sntejo saw Raghe walk out into the town proper he thought of them, the children Raghe took to mollify the anger of the gods, because that sound, the crying of the living child, was still clear in Sntejo's memory. Everything from that moment was still clear; he remembered how the longhouse smelled, how the dust looked in the light at the doorway.

He had understood even then that the gods mattered, and that the dead did pass by the gods as they journeyed to the land provided for them. But when he thought about the doorway he wondered: why infants? He could understand better the sacrifice of adults who had either volunteered or were carefully chosen. Why would infants be more suited to guard doorways than anyone else? He had asked Raghe about that later in that day, the day of the sacrifice of infants.

"You see what has happened, Sntejo," Raghe had said back then. "You see what power infants have over us. What power that infant whom you had never seen before already has over *you*."

Those words were from a younger, more lucid Raghe, back when Sntejo could understand him. The sacrifice of the infants still bothered him. He could still hear that child crying as she was buried, after so many years had passed. It was a sentiment he didn't understand. He had it nevertheless, and it had power. Still, no matter how much power infants had in the world, would burying them in doorways help anything?

When he thought about his own eventual trip to the land of the dead, whenever it happened, he wondered whether he would spend the whole of his time watching doorways among the Téuta. Maybe he would. He didn't know. But he did know the dead rarely intervened in any obvious way in his own daily life, or at least not in ways that were obvious to him.

When he made bricks of mud and straw he felt the mud in his own hands and lifted the weight of the bricks with his own arms. When he hunted he drew the bow back with his own muscle and aimed with his own eyes. When he was in the hills outside the town he felt alone with the whole wild tumult of the world. Dyeus and Perkunos and Dhegm might be there; they *were* there. He could *feel* them there, in fact, feeling each god in his or her own way. But he felt no dead around him.

Sntejo was not a shaman, though. He knew little about these things. That Raghe knew far more about the gods, and about the land of the dead, than Sntejo did he had no doubt.

He also understood that both Raghe and Krepus had enough age to remember the old Téuta, to remember clearly what had happened there, and he understood that the horror of what had happened was enough to justify many difficult things. They were enough to justify nearly any sacrifice that was needed to be certain the trouble was past, and that whatever was needed by the gods was given to them. But the two men, Raghe and Krepus, were so widely different in their response to what had happened. Raghe looked to the gods. Krepus looked to the Téuta. Krepus spent his life and would willingly *give* his life to save the Téuta, to save the people. Raghe, it seemed, spent other people's lives, and would give any other life than his own, to pacify the gods. Of these two, Sntejo understood Krepus better.

The dawn had spread across the whole sky by the time Sntejo stopped musing about what Raghe had said. He turned back toward the longhouse and began to walk toward it. Krepus was waiting, he was sure, wondering why Sntejo was so long delayed. Or maybe not.

The delay had not been that long. But it was long enough for Raghe to scamper to the river, dip quickly under the water, and return; Raghe's baths were never more than that. As Sntejo reached the longhouse Raghe came striding back up the street, his eyes watching Sntejo with a strange, commanding, fearful look.

A smug, disturbing look.

Today Sntejo would walk the outer boundaries of the town around them, to consider if a new outer wall would be useful to them since the number of the Téuta had grown so much in thirty years, and he would see the sheep pens to determine if a new shelter would be needed for the winter. For the next two days he had work within the town. When that was done, he could again walk out into the hills, where he liked to be.

Sntejo ducked to enter the longhouse. At nearly that same moment, Raghe walked fully standing over the entrance to his temple, and over the flax-wrapped infants buried deep beneath it.

CHAPTER FIVE

"What really happened? Tell me again what you saw," Chaisa asked, and Kaikos explained again.

"Shafts of bholos were shooting from the ground in tall weeds into the air, like a wind was blowing from under the ground. They were spouting up everywhere, everywhere, everywhere," she said, and she swept the whole horizon with her arm. And she tried to describe the crazing film over the ground, to explain that the universe seemed to be crumbling.

"Why would this happen Chaisa? Maybe something under the ground is upset. Or sick," she said, turning to sense in all directions and then sensing at the ground as she said it. "Maybe that's it. Maybe the earth is sick."

She did not say: *"Maybe Dhegm is angry with me, as Raghe says she is, but I don't know what I've done wrong,"* even though that had always been her deepest fear.

The bholos around Chaisa swirled and twisted, but she said nothing for several minutes. She was quiet. She was thinking.

"I hope not," Chaisa said. "I hope not; I hope mother Dhegm is well. But maybe you're right. Maybe something in the ground is *not* well. Let me think about this Kaikos. It's not a good thing. I don't think it's good. But let me think overnight about it."

Chaisa put a handful of barley and a little salt in a crock of water and set it in their fire pit to cook while she prepared the fish. When the grain had softened and much of the water was gone, she placed the fish and a sprig of thyme in another crock with a little water to steam.

Because it had been a long day, because she had spent the day worrying, Kaikos was hungry. *Being afraid is hard work*, she thought. But her hunger was useful because the smell of cooking food was profuse in the hut. That drove everything, including fear, away for a while.

After dinner she and Chaisa talked, and Chaisa sang, and Kaikos danced quietly, listening to the song, and the fire, and the slow breeze around the hut. For a time they both relaxed.

But a dinner of fish and porridge could not keep worry away forever. There was still tension everywhere in the night. It slipped back to Kaikos, quiet as fog, to dim her senses. The ground was tense, and although it had settled from the storm of them in the afternoon there were still some shafts of bholos rising from the ground, the mist of them dissolving and flowing over her as she tried to sleep.

Her mother had been tense when Kaikos first explained what othersight was showing her, and after the glow of their meal faded she must have thought again about what Kaikos had told her. Her tension returned too. She remained tense into the night. When they slept her mother held her very close, as though she were too afraid to release her hold, even though she couldn't see the bholos. *Afraid of what?* Kaikos wondered.

Kaikos had odd feelings as she slept. She had dreams of tilting. She felt dizzy, as though she had drunk too much beer. In the middle of the night she woke and put her hand on the ground, and felt its tension under her palm, like a branch pulled to the ground and ready to spring back.

The next morning Chaisa held her before they went to the river to bathe. When they returned Kaikos walked in the morning while Chaisa again made rounds of barley bread with walnuts. Kaikos could smell the bread, and the river still on her skin, and the ground. And she could smell the dawn.

Chaisa and Sntejo had told her many times that it was beautiful, that it changed the color of the sky. During the day, when she was busy, she didn't miss sight with eyes. She didn't think about it; she could find her way, and she didn't run into things. She knew who was near her. What else mattered very much?

But she didn't like to step on unseen stones when she walked with bare feet. She wanted to see what people looked like, and stones, and rivers, when eyes saw them.

And she wished she could see color in the dawn. Kaikos liked the early day, when she swam with Chaisa, when the world smelled cool, smelled fresh; she liked waking to the smell of the ash from the fire pit, of the earth outside, of the rock and mortar of the hut and the still warm mud bricks of the oven. She liked the feel of the air. She liked the bholos spread thin and cold on the long ground and drifting through the low places in the hills. But she wondered about the beauty that Chaisa and Sntejo called color.

After they ate their bread Kaikos stood up to go to her chore, but Chaisa stopped her. She asked who Kaikos had told about what she saw; she asked that even though there was no one else Kaikos *could* have told. Who else had she seen except Chaisa?

But Chaisa cautioned her: "Tell no one about this, Kaikos. Tell *no one*. This must be a secret between us."

Kaikos promised, and it was easy to promise: no one came to their hut except Sntejo, and sometimes Prsedi. But she didn't come often. Prsedi's visits were happy and seemed to be important. Chaisa made special bread and served beer when Prsedi came, and she was respectful. Rarely, maybe once a year, Sntejo would bring one of his friends, An or Do, to help Chaisa with some task. Sntejo and An had helped to build the hut, Kaikos knew, although that was long ago, the year she was born. To Kaikos the hut had always been there.

An seemed to like Chaisa, but he was nervous around Kaikos. He was too close to Raghe, so he was even surer than most of the Téuta that the whole hut and everyone in it was cursed. Because of Welo. Because he was a terrible giant, and they didn't want him to rage again. *Because*, Kaikos thought, *they are afraid of Welo even though no one has seen him for more than twice as long as my whole life.*

But Do wasn't afraid. To Do she was just a child, like any other child, and he was himself not so far past childhood that he had forgotten it completely. He was very nice to her and was always happy. He laughed so much it made everyone else near him laugh. Kaikos would be glad of a visit from Sntejo, or from Do, or from any of them, but she had no reason to think one of them would come anytime soon. If no one came to see Chaisa, there was no one to talk to, no one to tell.

So Kaikos tossed the grain to clean it, and Chaisa spent most of the days behind the hut making pottery and setting it to dry in the sun and firing already dry pots in the great covered mud-brick fire oven outside. Festival day was coming. Chaisa's pots were so excellent that on festival days the Téuta would come to her to trade for them, even though they were nervous about the curse. Sntejo told Kaikos that the pots her mother made were wonderful to look at, that she made tops for them that fit tightly so pests could not get inside.

Kaikos couldn't know very much about that, except the part about pests. She knew Chaisa fired her pots very hot, and that made them strong. But Chaisa never let Kaikos help her fire them; she thought blindness would make it hard to see the fire, hard to avoid burns. Kaikos could see the fires; bholos was very active around fires. But she didn't want to do pots anyway, so she didn't say anything about that to Chaisa.

The days passed. Kaikos watched the fields, watched the ground, and waited. With each day the spouts rose higher out of the ground. Each day for the next two days Kaikos tossed the grain into the air to separate the chaff, except the morning when she tended the small garden of peas and lentils Chaisa had set aside for her. Kaikos had always helped Chaisa in the big garden, but she liked having one of her own, even a small one.

Most of the time she winnowed the grain; they had to fill their grain jar for the coming year. She worked, but she was troubled through the next day and the day after. The tension in the ground was hard to bear; it was hard just to sit on the dirt or on rocks, or on anything. It was hard to stand with her feet touching the ground. She spoke to Chaisa again, and again her mother said, "This is a secret, Kaikos. It must be a secret."

"I think this means there is some danger. We should tell people."

"No, Kaikos, please, do as I tell you. You don't understand what people are."

"We should warn them."

Her mother sighed. She knew Kaikos well.

"Kaikos…here. Alright. You can tell one person, Kaikos, *only one*. Go to Prsedi and ask her advice. She will tell you what I am telling you. There is a reason you must stay quiet about this."

Kaikos stopped still. She sensed everything she could about her mother with her othersight, and with every sense. Her eyes focused on nothing, but she was alert.

"Go to the village?" Kaikos asked, bewildered.

"Yes. Go to Prsedi in the village. Go tomorrow."

"By myself?"

Chaisa didn't respond, but Kaikos wanted an answer to that.

"You said go—not we will go. Did you mean that I should go by myself?"

"Yes, Kaikos. Go by yourself this time. I'll walk with you most of the way, to the edge of the village, to keep you company. But go to Prsedi alone so you know Prsedi is speaking only what *she* thinks is true, not saying things because of me. I know you know the way; when we go to celebrations you run far ahead of me or pull me by my hand to get there faster."

That quieted Kaikos. It both frightened her and calmed her. It frightened her because Kaikos had never been to the village without Chaisa or Sntejo. They didn't let her wander very far from her hut without one of them. Chaisa and Sntejo thought the world was full of dangers she couldn't see. It probably was; that was something she couldn't know. They were grownups. They did know.

But Kaikos wasn't afraid of being out in the world alone. What frightened her more was being *with Prsedi* alone; Prsedi was an important person in the village. She didn't live in a big hut with others, or near the center, and had nothing to do with leading the village, but long ago in the old Téuta, Dhegm had come to her, had helped her then and liked her. Dhegm still came to speak to her. So although she lived outside the wall, no one wanted to offend Prsedi or anger her, for fear that Dhegm would be angry too. Even Krepus the king, the hunt leader who was afraid of nothing, was wary of her.

Kaikos had only been to Prsedi's home a few times in her life, at the celebration times with Chaisa and Sntejo both, and had never thought she would be there by herself. If Chaisa was saying to go see Prsedi in the village, and on her own, without being invited, then this was something very important.

But the idea calmed her also, because Prsedi would believe her. Prsedi would know how to fix whatever it was that was wrong with the world.

CHAPTER SIX

Krepus had risen long before dawn, as he usually did, but this morning he had a purpose: he wanted to join Sntejo in his patrol through the hills to the north. For Sntejo this was a working trip, but for Krepus it was pure joy. He was often too busy to walk very far from the Téuta. A king's days filled up quickly with tasks, so he wanted to get out into the wild, far above the village, before anyone pulled him away to solve some petty dispute or engage him in a discussion of building or crops or whatever was on their minds when he happened by.

And Raghe was walking the town this morning. Why shouldn't he? But seeing him out of his smokerooms was unusual. Krepus had stopped him to ask if he needed something.

"Nothing."

"Are you looking for something I can help you find?"

"I don't know."

"Where are you going, then?"

"I don't know."

He had stood still then, his eyes staring at the streets, as though something were going to come out of them to attack him. Krepus looked too, up and down the pathway.

"Are you waiting for something?"

"Yes."

"What are you waiting for?"

Raghe was silent for some time before he answered, "I don't know. The gods are silent."

"About what? What do you ask them?"

"I don't know what they are silent about."

Krepus had felt an unease for days, so he asked Raghe if something were going to happen that he had to deal with.

"I don't know."

Krepus had been exasperated. "What *do* you know? Why are you out here in the streets, wandering with no place to go?"

"I don't know what I don't know. There is some secret blowing in the air, in the secret wind, but it says nothing. I can't hear words in the wind."

Krepus had told Sntejo of the encounter, every word, and Sntejo had wondered if Raghe had finally been completely overcome by his mushrooms and smoke. He had asked that: "Is he finally crazy?" and Krepus had done his best imitation of Raghe's voice when he responded:

"I don't know."

They laughed together about that, but Krepus was clearly stressed by his responsibilities. Sntejo watched his friend with concern as they walked.

"Why do you still do it?"

Krepus didn't have to ask what the question was about; he knew. He walked on slowly as he thought about how to answer, because he also wanted to know: he had never wanted to lead the Téuta. He did it because no one else did. Because no one else would. Or more exactly, because no one acceptable would.

He looked at Sntejo. Finally he asked, "Can you control Raghe and all his admirers?"

"I don't think so. I've never tried."

Krepus took a breath, slowly, and released it. "He *is* crazy, yes. It was easy to be crazy when the cliff fell. Everyone was crazy. Some recovered, slowly or quickly. Others never recovered. Raghe is one of those."

Smells around them, and the sun, and breeze on their faces, kept them peaceful even when the subject was not. Sntejo was silent, waiting for Krepus to order his thoughts.

"Half the village thinks he should lead, since he is the one the gods speak to. For thirty years, since he was twelve years old, he has been all we have as shaman. All the others were—they are still under the cliff. So I need him. The gods do tell him things, and a leader needs *some* way to hear the gods. But what would the Téuta be if Raghe were our leader? He accepts only worship. Not of the gods, worship of him. But if he were leader, those who worship him would be servants to him, and those who did not—I don't know what would happen to those who did not. If Raghe were leader, there would be no hertus, no balance in the Téuta. No goodness. It would be hard to live here. I still lead because if I didn't Raghe would, and the Téuta would dissolve and be swept away like mud thrown into the river."

The sun rose through the sky, and the morning warmed. But there was something else Krepus had to say to Sntejo.

"I don't know what has changed, but Raghe is getting more active. More assured, or something. Something has changed, maybe. And you know what he wants."

"Everyone knows what he wants," Sntejo said.

"Watch them, Sntejo. Chaisa, I mean, and Kaikos. Raghe watches them, or people who follow him do."

"They don't. That can't be true."

"Yes, Sntejo, it is. Raghe, crazy as he is, hasn't forgotten, and won't forget. He does watch them."

Sntejo wasn't convinced. But his reaction was anger anyway.

"If Raghe harms them, he knows I will come after him. He would have to cower inside his temple for the rest of his life."

Krepus was quiet while they walked, but his mind was still on Raghe and Kaikos, and that it was good that Chaisa's hut was far from Raghe, and out of his sight, and that it was good that the two women so rarely came into the village. Everyone did know what Raghe wanted, and many followed him. Raghe wandering the streets looking wild and bewildered disturbed every settled thing.

"Do you ever think about that morning? The morning when we first saw her?"

"Sometimes."

"I think often about it. When I saw Chaisa and Prsedi standing there, I felt only awe for them. I loved Chaisa in that minute, and I loved Prsedi, and I loved their courage. At that moment I wondered which I loved more, Perkunos' beautiful anger, his courage in the sky, or the courage of these two women to stand against Raghe and all his adherents, against half the Téuta, to protect that tiny child covered in flour."

"I'm glad you were there to help her," Sntejo said.

"Kaikos? I liked her then and I like her now. I never wanted to harm her."

Sntejo smiled at this unusual eloquence from Krepus about feelings he rarely shared.

"It's good that you came out with me today. The peace in these hills is good for you."

"The village can get along without me for half a day."

The two friends were quiet after that. Walking with Sntejo was pleasant, partly because Sntejo's eyes were sharp enough that no danger would escape them, so Krepus could walk with his own thoughts, and partly because Sntejo had enough sense to be quiet when the nature around them gave them all the conversation that was needed. They walked through the smell of the end of summer, the rustle of small animals in the fallen leaves, the beauty of the dawn as it came to them. This was not a consultation. It was simply a walk with an old friend. It was solace, and rest—and a time to ponder a stubborn mood.

He hadn't said this to Raghe, but he understood the man's nervousness. He was nervous too. Something he couldn't quite name had been troubling him for days. Even here, away from the Téuta, he felt it, although it was less here. Here he sensed distant rain, hard rain; maybe that was what had been disturbing him, although he thought not. He liked weather, all kinds of weather. But maybe the coming storm was a bad one, a storm that could threaten those who lived too near the river. Maybe that was why it smelled like worry.

Worry, worry, always worry. But whatever it was he would handle it, as he always handled whatever came.

Through the morning he walked with Sntejo, occasionally, but rarely, exchanging a few words about the beauty of the world, and of the dawn when she came, and of the strange behavior of the animals. This was a good morning for walking and for watching, but would not be good for a hunt; the animals also felt that something was coming at them. They spooked at the slightest sound, the slightest movement, and bounded away through the bushes or flew into the sky.

At the end of the morning Krepus felt soothed, but still wary. Still waiting. He left Sntejo to continue his patrol through the hills and went back to the Téuta to find out what had fallen apart while he was away. A vague anger settled over him as he walked away from the peace and beauty in the hills, and instead approached the village with all its chores.

His first chore was to consult Raghe, if he could find him. To corner him in his rooms if he could. He wanted Raghe to ask the gods directly, to see if the gods had anything at all to tell him. It was a frequent chore for him, and one he dreaded.

A trip to the depths of Raghe's temple was never pleasant. The rooms were dark, heavy with smoke, and far too near the water;

some of the inner rooms extended outside the village walls, dug into the slopes toward the river. The rooms, with their damp and their smell, were not the worst of it. There was the sense of the presence of gods, of course, which was disturbing, but even that was not the worst. It was the man himself Krepus found distasteful. They had been friends, once, when they were children in the old Téuta, but the falling cliffs had changed them both. Now they could barely speak to each other.

But the trip had to be made. The king had to know what the gods needed.

rt̄ (I) H̄

Sntejo lay on his back with his bare feet cooling in the creek. He could smell moss on the rocks near the water, and in the quiet here, in the distance, he could sometimes hear Chaisa singing. It was only a tiny trickle of sound mingling with the creek's burble, only a quick tang of melody in the air from time to time. He put his hands behind his head and watched the few streaks of cloud moving in the sky, light gray but now tinged with evening pink along the edges.

He had spent much of the day walking in the foothills to the north, across the river, on the lookout for the raiders who sometimes came down from that direction looking for unguarded stores or sheep, probably pushed here by the cooling years.

In the first hours, from before the dawn until nearly midday, Krepus had walked with him, and he was glad of that company. Krepus was a skilled hunter, a skilled warrior, and a motivated lookout since the safety of the village rested on his back as king. In any case, he was good company for a walk in the world. He stayed quiet when that was good to do, which was most of the time, and spoke when that was good to do.

They had walked to the tops of the hills and looked in all directions for any dangers, and they had seen nothing that troubled them. It was the kind of day, after the heat of summer, when it was a pleasure to walk, and it was the kind of day that Krepus loved: the season of storms was nearly here. He had stopped often to breathe the early autumn air. Sntejo had too, although Krepus seemed to feel something in the wind that Sntejo hadn't.

Krepus had left him to the day's watch when the sun was high overhead, walking back toward the village to attend to other business. When the afternoon began to wane, Sntejo had crossed the river again, and he had walked on the village side. Now, at the day's end, he was here beside this creek, with his feet in the water.

The day had been strange, though. He had hoped to return home with game for dinner, but animals were scarce today, and skittish. Even the birds seemed nervous, easily startled, and quick to fly. And now, finally, he could sense what had excited Krepus in the morning. The season's weather was coming; he could feel it now.

Perkunos' axe was a hint in the wind, far away now, but that god was coming toward them, he could feel it in the thinning of the air, in the hair rising on his arms. He could smell it. It was the smell of hunt, and war, and robust life; he felt excited, alert, fearful, watchful. He felt the purpose in being strong.

For the moment the wind was calm, no more than a steady shifting of air that pestered the leaves. It was a gentle pleasure on his face. Perkunos was days away, so for now he enjoyed the peace he found in this evening and soaked his feet in the creek.

Sntejo knew this place well. He often came this way, whether he was out on watch, or hunting or just walking in the hills. He liked being out of the village. It was lonely here, but he liked the loneliness, and often after a day of it this place lured him, this exact place, because up on the flat, away from the stream, there was a place where he could see Chaisa's hut, and because at just this spot next to the water he could sometimes hear Chaisa's voice. The sound was a lonely echo along the rocks. He didn't know why that happened. She did live near the mouth of this ravine, but the mouth was a ten-minute walk from this spot. If he climbed to the top of the rocks, where he was closer and could see her hut in the distance, he couldn't hear her. But in this place he had discovered that her voice seemed to carry along the gully, sometimes, a tiny sound to compete with the burble of trickling water.

Sntejo had few tasks to do in the village tomorrow, and none pressing, and when that was true he liked to be out of the village in the hills. He had spent more than a few evenings here, staying down in the shallow ravine until night and then sleeping up on the flat where there were trees to give him some shelter. For the moment he rested his feet in the rill and tried to hear the small sharp glimmers of Chaisa's song.

When Chaisa was finally still and probably asleep herself, he climbed up the side of the ravine, built a small fire for warmth and to keep the predators away, and lay on the grassy ground against some rocks. The fire's heat, reflected from the rocks, created a warm bed for him. He spread his cloak at his side; he had no need for it now, but he kept it close in case the morning was cool. Stars were dense in the clear air, the wide road of stars down the sky as clear as the path through the Téuta village inside the wall. He spent some time looking through the tree branches, watching the moon climb over the sky. Finally his eyes closed, and he slept.

Sntejo woke with thin early sun in his eyes and with his cloak covering his chest; the rest of him was cold. He sat up, put his cloak around his shoulders and pulled up his legs so the cloak could cover them. He rubbed his legs for a few minutes to warm them. Then he stood and looked over the rocks toward Chaisa's hut. But his focus shifted quickly. Someone came out of the hut, and from the size, from how she dressed and how she walked, it was Kaikos. After a moment Chaisa came out behind her. The two of them began walking toward the village.

He sat, watching them walk, until they looked like dots in the distance—and then one of them stopped. Chaisa, it looked like. Chaisa stopped—and Kaikos kept going. Kaikos was walking alone toward—toward what? Why was Kaikos straying so far from home? Why was Chaisa not walking by her side or turning her back?

What had happened?

The girl walked calmly, but he knew it was Kaikos because she sometimes paused, uncertain about where to step. She knew the way to the village. Her hesitations were not about what direction to take, only about what would be under her feet when she put them down.

Still, Sntejo wasn't sure he liked the idea that Chaisa had allowed her to go alone. It seemed risky, not because she couldn't see her way; he had long ago learned not to worry about that. It was risky because the outskirts of the village beyond the gate were sometimes rough, and Kaikos was not protected by any high status, or any honor. She had neither of those. What reputation she had was not in her favor there. But, he thought, even though the people in the village might resent Kaikos they knew and respected *him*, knew who he was and that he was close to her. They might hesitate to harm her because of that. This, too, was a purpose in strength.

Then he realized there was a greater strength than his at work to keep Kaikos safe. There was only one place she could be going, and none of the Téuta outside the wall, or inside either, would risk angering Dhegm by harming someone who was on their way to visit Prsedi. The walk back home might be a little riskier, though. If Kaikos' visit was long enough, and if he hurried, he might be able to be there to walk back with her. It would be good to see Prsedi anyway.

Something in his peripheral vision was troubling. Sntejo turned to look, took a step and stopped. Not twenty paces away stood a large stag, watching him. Normally deer were careful around men and wouldn't provoke a confrontation unless they were cornered. But this stag stared at him and didn't retreat. It seemed defensive, and defiant. It seemed, perhaps, dangerous.

His bow was still leaning against the rocks where he had slept. He would not have time to get to it and also aim and shoot if this animal decided to charge him.

Watching him—the stag stood looking in his direction—was it watching him? He wasn't sure. It behaved as though it were disoriented. It started to turn away. Sntejo paused, waiting. The animal was, or appeared to be, confused. It turned more and took a tentative step away, up the hill.

Sntejo moved very slowly toward the rocks. Slow or fast the movement was a mistake. The minute he moved the stag turned and charged toward him, head lowered, antlers forward to spear anything they encountered. He dove out of the way at the last minute simply by instinct; he had no thought that the move would help much, since the stag, although much heavier, could turn nearly as fast as he could. But turning toward him it slipped in the dirt from the momentum of its charge, and disappeared over the edge into the ravine. Sntejo watched the big animal sliding down the hillside toward the rill.

It stood at the bottom staring up toward him, huge, wet and snorting with anger. He thought the animal would charge again, would bound up the slope, and Sntejo backed away toward the rocks to get his bow.

Nothing happened. After a moment he edged toward the slope again, expecting the creature to be there waiting—but there was nothing there at all. He looked around, up and down the creek, and climbed down into the ravine. If the animal had gone toward the plains he would need to follow, to kill it since it was crazy, so it didn't threaten Chaisa and Kaikos when they returned. But there was nothing down the creek, and he continued to look. At last he saw it in the other direction, far up the creek heading back toward the hills, and he watched until it was out of sight.

Sntejo climbed back up to the flat and organized his gear for the walk home. The animals were behaving very strangely, he thought, yesterday and now today too. He wondered if others had seen the same thing.

Wood shavings. That was what it was, what he had seen and

turned toward at the cliff edge. He went back to the place where he could see Chaisa's hut to look. Ten paces to his right there was something in a cleft in the rocks, so he went to look. Yes, wood shavings. Someone had been here. They had stayed long enough to start whittling to pass the time. Here there was a place to sit. And from here Chaisa's hut and much of the ground around it could be watched.

CHAPTER SEVEN

After their river-bath but before they made breakfast Chaisa and Kaikos left their hut and walked toward the village. Breakfast would have been a foolish effort and a waste of food, because neither could have eaten it. They spoke very little. The long walk was strangely quiet. Only their footsteps and insects in the trees near the river broke the unusual silence between them.

Chaisa stopped when the village was within easy sight so she could watch Kaikos the rest of the way, and pressed Kaikos to go on from there alone. Although it frightened her, Kaikos did what she was told. She walked into the outskirts of the village, and felt the people become quiet as she approached. They watched her as she passed, seeming to her to be resentful, and a little afraid. She couldn't see them, exactly, but the bholos clumped up around them so that they seemed like tall grey flames if they were standing, or short squat grey flames if they were sitting.

When she came to Prsedi's hut she went in and knelt on the ground and waited, her head bowed and her hands for now quiet in her lap. Prsedi was very old, more than fifty years, and Kaikos liked her. Also, she was the only person Kaikos knew who had ever seen

Dhegm with her own eyes, so she always showed respect to Prsedi.

The older woman was quietly making bread beside her fire from barley flour and water and salt and mashed boiled roots. It smelled wonderful, partly because Prsedi made wonderful bread, but also partly because Kaikos had not eaten yet.

She waited quietly for Prsedi to look up and see her. But Prsedi didn't need to look up to know who it was.

"What is it, Kaikos? Please, no formality for me. No ceremony. We are friends."

"Prsedi, I'm sorry to bother you so early in your home. I have to ask your advice about something. Chaisa sent me to ask advice."

The old woman turned then to look at Kaikos, and then looked past her.

"You're alone?"

"I'm sorry Prsedi. Chaisa said I should come to you alone, be here with you alone, if you will let me."

"Let you?" Predi said, almost laughing. "Of course I will let you, Kaikos. I'm glad you came to me here. I'm always happy to see you, here or anywhere."

Prsedi watched her, for a minute, concerned. She came to ask advice? Kaikos never asked advice. She usually just wanted to talk when they saw each other, because it was a lonely life to be separated away from the village as Kaikos and Chaisa were.

Kaikos sensed Prsedi with her othersight; she seemed tense now too, like Chaisa, and like the ground. But Prsedi waited silently to hear what Kaikos had to say. So Kaikos took a breath and spoke to her.

She told Prsedi about the bholos, about the first sprouts three days before, and the great field of sprouts in the evening of that day, and about how they came and went but that they were getting higher. As high as the tallest grownups now. She put her hand on the ground in Prsedi's hut and told her that even here the ground seemed—not angry, but strained, stretched, waiting. It had to mean something.

The dim flame of bholos around Prsedi shook and leapt and then was still. That meant she was surprised and upset. Maybe afraid. Prsedi put her hand on the ground too but seemed to feel nothing different there. She was quiet for a long time. Kaikos stayed where she was and waited. Her hands were never still though, touching the ground and pressing the tops of her legs and brushing against each other. The ground's tension seeped up into her and seemed to settle in her legs and in her hands.

Finally, Prsedi asked, "What did Chaisa say when you told her?"

"She said I have to keep this a secret."

"Yes. A secret. That is very good advice Kaikos," Prsedi said. "Keep this a secret between the three of us, you and Chaisa and now me."

"Why?"

"Because. Do as your mother says, and as I say. It's hard to tell you why. But it's important. Even coming to tell me was foolish, Kaikos."

"But if..."

"Kaikos! No more talking now, and no more talking to *anyone* about this!"

Kaikos was surprised by the stress and energy in Prsedi's response. The words weren't harsh, and weren't said harshly, but they were unexpected. Prsedi never felt stress. Kaikos said nothing, though, and felt some comfort in the quiet tone when Prsedi continued.

"I know, it's hard to be still. You're not good at being still, and you don't ever really have secrets, do you? I'm not sure you've ever had any that you didn't finally tell Sntejo, or your mother. Often your mother last, like any child, but eventually even her, always. And you're right I think. There might be some small danger to others. But that danger won't go away if you say anything, because they won't hear you. They won't listen. They will ignore you, partly because you are still a child, and partly because you are Kaikos. They will be deaf, but they will still blame you when danger comes. They will blame everyone around them, because they won't want to admit they were told it was coming but still did nothing."

Prsedi was silent for five minutes, rolling her bread out and putting it onto the flat of the rocks inside the fire pit to bake. She watched, and waited, then turned it over to bake on the other side. Kaikos kept kneeling, still with her face down even if Prsedi said no ceremony. She was frightened.

"Kaikos, I've seen something like this before, and it was terrible. This thing you described, the rising whatever-it-is, is almost exactly what those who knew him say Welo described before the earth shook at the old village. What happened then was terrible; what it made people do afterward was terrible. But I think the danger you feel won't be very bad here," Prsedi said, breaking the silence without warning, and making Kaikos jump.

"But Welo was a giant."

"People say that, don't they?"

Prsedi paused, then said, "Kaikos, think about this. Here, on the plain, away from the cliffs, it won't be so bad, even if the earth does shake. But if you tell everyone what you have seen—well, there will still be some small danger to them, but maybe a very big danger to you, even if the earth never shakes. Keep your secret, Kaikos. Say nothing about this. Let Chaisa and me think about what to do."

Prsedi stood and walked in the room, straightening things that were already straight, and talking as she walked.

"Maybe if we don't use your name, if the warning comes from me—but that won't work now. I don't think that will work. Everyone has seen you come to me, by yourself, so they will know where the warning comes from. And if the earth does shake—where is Chaisa?"

At the last question Prsedi stopped walking and turned to look at Kaikos.

"Just outside the village, that direction," Kaikos said, and she pointed toward Chaisa's bholos-flame.

"Has she eaten? Have you?"

"No. We came here first."

Prsedi went on cooking, making several round flat loaves of bread, more bread than she could eat in a morning, and making Kaikos even hungrier. Prsedi was still thinking, and she stayed quiet even after the bread was done. Finally she looked at Kaikos.

"I'll walk with you back to your hut," she said, "and we can all share this bread on the way."

Kaikos could find her way back to Chaisa without help, as she had found her way here alone. Her blindness was less restricting than people seemed to think. She could sense the bholos blowing past the huts, and inside the huts, and she could sense the bholos swirl around the people in them since her othersight didn't stop where there were walls. With othersight she could see the paths. But Kaikos thought to herself, as she often did when she walked, *with eyes you can see stones on the ground so you don't step on them.*

Prsedi took her hand, and they wound their way through the spaces between the huts and ate their bread together. People watched her again, watched Kaikos as she walked. Usually the staring people bothered her. But today, walking in the warm sun with Prsedi back toward her home, she was content. Kaikos felt relaxed for the first time in days. The sun relaxed her, and the hot bread also, and Prsedi, who held her hand and would know how to fix everything.

The bholos still sprouted high, though, everywhere she looked. Even inside the huts there were tall sprouts of bholos that rose and blew away unnoticed by the people who lived there.

There were eyes that did notice something though. Raghe's many eyes in the village noticed that Kaikos, who was never alone, walked alone to visit Prsedi, and that she walked *with* Prsedi to go home.

That would be remembered.

They found Chaisa where Kaikos had left her, and the three of them walked back toward the hut tucked in behind the hills.

Prsedi stayed through the afternoon talking to Chaisa. They spoke about this closely and quietly inside the hut, and as they spoke their bholos shook like worry. Kaikos, sitting outside cleaning grain again, listened to the murmur they made, feeling the ground's tension wherever she touched it. Once she felt what seemed like a shiver in the ground, very tiny, but it was there. Surely Prsedi and Chaisa felt that? But they didn't seem to. After that though, as the day moved on, the bholos seemed to settle a little. By the time Prsedi left to walk back to the village the puffs from the ground were small, and were much less frequent. When Kaikos placed a hand on the ground the tension was less.

She went in again in the afternoon. That night she slept, but again she felt as though she were tilting, so her sleep was restless.

When the morning came, Kaikos went outside to clean grain again. She was uneasy, but the ground seemed less so, and the bholos puffs were gone. Maybe it would be alright. Maybe Dhegm had been sick, but the sickness had passed.

Kaikos worked through the morning, and through the early warmth just after noon. As the afternoon passed by her the breeze slipping around the corner of her hut came endless and gentle, to perform what, to Kaikos, clearly seemed to be its true purpose, its only purpose, the reason it came down from the snows at the mountaintop, which was to help her do her work: to cool her and take the chaff away and leave the grain clean.

Then someone came toward them from the village.

One of the things that made people nervous about Kaikos was that she didn't turn her head when they approached her. She didn't turn her eyes to look at them. To her this was simply normal; her eyes couldn't see them if she did turn her head, and she had no need to turn her head very much to sense the bholos around them. So when she saw the bholos ghost-flame of someone approaching she just kept on with her chore, seeming not to even notice, even while she was watching with curiosity.

She wondered at first if Prsedi was coming back to talk. But it was not Prsedi; Kaikos could tell from the way the bholos moved that it was a man, so that meant it had to be Sntejo. Among the men only Sntejo came alone this far out to see them. She sat and continued her work, seeming oblivious to him as he approached.

It was unusual for Sntejo to come this late in the day, unless he came very late to stay with Chaisa, she thought. As late as it was in the day he would surely go straight to her.

But he didn't. This time he just sat outside the hut to watch Kaikos as she worked. She sensed him watching her, sensed his movements and his mood, and smiled a little to herself. She knew what he felt as he sat there in the warm afternoon. She knew he didn't see the bholos rising around him, and he didn't feel the tense ground. This was Sntejo, and she knew him, knew he loved the world. Now, she knew, he simply felt the day. He felt the earth and the wind. He felt the sun.

CHAPTER EIGHT

Restless, cheerless when he thought about his purpose here, Sntejo reflected on where it came from, and why it was his. Krepus had asked. But he knew it wasn't Krepus whose purpose he served. He knew that, as always, it was Raghe who raised suspicions, who raised alarms, who needed to spy on Chaisa, and on Kaikos. Raghe who needed to spy on everyone, who split the Téuta for some purpose he could never name.

It had so little of reality in it that Sntejo couldn't really comprehend it, so sometimes as he sat watching he lost his focus. He couldn't hold it all inside his mind. With Chaisa singing so near, with the afternoon air and the still warm earth at the end of the grain-gathering season soothing him, he fell easily into luminous reverie. He closed his eyes sometimes, to smell the river, the hut and the fire inside, the baking, and the dusty chaff in the air as Kaikos tossed grain to clean it.

Afternoon sun fell on his arms and on his face. He took in the beauty of the scene just at the start of the foothills, listened to the wind in the leaves nearby and to Chaisa singing. He watched Kaikos tossing the grain in the air over and over, and sometimes swaying gently from her waist to the rhythm of Chaisa's voice. The day was so serene that Sntejo lost track of the passing time, and he sat silent in the restless air. Twice Kaikos took bowls of clean grain into the hut, returned, and filled her bowl without seeming to notice him. She simply sat, her eyes open and pointed toward the river, or toward the mountains beyond the river.

Sntejo sat on an old fallen tree a short walk up the hill from Kaikos. The day had been hot at mid-day. Now daylight was thinning in the late afternoon. Kaikos would have to stop her work soon. Not because of the darkness, which made little difference to her. But it would be cold when the sun set, and the breeze had dropped to almost nothing which made her work difficult.

He opened his eyes to watch her. She didn't look angry, or unhappy. She looked like the same Kaikos he had cared for and played with when she was a small child, but now she looked worried and moved with worried caution as though she expected the sky to fall on her. He watched her sense the breeze.

Now and then she stopped her work and reached out her hand to the ground to feel it, as he had seen her do many times when they were hunting for burrowing animals. No one else could find the animals under the ground as she did.

As the chaff drifted on the wind her disturbing eyes didn't follow it. They didn't follow grain falling back into the bowl either; they didn't follow anything, which is why they troubled people. Her hair, black and soft and tufted, blew in long, thick strands, and it was filled with chaff that had blown into it through the day.

Sntejo realized, for the first time, that she would be a pretty woman when she grew old enough. Beautiful, maybe. That made sense. She was Chaisa's daughter. But it was hard for Sntejo to think of her that way. He had held her as an infant, and he still thought of her, almost, as an infant.

But Sntejo wasn't thinking about Kaikos, or not only about her. He was thinking about the erratic benevolence and sometimes perfidy of gods, and about Welo, the nightmare of the Téuta, who had tipped and split the whole earth thirty years ago, killing many people.

Welo had told the other village leaders then that they should move the people, the whole of the Téuta. He had warned them, but they had scoffed at him. Move the whole Téuta? More than a thousand people and all their goods and huts that had been built over generations? Leave all the generations that lay in the ground beneath their huts, their long familial connection with the land around them? Crazy, they had told him. You must be crazy to say such a thing.

That must have made him angry, because then he shook the ground, and the whole cliff above them cracked and slid down on top of the village. Even houses that were not covered by the falling rocks shook and fell in on the people inside them. It was an offense against Dhegm to shake her ground, but Welo was a giant, powerful and huge, and he did not fear the gods. After the earth shook the Téuta left the old village and left him there among the ruins he had made.

Absurd, Sntejo thought. He had been a small child when the ground shook so long ago, too young to remember it clearly, and Chaisa had been a baby. He didn't remember Welo. He remembered houses and cliffs falling, and he had no doubt about that. But he doubted the story about a curse.

He knew Chaisa. She was good, and she was beautiful. And Kaikos was blind, but she could do many things on her own; she laughed and made him glad when she was a small child, and she made him glad now. Why would any god worthy of being a god curse either of them? But maybe not all gods were worthy. Sntejo knew nothing about the nature of gods except what he was told, and he was not always certain about that when it was Raghe telling it.

Sntejo's friendship with Chaisa had been known to the elders for many years. They were concerned, and they watched him for any suspicious signs of curse about him, but he was well liked other-wise, and he was not completely alone in this friendship with these two. Even Prsedi welcomed Kaikos into her house on celebration days, and sometimes visited Chaisa. No one in the village could condemn an elder as revered as Prsedi, a woman who had met the living Dhegm when she was young and had become friends with her. It was because of friendship with Prsedi, people said, that Dhegm gave the Téuta grain to eat, so the Téuta treated her with deference, as a valued elder, and a power.

He shook his head when that thought came to him. He wasn't sure he believed that either, really. It was a strange thought, that a woman in the world could be a friend to a god. The Téuta said it was true. Yet Prsedi didn't talk about it, or brag about it.

Prsedi was Chaisa's friend, and was his friend too, and he was glad of that. But his friendship with Prsedi, and with this house and these people, was why he was here. More exactly, that was why he had been *asked* to be here. He sat thinking hard, remembering all he knew about these two, the woman Chaisa and the child Kaikos who showed some signs already of becoming a woman. Because he was so deep in his thoughts, and because Kaikos didn't turn to him but simply continued with her work, he didn't notice at first when she spoke to him.

"Why are you sitting out here?"

He watched the chaff drifting.

"Sntejo!"

He still sat, his mind on other things, and Kaikos still seemed to watch the air in front of her. She called to him again, louder now.

"Sntejo!!"

"Oh...Kaikos, I'm sorry. What is it?"

Kaikos seemed a little amused, lifted for a moment out of her worry.

"Why are you sitting out here? Chaisa is inside, probably waiting for you. You've been sitting over there watching me for a long time.

She must know by now that you're here."

He sighed to himself and stood to walk closer.

"I came to talk to you, Kaikos."

She stopped her work and sat up straight. "To me? Why?"

"Why should I not talk to you, Kaikos? You are a wonderful girl, and always a pleasure to talk to."

Now she turned slightly toward him with an amused smile, but still seemed to focus her eyes on something in the air far away.

"I think I am always a pleasure to talk to *after* you visit Chaisa, Sntejo. And you have not been in to see Chaisa yet. If I'm a pleasure to talk to why have you been so quiet?"

Sntejo looked down and said nothing for some time. Kaikos put her bowl of grain on the ground next to her and waited, her hands in her lap. *Why*, he thought, *are women so good at asking questions that make men feel they are at fault no matter what they answer?*

But he did have business, and he couldn't put it off forever.

"You were watched when you went alone to see Prsedi yesterday, Kaikos. And watched when Prsedi walked back here with you. People are saying you must have told her something important to make her leave her hut in the morning."

It was not a frown, exactly, that crossed her face. It was just a twitch between her eyes, quickly gone. But her speech was more careful than it had been, and less amused.

"I'm always watched when I walk in the village. Everyone stops talking, and they watch me until I pass them like I'm a monster walking outside their huts."

"You seemed worried," Sntejo said. "While you walked yesterday, at least when you were on the way to Prsedi, you seemed very worried, and now today you also seem worried. You keep feeling the ground. Is something wrong? What worries you?"

Kaikos was silent for a moment, thinking, her head tilted a little. The chaff in her hair sparkled, tinted orange in the afternoon light. Then she said, "Krepus sent you to ask me that. He sent you because you know me, and know Chaisa, and because you are trusted here."

Sntejo stood up, uncomfortable with how much this little blind girl could see. But he couldn't lie to her. He would never do that.

"Yes, Kaikos. That's true, he did send me. He wonders if you are worried about something he needs to know about."

He and Kaikos were silent then, since she didn't know what to say to him, whether to tell her secret to him, and then all the people she trusted would know it. But Krepus would also know it, because Sntejo would have to tell Krepus whatever he heard here. And then Krepus would tell Raghe.

They were both startled when a third voice spoke.

"Kaikos is right, Sntejo. You should have come to see me first. If you are here to spy for Krepus, you shouldn't talk first to a child. To *my* child."

Sntejo turned to look at Chaisa standing outside the doorway of her hut, and Kaikos kept gazing at something beyond the mountains, looking at neither of them but watching both.

"Your child," Sntejo said aloud. He thought to himself that Chaisa looked worried too. Worried about Kaikos? About him?

"Yes, your child, Chaisa," he said, "but you are my friend, and I've known her almost since her birth. I spoke for her then, and I will still speak for her. I would never harm her or do anything that would harm her. You should know that."

"No? What if Krepus told you to harm her, would you do it then? Krepus is your king, your hunt leader, ruler. What if Raghe tells you that Perkunos or some other god commands it, commands Krepus, and you must follow where he leads? If he said the safety of the whole Téuta depends on it, would you harm her then? I think you need to come inside, Sntejo, and leave Kaikos alone for now."

CHAPTER NINE

Sntejo and Chaisa spoke quietly inside the hut. Kaikos couldn't hear their words, but she watched through the walls with her othersight. They leaned close to each other. They didn't whisper, but their voices at first were very low as they spoke. Then Chaisa became more active, more animated, and their voices rose with tension, and Kaikos stood and moved farther from the hut so she didn't have to hear them argue. Chaisa wasn't like that with Sntejo. Kaikos found it upsetting to hear Chaisa's tension erupt toward him. But Sntejo spoke calmly, and Chaisa's tension slowly left. She sat near him, and they spoke quietly again.

Kaikos watched as they sat together, then as they lay together. She watched their motions and the strangeness of the bholos around them. She was always intrigued when they did this; it made their bholos swirl and tilt and wrap over them as though they were one huge creature, perhaps a bear rolling on the ground in the forest. She could hear them then, but they weren't speaking words. Kaikos was glad to see them do their rolling-bear thing; that meant they weren't angry, that they were friends again. They were soft with each other. Later they spoke words again. They spoke for a long time.

It's because of me, Kaikos thought. *Because I saw the bholos rise and couldn't keep the secret. Because I had to tell Prsedi. That's why Sntejo came to spy, and why Chaisa was angry with him.* She sat thinking, cleaning the grain, and watching the two grownups talk inside. *It's because I am a curse. That's why people watched me go to Prsedi, why they remembered, and why Krepus sent Sntejo here.*

Kaikos cleaned the grain, and waited, and felt the guilt of what she was.

When night had come, or nearly come, Sntejo came out of the hut. Kaikos knew that night was near from the sounds and the smells around her. Usually when he came out to start his walk back to the town he might tell her jokes, or just talk a little, and then he would go. But instead he walked to her and squatted in front of her. She was still, and again set her bowl next to her on the ground. She placed her hands in her lap and waited, facing the river, turned slightly toward him.

Kaikos waited, and waited, and felt the guilt of what she was, her face blank but her eyes toward the far mountains across the river; she felt the close crush of the night around her. She waited in the crushing night to hear what he would say.

† ⓪ ↦

Sntejo sat quiet for a time. He was feeling the cool of storms coming after the long summer. He was unsettled.

He watched her, but she was still.

"Kaikos, what do you feel in the ground?"

Kaikos said nothing. Her hands were quiet in her lap, and her eyes seemed fixed on the mountains she would never see.

"Then tell me, Kaikos. Do you think something bad might happen? Something terrible?"

"Why does Raghe hate me so much? Why does Krepus hate me? Why does everyone in the village hate me?"

Kaikos seemed disturbed, not only with what seemed to be her worry about the earth, but about her life. She wouldn't cry. He knew that. She never cried if anyone was watching. But he felt the tension in her heart.

"Krepus doesn't hate you," he said.

"He does. And everyone stares. Krepus hates me because of Welo. Well, *maybe I hate Welo too;* did he ever think about that?"

Sntejo stopped and looked at her. Hate was not an emotion he had heard from her before, and it bothered him. He understood, but he was curious what she would say.

"You hate Welo? Why do you hate him?"

He saw tears start in Kaikos' disturbing eyes, and he saw her stop them. The tears were in her voice, though, when she spoke.

"He killed my grandmother! He made me blind, so I can't see the beautiful color of the goddess when she comes in the morning, or goes in the evening! Why should I not hate him? And because of him Raghe hates me, and Krepus hates me, and because of him all the people, all the Téuta, hate me and stare at me when I walk!"

Kaikos turned her face away a little, maybe because she was afraid the tears would come out. She took some deep breaths to keep them from coming out, and they stayed inside her.

Sntejo was quiet for a moment, and then he said, "Krepus doesn't hate you. I think you remind him of something that makes him afraid. Kaikos, you are too young to feel this. But you know the years are colder now than they were. The crops are weaker. Why? The gods want something from us, but we don't know what. Krepus only wants to know what he needs to do to make the Téuta safe. And Kaikos, you shouldn't hate. I fear Welo, and I fear what the gods might do because of Welo, but I don't hate him."

They were quiet again while Kaikos considered that.

Ridiculous. Ridiculous, he thought. Welo was immense and terrible; he was powerful beyond measure, and when he was angry he challenged the gods, he shook the earth and many died. It was easy to understand why the gods would punish Welo.

But Kaikos? How could Kaikos do this? Ridiculous. She was not immense, not terrible. She was small, and blind. And good. And why?? Why would she do this? He could not understand what Krepus thought about Kaikos or how he thought. He wasn't sure even *if* Krepus thought about her in any way that Sntejo could understand as thinking. Even though they were friends he knew that Krepus thought mostly with anger and impatience.

But he also knew that Krepus deeply felt his duty to protect the village. And, in this case, even thinking mostly with anger Krepus was right: Kaikos and Chaisa were hiding something. Something was not calm, not good; something here was not beauty in the world. *But this must be a different thing,* he thought. *She is not like Welo. Kaikos would not cause danger to the village or the people.*

He didn't believe she would hurt the Téuta. And he did not believe that Kaikos could shake the earth.

He did believe she felt something there, though, when her hand met the ground. What she felt there frightened her. Something was worrying both Chaisa and Prsedi, and Kaikos was the source of it.

"Kaikos," he said finally, "Raghe thinks you are like your mother's grandfather. He thinks you feel the earth and control the earth. That sounds stupid to me, but Chaisa won't tell me anything, and you won't tell me anything. I haven't talked to Prsedi, but I am sure she will tell me nothing too. What should I believe? You didn't answer me, Kaikos. Do you think something bad will happen?"

Kaikos raised her head and turned it a little so it was clear she was sensing him, everything about him that she could. He thought she might stay silent.

But at last she said, "Yes, Sntejo. I do think something bad might happen. I think something bad has already happened."

She sounded sad. Tears shimmered on the edge of spilling over her lower lids, but still she would not let them out.

"Something in the ground?"

"The ground? Oh. The ground." Kaikos shrugged. "Maybe,

Sntejo. Maybe so. That's always possible, isn't it? Sometimes the ground is dry, and sometimes not, and sometimes it gives us grain, and sometimes not. It's hard to know about the ground."

"Something else, besides what you feel in the ground? What else?"

But Kaikos was quiet. She shook her head once and wouldn't speak again. She was disturbed by something he couldn't see.

So there it was. Sntejo could see no way around it. It had to be that. Even now, as he watched her, she was holding her hand to keep it from touching the ground to feel whatever it was she felt there, as it had twenty times while he watched her winnowing the grain earlier. That she sensed something in the ground there could be no doubt, and what else could it be?

Something else, maybe. Something else, something else, something else he hoped. But maybe also, as Welo had before her, Kaikos was sensing that the ground would shake, sensing it before it happened. That had to be what she and Chaisa were keeping secret. And if that was what it was, Chaisa knew better than to let Raghe know what Kaikos felt; Chaisa feared everything about Raghe. She would surely fear that he would declare that just as Welo her ancestor had been an evil thing, which was proven by Kaikos' blindness at her birth, so she, Kaikos, must be evil now. Chaisa thought that if Raghe said this Krepus would be very angry, even more than his usual anger, and this time his anger would be aimed straight at Kaikos and at her mother for making her.

They would keep their secret, the three of them, and that was good. It wasn't hard for him, for Sntejo who knew them well, and who had watched Kaikos through a long afternoon, to guess what it might be. But everyone in the village knew something was strange, something was upset in the world, if revered Prsedi walked cursed Kaikos home to talk so long with Chaisa.

He remembered the wood chips in the hills, and that others watched Kaikos through many afternoons. Those who watched didn't know her, though.

Chaisa and Kaikos and Prsedi could keep their secret for now. But if what he feared did happen, if the ground did shake, then it would not be hard for everyone to guess this secret, and that Kaikos and Chaisa, and Prsedi too, had known it and kept it hidden. People would be hurt. And Krepus then really would be angry.

He stood up and walked toward the village, and Kaikos picked up her bowl and went into the hut. But they both knew this: it's possible for two people to keep a secret. It's hard for three. But when four people and the whole earth under them know a secret, it can't be kept.

CHAPTER TEN

⊓⊓

Full night had come before Sntejo finally got back to the village, but the sky was clear. Thin, rich smoke from many huts hovered in air thick with the smell of bread and roasted roots and soup and other things cooked earlier. This moment persuaded him again that it was good to love the village, and reminded him of why he lived here—but the other smells of households, smells of refuse and waste, also reminded him of why he sometimes left it to wander in the open hills. Huts here outside the village wall were just scattered across the ground with no clear path in any direction; inside the wall there were more defined paths with huts and other structures along the sides. He walked through the dark, and through the quiet, with nearly everyone inside, most of them already lying on the pads they used to sleep on. That was not a surprise. He had expected everyone to be asleep. But as he passed Prsedi's hut he saw she was there, awake and alert, sitting just outside the doorway.

Sntejo approached gently, and sat quietly, looking at the ground. It was good sense and proper, and also, it seemed to him right to come to Prsedi with peace and respect. In the quiet of the night around them his voice, even as low and soft as he could make it, seemed like a violation.

"Can I speak with you, Prsedi?"

"Of course. I've been waiting here for you."

"You've been waiting for me?"

"Yes, Sntejo. I've been waiting for you to return from your errand with Kaikos."

He looked up, looked at her directly. "With Kaikos" she had said. Not "with Chaisa." Of course she would understand that. That he walked such a distance to see the mother was commonplace. But Prsedi knew his purpose in going there today, his business, was with the daughter. He paused for a moment, unsure of how to ask what he needed to ask.

"Are you well, Prsedi?"

Prsedi smiled at him. "Yes, thank you, Sntejo, I'm very well. But I'm tired too, and perhaps getting a little old, and it's late for me to be awake. We should talk about what you came to talk about so I can go to my bed."

"Yes, alright," he said, and paused to gather his thoughts. Finally he said, "Kaikos and Chaisa seem worried. Kaikos told me before I left that she was afraid something bad was going to happen, or had happened, but she wouldn't tell me what worried her, or why. Do you think something bad is going to happen?"

"Bad things happen from time to time. No time is perfect, although this time of year seems almost to be perfect, doesn't it, on a clear night with the clean cool wind all day across the fields?"

She was teasing him, he realized; her face was very serious, but her eyes were not. He looked at her, and at the sky, and back across the fields toward Chaisa's hut although he couldn't see it from here. At night he couldn't even see the hills that hid it, even on a clear night like this. He started to speak, but Prsedi held up her hand to silence him, and now she was serious all the way through.

"I know, Sntejo. You were asking why Kaikos came alone to see me yesterday, and why I left with her to walk to Chaisa's hut. I won't tell you what we talked about; that is private between Kaikos and Chaisa and me. But I will say that I also think more than one bad thing *might* happen, and maybe soon. Or maybe not. Maybe not at all. I don't know. Before you ask, neither does Kaikos know what bad thing might happen, or when. She doesn't really know anything at all; she came—as you do now—to ask for my thoughts, not to tell me hers."

For a time they sat silently, simply enjoying the freshness of the night. But Sntejo had to ask his questions, whether he wanted to or not.

"Kaikos seems to feel something in the ground. Did you think that too? Did she seem to feel the ground while you were with her?"

Prsedi sighed. "You are observant, and perceptive, and a smart man Sntejo. Be smart now. Don't ask questions you know I won't answer, questions you know I *shouldn't* answer."

"Why don't you trust me? Why doesn't Kaikos trust me?"

"Doesn't—*Pteh!!*" Prsedi issued a sound of incredulous frustration and turned to look him in his face. *"Doesn't trust you?* Really, Sntejo? *You can ask that??* Kaikos trusts you more than any person on the earth, except Chaisa, and even more than Chaisa sometimes when she thinks she's going to be in trouble for something. She thinks you're perfect. She loves you without any doubts. You are an adult who acts like a playmate to her, like a friend. She trusts you more than she trusts me, many times more, almost always."

Sntejo looked at her, astounded by her display of emotion.

"Nobody trusts me more than they trust you, Prsedi. You speak to Dhegm. You are Dhegm's friend."

"Which means everyone thinks I'm something special. I'm not. Anyone can talk to Dhegm. There's nothing special about that. You can talk to her if you want to. But when Kaikos comes to me, she sits and waits with her head down. When she sees you she just loves you."

"But she won't talk to me about this. She won't trust me on this."

Prsedi made a sound with her tongue, almost a scolding sound.

"We all trust you to do what you think is right. *You*, Sntejo. We trust you. But that's the problem, Sntejo: what do you think is right? I don't know whether this has ever happened to you before. How did it feel today, going to Chaisa, to Kaikos, to gather gossip for Raghe? Did that feel right to you?"

They were silent for a time; the sounds of the night surrounded them. Sntejo didn't want to answer that. But it was impossible for him to look away from the truth. He had never had the ability to do that.

"You know it didn't. Well, right, yes, it did feel that, but also ugly."

"It felt ugly to Kaikos too, I think, and to Chaisa. Think, Sntejo, what this is like for them. You have a divided duty, don't you? You're Chaisa's friend, Chaisa's lover; you would be her husband I think if you didn't know that would mark you and expel you from the council. You feel almost that you are Kaikos' father, and Kaikos feels that too. It's right for you to protect them. But it's also right to support the leader of the Téuta, the king, isn't it? It's your duty, and it justifies your presence on the council. If I were talking only to you, Sntejo, I would be happy to talk all night about Kaikos or anything else. But I'm not talking to you now, am I? When I speak to you tonight, I'm speaking directly into Krepus' ear. That is not so bad. But Krepus will consult Raghe."

"You don't trust Krepus, then?"

"On most things, yes, of course. He's very strong, and very brave. But he's also often angry, maybe always angry. He isn't comfortable with being a king. He doesn't want it, which is one reason he's a good king for us. But he also depends on Raghe for advice, for a link to the gods.

"Chaisa is afraid of him with good reason, as you know. It's Raghe, mostly, who says they're cursed. Krepus follows Raghe in all things about gods or curses. Krepus is king, but Raghe leads him on a leash in some ways. Oh, others think it too, but most of the people would forget Welo over time. Raghe doesn't forget him though, and so Krepus doesn't either. Welo is in his mind often, and often those thoughts lead him to anger. Because of that, Krepus chased Chaisa and Kaikos into the wild, to a place where we can't even see them."

"Krepus had..."

"No, Sntejo, don't. Krepus had no reason at all, at least none that is real. Raghe had obsession and lust, and Krepus had anger, always anger and more anger. And maybe he even had fear, so he sent them far away where he thought they couldn't 'curse' the rest of us. And even that was only because you and I intervened for them. If he had any strong reason, he might finally do what Raghe wanted him to do when he came for her here, in this hut. Raghe has killed people who troubled him before. You know that's true."

Crackling of dying fires in the huts sounded loud in the night, and of insects near the river, but the two of them sat silently for a few moments after that. Then Prsedi spoke to continue her thoughts.

"If it were not for Raghe's lust and Krepus' anger we would have Kaikos and Chaisa living here, not inside the wall, but here, next to me, and I could see them and talk to them every day. I would like that, and I think they would like that. But instead they live out there," and Prsedi waved a hand into the empty dark. "I don't want to be harsh with Krepus. I don't. He's good in his heart. He wants to be good. But he lets Raghe tell him how to be good, and Raghe can't even understand what good means."

She was quiet then, and from her posture it was clear that she was done. She had said what she needed to say.

Sntejo stood, walked a few paces, and walked back, and sat, and spoke in a whisper barely audible even to Prsedi.

"Prsedi, I can guess what has happened, partly because I know Kaikos and partly because the animals in the hills have behaved strangely for days. Some are afraid of everything; some are confused. No one else, I hope, will guess this while it is a secret, but if it happens—I still don't think so; I think this is all about nothing—but if it does happen, this shaking earth you're afraid of, then every-one will guess. Raghe above everyone will guess, and there will be no escape for either of them. I won't be able to restrain Krepus, and neither will you, against his own rage and Raghe's demands. Krepus will have no choice left. The whole of the Téuta will side with Raghe, or nearly so."

"And you suggest what? That they should run before any danger presents itself?"

"Yes. No. I mean, not run. But maybe, if your secret is what I think it is, then they should prepare. Make a place to go if they need it, a place where no one will find them. Stock it with food, with skins, with whatever they will need to live for some time, maybe the length of a moon or even more. They can come back when every-thing is settled down." He thought for a moment, then added, "And they should make sure no one sees them go."

"Where would they go, Sntejo? Krepus is a good hunter. There is no place for them to hide."

Sntejo smiled a little, although he stayed serious, and he shook his head. For once he knew something that Prsedi didn't.

"Krepus is a good hunter, yes. But you have never been hunting with Kaikos," he said, still in a whisper so quiet that even he could hardly hear it. "She's a child, it's true. But children are more flexible and more fearless than we are in some things. And she's Kaikos. She's *Kaikos*. She is a child more able than most in spite of her blindness. If she knows she has to, she will find a place to hide with Chaisa, and it will be a place the rest of us can't even see."

Prsedi watched him for several moments and said nothing. But finally she found a smile in her eyes to give him, to give the universe, and nodded, accepting his point.

Prsedi sat watching the night, and Sntejo stood next to her, watching the quiet stars, watching bugs in the small light from Prsedi's damped fire pit.

"I still don't believe Krepus will be a danger to them," Sntejo said, breaking the silence. "Why should he? But they should be ready for whatever happens."

Sntejo paused, thinking. Then: "Prsedi—you're right, as you usually are. Krepus protects the Téuta, and I help him. But *he is king*. They should find a place to hide where they can't be found, and they should not tell even me where it is. Tell Chaisa that. No, not just Chaisa; she is wonderful, but she won't completely believe it. No. Tell *Kaikos* that. Tell her *I said it*. She will understand, and she will do it."

Sntejo stood up straight, and he walked toward his home in the heart of the sleeping village. Prsedi watched him until he was out of sight, inside the village wall. Then she rose on old, reluctant legs and walked the other direction. Tired, late in the night, she began the long dark walk to wake Chaisa and Kaikos. They had work to do.

CHAPTER ELEVEN

IIII

The day Sntejo reported back to him about nervous Kaikos and silent Prsedi, Krepus walked to Raghe's rooms to talk with him. As usual, Raghe and a boy he was training as shaman were secreted far inside the temple, in the inner rooms near the river where only they could go—except those who went as sacrifice to die.

As king, leader of the Téuta, he might have resented that he couldn't just crawl through the access hole to the inner rooms. When they moved to this place he was not yet grown, but he had lent what strength he had to the work of building this room and the rooms behind it, the rooms that could only be reached by crouching and crawling.

He looked, in the dim light from the opening above, at the bull's heads stacked in columns. Each was covered in dried marl-mud and colored with white plaster and ochre to look real, and Krepus knew that inside each was a real bull skull retrieved from a sacrifice made to sanctify this place, to bring the gods here to explain their needs.

But resentment was not what he felt when he entered here. He could barely endure this room; the damp walls, the darkness, the clinging strangeness of the place depressed him, and the smoke of burnt sap and the smell of boiled dung-mushroom that Raghe used to help him find a connection with the gods made Krepus feel sick, even from two rooms away. Krepus had no desire at all to get any closer. No. This was Raghe's place. Here Raghe was king, and he was welcome to be king here. Since they had been built and covered, only Raghe and his apprentices had been allowed to pass through those holes to the back spaces, with rare exceptions, and the exceptions who crawled into those spaces did not return.

He stayed here in the outer room and waited, because there was no doubt in his heart that he needed to consult the gods—not as a casual friend as Prsedi did, but to deeply consult them—which could only be done here, and only through Raghe. He needed this because he felt something coming across the world toward them. He didn't know when it would come, or whether it would be a good thing or bad, or whether there was anything he could do to control it.

But he did need to understand it. He wasn't sure even Raghe could help, though; when Krepus last spoke to Raghe he seemed as confused and skittish as the animals in the hills.

When Raghe finally emerged from the crawl-hole to talk he stank of sap-smoke and sweat, and looked, as he always did, like the inside of a long-abandoned badger's nest with his long, tangled black hair and beard. His rooms here were closer to the river than any other room in all of the Téuta, but he never seemed to really bathe. Maybe he thought being dirty made him closer to the gods.

When Raghe spoke, he said what he always said: the girl, the girl, the blind girl. Raghe had never even seen her, as far as Krepus knew, other than that single time he went to Prsedi's hut to take her. But he feared her curse. That might have been enough to decide the matter. He was shaman. But Prsedi, who counted Dhegm among her friends, spoke in the girl's favor. Sntejo also found the girl to be innocent of any curse, and Sntejo knew her well. Who to follow, then? Raghe who knew the gods, or Sntejo who knew the girl?

Krepus left, putting all decision off for now, putting off the decision he did not want to make, as he had for twelve years. Nothing had happened yet, and Raghe had not said anything new. The long contest between Raghe and Prsedi continued, deeply felt by him but not felt at all by Prsedi. At least she never spoke of it, and only rarely of Raghe. He put the question out of his mind and went to the longhouse to see what tasks the day would bring.

For two days he worked in the longhouse, or in the streets of Téuta, absorbed in his normal duties. But his sense of apprehension never left him. So, finally, he thought, *I've consulted the shaman. Tomorrow let's see what our other speaker-to-gods has to say.*

On the third morning, early, Krepus walked the village paths in the dark, wary and alert. It was the time when everyone but the watchmen were asleep. Twice in the summer raiding parties had come from the north, both times in the early, dark morning, and since those raids he had made sure there was someone in the north hills watching every day, every morning before dawn.

This morning his mood was darker than usual. He was more on edge. Maybe it was the heavy clouds, the storm ready overhead. He felt Perkunos' anger all around him. That was not what disturbed him. Perkunos anger? *He liked it.* He *shared* it. Of all the gods he understood Perkunos best.

Raghe, the priest, plagued him with talk of the anger of gods, but he understood little of it. Dhegm? Dyeus Pter? What had they to be angry about? When had they ever shown anger that he could understand? Anger, yes, but anger that *he* felt, anger that was in *him*? Perkunos he understood. Perkunos was *always* angry; he *was* anger.

The storm exactly matched the feeling that had built for days, except the storm was there in front of him where he could see it. Perkunos was direct; he displayed his anger in great arcing flashing strokes, striking across the sky, striking his flint axe against the iron ground again and again, casting sparks in all directions.

But the years were colder now, the winters much longer than he remembered them as a child. That much of Raghe's talk was true.

The crops were failing, slowly failing as the years passed. What was there to make of that?

Krepus watched the hills far to the north and west, watching the axe come closer, and as he waited the storm came toward him. The imagined storm had been anxiety and tension for days, but the actual storm now, seen in the distance, was a release. Perkunos struck hard in the distant hills; he lit the world and raised Krepus from his gloom, raised him above the common earth. When Perkunos struck he could see across the plains as though the day had come. He watched, and the world lit and lit again. In those instants darkness and worry were dispersed.

After watching for some time he wondered: *What is this? What am I feeling now?* Distant thunder grumbled across the plain, approaching, approaching. Even from that great distance the strikes dimly lit the walls of huts, lit the village, and a subdued thunder echoed through it. Krepus stopped in the middle of the path, captured by the light and the growl of the storm, and waited to welcome his god. *Happiness. This is happiness*, he thought. *This is what happiness is.* His laughter stretched across his face.

As lightning struck again and again in the hills Krepus watched; the distant tempest filled him with awe and seemed to fill his life with purpose and meaning. He waited in the quiet street as Perkunos came to him.

The air, the light, the sounds of storm gave him long warning, but it was still vibrant, still exciting, when trees along the river shore bent suddenly. Branches and whole trees pitched in a new and violent wind, and the rain that had threatened for days finally followed close after and fell hard on him. He stood in the rain, his ecstatic face rising toward the sky. Noise, not just thunder but the heavy, hard noise of real rain, strong rain, *Perkunos* rain, hammering against the ground, lifted him and made him feel *right* in the world. It made him feel balanced. Hertus, hertus, right order of the world came down to him, came down onto his face from the sky.

His other concerns, strange behavior among the animals, and strange behavior from Kaikos and Prsedi, seemed less important. He had been on his way to Prsedi's hut, to see for himself what she would say, expecting to arrive there at dawn. Prsedi was an early riser. She would have been awake. But maybe now there was nothing to talk about. Maybe the storm explained everything. Maybe the animals and Kaikos and Prsedi all only felt this, the slamming rain, the rumbling raging joy; maybe they only felt Perkunos' cleansing anger surging toward them across the earth. What they had felt, Krepus thought, he was feeling now, and he could never blame them for that.

The storm blackened the skies even more than night did, although the dim along the hills to the east was a fraction less dark than the rest of the sky. Dawn. But the storm overwhelmed it, the dawn goddess, that delicate child, hid from Perkunos this morning. The storm was life, so Krepus paused to savor it, and to think about it. The river would be full soon, he thought, with rain as heavy as this. He would have other duties. A conversation with Prsedi would have to wait.

Krepus turned back toward the village center and walked toward the longhouse, the center of his domain, the center of his authority. A storm like this would bring those who worked to secure the Téuta to the longhouse to talk, and to plan. The lightning was striking all around the village by the time he got there, striking so close he could smell the flint of the god's axe in the night. Sntejo was there already, and others were coming.

It rained hard for most of the day. As evening arrived the rain eased; it came down steadily, but not violently. The thunderstorm and its drenching hard rain had moved up into the mountains, up the river. They would see it again in the coming days, Krepus thought, as the river rose past its banks.

Krepus worked all day ensuring that the longhouse and all the dwellings in the center of the village were sound and repairing roofs and draining the flooded firepits under them here and there. He and Sntejo and Do and others worked whenever the rain was light enough to permit it.

He slept well that night after his early morning and his long day of work. The next day was much the same. The rain stopped only briefly in the morning, and then returned in the afternoon, but a much softer, duller, windless rain, which did less damage. At that day's end Krepus saw that the village was under control, the longhouse and sacred places were safe and intact, although Raghe's smokerooms could be in danger, he thought, if the river rose too far. Some years ago a long rain and a fattened river had soaked them, their floors inches deep in water, or so Raghe said. Now the rains were stable, and the river was only a little higher than normal. The remaining work to maintain dwellings could be left to those who lived in them.

As he walked back to the longhouse he smelled strong smoke, not just the damp embers of the drowned fire pits, but bigger smoke, and the air was thick. He looked into the hills and saw that Perkunos had fired them, fired the trees. Since it was the end of a dry season that should have been a catastrophe of its own, but the steady rain was slowing the fires. Still, it was a concern. The rain might put them out. But it might not. It was one more thing to watch.

He decided that the next morning, early, he would complete his errand to Prsedi. He had to talk to her, and to Raghe again, because something, *something*, was truly wrong in the world. Something was wrong that had to be fixed.

⫟ Ⓤ ⊬⫟

After Sntejo left her, after her long day of work and her kept secret, Kaikos slept, and Chaisa let her sleep even after Prsedi came, promising to tell Kaikos everything, to pass Sntejo's message fully to Kaikos the next day. Chaisa didn't sleep, or she slept only a little; she let Prsedi sleep in her place next to Kaikos. She smiled when

Kaikos seemed to shift, to be puzzled in her sleep, but after a moment, never waking, she settled and accepted the substitution with no complaint.

In the morning, long before dawn, Prsedi rose and left them. When Kaikos woke they went to the river. As they bathed, Chaisa spoke to her.

"No running today, okay Kaikos? I need to speak with you. I have messages."

They had just finished swimming hard, so Kaikos was shaking water from her hair and was just a little out of breath.

"From who?"

"From Prsedi and Sntejo."

"From Prsedi?"

"Yes. She came to our hut last night, very late. She had to wake me up, and you were fast asleep."

Kaikos stopped shaking her hair and stood still. She was alert.

"Prsedi came to our hut after we were asleep? The long walk to our hut and back in the middle of the night?"

"She stayed with us last night. She slept next to you."

This was more information, or stranger information, than Kaikos could absorb standing without clothing in the cold river. She climbed out and put on her waist cloth and belt, trusting them to dry on their own, thinking, but with a puzzled smile.

"Chaisa," she said, when she had dressed, "let's run back and we can talk at home. I'm cold just standing after our swim."

So they ran back to the hut after all, and continued there as Chaisa made breakfast. Kaikos was sitting on the sleeping platform.

"Were we all sleeping together? I think moving to let three on would have wakened me."

She knew there was room for three, even for an extra person who was big, because Sntejo had stayed to sleep a few times after a day of hunting with Kaikos and being with Chaisa after. Usually that happened in the winter so Sntejo didn't have to walk back in the cold.

It was nice when that happened in the winter. The extra warmth of Sntejo with them made sleeping easier.

"I got some skins to make the floor soft and slept there so we wouldn't disturb you very much Kaikos. You didn't have to move at all. Prsedi just lay down in the place I had just left."

This information about sleeping with Prsedi was already overloading Kaikos. The world seemed turned inside out for that to happen.

"Why did she come so far in the night?"

Chaisa told her about Sntejo's talk at Prsedi's hut, and the message that Sntejo sent. They needed to find a place to hide if there were trouble. Prsedi thought so too, partly because of her talk with Sntejo, but also partly because there was other talk in the village, about things Raghe had said to his acolytes, and talk that he had been seen walking in the town several mornings. Even without the bholos storm something was changing. Maybe it was alright. But maybe not. Sntejo said they had to prepare for anything.

Kaikos stood up, half turned toward Chaisa. "*Sntejo* said that? He said that was a message for me, not just for you?"

"Yes."

They abandoned work for the day and talked through the morning. And that afternoon they walked in the hills to the northwest, up the hills toward the mountains, letting Kaikos search for a snug place for them to hide if they needed to. Chaisa went, she thought, so Kaikos wouldn't get lost, but Kaikos was alert, sensing everything far around them, and Chaisa just followed Kaikos wherever she decided to go.

They spent the next day looking, and the next, before Kaikos found a place for them that Chaisa, even looking at it and knowing it was there, couldn't see. A small crack in the rock wall beside a creek, a crack barely big enough for them to squeeze through once they knew where to find it, with rocks that overlapped and were covered with tangled brush—and behind, through the crack, was a cave bigger than their hut, and through a tight passage an inner cave three times as high and ten times as wide as the first. It was a long walk from their hut, as far from their hut as the hut was from the village, and in a direction no one was likely to come.

It was sufficient.

That night, or in the early day before the time to bathe in the river, Kaikos was wakened by thunder and the loud rumble of rain on the roof, the sound of rain all around the hut. For some time she lay awake listening. She didn't know how much time passed before she slept again, lulled by the rolling rainy night, and by the normal, normal, sweetly normal bholos all around her.

At the first sound of Chaisa flattening dough on the grinding stone, Kaikos woke and looked around, and looked again. The storm of rain had passed over and into the hills. And the storm of bholos seemed to have passed too. There were no sprouts, and although the ground was not calm, it was not as tense as it had been. Was it over? Was Dhegm well now? She spoke to Dhegm, although she had no reason to think the goddess heard, or would ever hear, things that Kaikos the cursed girl said. She whispered softly, *I hope you are well.*

She rose and would have gone to work, but the world smelled too good, and the stormy world felt too peaceful to work right now. She watched the gray flame of Chaisa moving near the fire pit, moving, slapping small rounds of bread on the hot stones, turning them. Kaikos smelled the charring bread and the world was almost too beautiful to live in.

She spoke, startling Chaisa, who didn't know she was awake yet. "Chaisa, can we swim again after we eat? Can I put off the grain-cleaning for long enough to swim?"

Chaisa felt the warm day, tasted the clean-smelling air after the thunderstorm had passed, and decided work and worry could be put off until the afternoon.

They ate, after Chaisa finished making her bread, and then they raced each other toward the river—Kaikos won and threw her clothes to the ground on the run. She was already swimming hard before Chaisa even got to the river's edge, laughing and calling after her. Chaisa loved Kaikos' independence and knew that after all their morning baths she was a strong swimmer, but it still worried her that her blind child was swimming alone in the long, quick water of the river.

Kaikos had no such worries—she just swam joyfully and felt the water sliding around her. True, she was blind, but her othersight left her in no doubt about where she was on the river, where the bottom and the banks were, where the big rocks and the fish were, and where Chaisa was.

That afternoon they began moving things they might need to their hidden cave in the hills. They didn't believe they were doing it. It seemed unreal to them. But Sntejo and Prsedi both said to prepare, even though there might never be a need. So they prepared.

In the weeks ahead they would be glad they had listened, and glad they had done what Prsedi asked. It was often good, Chaisa had found, to take Prsedi's advice.

CHAPTER TWELVE

Kaikos was tired after days of shifting and moving; after Prsedi's night visit, after seeking a new shelter, after moving grain and bedding through the stormy days. The hiding place had begun to seem real, and it had even started to feel like a home to her. She understood but did not understand. Nothing in her life had prepared her for this. Could this ever happen, that she and Chaisa must live alone, without Sntejo, without Prsedi? She was not sure how they could do it.

She, blind and small, would live with only Chaisa to help her; alright, alright, she could understand that. She could do that, she thought. But she was afraid, and she felt the guilt that this was all because of her, because she saw the bholos. Because she had told Chaisa and Prsedi about the bholos. Because she was a blind girl who was the curse of the Téuta. Because Dhegm was angry. What could have angered her? That, again and again, was the thing Kaikos could not understand. It was the thing she wanted most to change in the world. She wanted Chaisa to be safe, and Sntejo, and Prsedi. And Do. Yes, she wanted Do to be safe. And she wanted Dhegm to be well, and to not be angry with her anymore.

Through that first night after the thunder they had worked. They had slept most of the next day. Then they worked again through the night. A fear that she had never imagined had crept into their home. They worked through the next night, and the next, and then the storm came again and the rain came down on them and the wind blew them like dry leaves tumbling through the sky, but still they worked. The first night of lightning there had been fires in the trees, and the next too. Tall columns of fire marched across the hills. Chaisa said the whole plain reflected the fire's light, fields of high wet grasses restless under the wind tossing like an ocean and shining red and gold in the night. For Kaikos there was no light on the fields; light is something only eyes can see. There was no light from fires in the hills for her. There was only the sifting, soaking rain and the smell of wet smoke all around them, and constant work.

Then the work was done, and nothing had happened to disturb the Téuta.

Days passed. The bholos seemed to be quiet, and the sun was out most of the time after the first days. A few rains passed through, but that was welcome too. Kaikos began to forget the bholos storm that had so distracted her, that had sent her, for the first time in her life, to see Prsedi alone. The winnowing task was done; the grain-jar was full to the top, the hut and everything in it, and the small shelter behind it and the big covered outdoor fire pit that Chaisa used to make her pots, were all in good repair. Their cave in the hills was stocked for a month. The last few days before the autumn festival passed with Kaikos and Chaisa playing, swimming, running, and talking into the night.

Festival day was cloudless in the early morning; Kaikos smelled no rain, and Chaisa said the stars were clear. Kaikos was excited during her morning bath with her mother, and excited at breakfast, anxious to start festival day, but also still anxious about what had happened even though the bholos was still now.

Walking toward the Téuta was quiet. Neither Kaikos nor Chaisa felt any need to talk, and Kaikos walked where she usually ran. They arrived late in the morning, and the festival was already well underway. Some of the people who lived outside the walls had gone into the village to celebrate there, but some of those who lived within the walls had come outside the wall to see what goods were being traded. Braided belts, stone oil lamps, woven mats; two huts were trading beer, and four were trading bread or roasted meat or boiled meat with grain or with roots. All these goods were available from traders who sat outside their huts to show what they had. Chaisa had brought several finished pots, a bag of salt and a small bag of obsidian chunks, most of them small, to trade for things they wanted.

One man sitting outside his hut was trading flutes made of bone, and he played music to help raise interest in them. Chaisa had baked bread for them to eat during the day, so Kaikos sat with a small piece of bread, smelling it—she had eaten breakfast, but the barley bread smelled delicious—and listened to the jostled, hectic sound of the crowd, and to the music of the flute. Another man joined the flute player, beating a rhythm with something, maybe, Kaikos thought, some hollowed wood made for that. It sounded like wood.

Chaisa walked on into the crowd for a time, trying to find Sntejo. A child who must have lived inside the wall wandered toward Kaikos until his mother noticed her sitting there and recognized her; then she ran to take her child's hand, to pull him away so he wouldn't speak to the cursed girl. Kaikos hardly noticed that. She was used to it. She simply listened to the day and to the music. She smelled her bread and the food cooking at the festival, and she heard the river playing with the rocks along the shore, and she swayed to all the music. Her bread smelled quiet; it smelled like evening in her hut with Chaisa. The river simmered and slid to the top of its banks because the rain had filled it until it couldn't hold any more water.

The drum was a single bull running along hard ground. The flute sounded like the shapes that leaves made when the autumn wind blew them through the sky. Kaikos swayed, moving to the music.

Sntejo came to her from nowhere—there were too many people here; she couldn't keep track of all of them, so she hadn't noticed him coming. He asked where Chaisa was. Kaikos pointed into the crowd. She could always tell Chaisa's bholos from any other. She could see her not far away talking to a woman about something, possibly trading with her.

Sntejo couldn't see Chaisa but he knew Kaikos well enough to simply go where she pointed. Soon he was back, with Chaisa, and with some meat still hot from the fire and wrapped in leaves so it could be carried.

He had four packets of it with him. That meant they would visit Prsedi, so Kaikos stood, still swaying to the music, and they walked toward Prsedi's hut. The man playing the flute stopped when he saw Kaikos was listening to him, and he didn't start again until she was well past.

But that was expected, and he would play again while Kaikos was inside Prsedi's hut where he couldn't see her. She could dance there, and she did. After greeting Prsedi with her face toward the ground from respect and hearing Prsedi say "no ceremony, Kaikos!!" with a laughing voice, Kaikos stood up and danced to the flute music from outside while the grownups talked. Prsedi gave her some beer, and she sipped at it slowly.

The afternoon gradually became all music for her, all dance, and the chatter of grownups became background noise. When her cup of beer was empty Sntejo filled it again, even though Kaikos didn't ask for any more beer. She continued to dance and sip her drink.

At one point she thought she heard a different voice, and realized Krepus was there, wanting to talk to Sntejo about something. She began to turn to honor him, but something on the ground must have been uneven because she started to fall. She would have found a way to stay upright, but before she could think she felt a huge hand on her back, and Krepus' other hand under her arm to steady her.

"Careful, Kaikos," Krepus said to her. "No more beer for a while,

I think." He seemed amused. His voice was quiet, and even nice, and she didn't hear any of the anger she usually heard when he spoke, the anger everyone said was always in him. Maybe he wasn't angry on festival days. But he was also busy on any day, and he left soon after that.

In the late afternoon they were all full, and full of the feeling of friendship, and Kaikos had sipped enough beer to be a little too bold. She asked Prsedi questions she would not usually be brave enough to ask. She asked many things. She burbled on like the river without waiting for answers.

"Prsedi, what do you talk to Dhegm about? That thing in the music that goes tok, tok, tok, that sounds like wood, is it made out of wood? What is she like? Dhegm, I mean. Are you afraid to speak to her? I think I would be afraid of her. What is in the meat we ate this morning? It tasted like flowers. Does she have a big voice? If she speaks with a big voice why don't all the people in the other huts hear when she speaks to you? Is it hard to make a flute?"

Later she sat with Prsedi alone, because Sntejo and Chaisa had walked into the dwindling crowd of the late-day festival. They had decided to walk because there was time. Kaikos and Chaisa would stay until the crowds were mostly gone because some of the people outside had taken too much beer. The adults said they didn't want Kaikos to have to walk back through the rowdiness. Some of the festive people laughed, and some squabbled, and others touched each other and leaned together until they wandered off to find a quieter place to do what they wanted to do.

When they were alone, Prsedi came over to sit next to Kaikos. Later Kaikos would be reluctant to think about what happened next, but the day was so comfortable it happened without thought. With Prsedi so close, and so calm, with Kaikos so relaxed, and Sntejo and Chaisa only just outside, she accepted the feeling of close warmth. She simply leaned and rested her head on Prsedi's arm. Only weeks ago she had been afraid even to be alone in this hut with Prsedi.

But now, today, at the end of a day of festival, leaning against her seemed natural.

Then she asked something more serious.

"Prsedi, Sntejo says that Krepus doesn't hate me, but sometimes I think he does. I've only seen him a few times, but except for today every time I have seen him he seemed to be mad at me."

"Krepus is almost always angry, Kaikos. He's less angry with me I think than with most others, and with Sntejo he's almost happy. And of course today is a celebration day. But deep inside him the anger's there even today."

"Why?"

"Why is he angry?"

"Yes."

"I think he's angry, most of the time, because he can't fix something. Because something is wrong in the world, something his size and strength can't change, and that makes him a little afraid of it. It's not because of anything you ever did; it's because he leads us, Kaikos. That's not an easy thing for him. The whole Téuta depends on him for safety, he thinks, and so he feels he should be able to fix anything at all. Sometimes he can't."

"I think I am something that's wrong in the world, something he can't fix. He's mad when he sees me because of that," Kaikos said.

Prsedi paused, watching Kaikos. *It's her age*, she thought. *She leaps from childish curiosity to very adult seriousness and back again without even seeing that they're different. And she sees and knows far more than we tell her.*

Finally she said, "Don't say you're something wrong in the world, Kaikos. It's not true, it's never been true. I know there are some who say things like that, and Krepus hears them, but Krepus doesn't *want* to do anything about their talk. He doesn't hate you, Kaikos. He's just heavy with responsibility. But why are you asking about Krepus? Let's enjoy the festival."

Some? There are some who say that? There is Raghe, Kaikos

thought, and the name made her stiffen. But Prsedi said something then that sounded like it had meaning to her.

"I think you are something that makes the world right, Kaikos. I think you make balance in the world."

Prsedi put her arm around Kaikos' shoulders, and Kaikos' head leaned against Prsedi's soft, warm breast. They were quiet for a long while, drowsy from a day of festival, and from the sounds of people outside doing all the things they were doing, all the things the festival beer made them do.

Kaikos asked again, because Prsedi was the only person she knew who could tell her things like this: "Dhegm is very big, isn't she?"

"Very big. She is the mother of all the earth, Kaikos. She has to be big. Think how far away the mountains are that we can see from here. There are other mountains beyond those, and others beyond those. No one has ever been to the end of it."

"The mountains are far away."

Something about how she said that made Prsedi pause.

"Do you see the mountains, Kaikos, with the sense you have, what you call your othersight?"

"No, they are too far. The mountains are farther than I can sense. I have been into the hills with Sntejo, but he says the mountains are far beyond the hills. He says they are beautiful to see. I wish I could see them."

"How far can you see, Kaikos? Can you see your hut from here?"

"No. I can see the river, though. I think with eyes you can't see the river from here, right?"

"Right, that's true; the other huts are in the way, and eyes can't see through them. Can you see the center of the village, the longhouse?"

"Sometimes I can, kind of. It's cluttered, though. There are many things in between, and they get all mixed together. Today it's too confusing to see in that direction. Too many people outside walking at festival time."

"I can't see that either. My own hut walls stop my eyes from seeing. In some ways I can see much farther than you; I can see the mountains if I step outside the door of my hut. But in other ways you can see farther than I do. You can see the river while you are sitting here talking to me. So there is value in both ways of seeing."

Kaikos sat up. She needed to ask this.

"Prsedi, you and Raghe both talk to gods but you're different. You're not like him. I've never even seen him, but I think you and he are different. Why are you different if you talk to the same gods?"

Prsedi didn't have an answer to that. At least she didn't have one she wanted to give to Kaikos.

She had started to wonder what had happened to Sntejo and Chaisa, but at that moment Sntejo spoke from the doorway:

"I can answer that, Kaikos. When Raghe speaks to gods, he thinks that makes him bigger than the rest of us who don't speak to gods. He speaks to gods and comes back feeling that he is more like them than like us, that he is a creature of the gods, not of the Téuta. But when Prsedi speaks to Dhegm she sees how immense a god is, and she comes back feeling how tiny *she* is; she remembers she is far more like us than like a goddess."

Then another voice spoke behind Sntejo: "Sometimes I think she's silly about that. She once told me that speaking with Dhegm makes her feel as small as the beetles on the ground, that she and the beetles are the same."

"Well that's true, Sntejo," Prsedi said, thinking Sntejo had said that. "Compared to a god, all of us who scamper around here on Dhegm's earth are very small, and—oh." She had noticed Sntejo's face, and he was near laughter.

Do stepped out from behind him, and it was clear that Do, full of mischief and beer, was teasing her. And he was astonishing Kaikos, who could not quite believe that anyone would tease Prsedi. But Sntejo and Prsedi both laughed then.

Sntejo turned to Kaikos, a little more serious.

"There is another difference. Prsedi speaks to her god simply for friendship. Prsedi *likes* Dhegm. But Raghe neither likes nor dislikes gods. He speaks to them, as he does everything in his life, so he can gain something for himself. But enough about Raghe. I don't want to talk about him, and we don't really have time to talk about him, or about anything, if you two are going to get back to your hut and still be dry. There is another storm on its way. The end of summer is full of storms."

Prsedi and Kaikos both realized they had been hearing faint and distant thunder for several minutes. All of them scrambled to gather what Chaisa and Kaikos had to take with them, and then they quickly left. As they were almost ready to walk through the door of her hut, Prsedi called after Kaikos.

"I can help you make a flute," she said.

"What? A flute?"

"Yes. You asked about flutes. There was a kind man once who showed me how to make flutes, and I will show you. Would you like to learn? But you will have to learn to play it without me. He never taught me that."

"Yes, I want to make a flute! Thank you, Prsedi."

Chaisa spoke then, saying they had to leave before the storm came, that they had a long walk—or run—to get back to their hut. Then Kaikos and Chaisa ran hard toward home, and Sntejo ran with them.

But Perkunos was faster than they were. When the storm came down on them they were still far from the hut. It wasn't really cold, so they ran laughing together, ran simply for the joy of running in rain.

When they reached the hut they were soaked, and they all tried to dry themselves in whatever way seemed feasible; Chaisa and Kaikos simply changed into dry clothing. Sntejo watched Chaisa, and Kaikos recognized the form his bholos was taking, so she went to the doorway, ducking her head to enter the opening, and she sat, sensing Perkunos, sensing the gradually receding thunder, and the smells of the wet earth, hearing all the sounds of rain spattering against the hut and of trickles of water finding their way across the ground to the river.

She leaned against the side of the door and waited for dizziness to slow; she had tasted too much beer at the festival. Only a very small amount compared to many others there, but enough for her to have the lost feeling. In the corner of her othersight she did sense Chaisa and Sntejo doing their rolling-bear thing, their together thing. But that was far in the background for her, even though they were really only a few steps away. It was the rain she was sensing, and all the thousand creations of the night.

Chaisa shook her awake. She was sitting and leaning hard against the side of the door opening, her head against it, and had not realized she was asleep.

"I'm sorry we chased you to the door, Kaikos."

Kaikos could sense Sntejo out in the rain, running back toward his home inside the walls. She wasn't sure how he had squeezed past her through the small doorway without waking her.

"It's alright," she said to Chaisa. "I like when you do that with Sntejo. You're soft afterward."

"Soft?"

"Your bholos. It's soft as rabbit fur right now."

Chaisa thought about that. She laughed gently at the idea.

"Is Sntejo soft as rabbit fur too?"

Kaikos thought, and watched Sntejo running in the distance, a dwindling bholos flicker almost completely hidden by the rain. He was soft too, but thinking of Sntejo as rabbit fur was funny; Kaikos grinned and pushed her mother's arm.

"Maybe Sntejo is as soft as sheep fur," she said.

That made Chaisa laugh harder.

"Don't ever tell him. I don't think Sntejo wants to be a sheep."

"I'll tell him he's a ram."

"That might be better for him."

"A big ram with giant horns."

Chaisa shook her head, but her bholos was soft as rabbit fur and was also rocking with amusement. They sat together listening.

Finally Chaisa asked, "Are you ready to come inside?"

"Okay."

The two of them went to bed to end a long day, a good day. The best day for Kaikos in weeks.

And the best day for a very long time to come.

It was the night after the next night, the second night after Perkunos drenched the festival's end, soon after they had settled into hard sleep, that Kaikos woke, startled. Rain was falling again. Kaikos sat up and thought for some time, but her thoughts were scattered and tossed like the tall red grasses that Chaisa had seen when there were fires in the hills. Why did Kaikos think of that? Everything was tense in the night. Everything. The village, the ground, the air around her, the rushing bholos in every direction.

Twice Kaikos put her hand on the ground to feel the earth. In the late dark, while Chaisa slept next to her, the bholos jumped up high. Then Kaikos watched the bholos across the whole plains. She bent down to shake Chaisa awake. Still groggy, Chaisa turned in the bed to face her.

"We should go," Kaikos said.

"What?"

"We should go, Chaisa. We need to go."

Chaisa took a moment to wake up, to focus. She looked at Kaikos, and saw that she was serious, although as usual Kaikos looked to the distance, not at Chaisa's face.

"We should go *now*," Kaikos said again.

Chaisa didn't question it. Her daughter was anxious; her voice was filled with it. Chaisa simply stood, gathered what last things she could, and walked out of the hut toward the hideout they had prepared weeks before. Neither of them knew when they would be able to return.

CHAPTER THIRTEEN

They walked the path they had walked twenty times in the days after Prsedi had come to warn them. They found nothing to be bothered about on their trip but the rain, and for the rain they were grateful: it hid them, and it washed away their path behind them. Chaisa saw nothing to worry them on their way. She began to wonder as they approached the second big hill, approached the creek where they planned to hide for a few weeks while Sntejo tried to calm the village, what had made Kaikos so anxious on this particular night, at this particular time.

As a gray dawn lit the sky dimly to the east Kaikos and Chaisa rounded the last hillock on the trip to their hiding hole, their secret space, Chaisa wondered. They had passed the last place where the village could be in sight even on a clear day, and only because they had climbed to a hilltop well above the plains. Kaikos looked grim; she looked almost dazed, and she was very clearly trying to sense everything in the hills, everything in the air. Kaikos looked as though she did sense some danger. The night seemed only calm to Chaisa, only peaceful, other than the drenching rain falling all around them.

Then her foot seemed to miss the ground on her next step. The ground seemed to slip from under them, and the world seemed to tip, and Chaisa stumbled and fell. Her knee met the ground instead of her foot; she cried out and fell to the side holding it. Chaisa was bounced on the ground like a tossed rock.

Kaikos crouched to keep her balance; she put her hand on the ground and then both hands and waited for the shuddering earth to swallow them. The shaking seemed to go on for a long time. They waited, holding tight onto the ground under them even though that seemed to be the least stable thing in the world.

Swirling, disorienting bholos gave Kaikos no clear knowledge of what was happening around her. She could see the lump of Chaisa on the ground, but she couldn't know if the rocks above them would roll across the hillside, if the whole hillside would tumble down and crush them. She waited for that. It never came, so the ground here was at least stable enough to keep the rocks above them in place.

In the village, she thought, the huts would be cracking and falling. And although neither she nor Chaisa nor any other in the Téuta could know it, high in the mountains rocks did tumble, and snow and ice tumbled. Some of the creeks were blocked, and water made little lakes behind them in the rain. That slowed the rise in the river, but there were plenty of tributaries left to feed it. Water flowed over the ground, and ran down the rocks, and the river that flowed past the village was still rising steadily.

When the ground finally stopped moving, Kaikos stood and held her hand out to help her mother. After their fearful moments with the shaking earth, everything seemed suddenly quiet by comparison, so it was almost a surprise to recognize that the rain still came spitting down around them, washing the rocks, washing the hillside, washing the mountain above them and their hut and all the huts below them, washing the hills and the fields and the Téuta clean.

"Are you hurt, Kaikos?" Chaisa asked

"No. I'm okay."

Chaisa sighed, and remained seated, rubbing her knee.

"We will do what we need to do now," Kaikos said. "Come on, Chaisa. Can you get up? We need to go. We need to be settled before they start to look for us."

Chaisa got her footing and stood. Her knee hurt badly where she had fallen on it. Then she turned toward the village, wondering about Sntejo and Prsedi. She couldn't see around the rocks and trees, and she wouldn't be able to see the village through the darkness and rain from this distance anyway.

⊓ (] �

Darkness, smoke, silence except for the burble of the river outside, Raghe lay back on the stone he used for long travel and found his way out of the world. He would speak to the dead tonight, travel to their world where there was no sun, where shadow was all they knew. He lay still like a corpse himself. He had spent the time before morning over the sap lamp, and the smoke had lifted him, as it always did, and sent him careening out to emptiness. Quiet. Silence. No, not silence. A chant behind him; that was a boy keeping watch over his empty body while he was swept out of it.

But something drew him back; something moved under him; something moved under him; what was that? Something, and he moaned it away but it came again. And then it threw him to the floor. He rolled over and a shaft of harsh light came from a crack in the wall—what crack where did that come from? And the ground shuddered and sifted him; he rolled limp against it against the light and the shaking ground, and then he came back—not from the dead land because this shaking and light jerked him back before he got to that, and he rolled on the ground and came to himself. A little. A little. A little at a time he realized what was happening; by the time he knew, it was over.

Raghe looked at the tiny crack in the wall. His watch-boy had stopped his chant and was trembling in a corner, knowing nothing.

To him this was the apocalypse, the legend, the nightmare. But Raghe knew.

He knew what had happened, and he welcomed it. He laughed at it.

Now they will listen, he shouted to the single shaft of light in the dark narrow room; *now finally they will know*. No, he didn't shout. There was no sound. That was his thought.

Now they will know, he thought. *Out of their terror they will bring her. Out of the long years they will bring her. After the dark time they will bring her.*

Now it will be done. They will bring. They will bring. They will bring her. It will be done; Prsedi cannot. The shaking world is here, she cannot stop it.

Now at last we will take her, and then we will be safe.

Raghe slept. A light shaft filled with joy covered him.

ꙏ ◖ ꙮ

Krepus walked again toward Prsedi's hut in the early morning and the steady rain. But once again, Krepus never got to Prsedi. As he walked toward her, he seemed to stumble, caught himself, and realized that the ground was moving under his feet. It was a tremble first; then the ground lurched, then lurched again and then a third time, knocking him down to fall on his side, then it shuddered for a time before it settled.

He looked around him and saw huts with walls fallen, or roofs tumbled in on the sleeping residents; he looked toward the village wall and as he watched a great section of it leaned outward and fell to the ground. For only a moment there was quiet except for the sound of the steady rain falling, and the rushing river so full it sometimes nearly leaped over its banks. Then there came cries for help inside fallen huts, and sudden shouting from all around.

So, again, he turned back from a trip toward Prsedi, as people began to emerge from their doors, wondering what had happened.

They saw him, looked to him to explain. Most of them were far too young to remember the day thirty years before when Welo had shaken the ground, so they knew nothing.

Krepus remembered. At the first moment when the ground shook him down he remembered all of it with perfect clarity. He looked through the debris and the mud and heard the surprise in all the Téuta around him. *They are babies in this*, he thought, *nearly all of them.* Until now the idea of shaking earth had been a story to them. Now they knew it was real. He gave them only silence and strode away in the dark, toward the longhouse.

It was not until late in the day that he looked beyond the wall, out across the plains, toward the hut he couldn't see from here. Toward Chaisa's hut. *Welo is too far away, and probably dead by now,* he thought. *And Kaikos is small. She is no giant. No matter what Raghe might say, she hasn't the strength to shake the earth.*

As he looked, he saw a thin column of smoke where Chaisa's hut should be behind the hills. Looking higher he also saw the fires in the hills themselves, still strong even after the day's rains, and high in the smoking fires was a tall, whirling wind of fire reaching to the sky. He had never seen anything like this before. It was a fire giant walking across the hills.

His senses suddenly were stark and alert. Was this a new form for the giant Welo? Should he run from this giant in the hills? Should he gather the people around him and run? But for some reason he couldn't think about the fire. Instead he thought, *this rain seems thick. There's dust in it. And the river smells strange.* And he stood where he was, watching this thing that looked like it could sear the whole village, and rid the gods of it forever.

He would talk with Sntejo, and with Raghe, and tomorrow he would finally visit Prsedi. Then he and others would go to talk with Chaisa. The changing weather, shaking earth, the river rising above its banks, raiders coming down from the north, and now a fire giant. His people, the whole Téuta, suffered from these things. Something had to change. Something had to be done.

The girl, the girl, Raghe will say. Well, maybe it *is* the girl. Maybe it is. Maybe we've waited too long.

ᚻᛏ ᛰ ᚻᚱ

Sntejo's sleeping platform tilted and tossed him to the floor with skins falling onto him, and he was nearly standing before he realized what was happening. As he watched, the wall next to his bed cracked, and he ran to the street outside to see what was happening to those around him. Without thinking he turned to look toward Chaisa's hut, although there was no way for him to see it; the rain, the dark, the walls, the dust, the distance and the hummocked ground all hid it from him. *They will be alright*, he thought. But they stayed in his mind, and he couldn't get them out, as he walked toward the longhouse to find Krepus.

That evening he heard rumors that Raghe had not waited an hour before going to find Chaisa and Kaikos, that he had sent men to find them, and that the hut had been empty when the men arrived. Sntejo went to investigate. The hut was a charred ruin; all the pots were broken, and the grain Kaikos had spent so many days winnowing was scattered on the blackened ground.

Raghe's followers had been angry, Sntejo thought, that Kaikos and Chaisa had at least temporarily escaped them. So the men did what they could; if the two women tried to return there would be nothing there to hold them, and nothing to feed them through the winter.

An, who had helped to build the house, had been there to help destroy it.

ᚻᛏ ᛰ ᚻᚱ

Kaikos took Chaisa's hand again and tugged against it. They had to keep going, another climb, through a ravine that would be running now with water, up the opposite side to the place Kaikos had found for them with her othersight. Halfway up the ravine wall, as high as Chaisa's head, well hidden by brush and tumble around it—if it was still there—was the entrance to their sanctuary. The need had come, and Kaikos thought about all they had stored there: food, a fire kit, skins, grass mats, a pot made of hide so they could flatten it to fit it through the opening to their cave and a frame to hold it over their fire, a pile of wood and dry dung to burn. There was no real fire pit, so they would have to build their fire on the ground this first night, and they had no flat stone to grind flour on. For that they would use the rocky ground too. But they could live for a time with what they had brought over during the days of preparation.

They walked through the rain, through the creek running fast and as deep as their calves in the ravine, until they came to their chosen place. When they were inside the inner chamber, when they were hidden from everything outside, they took their wet robes off, built a small fire to warm themselves, and huddled together under some dry skins from the small stack of them they had left here.

The chamber was high, and there must have been small cracks that led outside, or led to some other passage with moving air, because the smoke drifted toward the top of one side of the cave and disappeared. That would have been a concern for them, but for now the wet smoke everywhere in the hills would hide the smells from any small campfire they might make.

When they were warmer, they dug out some dried meat and boiled it in water with a handful of grain. They waited for the meat and grain to soften, and then ate. And then they finally talked, about the shaking ground, about the future, about what might be happening at the Téuta village. There would fear, and rage, and the rain would make it difficult to repair whatever was damaged. Maybe people were hurt. There was no way to know, there in their secret chamber under the hills.

The chaos at the village was far away now, and the world was quiet, and Kaikos thought the day smelled early.

"I'm afraid in here," Chaisa said. "What if the ground shakes again? The hill can come down and trap us."

"It won't shake again. Not tonight."

"How can you know this?"

"I know," Kaikos said. "The bholos is quiet. It's swirling in circles; it's still tumbling from the shaking, but it is not shooting up high out of the ground like it did before. When I lay my hand on the ground, I feel almost nothing. The night is quiet now. The ground is quiet."

Chaisa looked at her daughter's serious face in the firelight and believed her.

They lay down inside the cave, with Chaisa's soft dry shawl beneath them and Kaikos' dry shawl and one more dry fur on top of them, and they lay close to warm each other. The fire had taken some of the chill away from their cave, but it was still cold.

Kaikos felt the moment, the still night, held close by her mother under the furs. She didn't know what to expect tomorrow. But this moment, in the cave with her mother—*this* felt good to her. She wanted the sweetness of this moment, this moment holding her mother, this tiny moment of safety and warmth, this tiny, good moment—she wanted this to last forever.

Warm, yes, warm in spite of the cold rain, and safe in spite of everything. No one would find them here, and she could not quite believe the village would really hurt them anyway. Not even Krepus, even if Raghe said to. She could still feel the warmth of his great hand on her back when he kept her from falling at the festival.

This would be alright tomorrow. They would wake later in the day and Sntejo or Prsedi would find some way to tell them they could come home, and it would be alright. Prsedi and Chaisa had planned a signal that Kaikos couldn't see, but that Chaisa, with eyes, could.

But they heard nothing, and saw nothing, from either of their friends that day, or the next, or the next, even though twice they climbed up to the hilltop where Chaisa could see the village in the distance.

CHAPTER FOURTEEN

Welo stopped as he approached the ruined town, the tumbled huts of the old Téuta village. The sight of it always made him pause.

Rubble and rock cluttered what had been paths through the Téuta then. Few of the huts still stood; many had vanished under the sliding cliffs, and others had been crushed by boulders. Still others had been weakened and had simply fallen in on themselves as the years passed. The dust, long settled, covered them.

But the Téuta might have moved south anyway, he thought, toward longer summers. They liked their warmth, and the years were cold now, and always colder. Through his whole long life they had been getting slowly colder year by year. When he was a child, he seemed to remember, snow was uncommon here; even during the winters the ground was clear most of the time. Now the ground had snow or ice much of the winter. It was usually not deep like in the high mountains, but now even here in winter, for four or five moons at a time, the snow and ice were expected, and it was the times of clear ground that were uncommon.

Maybe the endless world was ending. *It might be*, he thought.

Deep in his heart his bitterness wanted to say, *maybe that is good, since people are so cruel.*

"What becomes of the dead when the world ends?" he said aloud, to only the ruins around him. "What becomes of the gods? There will be no earth, and no sky, and no weather if there is no world. There will be no dawn. There will be no sunset. What gods can there be in such a place?"

He watched the disk of red sun and the clouds, and the high cliffs, still sharp and ragged from the slide half a lifetime ago, and he didn't want any of that to end. *And,* he thought, *maybe I will die before the earth dies. The world might end, but maybe not for many days, or many years. This evening is here now, and this sky and this earth.* He told the bitterness in his heart to recede, and to let his joy in the beauty of life come out.

Only two huts looked cared for as Welo strode through the ruined streets. He walked toward one of them with his kill, a small red deer, in a sturdy sling across his back. He was grateful for this at least: his back was still strong enough in his old age to hunt and to carry his kill home. He tired more easily now, but he could still use his strength to lift what he needed to lift. He had cleaned the deer already near the stream, so the weight was not too great.

Welo had spent two months after the event living alone in the hills, and then he had lived at the top of this new cliff. He had built a hut up there a lifetime ago for Eksi when she first came before she was accepted by the Téuta, and before she became his wife. It was big enough for him, but for only him. That was enough. He knew he would be alone forever. There was no need for any greater space than that.

And for the first months after his return from the hills he stayed there, angry and bitter, before he came back to this ruin to take whatever he could find that might be of any use to him. He had taken hides and grain and pots and flint, some axes and knives that had been left behind because their owners were buried under masses of rock where they had no need for such things, or they had left with the Téuta to go wherever the Téuta had gone. Then he returned to his high hut and stayed there.

But his daughter had been buried in this slide too, so when his grief at long last allowed it, he had come back to care for her. He dug her out from the place where she died, from the hut where she had lived with her husband and with her infant daughter Chaisa. He was lucky that the big rock, the cliff itself, had not come down on it; nothing could ever move that. Still, some of the rocks on top of her were very heavy. He had needed long poles to pry them away enough to find her. With Chaisa gone to some far place she was all the family he had left. She, and Eksi, with all the ancestors buried in their graves, with the graves buried under the fallen cliff.

He dug a place for his daughter in the earth and buried her with furs and pots of grain. He had taken the grinding stone from her hut and buried that with her too, so she could grind flour to make bread if she needed to, if such things were ever done in the land of the dead, and he buried her needles and spinning whorls with her to make thread, and to sew her clothes.

Then he had built a new hut over the ground where she lay, and he built a new hut next to her for him to use when he came to visit, since the hut he had built for her belonged to her and to her family. He had not lived in their hut when she had been alive, so now he thought it was proper for him to live in a separate hut next to her, as he had then.

They may all be dead now. It was possible he had no living family at all. He had no way to know. But if Chaisa ever returned—she would not, but if she ever did—she could live there, in that hut, with her mother. It would be hers now.

He spoke again to the hut, to the ruins, to the evening:

"It would have been good to see Chaisa grow up," he said. "It would be good to know her now, if she lives. Families are difficult sometimes, but life without a family is also difficult."

It was not a new thought for him. He thought it whenever he came here.

This work of building huts took him all of that summer to do. For twenty-nine years after that he had come back here to spend the winters on the flat ground, where the snow was less deep and there was shelter from the north winds. In the summers he moved to higher ground, building huts and shelters among the lonely rocks. He had no fixed place anymore, no village that bound him, so he had several huts up in the mountains too. He wandered where he wanted, wherever the winds and his curiosity took him.

He lay the deer on the ground outside and built the fire up in his hut. Then he went to his daughter's hut and built a fire in her fire pit too. Why should she not have a fire? He spoke to her for a time.

He returned to the deer carcass and spent the evening cutting strips of meat from it. He salted them and laid them on the hot flat rocks next to the fire to dry. Finally he decided to make his dinner. He used the method he and others had used when they were far from the village, when they were hunting overnight and carried no pots or stone vessels with them: he used the washed stomach of the deer as a vessel, and boiled both meat and bones and roots in it until the slurry was ready to eat.

He cooked this way often. He had become used to treating every day as a long expedition, a long exploration into the wild. Because every day *was* an expedition now, and everything around him was wild. *He* was a wild thing now, only another wolf in the wilderness, since he had no village to belong to.

When he had eaten, he sat outside the hut to watch the evening. *It is good,* he thought.

"It's good to be here," he said aloud, "and good to be alone here. This is where I was born, just over there in a hut now buried, but in this village. I live here, have always lived here, and I will die here. Soon, probably, because I'm already too old. I hope I die here, in this hut. But I will have no one to bury me. I have no living family. I have this ruined village, and I have the mountain. I have my daughter in her hut beside me. That's all I have."

Clouds spread across the sky, and the day's end stained red across them. Welo sat, waiting, until the sun was well down, and the dusk was in the old streets.

"My ancestors, my daughter, my village. That's enough. For what's left of life that's enough for me."

He woke the next morning early, in the dark. The world in his other sense was a dizzy disk around him, horizon to horizon. He rose from his bed and watched. Time passed, and passed, and when the dizziness ebbed he went out to the street looking for what had wakened him. Why was he here in the village, in late summer, not winter, and why was he in the street so early, as dawn, earth's daughter, was just waking to open a new day? He should be asleep in the hut high on the cliffs. But something had made him nervous. Something in his senses felt off, felt strange, and reminded him of this place, so he came to try to figure out what it was.

Then the ground shuddered under him, not violently, but the shudder was there. He turned to look west and south and saw—something. He wasn't sure what he saw. So he sat and closed his eyes, concentrated as he had learned to do to sense into the far distance, and again even farther. The shaking wasn't terrible here, but down on the plains it was much worse.

That was where the Téuta went, he thought. *The Téuta, the Téuta, the Téuta—the ground shakes under them wherever they are. Now they must know it wasn't me.*

Welo sat in the street thinking for a long time. He sat until the light from the east roused him. Then he stood. For a time he watched the red dawn, singing softly to himself. Now he knew what had troubled him for the last days, and why he had come here.

He walked back to his hut to gather his things; he had no need to be here anymore. But he didn't want to simply leave, now that he was here, so he went through to his daughter's hut and sat on the floor talking to her. He did not expect a reply since he was not a shaman. He had no way to see through to the land of the dead.

But his home, the place where he lived during the summer, was elsewhere. When he had told his daughter all he meant to say, he stood again, moved slowly out the door of her hut, and then, with his dried meat in his sack and what remained of his deer in the sling on his back, he walked through the ancient streets, past the rubble of the fallen cliff, back along the river toward the path that led to his summer hut high above.

PART II

Early Autumn Among the Téuta

CHAPTER FIFTEEN

The girl and her mother stayed in hiding during the days, since in the light they might be seen. Chaisa spent much of her time in the outer cavern; she was comforted by the thin ribbon of daylight that came in through the entrance crack.

There was no sign from Sntejo or Prsedi.

They tried to eat once each day, and once each morning they came out of the cave to bathe in the rill and to breathe fresh air. They had a single sack for water, and they filled it when they bathed, and then Chaisa went out each evening to fill their sack again with water from the rill below. They emerged only when Kaikos' othersight told her there was no one near them. No one. Not even a stag in the brush.

They foraged a little, but mostly they ate what they had: some dried meat, grain, some bread that had quickly become hard. When it was too hard, they could dip it in water or broth to soften it. When even that was not enough to soften it, they would throw the dry bread into the soup to thicken it. They ate as little as they could because food, now, was precious.

Four days passed before the second earthquake. Kaikos had

watched the bholos rising for days from the ground before she told Chaisa they should go outside to bathe in the stream that ran by them; she didn't want to be in the cave when the earthquake struck, fearing the cave would collapse.

"It's daytime, Kaikos," Chaisa said to her.

"Yes. But we need to go anyway. We can't be here inside the cave right now."

Chaisa saw how troubled the girl was, so she knew it mattered. Again she chose to be guided by her daughter. She stood, took Kaikos' hand, and walked out into the day. Kaikos took them away from the steep rocks, which meant they had to walk into the stream. They had reached the deepest part, wading up to their thighs, when the ground shook under them, spilling both of them into the water.

But the second quake was milder, and the cave remained intact. When the ground was quiet again, they went back inside.

⊓ ⏺ ⊬

Krepus looked around at the village, frustrated, angry, tired.

The damage to the Téuta had been everywhere across the village, so for four days Krepus and Sntejo and most of the younger men in the village worked to repair it. Many others had made bread or root or lentil soups to feed the workers. Sntejo and three others had gone to hunt; they returned with two deer and many rabbits, and there was a lighter moment as the workers feasted on this food, and on the bread brought to them by many people grateful for their help.

Through all of it, though, even through the feast, there was a common sense of loss, and a common sense that loss was still waiting for them.

It wasn't the kind of devastation that Welo caused thirty years ago, because now there were no cliffs to crack apart and slide down on them. But it was still hard, and there were still some dead and many injured. Krepus' back hurt, and his hands hurt.

And things inside him that he would never admit also hurt. He had few friends, and no wife, but he had known the woman Delki for many years, and she had often been a comfort to him when he most needed it. She had been wounded when the ground shook. How long ago? Six days, seven days? Twenty days? He was too tired to remember.

On that day her hut fell inwards trapping her. A small child, her child and possibly his as well, had been buried in the rubble. When he let himself think of that—and he thought of that if he thought at all—his anger rose, and it was not pleasant anger. Not Perkunos anger. It was something else, something he didn't want, something that was of no use to the Téuta. He tried not to think of anything at all. He tried to just do what had to be done and let all the rest go for now.

But he had to think. He had to find an answer to this. Now he was angry at the gods. All of them. *All of them!* Angry at those who were cursing the Téuta because they cursed, and at those who were not because they did nothing to help.

Prsedi, of all people, had found him early today and had given him bread soaked in honey to eat, and told him he should rest for an hour before he fell down from exhaustion. So now he sat resting in the middle of the day watching the swollen river flowing strong, well over its banks now and still rising toward the village, and he tried to think of nothing. The rains had stopped over the Téuta for now, but rain *here* was not his concern. His concern was the rain to the north: that was where the rain had gone to come down hard and constant in the mountains. Krepus knew, though, that the water in the mountains would come down the rills to the creeks, down the creeks to the canyons, down the canyons to the river here, and the river would rise even more. He had no idea how to stop it, or how to protect the Téuta from it.

He couldn't think now. He had to rest, and he could, for the moment. Nothing was really pressing. The sun was warm on him, and he was ready to lie back on the ground and sleep.

As he watched the river it seemed to ripple, settle, ripple, sway. Then the water in the river suddenly leapt, with great rocking waves smacking against rocks and sending spray far into the air. He was puzzled for a moment, until he felt the ground under him shift and buck again. This time it didn't knock him to his knees—he was already sitting—but he knew in his angry bones that this day, this endless day, was not over. Behind him he could hear cries of people whose huts, just repaired with the new mud in their walls still wet, had fallen in again, and other, pleading voices of those who had been hurt.

Krepus cursed hard.

Raghe, Raghe, tell me what I need to do! Prsedi, tell me what I need to do to protect my Téuta from the curses of gods or giants! Give me something to fight against, or tell me how to fight against something I can't touch and can't see!

Krepus put a hand on the ground and pushed himself to his feet. He stood, stretched his sore back, and walked toward his village.

ᛏᛏ ⑴ ᚻ

More than half a moon after the first earthquake they were still in the cave. All the bread was gone, and the meat more than half gone. They still had two small crocks of grain, which might last another month, but both of them thought, then what? What would they do when the grain was gone and winter was threatening? What would they do when winter was here? They had lost their belief that this would pass, that Prsedi would signal them and Sntejo would come to take them home.

Foraging at night when they thought the Téuta would be asleep they found late summer berries, and walnuts, onions, sage and thyme, and some roots they could eat once they were boiled. Salt reserves were finally low, since they hadn't thought to bring very much to a cave they thought they would occupy for less than a month, so they took a long trip—their longest trip in distance—to get salt from Chaisa's spring.

On the way back from that trip, walking through the trees as they approached their cave, Kaikos suddenly took Chaisa's elbow and signaled her to be silent. After a few moments Kaikos pulled Chaisa down to crouch hidden in the bushes. They waited there for a long time.

Twice Chaisa turned to ask what was happening, but each time Kaikos signaled for silence, looking serious. Then Chaisa heard men walking along the stream, talking quietly to each other. What they said was easy to understand but hard to hear: they were not simply out hunting for game. They were hunting, as Raghe's legs and eyes, for them, for Kaikos and Chaisa.

When the hunters walked on, and Kaikos signaled that they could move again, they went as silently and as cautiously as they could to their cave entrance, taking their onions and berries and salt. They slept uneasily that night. Their stay in the cave suddenly seemed less like life, less like adventure, and much more like hiding.

Chaisa was quiet through the next morning. She didn't have to speak, though; Kaikos knew what she was going to say. She waited. She didn't want to hear it.

Finally Chaisa said, "We can't just stay here like this Kaikos. I need to find help. Who can we trust? Sntejo?"

"Maybe. I think so. *You* can. I think you can trust Sntejo. But I don't want you to go. If you go then I'll be alone."

"I'm not going for long, Kaikos. I'll return right away."

Kaikos was quiet.

"What else can we do?" Chaisa asked.

"We can stay here. I can find burrowing animals and you can make a fire to cook them. Even in the winter I can find them; I can sense the bholos around them in their burrows. Right now the hills all smell like smoke, so we can build fires, and in the deep winter no one goes far from the village except to hunt. There is still grain in the fields for now; we can gather that at night. Or maybe in the winter when everyone is inside their huts at night we can go down to our hut and take the grain that's there. I don't know, Chaisa, we can think of things; we can make porridge with meat in it, and you can grind grain on the ground to make bread. We can catch frogs in the creek. Maybe find fish; there are fish even in winter. We can live here and be secret. But if you go you near the village you will be seen. They will take you, or you will be followed back."

Chaisa was quiet and thought about that.

"What kind of life is that Kaikos," she said finally. "And I don't know if that would work. We're too close to the Téuta. Sooner or later they will know we are here."

"Then we can go over the mountain to the other side, find a better place. A farther place, where they will never find us."

And Chaisa thought about a different life, over the mountain. She thought about a life, a whole lifetime, without Sntejo or Prsedi.

They waited through the day and slept. Kaikos didn't want to be alone. She clung to her mother in the night as hard as she had clung to her doll of fur when she was a small child. She held to her as if this were the last moment of life. She held as though she wanted to keep her right here, in this place, through all the rest of time.

Night insects kept a constant chorus around the cave opening, and bats came out to hunt them, and horny owls called out. High on the bank above, a group of deer crashed through the brush, followed silently by a big cat. Kaikos watched all of this with her othersight.

The buzz and busyness of life in the night lulled her. Her eyes finally closed, and she slept deeply. In the morning when she woke she looked around the cavern, and around the outer cavern. Chaisa was gone.

CHAPTER SIXTEEN

That whole day Kaikos was alone, afraid for her mother and afraid for herself. She was miserable, and she slept miserably that night. All the next day she waited, and she ate some of the last of the dried meat, and slept again. She would have to give up, to give herself to Raghe, she thought. A blind girl-child could not survive alone in the world. She knew that. Everyone knew that. She needed Chaisa, at least. She needed Chaisa and Sntejo and Prsedi, and Do, even Krepus, the whole village that hated her, she needed all of them to survive. In her whole life she didn't remember being so alone.

She slept, and wakened, and waited again through the day. When the day was almost done, she was very hungry, and she thought she had no more time. She would have to give up.

Then there were two people outside the cave. She saw them with her othersight but couldn't tell who it was. She crept silently into the outer chamber and to the hidden opening to listen, to try to understand who was there. She watched as the two seemed to wander back and forth, looking for something, or looking at the things around them. Finally they settled some distance down the stream from the entrance to her cave.

A voice spoke to her, loudly so she could hear, "Kaikos. Are you there?"

Kaikos was quiet. It was Sntejo speaking, but who was the other? She sat silently.

"Kaikos, it's okay. It's Do with me. We have food for you. We'll leave it for you here outside. You should know your mother is safe. She is in Prsedi's hut, kept safe there."

Sntejo was giving her news; he spoke in a stream to let her know what was happening.

"She went back to your hut to get grain and other things, which was foolish. Raghe and those who follow him had already burned your hut, and they are watching everything now. They were waiting for her, and for you, but only she came. But Krepus and I were at the gate when they brought her in, and Krepus stopped them there. Prsedi and I have promised to keep her, to care for her and be vigilant.

"Raghe is angry. He's angry at Krepus for keeping Chaisa from him, angry at Prsedi for sheltering her, and angry with her for hiding you; he is sure she has done that although she says not. He sets people to watch her in case she tries to come to you again. You should stay away from him, away from the village, for now. Krepus is tired. There is so much damage, Kaikos, and eleven dead, and many hurt."

Kaikos still sat silently.

"I don't know if you hear or not Kaikos. This is where Chaisa told me to leave food for you. I think this is where she said. I don't know where in this place you might be, since there is no place here to hide that Do or I can see. I know you, though. I know you can find places I can't. But stay silent. Even if you hear me, you're smart to stay quiet, and stay hidden.

"It's bad among the Téuta, Kaikos. It's so bad, I can't explain what is happening. But listen, please. Don't trust anyone. We all spend our days repairing things, but what Krepus really wants is something to tear apart. Everyone is afraid of Krepus and Krepus is afraid of the ground. Afraid of Welo. Maybe afraid of you, since Raghe is crying out for your death. I don't know what Krepus plans to do but he won't sit still and be afraid. If you hear me, stay hidden, Kaikos. I might be able to bring more food for you, but I might not. It's not just Krepus. *Everyone* is angry; *everyone* has lost something. Everyone is watching everyone else."

There was quiet for some moments, then Sntejo said: "We will leave the food in the bag. I hope you hear and can find it. Don't leave it for others to find, or they will know where to look for you."

Do and Sntejo stood and turned to walk away.

"Sntejo," she said, calling his name quietly.

Sntejo's hearing was acute. He paused for a moment and squatted down on his heels again.

"Yes, I'm here. But be more careful, Kaikos, and you should move to a different place, so I don't know for certain where you are. Now that you've spoken, I know this is the right place. Please, Kaikos. Don't trust anyone at all. Not even me. I—you are like my daughter, Kaikos, but I must do as my king asks, as the Téuta need me to do. Krepus doesn't really want to ask me anything about you, or ask Chaisa either; that's another thing stinging him, because Raghe walks the village often now, creating hatred against you and Chaisa wherever he goes."

"Sntejo, will Chaisa be able to come back?"

He was quiet. He didn't want to say what he had to say.

"She will not be able to come back for a long time, until Raghe goes back to his dark rooms, until the anger is less, and people watch less. I'm sorry, Kaikos."

"I want to come home Sntejo. How can this happen? I want to be home with Chaisa, with you and Do and Prsedi to visit us. When can I come home?"

"Kaikos, please don't do that. Don't come to the village at all. Krepus thinks the whole world is in danger, and he wants to stop whatever threatens us. Raghe says that is you, and Chaisa, and Welo.

But it has been so long, Welo would be far too old. He is surely dead
by now; he has been alone for thirty years. He was old when he was
left behind; by now he would have lived two lifetimes. So he must
be dead. Krepus thinks you might already be dead too, a blind girl
alone in the world."

Sntejo paused, and Kaikos was quiet.

"But Welo was a giant, they say, so he may have a long life. It's
possible he's still alive and causing this. Raghe says the gods tell him
Welo is alive. I don't know about that. But Raghe says it is so."

There was a long silence. Kaikos waited.

"I don't know, Kaikos," Sntejo said. "I can't believe Welo is still
alive. Krepus listens to Raghe and wants to believe him about that.
He wants to believe, because if Welo is dead, was dead when this
happened, then it would not have been Welo who caused it. If Welo
is dead then Raghe would claim this shaking ground, and the long
years getting always colder, is because of you. Krepus would have to
listen to him."

Kaikos erupted in confusion, in fear and anger, almost in tears.

"*Why would he think that?? How can he think that?!* How could
he think I could do this? *How can you think that Krepus??*" She
shouted loudly, as though she was trying to make Krepus hear her
from the village. "I can't shake the world or make it warm or cold!"

Then, more quietly, but her voice still shaking with grief and
anger, she said, "The years were getting colder before I was born,
before *you* were born, Sntejo! *Since before Krepus was born. How can
Krepus think I am doing something that was happening before even he
was born??*"

"Yes, since Welo was born the years have been changing, they say,
so maybe it is him. But you knew about the shaking ground before it
happened, Kaikos. Everyone knows that now. No one said anything;
Chaisa didn't, I didn't, Prsedi didn't. But everyone knows."

Sntejo's frustration was clear, and Do was silent. Do wasn't
laughing now, and that frightened Kaikos more than anything else.

But it was Do who finally said what silenced her:

"Kaikos, listen," Do said. "I know it doesn't seem right. I know it *isn't* right, but it is how things are. Do you understand, Kaikos? Raghe thinks the gods demand a punishment or a sacrifice for whatever is making them angry. Krepus might hesitate but the village is convinced by their shaman. Only Prsedi is holding them from swarming out to find someone to punish. From finding *you*, Kaikos. And they would find you here. You are well hidden but sooner or later, now or next year, or the year after, if you are still alive, they will find you."

Do stood, and then sat again, and Kaikos could hear the tension in his voice. "I will not hurt you, Kaikos, never. Never. I will do anything I can to keep you safe. But I am one, and Sntejo is one, and the Téuta are many."

Sntejo sat and it seemed that he wanted to say something else, but he didn't. After a moment of quiet both men stood and walked away.

Kaikos watched them with her othersight until they were far down the hills. She smelled the evening smells around her. Still she waited, until it smelled like night, when she knew that people who used their eyes to see found doing that more difficult. She used her othersight to peer as far as she could in every direction, to make sure there was no one there waiting to take her. Then she slipped out of the cave.

She kept low and quiet, even though no one was near. She spent some minutes brushing the ground with her hands, until finally her hand found the sack they had promised. It had bread and fruits, a big sack of grain, and a lot of dried, salted meat. As long as she kept her fire alive, she could make soup with this, and survive, and for now she had dry wood.

She was glad to have the food. Glad to have someone like Sntejo who would bring food for her. But the world was suddenly a lonely place, and a frightening place.

She wanted to feel her mother putting a shawl around her

shoulders. She wanted to hear her turning in her sleep during the night. She wanted to feel Chaisa's arms, and Chaisa's breath against her as they slept.

She wanted to lean her cheek softly against Prsedi's breast.

She put the woven mat on the rock floor of the cave to sit on and wrapped herself in her shawl, rocking silently in the dark.

CHAPTER SEVENTEEN

Noon, or nearly noon, and the river smelled muddy; it smelled of dead fish and of vegetation uprooted by the risen water and left on its banks to rot. Those who had work to do were working, and those who didn't were inside their huts, when Prsedi walked through the gate into the inner village. She rarely came here. As a rule, when she wasn't home she was walking along the river or tending a garden she had made near the river; it was flooded now, but she didn't really need it. People gave her food, often. People would come to her house to ask her things and would leave food and other things with her. Often they were things she didn't need or want, so she gave them away to her neighbors.

Now she walked intently, ignoring the nearly empty paths, looking at her destination. Raghe's stone stood tall above the huts. Why did he have it? Why did others, many others, work so long to bring this stone here and tip it up to stand so high? Why did they carve strange things into it, animals, and people without heads, and vultures? Did they think that would entice the gods here? That the gods who made sun and rain, who made dawn and mountains, would flock to this place to see this little piece of rock? Did Raghe think that?

Well, she thought, the man needed all the help he could get. It was impressive, she admitted as she passed it, and it drew every eye in the village. It was a monument to Raghe. It cemented his power—not his power with gods, but his power here in the Téuta.

The smell of the place was faint, here in his outer chamber, the one of all his rooms that was available for anyone to see. But it was here: the smell of strange burning things and sweat. Her nose rebelled as soon as she walked in. But she was disturbed at what was happening. She walked to the center of the room and stood waiting. She knew he would hear of her presence soon enough. Prsedi, Prsedi, Prsedi is here! The rival god-speaker, standing in your castle, your holy place, her presence like a gash, like a wound in the Raghe-worship!

Soon he came and stood looking at her.

"What do you want, Prsedi? Why have you come here?"

"Why are these people skulking around the buildings, Raghe? Doesn't Krepus have enough watchmen out?"

"I think he doesn't," Raghe said. "Krepus watches for enemies, but he doesn't watch his friends. He watches Chaisa, but he doesn't watch you, and he doesn't watch Sntejo. He thinks you are both blameless perfections. But I know you find ways to help Kaikos. I know that. If Krepus is blind, I'm not. I will be sure you are watched."

Prsedi paced away, then paced back.

"Raghe, think. What have you created, here among the Téuta? Are all the streets clogged with your spies now? Is that what the Téuta is?"

Raghe snorted, turned, and began to walk away. Then he turned back just long enough to say, "If you have nothing to hide from me then you have no reason to resent being watched."

Then he crouched to disappear back into his inner rooms, back to the smoke and the stench.

Prsedi gazed around the walls, with all their decorations, the bulls' heads, the murals. *Yes*, she thought. *Very impressive, for those who are easily impressed.*

She walked back toward the gate, watching around her now, watching the almost empty streets. But they were not completely empty. Two of Raghe's spies were standing near Sntejo's hut, and only a single spy near Do's hut. *Do must feel slighted*, she thought, *to have earned only one.* They were waiting for anything to happen that they could report. No doubt they were sure they would gain favor with the gods by reporting it.

Mountains stood brilliant in the sun; the rains had paused, for now. Sun lit the huts, and the walls, and the dust in the streets. Light gleamed off rocks normally dry but now washed with water from the river. Prsedi breathed in the wonder of it and shook her head at the confounding arrogance that would make Raghe think the gods who did all of this without effort—to the gods this wasn't a thought or even an afterthought, it was just what they left behind them as they passed—to think that gods who did this would worry about the actions of Sntejo, or Do, or Prsedi.

Or Kaikos.

Well, she thought, *the gods leave what gods leave. And we leave what we leave. And Raghe leaves everywhere a corruption in the world.*

The days passed, and Prsedi did what she could. Fortunately, Raghe's spies were easy to see, and easy to evade.

ᚻᛏ ᚹ ᚻᚱ

Night air was cooler now. It felt good, and walking felt good after the long weeks huddled alone in her cave. Kaikos knew she shouldn't be out. Each minute she was aware of that, but she had eaten most of the food Sntejo had given her, and he had not come back. Do had not come back.

She still had lentils they had brought from the garden near their hut, but those too were hard to eat without a fire to boil water to soften them. The peas had been eaten raw long ago. So she needed to find food, or better food; she had found roots that could be eaten, but she had no fire to cook them since the fire Chaisa had started had gone out one night while Kaikos slept. Starting fires was one of the tasks she had never been allowed to do. She had the fire kit, but she couldn't see the sparks when she struck the iron and flint together. No matter how many times she tried she could not make the fire happen.

She waited until the village was asleep, and walked, far around the village to the side away from the doors. There were rocks on a small hill there, thirty steps from the nearest huts in the village, and she sat behind them, searching the night smells, and hearing the night sounds, and looking with othersight into the village. As far as she could tell everyone was sleeping. She could see their bholos clumps huddled near the ground.

She wasn't sure why she was there. She did need food, but she couldn't risk going into any hut to get it. There was no way to get in to see her mother; she was guarded. And the risk of being here was high. But it felt good to be near the Téuta village again, to be near other people again, near Prsedi and Chaisa, even if they were all asleep. She missed her village. She missed everyone, even those who hated her.

She was hungry, and that mattered, but just being close to all of them mattered more. She would try again to start her fire, and she would stay alive as long as she could. Without Chaisa there wasn't much joy in it. But as long as she was alive, and Chaisa, and Prsedi, as long as Do and Sntejo were alive, there was hope.

Someone was just outside Prsedi's hut, just at the door, but lying down. She thought whoever was there was snoring; the sound carried far so late in the night's stillness. He was the only one who lay outside, so the snoring was probably him. So he slept. Still, it would be impossible to get into the hut, or out, while he was there.

Kaikos looked at the back of the hut, and thought, *Chaisa is just*

there, just on the other side of that wall. She slid quietly from behind
her rock and crept up behind Prsedi's hut, which was near the edge
of the Téuta, well outside the town wall, and also no more than a
hundred paces from the hill, and from the rocks Kaikos had hidden
in. Since she could see that no one stirred, and everyone was inside
their huts except the man who slept in Prsedi's door, she walked
upright, as silently as she could.

She put her hand on the back wall of Prsedi's hut, knowing
both Prsedi and her mother were just on the other side, just a few
feet away. She could sense them asleep on mats on the floor; they
seemed so simple, so restful, just silent bholos lumps quietly breathing. She too breathed deep, and silent, silent, silent. What could she
do? Nothing. Her mother must worry, and Prsedi too. At least she
might be able to leave a sign for them that she had been here, that
she was alright. But what? What could she leave that Prsedi would
see but others would not?

As she moved along the back of the hut, thinking, she nearly
tripped over something soft. She knelt down to feel, to see what
it was, afraid that it might be another sentry who, somehow, she
had not noticed with her othersight. Soft, heavy—something made
of skins, it had fur on the outside. A pouch? Yes, a sack, filled
with something. It was heavy to lift. She found the opening and
felt inside.

Food. She smelled it to be sure. Food! They had left something
behind the house—for her? It had to be for her. And it must have
been Prsedi; according to Sntejo, Krepus would not allow Chaisa
outside without close supervision. And only Prsedi would think of
this. Only Prsedi would expect this. In all the village only Chaisa,
Sntejo and Prsedi knew, really *knew*, that she could find her way
around without eyes, and only Prsedi would expect her to come
anywhere near the village.

Take the bag, she thought. Take the bag, and that would be a sign
for Prsedi that she had been here. Or that someone had been here to

take it, and who else would be out here behind her hut when there was nothing back here but the hills? A hunting party might go up into the hills, but they would leave from the far end of the village, not here, and they would not come this direction. This had to be for her. And if Prsedi was leaving gifts for her then she had not given up hope, and Chaisa had not either.

Hope. Hope was what she missed. The Téuta too, the village, she missed sitting with Chaisa inside their own hut, and knowing that Prsedi and Sntejo were near, that she could find them if she wanted to talk. Those were the things that meant hope. They *were* hope, to Kaikos. What else was there in the world that was worth hoping for?

She took the sack and silently moved away from the huts. As she neared the rocks she heard the snoring man turn over and stop snoring, so she ran quietly but quickly, and ducked into hiding, casting her othersight back toward the hut. A giant bloom of bholos was moving through the village, one so large it could only be Krepus. As he walked past Prsedi's hut he roused the sleeping guard. Then he moved on, watching the village, watching the earth around him, watching for dangers, for enemies.

Krepus. How could she miss Krepus? But she did. Krepus was the guard who kept them all safe.

When Krepus had returned behind the wall of the city she took her sack of food back up the hill, walking as much as possible on rocks that would leave no trail, and back around the long path to her cavern. It was the middle of the day by the time she arrived. She sniffed the air and felt the sun; it was noon, at least. But she also smelled rain, somewhere. It would rain tonight, she thought. That was good. It would hide any trail she might have left.

She crawled back through the narrow opening and walked easily through the dark to the back chamber, walking as she did anywhere day or night: guided by her othersight. Then she explored what she had been given by touching and smelling it. It had some fruits, some dried meat, some lentils, a sack of grain and some flour already ground.

Kaikos ate some fruit and sat next to the old, dead firepit. Without fire it would be hard to eat the grain, or the flour.

She got the fire kit and tried again to get something started.

CHAPTER EIGHTEEN

⊥

Rain again. Not hard rain, but long, steady, deep rain that would douse whatever fires might be left but would leave even more water in the hills. The river was already far over its banks. It was lapping already against the far wall of Raghe's temple, which had seemed safe enough when it was built. It was well above the normal banks of the normal river.

This was not the normal river.

Why did this not stop? It had to stop. Krepus stalked the street before the day, again, watching, waiting; twice in his walk someone came out of a hut to ask something of him, but looked at him hulking, looked at the frustration in his face, and returned silently into their hut. He walked the length of the Téuta, the width, the whole village. He walked to the gate and stepped outside the wall.

He knew where he was going; he had known from the start. But he didn't want to confront her. The truth was that he *liked* Prsedi, as difficult as she was, and he could hardly stand to be near Raghe. But he needed them. He couldn't know the minds of gods. Whether the gods' needs were deep or shallow, vital or whims, he couldn't know them without his god-speakers. So he needed his god-speakers, and he needed them to agree.

But they didn't. Raghe told him, and had told him for twelve years, that only Kaikos' blood would save the world. Prsedi told him Kaikos was an innocent child, helpless because of her blindness, who needed his protection instead of Raghe's zealotry. Both claimed they gave him the word and purpose of their gods.

It seemed the gods were not in agreement on the topic of Kaikos. But he had no deep interest in the squabbles of gods; he needed to know what he should do *now* to keep his village safe. He didn't want to anger Dhegm. But right now it was Perkunos who worried him. It was Perkunos who sent the rain to drench the mountains, and who threatened to flood the streets. Dhegm might slow the crops next year. But that was next year; maybe even if he angered her now, he could soothe her again by spring.

He entered Prsedi's hut without asking permission and found her poking and blowing at her firepit with her back toward the door. Chaisa was still asleep near the far wall. Prsedi ignored him and got her fire going again. When that was done she sat up, fussed with something there beside the fire, and said, without turning, "Krepus. It's good to see you, although I have to say that it's taken you long enough to find your way here. Was Raghe so long-winded in his bloodlust?"

Blunt. It was blunt and provocative, and that meant Prsedi was not in a mood for idle discourse. Krepus had rarely seen her stressed about anything; he didn't know anyone who had. Apparently it was possible though, because she was in a mood for combat.

But if Prsedi was blunt so was Krepus. He needed an answer. He needed *the right* answer.

"Prsedi, you must speak to him. I need you and Raghe to agree on what we need to do. This isn't just one person, or even the village, although I would defend this village against all the rest of the world together. But the years are getting colder *everywhere*. The whole world is becoming ice because of something we have done. Or at

least it might be because of something we have done, or something
we have failed to do. Or because of something some other town has
done or failed to do. We need to know. We need to know how to end
this. *I* need to know how to end this. Do I need to sacrifice, or go to
war, or is there nothing at all I can do?"

The older woman huffed at her fire, although it was already well
started, and then she turned to look hard at Krepus.

"I will *not* speak to Raghe in that place, Krepus. The whole place
stinks. And Raghe stinks. He is a repulsive thing. He has spies all
over the Téuta. Haven't you seen them? *He spies on you*, Krepus."

"I know. Let him."

"Let him. Let him. Everyone *lets him*. Krepus, he kills because he
likes to kill, not because the gods demand it. Do you really think the
gods want to shorten Kaikos' life? Or the lives of bulls, for that matter? Why would they? Dhegm is the mother of the earth; she *is* the
earth, she existed before the earth began and will exist until it ends.
To Dhegm the whole life of Kaikos, or of Welo, my life or yours,
the life of the Téuta village, is less than the time between the end
of one breath and the beginning of the next. Why would she afflict
the world to shorten a single life? *Any* single life, since *every* single
life will come to her before she knows any time has passed. Now,
fifty years from now, it doesn't matter to Dhegm. She loves Kaikos,
but she is patient; in the end Kaikos will go to her no matter what
Raghe does. I will go to her, you will go to her, everyone will go to
her. No. *No. No! I won't accept it.* I don't know what you should do
to fix what is wrong, but *that is not it.*"

Prsedi stood and walked back and forth in her hut. It shocked
him to see her like this, to see her usual serenity in such tatters. She
seemed to be as intense as he was, as intense as Perkunos striking the
ground and it almost felt like she was Perkunos when she looked
directly at him, her eyes like an axe striking him.

"Here's the truth, Krepus," she said, watching his face with fierce
eyes, "Raghe doesn't want Kaikos because of anything about Kaikos,

or about any gods. He wants to kill Kaikos *because Chaisa is beautiful.* Because she is beautiful, and that is the only reason, other than the general joy he takes in killing things. He wanted Chaisa from the start and couldn't have her; he rages because she had a child with a better man than him. Not that there are very many men worse."

Trying to calm Prsedi seemed so bewildering he wasn't sure how to start.

"Prsedi, I understand this," he said. "I'm not comfortable with him. The truth is that I dislike him. But he does speak to gods. He is right too often to think otherwise."

"Maybe. But I never had to breathe smoke from flower sap to talk to Dhegm. She is a friend. She speaks to me near my fire, while I eat bread in the morning."

"*Prsedi!!*" The stress of weeks erupted from Krepus like the flare of pitch from a fire. "No more competition among the gods, or between the god-speakers, Prsedi. I need to find a way forward; I need to know what I must do now, this morning, not tomorrow, not in the spring. The ground is shaking our huts down and the river will drown us soon. You must speak to Raghe; you must both speak to the gods together!"

He had spoken with such fervor that she stepped back, watching him. Chaisa was wide awake then, staring at them, afraid, trying to press herself into the back wall of Prsedi's hut.

Krepus paced, back and forth and back.

"Prsedi, I know you have helped Kaikos. You may not know where she is—maybe Chaisa does, but she won't tell us. Chaisa will never tell us. Good, I admire her for that. But you left food for her. Raghe says that's so. It is so, isn't it? You would do that."

Prsedi said nothing.

He started to turn, to leave, because he knew he was too stretched to speak with anyone at that moment. He turned away from her, pressed his lips together, a forest fire of frustration inside him. He was ready to walk out of the hut. But Prsedi was not a stupid

woman. She knew she had to get his attention, had to get his agreement. Kaikos was alone, somewhere in the hills. Sntejo said she was
more capable than most children. She was. But a blind girl wouldn't
last forever alone in winter's cold. She had to get Krepus on her side
or Kaikos would die in the hills, or, if she returned, Raghe would
finally get his way.

"Krepus, I will not go to Raghe's miserable cavern! If he wants
to come here, let him come. I will accept him here. I'll accept anyone here, even Raghe. But I've told you what to do about Kaikos:
bring her home, support her, let her be. Let her be! There's no harm
in her, no curse. All she asks is that you and Raghe let her be. Oh,
she wants more; of course she wants more! She wants to be a normal child with friends her age. But all she would ever ask for is a
peaceful life with Chaisa. A burden to the Téuta?? What burden?
What burden? When has she *ever* been a burden? Tell Raghe to kill
another bull if that will satisfy his need for death."

She walked toward him, her bare feet silent on the floor. But
she walked with a purpose, desperate to convince him. She remembered the warmth of Kaikos leaning against her at the festival's end,
and the warmth of Kaikos nestled against her while she slept. She
remembered the baby covered with flour. She walked quickly with
insistence in each step, but each step utterly, terribly silent.

"Krepus, you wander the paths—I've seen you, everyone has seen
you—all night you wander because you are afraid! You are afraid of
the ground you walk on. You know it can knock you over because it
did knock you over. The Téuta?? You are afraid for yourself! That is
why you want to kill Kaikos! Raghe from soured lust, and you from
swollen fear!"

The statement was a little unfair to Raghe, and completely
unfair to Krepus; she knew that as she spoke, but she needed him to
stay and talk. She needed him on Kaikos' side. And she walked still
toward him until she was nearly touching his back.

Later Krepus would tell himself he didn't mean to do it, and that was true. He didn't. But at the time, and just after, he wasn't sure whether he meant it or not, his anger was so great. He loved Prsedi, though; he revered and was humbled by her. Nothing in his heart meant to harm her. She was simply closer than he thought she was when he turned. But his mind was numb; he was a thunderstorm. The tension from many weeks boiled in him, and he was not a king, not a man, he was only anger, only frustration about his village and all the threats it faced. So he turned fast, turned with fire in his heart. The great meaty arm rose before he turned; the great bulk of Krepus swept around, his finger already extended to point to her when he replied to her insult. He hardly felt it when his elbow struck her. But his gut felt like it fell to the floor at the crack of it, the sound of it.

It was not a terrible blow, by the standards of a hunter, of a warrior. If it had been Sntejo who was struck he would barely have felt it. Sntejo would have stumbled a little and laughed at the comedy of it. But it wasn't Sntejo. If it had been Chaisa, or even Kaikos, they would have fallen from the blow; they would have been bruised, maybe, but they would have risen—Kaikos, who was Sntejo's hunting friend, might have laughed it off too. She was a tough girl in many ways.

But it wasn't any of them that his arm struck. It was Prsedi, and she was old, and her bones were ready to break. He watched every instant as she fell, as her small body smacked against the rocks near her firepit, and as she lay there with her head back strangely, back too far. She made a noise like a foot pulling out of deep mud. Her hand jerked once, twice, and she lay still.

He knew, from long experience with death, that Prsedi would not argue with him ever again. He knew that she would never speak with Raghe, and that they would never agree on how to lift the curse that lay over the Téuta.

�ᛟᚺ

Chaisa had watched the scene as it developed, had watched Krepus as he paused with his back to Prsedi. She had watched them both, two bulls facing each other, pacing, watching. *This should be finished*, Chaisa had thought. *Let Krepus leave, so this fire can settle.* But Prsedi had not stopped. And then the turn, the elbow not lifted that far for Krepus but enough to meet Prsedi on the side of her face, the hard side of her head. And then the sound.

For a moment after that neither Krepus nor Chaisa moved. Then Chaisa was down near Prsedi, with her head buried on her, and Krepus dropped to his knees, holding his face hard with both hands. Prsedi was silent. Krepus was silent. And Chaisa quietly wailed her grief.

Chaisa's keening, small as it was, attracted attention from the outside. Several people passing by looked in, saw the tableau before them and stumbled back away, in part because they didn't want to believe that such bad fortune was descending on the Téuta, and in part because they were pulled away by Do as he tried to reach the door.

Later, none of them, Chaisa or Krepus or Do, could remember how long they were motionless. But in the end Chaisa sat up and turned to Do. She had tears on her face, but she was not tearful. She was calm. Grief was a fire in her, but she had a goal to focus on. Her goal. Prsedi's goal, which was the same.

She looked at Krepus and knew he was spent; her fear was gone, and her tone was command. Here, for now, Chaisa was the king.

"Get Sntejo," she said, looking at Do. "Go get Sntejo. Now. Quickly, Do."

She didn't have to raise her voice. Do was gone in an instant, running to do what she asked.

Chaisa laid Prsedi along the floor, straightened her head and put her hands on her chest. Then she went to Krepus and took his face in her hands to get his attention.

"Krepus. You should not be here. Wait outside the doorway, and

I will come to speak to you after I have seen to Prsedi's needs. Sit there beside the doorway, and don't move."

Krepus took a moment to become aware of her, and then he nodded. He recognized his position now. He had brought the wrath of Dhegm down on the Téuta. He was not king now. He wasn't anything. He was lost. He was lost. He was lost, and he did what he was told to do.

Then Sntejo was there, and Chaisa spoke, quietly.

"Sntejo, please, look here, look at Prsedi. Look at her. Understand. Then come sit here with me."

For a moment Sntejo simply stood looking, unable to take this in. Then he went to her, and he, too, recognized that she had taken charge, that she was leading them.

"Chaisa, what can we do?"

"Sit here, Sntejo. So I can speak to you."

He sat close to her. He was aware of her, but his brain would not focus on her, or really on anything because this could not be real. Death, yes, death can happen. Everyone dies.

But not Prsedi. That could not happen. He waited for her to sit up. She did not sit up. Chaisa spoke, but it was a sound like the river, soothing but with no meaning to him at first.

"There is no way to change this, Sntejo. No, look at me," she said, as his eyes wanted to drift to the stillness that was Prsedi. Chaisa put her hand on his face and turned it toward her.

"Look at me. Prsedi is dead, and Krepus killed her. We can only accept what has happened. But you know what we must do for her: speak to the council. Make them care for Prsedi, make them give her great honor so Dhegm might find a way to forgive us, but not only for that. Tell them to provide for her because she is Prsedi. Because she is your friend, and my friend, and Kaikos' friend, and even Krepus' friend. She will need things now that she can't get for herself. She needs clothes, food, other things to help her on her way."

Sntejo, still a little stunned, was silent, drifting away to look at

Prsedi not at Chaisa. Chaisa pressed her hand against his cheek again to turn him, but his eyes were pulled back to Prsedi lying still. So she reached behind him and took the hair on the back of his head in her grip and pulled his face to her. She put her eyes close to his.

"Sntejo, listen. No, look at me, at me. Prsedi is gone. There is no escape. There is no escape, Sntejo, and no way to fix what has happened. None of us left here can escape; Krepus, and you, and I, can only be where we are, and what we are. Raghe won't be put off now. He wants blood, and Krepus can't stand against him now. Prsedi can't stand against him. He will have a strong sacrifice. One more bull-head to put on his wall won't be enough for him."

His eyes focused on her now, and his blank look turned to a stare. "No! Chaisa..."

"Shh. Quiet. Listen to me Sntejo," and she had to tug his hair again to turn him to her. "Sntejo! Look at my eyes. *Look at me.*"

When he was settled, she went on. "Don't struggle with this; I know, I know, I've already done it, do you think I want this? I've already struggled. I've struggled, but there is no way out. There is no way out. So listen. Please. Let Do stay here with Prsedi. You will go to the council to speak to them. Sntejo, this is important," and again she forced him to look directly at her. "Let the council give Prsedi what she needs. I will give Krepus and Raghe what they need." She dropped her voice then, so only Sntejo could hear. "And *you must give me what I need!* Promise me, Sntejo. I need you to promise, *now*, because there is no other time for this."

He looked at her, knowing what she meant to do, but numb from grief.

Chaisa spoke in a nearly silent whisper to him. "Sntejo, they all think she is helpless, that she is dead by now. But you know. *You know her.* You know she's not dead, not yet. I don't know that you can ever do anything to help her, but if you can, you must do it. You must help her and protect her because she has no one else at all now.

Prsedi is gone; I am gone; even Krepus is limp now and can do nothing. Raghe runs the Téuta for now, for this moment at least, and he won't relent. Save her, if you can."

Sntejo looked at Prsedi, and then looked long at Chaisa. The events were just too big to accept; his grief was too big for him to endure, and now she needed him to choose between Kaikos and the Téuta, loyalty against loyalty, with no time to weigh one against the other.

Finally, he bent his head, and said to her: "Yes. Yes, I promise."

He felt a release inside himself; he knew, suddenly, that this was what he had always meant to do. It was what Chaisa always wished he would do. And it was what Kaikos always hoped, and what Prsedi always *knew* he would do.

Chaisa rose and pressed to him, and her face was hot against his cheek when she gave him her last human embrace.

Then she turned and left the hut. She knelt down to the husk that had been Krepus, and she took his face in her hands.

"Krepus."

He gave her no response.

"Krepus."

No response. It took three attempts to get his attention. But she did not raise her voice, she simply spoke to him.

"Krepus."

The huge head turned to her.

"You have a duty now. Maybe many duties, but this one first. You, and Raghe, and everyone, all think Kaikos is dead, and I'm not going to try to convince you she's not. In fact, I don't know. I didn't see her dead, but she has never been allowed to start fire, never been allowed to grind grain; she has no one to hunt for her. If she isn't dead already maybe she will be soon. Welo must be dead by now too, after all these years. And Prsedi is dead. I am all that's left, Krepus. I am all that remains of Welo's curse, and I am what Raghe wanted from the start. Leave Kaikos to her own death. Take me to mine, and then all Welo's children, all his friends, will be gone, and the gods will be satisfied."

Krepus watched her, barely understanding the words.

Sntejo walked to the door of the hut. He watched as Chaisa took Krepus' hand and coaxed him to his feet, and as she put her hand on his elbow and guided him between the huts to the gate, then through the gate. After that he couldn't see her. But he saw her in his mind. There, in his mind, he saw what he would never forget: that she guided a shambling Krepus along the streets toward Raghe's tall stone, toward his shamanic temple. Toward Raghe's trance-place. Toward Raghe's killing place.

Sntejo turned back to the darkness of the hut and went inside. He shut everything out and moved to do what he had to do, with nothing inside him, nothing in his heart, because he couldn't let anything in there or it would shatter.

Then he gathered Prsedi up and laid her gently at the side of her hut. He and Do and the council had to dig into the ground in its center, a big hole, so he could give her comfort and grace in her burial, and could provide her with all the things that were proper for a Téuta as august, as honored, as important as Prsedi.

CHAPTER NINETEEN

꓄

Raghe's inner rooms had their normal stench about them, but Chaisa and Krepus had no need to wait long there. Raghe was waiting for them when they arrived, and he spoke directly to Krepus, ignoring Chaisa.

"Prsedi is dead," he said. "Dhegm should be happy that Prsedi is with her, but she isn't. She wants retribution, compensation."

Krepus said nothing. He was still stunned by what he had done. So Chaisa spoke.

"Raghe, I am—"

Raghe interrupted her. "Stay still until I speak to you, Chaisa. You, who are cursed, should have the sense to keep silent in a place devoted to the gods."

Krepus shook his huge shoulders, and for just a moment he thought that if his visits had been in a different order it would be Raghe who was dead instead of Prsedi. He looked at Raghe hard. Raghe stepped back, seeing the anger in Krepus' eyes.

But Krepus spoke softly.

"Chaisa is here, Raghe. She is your sacrifice, by her choice. Kaikos is surely dead by now, Welo is surely dead, Prsedi is dead. Take

Chaisa and end this curse. End it. End it soon before the river rises enough to take the whole Téuta swirling and choking into the sea."

Raghe called to an apprentice who emerged head-first from the crawl-hole. "Take her. To the back, the center. Close the room." Raghe said this without taking his eyes off Krepus.

The young man looked at Chaisa, frowned, and would have asked Raghe questions about this, but Chaisa walked to him, and past him. She walked toward the crawl hole, and the young man had to hurry to keep up with her. Chaisa knelt to the floor and crawled through the hole to the back rooms. She crawled with calm acceptance, crawled with grace, toward the stench, toward the strangling smoke, toward the dark rooms where she knew her life would end. Raghe's apprentice crawled after.

Krepus watched her, wondering at her grace, and wondering which of the gods could ever love her courage as much as he did.

Not Perkunos; he was too busy striking the ground with his axe and blowing trees over. Perkunos loved courage, but he loved the courage of contest, the wild courage that sees no defeat. He loved Krepus' kind of courage; Perkunos was *his* god.

And not Dyeus Pter. He shone light on the world; his courage was simply the courage of endurance, of patience, of shining the sun on the ground day after day until the plants grew. But this, Chaisa's courage—this was a different courage: the courage of accepting and facing what can't be changed.

Dhegm. The rocks tumbled down the cliff, and the cliff was gone—well, accept the new cliff. The fire burned the hillside—accept the new hillside. This was Dhegm's courage. She would love this courage, and she must love Chaisa for having it. Chaisa, Kaikos, Prsedi—these three belonged to Dhegm.

Krepus admired them. He hoped he could have this courage. He needed it. It was not the kind of courage that came naturally to him, but it was the kind he needed now. There were things now that he couldn't change.

When Chaisa was gone, and the apprentice was gone, Raghe spoke.

"Welo is not dead. Find him. Kill him. Kaikos? I don't know. The gods don't tell me everything. But if she is alive, find her, and kill her. Then we will know that this is ended. I've told you for twelve years what you need to do."

"How can I kill a giant, Raghe?"

"I don't know. But that is your task. It's always been yours as king, but now it's yours to atone for Prsedi. And it's yours for not bringing Kaikos to me through all these years. *You* are why these curses continue, Krepus. Accept that and do what you need to do to end them. Take what you feel you need to do that. But find him. End him. Lift this curse from the Téuta."

Yes, thought Krepus. Lift this curse by leaving and staying away, by facing probable death while Raghe took Chaisa and all the Téuta to do as he pleased.

But he, Krepus, could do nothing about it.

Have some small part of Chaisa's courage, he thought. *Accept what can't be changed.*

He was ordered to go as a punishment for a terrible act, and Raghe would make sure the whole Téuta knew it. So he would go.

Krepus crawled through the hole that led to Raghe's public space. He walked out of it, walked into a bright, wet morning to prepare for his task.

††† ◖ ↤

Kaikos was sick of her cave. She had started a fire, although she couldn't say how. She had gathered dry moss in their fire pit, their depression in the rocks inside the inner cave, and she had struck the flint against the iron over and over, leaning close to smell if any smoke was made. Nothing. Nothing happened. Nothing ever happened when she did this. But this time when she went back a few moments later there *was* the smell of smoke, and she blew on the moss, and then there was fire. She had vessels and water in the creek outside the cave and dried meat and roots and grain. She could eat.

"I'm sick of eating," she said aloud, startled by how loud her voice sounded after days of silence in the cave. "At least I'm sick of eating alone."

It was not only that she missed Chaisa and Sntejo, and that she missed Prsedi. She wanted them around her; she had always had them near her. But she knew now that she missed Krepus too. She missed the Téuta. She wanted it all to be as it was before the earthquake. The Téuta was her village. She felt that, even if the Téuta didn't. They were family, and safety.

And now they were a mortal danger to her.

Small stacks of food were balanced on some flat rocks near her fire; she had only three small clay pots altogether, and one was used near the fire for cooking. And she had the pot made of leather, but that was too big, and it could only be used if it were always filled with liquid, so she only used the small clay pots for cooking. Prsedi had left bread and dried meat, and Kaikos had also found and gathered some onions, some late summer berries and sloes, and some roots that could be boiled and eaten. She had food for many more days; in fact she felt she could find food through the winter if she needed to, as long as she had fire to cook with. But she felt her isolation hidden in her cave. She worried she would be here forever, that Chaisa would be kept away from her forever, that she would never see Prsedi or Sntejo or Do again.

"I hope they are safe," she told the walls, ignorant of all that had happened in the Téuta. "Maybe in the Spring this will all have passed, and we can be like we were."

Then she remembered what Sntejo had said: her home was burned and scattered. Things would never be exactly like they were before.

And then she worried that in the winter or the spring, when the smell of the recent fires in the forest faded, the smell of the smoke from her fire in the cave would give away her hiding place.

She kept the fire as small as she could. But she worried also that the fire would die while she was out and she would not be able to get it started again, since she didn't really know how she started it in the first place.

"When winter comes the cave will be very cold if the fire dies. And there will be almost nothing to eat."

She could gather some of this summer's last grain, and she was good at threshing and winnowing, but she couldn't make a gruel without fire and she couldn't make bread without a grinding stone. And even if she could grind flour, she couldn't see it. It could be spread all over the cave, and she wouldn't have any way to find it. Instead, she might just step in it and leave big flour footprints whenever she was outside.

At night she wandered up into the high hills just to feel the outdoors, to have some feeling that she wouldn't be forever alone in her cave. And a few nights after her first visit to Prsedi's hut Kaikos walked back down toward the village and sat high on the hill but near enough to feel the presence of the Téuta, of the people.

She wondered what had happened to Chaisa, whether she was still kept in Prsedi's hut. She knew that it wasn't the hut itself that kept her, or not the hut alone. But as soon as she was gone they would begin to hunt her, and in that hunt she would certainly be found—and they might find Kaikos at the same time. Kaikos was sure that Chaisa stayed because of that. And that was not good; it meant that Chaisa had watched the men, watched Krepus, and thought it was better to leave her child alone in the wild than to let Krepus find her. That she had not found a way out meant that the danger, to her and to Kaikos, was real and very big. It meant also it was foolish for Kaikos to be here, this close, to risk being discovered and captured.

Again Kaikos crept away, back toward the relative safety of her cave.

But she wasn't sure how long she could be there. Sntejo knew where she was, and it would not be long before others would know. They were looking for her. Raghe was, or his people were. Twice since their trip to the salt spring she had sensed the bholos of people moving through the forest outside the cave. The cave was hard to see, the opening small and well hidden, but they were looking, and if they found it there was no way to escape. There was no other opening to the outside. She was afraid to stay alone in her cave, and afraid to leave her cave and risk being seen by any of the Téuta.

Sntejo himself had told her to move. So she spent the next few nights climbing higher into the hills, searching for another place to stay. On the third excursion out she did find something, not as hidden and not as big, but a closed space out of any rain, and even better, it was completely hidden from the village by more than one rise, more than one high crop of rock. It was hidden deep in the hills, so Kaikos could go out in the day if she didn't wander too far. She missed the sun on her skin. And it was high enough in the hills that Téuta hunters would not pass that way often. Maybe they would not pass that way ever.

The following night she moved some skins and most of the food up to her new place. She took two clay crocks. And she took a coal from the fire, wrapped deep in leaves, hoping she could move her only fire to her new place.

CHAPTER TWENTY

M ost nights she slept near the mouth of this cavern when the weather was dry enough. She felt the sun and the wind again. When the day was over she felt the night around her when she slept near a place that was open to it. That was good. It was sad without Chaisa, but she believed Chaisa would return to her someday. For now she accepted that, even while she was alone, nature had pleasure and beauty. Nature alone was a good thing—but gradually her stores of food dwindled. She wondered if Prsedi would leave another bag of food for her, and she missed the village again. No matter how long it had been, or how far away she was, she would always miss it.

For a third time she waited until the night smells were deep, waited nearly until all the Téuta would be asleep, nearly until the night began its first tentative turn toward morning. The air was cold. She wrapped herself in a parka with a braided belt, and she wore Chaisa's big cloak. When she was fortified against the night, Kaikos crept down toward the village. The dark, and the hills, hid her as she went.

From her new place it was farther, and she needed sleep, but she kept walking, bent low as she approached, and she finally reached her hiding-rocks behind Prsedi's hut. She reached out with her othersight to see everything she could, and she did think there might be a sack on the ground just where the first sack had been. The bholos mounded over something, and she knew the ground was flat there.

But there were also three men behind the huts nearby. Two were asleep, but the third was up leaning against a hut silently, waiting for something.

Waiting for *her*. What else would they wait for out here?

The man who was standing made no noise, but he wasn't hiding. Maybe he thought her blindness protected him. Most of the Téuta people dismissed her talk of bholos as just childish imagination, like the pretend friends that children sometimes have. But the clumping bholos around him made him stand out. She saw, with her othersight, not just him and the other two behind the huts, but all the people inside the huts outside the wall. She saw three people in the hut the man leaned on, and two in the hut nearby—and none in Prsedi's hut. Where Chaisa and Prsedi should be, where the bholos should cling to them, there was no life at all. No fire. The hut was deserted and cold.

Kaikos sat to think, leaning her back against the rock. They had discovered Prsedi's secret, that she was leaving food for Kaikos behind her hut. That must be why these men were here: they had discovered that and left this new sack as a trap. Maybe it was just a clump of rags; she had no way to know what was there, really.

They seemed to be very determined to catch her. Three men! But how did they know? Prsedi wouldn't tell them that, or at least Kaikos didn't think she would. And Chaisa wouldn't either.

Kaikos watched and waited. She would have to go back up the hill soon because morning would come. Morning was almost here, really; she could smell morning in the distance. In the light people might see her, even if she hid behind the rocks, although where she was the rocks wrapped partly around her. But she still sat, thinking.

Wondering. Waiting.

Maybe she dozed, or maybe she was just so lost in thought that she lost track of the time, but Kaikos was suddenly aware of the heat of sun on her arms, and on her face, still very early sun, but it was there. That meant there was light. People who saw with their eyes would be able to find her, and they would certainly see her if she moved. As she sat wondering what to do the men watching for her stirred, and rose, all of them, and they sat talking. Ragged phrases in unknown voices drifted to her across the distance. She put them together as well as she could. She was curious.

"Another night sleeping in the cold."

"This is a waste of time. The girl is dead by now. We'll find her body in the hills in the spring, if the animals don't take her. And Raghe—I don't know. He's thinking too many things. And Krepus walks like he has no eyes. He stumbles from place to place."

"You should watch what you say, Garsijo. There's trouble now; you should be careful. But I know what you mean."

The three men were quiet for a while, then they all stood and wandered closer to her. She crouched behind the rocks and stayed as quiet as she could. The men were stretching and yawning in the morning sun. The one who thought she was dead, Garsijo, was pacing, and his bholos fluttered as though he were upset about something. *He didn't seem upset about thinking I was dead*, she thought to herself, and that tasted bitter to her. She was glad they couldn't see bholos, because hers must be flaming in all directions. Her emotions were chaos.

One of the men walked down between the huts, and the other two wandered closer to the rocks, as though they were walking directly toward her, or away from the huts. Garsijo spoke again, and Kaikos could hear them more clearly now.

"Yes, we should be careful what we say, but look around. Look around, Wadhis. This—I think we bring curses in crowds around us when we act like this."

"What do you mean, curses? We have already had curses. We have had curses that make our crops fail; we have had curses that spill our huts on top of us, that make fire in the hills and flood the river. What more curses do you think we can have?"

"I don't know. But think about Prsedi. That is bad luck. That will bring a curse on us if anything does. Prsedi was a friend of the gods. You don't just kill someone like Prsedi in our midst and expect nothing to happen, expect that no curse will come back to find us."

Only the weeks of tense hiding, of practiced silence above all else, kept Kaikos from revealing herself by shouting in shock. Prsedi? *Killed* Prsedi? How, why? But her discipline of silence held strong, and the need to shout passed, and she wilted into her place behind the rock, shrinking inward in grief.

"He didn't mean to kill her. He just hit her too hard in his anger."

"Does that matter? It was Prsedi! No anger should have been great enough to hit her at all. I know I shouldn't speak like this, but—but I don't know. Now I'm afraid to anger Krepus, and afraid to anger the gods more than we have already. And afraid that both Krepus and the gods are already so angry nothing can save us."

The other man was quiet for several minutes. Both men seemed to be sensing the dawn, but not with pleasure.

"We've lost too many people in too short a time, in just this harvest. Lost to the shaking ground, people dead in their huts while they slept. And now Prsedi dead, Chaisa gone, the blind girl Kaikos gone too—she was strange, but she still was Téuta. All gone. So many hurt, so many without huts to stay warm with winter coming. Some of them will be gone by spring. And Krepus is as afraid as I am, I think, at what he did. Did you watch them walk to Raghe? He was lost. Chaisa led him by his hand to her own sacrifice."

Prsedi dead *and Chaisa gone to Raghe?? That means Chaisa is dead already, or will be soon, and nothing I can do can save her. No, no, no* Kaikos thought, or just felt; there was no real thought at all but everything inside her seemed to give way all at once. She had nothing left to hold her up. She didn't call out; that was just part of her from weeks of habit. She just slipped to the side and lay on the ground behind the rocks. If the two men had walked only ten more paces toward her, and then ten paces up the hill, they would have found her there. They would have found her limp behind the rock with her head covered by her arms. They didn't walk those paces, because that would have been the start of climbing the hill. The start of the upward slope was a kind of unconscious boundary. They had walked to the foot of the hill for privacy, but they wouldn't think of starting up the hill unless there were something they needed to do there.

While the men stood talking, the full day came, and the full heat of the sun came.

Kaikos couldn't go back to her shelter during the day, and she had no desire to move anyway. She didn't care if they caught her, if Raghe killed her. What difference could it possibly make anymore? But she lay, quiet, uncaring, sometimes sleeping she thought, but not moving. People walked within fifty paces of where she lay, often, and she overheard a little of what they said. It must have settled somehow inside her brain. She had no memory of having listened, but later she thought she knew something about what had happened. The whole of the Téuta was grave with grief for Prsedi and fear for the consequences. No one talked much of Chaisa, except that she led Krepus to Raghe, instead of him leading her.

Did it matter how long or short a day was? She expected to be found. If anyone had walked just a few paces up the hill they would have noticed her there behind the rock; there was no way to hide from them. But few people left the paths between the huts. Few people wandered behind them, and for those few the invisible barrier of the beginning of the slope held them away. She didn't think about it; she lay still, grieving, not moving, waiting to be found. When they found her, she thought, Raghe would kill her too, the cursed girl, the blind girl who saw the earth move before it ever happened.

But the day passed, and no one started up the hill. No one found her. The village seemed somber, quieter all day than she had ever before seen it because the Téuta were usually active people. Eventually, as the day waned, it became silent. People were drifting into their huts to eat and sleep.

Two men came and sat behind the huts to wait for her during the night, but they were not paying attention to their task, which they apparently thought was pointless. They seemed to be afraid, paying more attention to what was happening in the village than what they were supposed to be watching. They watched the ground, and the huts, and they talked quietly with each other. The cold came, and the late-night sounds, and the late-night smells all came, and Kaikos thought, *I will go now. I have nothing to go to, nothing left to wait for, but also nothing left to do but go. I can't lie here curled like a snake forever.*

Kaikos slipped away from her rock, less than a shadow in the night. She didn't care very much whether she was caught or not, and those behind her who were supposed to be watching didn't seem to care either. She started out crouching, as she had come the night before, but after only twenty steps she just stood to walk upright. If the watchers had bothered to look up the hill they might have seen her, even in the dark, even with her dark shape black against the blackness of the hills. But they didn't look up. They just chatted together, mindless as the night around them, settled in the safety of a village, secure that animals would stay away from so many huts, so many fires. Kaikos walked back through the hills to her little shelter, which seemed now that it would be her home for all that remained of her life.

⊓ ⑴ ⊦⊓

Days later the rain came again. Her shelter kept her dry, or mostly dry, but the wind was cold and blew hard, bending trees over sideways, and some rain blew in under the rocks. Kaikos set her crock out to gather the water, but she drank little, and ate only a little each day. She just waited, trying not to think. Something inside her tried to weave together the few bits of overheard conversation she remembered, though; something in her wanted to understand what had happened.

It was cold. *She* was cold. Under the shelter of the rocks at least the wind was mostly still. Her tunic was long, pieced together from the skins of burrowing animals she had helped to catch. She had Chaisa's long cloak too, but she was still cold. It was long enough to sit easily on the ends of it, and she moved her feet to put the tunic's edge under them. She rubbed her feet with her hands to warm them, and squatted on her heels so her shawl would cover her feet, with Chaisa's long shawl on top of that to stay warm, and she thought about nothing. She should think about what to do, where to go, how to live; all of that was urgent. She had to eat, but her food would run out; winter was coming, and the early autumn storm around her was proof that it was coming. But she couldn't think yet. She had to wait, at least until the storm was gone.

She lay back against the wall of her shelter, huddling under her cloaks, and she spoke to the walls, to the rocks around her and above her. She spoke to Dhegm.

"What do you need, Dhegm? I don't understand," she said. "Why do you want me to die? No, that's not it. If you only wanted me to die you could kill me now; you could bring this shelter down on me and I would die. But you don't want me just to die. *You want Raghe to kill me*. Why do you want that?"

The sound of rain against the ground was Dhegm's reply.

"You are confusing. Dhegm, you are confusing. Do you even hear me? Do you know I'm here?"

The rain fell all around her, on the hills, on the fields down below her, on the mountains behind her.

"When I was a little girl Prsedi came to visit us once, and I asked her how you could be the mother of the earth. I asked what that meant, because you would need to be very big to be the mother of the earth. She said you were not the mother of the earth the way Chaisa was my mother. You were the mother because you made the earth, not once but every day. Every day you make the earth. Then she said you *are* the earth, and because you are the earth you are our mother; you make us; that you suckle us; the fields and the river are your breasts and you feed us from them."

Rain and cold, the fire low in her shelter, the wind among the trees outside.

"How can you be the earth and be the mother of the earth? Dhegm, I have always loved the earth. I have always loved having my hands in it, helping you grow things. I have never harmed you. Never, never, *I have never harmed you*. Chaisa never harmed you. I don't understand why you have wanted Raghe to kill us."

If there had been any other person there, even Chaisa, she would not have cried. But Chaisa was gone. Prsedi was gone. Grief boiled up inside her, and there was no one there but her, and the wind, and Dhegm, and the cold rocks. There was nothing to keep her tears inside.

She cried, it seemed to her, forever, a loud sobbing that anyone passing nearby would have heard. Night came, and almost in answer to the sound of her crying the wolves howled in the distance. The sounds of night covered her and they were a lonely ocean that trapped her, that sank her. An ocean that drowned her.

Sleep came and went through the night, and in the times between sleep she thought.

The Téuta would catch her in the end, if they thought she was alive and tried to hunt her. They were good hunters, and her eyes were blind, and they had been far out across the world many times, but she had never been anywhere but Chaisa's hut and the outskirts of the village except for a few hunting walks with Sntejo.

She thought of Raghe, that fearful thing she had never met because he lived in his temple deep inside the village walls where she was not allowed to go. Down there, past Prsedi's empty hut, she imagined Raghe pacing and grumbling. Would he be alone? Who would be with him? She had never been to his rooms, or anywhere inside the wall, but Prsedi said they were smelly.

That he hated her she knew. That he wanted to find her, to sacrifice her, she did not doubt at all, although both his hate and his needs were only fragments of a notion that she had not bothered to imagine only a few weeks before. He thought she was cursed. Maybe he thought that Dhegm, or maybe some other god, was angry that they had let her live this long. Yes, she did believe that Raghe could want to kill her. And she believed that Krepus, whom she *had* met, might do what Raghe asked. Krepus would do anything he thought he had to do to protect his Téuta.

Raghe. Kaikos couldn't understand him. He had always hated her for being blind, because being blind limited her, and he thought the tribe shouldn't be asked to care for people who had limits like that. But he had also hated her for *not* being blind to the bholos that no one else could see, for having one tiny ability that no one else had, even though he claimed he didn't even believe in bholos. How did that make sense? Whatever the reason for his hatred though, he might think that now, at last, he had an excuse to rid the village of her, with Krepus weak and no Prsedi to stop him. If Raghe asked, she believed Krepus would do it. Of course he would. Krepus was brave in hunting, and cruel to the enemies of the Téuta.

And Krepus always thought he was hunting. Raghe, for now the leader of the Téuta, could declare that she was an enemy, and Krepus would act.

Kaikos thought through the night, and in the morning, she ate well and packed all that she could carry in the sacks she had, the one Sntejo had left at the first cave, and the one Prsedi had left behind her hut, and another one she had taken to the first cave with Chaisa. She couldn't stay here through the winter, and she couldn't go to the village for shelter. Prsedi was dead. Chaisa was dead or as good as dead. Sntejo would follow Krepus even when he hated what he did because he was loyal to the Téuta and would follow his king to defend them.

As far as Kaikos knew she only had one relative who even *might* be alive and free. Only Welo. Only the nightmare giant.

Death was coming for her. Death was here in her shelter, and in the Téuta; he was out with the wolves in the windy night and in the hills behind her. Well, if death was a certainty she would stop running from death. She would walk toward him, and in the end she would catch him, and then death would take her. It didn't matter. But before she died maybe she could see this strange creature, this Welo, her mother's mother's father. She could see what a bholos flame around a real giant looked like.

"Maybe Welo will just eat me like a berry," she said to the air around her. "I don't know what giants eat. But it's better to walk on top of the world and be eaten than to wait to die of cold and hunger in a cave underneath it."

CHAPTER TWENTY-ONE

She had heard many times where the giant lived: follow the river back into the mountains. This same river, the river Chaisa and Kaikos had bathed in her whole life, flowed by the old Téuta city, where the Téuta had lived for centuries. So she climbed down along the hills toward the river, watchful for hunters both human and animal. Then she walked along the riverbank away from the new Téuta, wearing her woven grass vest, her fur parka, her own shawl, and Chaisa's shawl on top of that belted closed with braided flax. She carried her three sacks but had no weapons with her except a single knife. She carried the flint and iron-rock in one of the sacks; it seemed good to have it even if she didn't know whether she could use it, whether it would ever work for her again. And again she carried a single hot coal wrapped tightly in leaves to keep it hot, then wrapped in a small hide from her shawl. And she had wrapped her feet in grass mats and tied the mats closed.

She walked without haste—why would she hurry? When she became tired in the afternoon she started to look for a shelter, any shelter, where she could stay overnight, somewhere up on the steep rocky hills away from any animals that might seek water at the stream. When she found a suitable place she looked for sticks, and built a small fire using the coal she carried. She chewed some dried meat and ate three sloes from her pouch. In the morning she carefully found a hot coal to wrap again to carry to her next fire. She did the same thing the following day, and the day following that. But on the fifth day, when she found her shelter, she also found that her coal had died. From then on she would sleep without fires, huddled under her shawls.

ꭲꞏ ꙭ ꝵꭵ

Work had been constant since the second shaking of the ground. Krepus had put his hunting trip off to help with repairs, and finally the village seemed to be doing well. The huts that were occupied had been repaired; the wall had been repaired. He could go now knowing his village was whole and right, physically at least.

And the sun was out. The day was shining around him. He felt good, for the first time in weeks.

But he was tired too. Only the hand on his shoulder kept him standing, Krepus thought. By the simple act of standing with him, Sntejo and Do held him up. The three watched the river, beautiful in the sunshine, and the leaves and rocks glistened wet from the short shower that had passed earlier in the day. It would come again. Rain seemed to be eternal now. But today the sun shone everywhere.

There had been heavy rains before, many times, and high water before. In the thirty years the village had been here in this place the river had only once come closer than ten paces of Raghe's walls. Now the outside edge of his building was as deep as Sntejo's thighs in water; everything inside must be awash, and must have been awash for a day, since the water had been even higher the day before. Then it had been as high as Sntejo's waist. Chaisa, or whatever was left of her, was trapped inside that wall. Whether she was alive or dead, she was trapped, and alive or dead she was floating, and with water this cold she would have to be dead now, even if she had been alive when the water rose.

The wall of the temple stood, even though the water slid around it, a powerful current washing away the ground around it. Sntejo felt a strong urge to stride over to it and knock it down to get Chaisa out. But it was a temple wall. Damaging it now, with the gods already punishing them, would be disaster for the Téuta, and it would do no good for a dead Chaisa. Even dead, though, he had to admit he wanted her out of that place.

Krepus, too, watched the river flowing. Sntejo wanted to tell him, and Krepus wanted to believe, the river was receding to its banks. It seemed to be doing that. But they both knew better. Even though the world was filled with sunshine now, Perkunos had sent another heavy storm over them two days ago, huge flashing arcs of light pounding around them one after another, and that storm, like all the others, had moved into the mountains. A tree not far from where they stood had been split into two pieces by Perkunos' axe.

Krepus no longer wanted to laugh or to share Perkunos' anger; he wanted to soothe it. He wanted to be done with it, but he couldn't. *He* couldn't. After what happened in Prsedi's hut he was not the man who could soothe any gods; Perkunos was sometimes Dhegm's lover, it was said. He would act if Dhegm asked him to.

It made no sense that the river level was falling, Sntejo thought. The storm should have made the river rise even more.

And as that thought came to him, high in the mountain the swollen river was seeping through the snowpack that was holding water back, worming through snow and rock that had come down to block the river when rocks in the mountain had fallen in the first earthquake. There were many small lakes created that way in the mountains. In the afternoon, in the sunshine, with the weight of weeks of rain behind it, the rock and ice that blocked the river's flow in one of them gave way. It was a small pond high on the mountain, a commonplace pond that hardly mattered. But the sudden weight of it broke the dam holding a second pond, and the combined water began its long journey down toward the Téuta, gaining volume again and again by smashing through the blockades that created other lakes farther down the river as it went.

��ᛁᛐᛞ

Chaisa sat high on Raghe's sacrificial altar, which was set waist-high for Raghe up on a platform. The water was receding a little; it had been near the edge of the altar once. Now she could almost dangle her feet over its edge and still keep them dry. She was hungry. She had been in this place for half a month, and it had been a full day since Raghe rolled the rock over the crawl hole and left her to the rising water. But he had left skins behind, not for her but simply because he didn't bother to look for them when the water started rising, so she was warm at least.

She could hear tiny snippets of noise from the village as people worked and talked. She could hear only because a few small gaps in the thick wall had been created by the earthquakes. These also let thin beams of light through—*that will have to be repaired*, she thought to herself. *Raghe must be upset to find his temple damaged.* And then she thought, *how strange that I would think about that when I'm about to die in the river, when all the huts in the village were also damaged.*

The day wore on, and she watched the light travel across and up the eastern wall as the sun moved, until the sun set behind the mountains and the light became more muted. Night came, and then all the light was gone.

Chaisa slept. So did the whole Téuta. On any ordinary night, any night before Krepus had lost his status as leader, there would have been at least three or four men awake, set by Krepus to watch for danger through the night. But now the village had no real leader until Krepus was restored or a new leader was found. Until then only Raghe was left to lead, and he would never think of guarding the Téuta unless he himself felt danger.

The streets and all the hills around them were empty for once. In the late night there was no one to see the wall of water as it rumbled down from the mountains. The surge moved faster than any runner, but it didn't matter on this night, because there was no one out in the hills to see it. There was no one even to try to warn the Téuta.

When the flood approached around the last of the hills the light sleepers woke up wondering. They thought it might be another earthquake, and they could feel some trembling in the ground, but at least the ground wasn't bucking and tumbling the walls. They were glad for that. Some of them walked out the doors of their huts, but with other huts and walls blocking their views they still didn't see the monster coming.

Chaisa, who slept soundly when she slept, didn't waken until the flood was almost on them. And then before she was fully awake it *was* on them, and it raged through the lower parts of the village, tumbling some very low-lying huts, toppling trees that stood too near the river. It slammed against the temple walls like a hammer, and they leaned inward very hard. The roof slid sideways leaving a large opening to the sky.

And then it was inside the temple, battering everything, battering Chaisa against the far wall as it tried to tear that down too, until that wall finally gave way. The flood carried trees, rocks, soggy mud bricks, and everything that would float or could be pushed and tumbled, along the river channel with it. Chaisa, trapped against the temple wall, became one more bit of floating debris, but one of the last as the first surge of water had nearly passed by the time it lifted her and sent her rolling and bouncing along with all the rest.

Although the surge used its first force against the outer walls, and the front of the wave had crashed around Raghe's rooms, what remained was still a flood. Chaisa was dazed by the rush of water, by being battered against the wall, and then battered again against the trees and rocks that were her companions in the rushing water. But she was a strong swimmer, honed, trained by all her morning baths with Kaikos to seek the surface. After the cold of the water had sharpened her senses, after her awareness returned from the first shock, she found a tree and clung to it for life. It dipped her often under the flood, but also often raised her out of it, and she gasped air when she could.

The night was nearly over when she finally found her tree snagged against a rock on the shore, stopped as the surge of water moved on away from them. And later when the current slowed a little, she made her way to shore. Her fur cloak was soddened, and shredded, and very heavy, and very cold. She was bruised everywhere, but she didn't think she was broken. She was too cold to be sure.

Then she looked around her. She was far from the village, far from anywhere she had ever been before. But she could see the mountains. She could see the direction she would need to take to get back to the village. And that meant she could see how to avoid the village as she made her way back to the place where she thought Kaikos must be, the hiding cave that Kaikos had found for them to live in. That, Chaisa thought, must still be Kaikos' home.

It would be a long hike. She dropped her fur, which was wet and cold and too heavy for her to carry, and she walked wearing only the tattered remains of her wrap of broken, woven grasses, which dried much more quickly. She tried to imagine that it was keeping her warm, but she was too tired, too bruised from the brutal surging river, to imagine anything as distant as that.

CHAPTER TWENTY-TWO

The swollen river flowed steadily, retreating from its surge but still far over its normal banks. Krepus watched, sitting on the ground, thinking. From time to time he glanced over at the ruins of Raghe's inner rooms, now washed clean but still stinking of decades of smoke. He looked behind him at the damage in the Téuta. Many of the people were wary of working with him, wondering if the flood had been Dhegm's revenge for Prsedi's death, wondering whether all the gods would strike the village down for what had happened. But he *could* work. He could help. When he was rested, when his mind settled, he would go to see what he could do.

He sat for much of the afternoon before Sntejo came to sit on the ground next to him. For a long time nothing was said, but Sntejo being there, being willing to be there given what he had lost, lifted Krepus and gave him courage.

Krepus' voice was soaked in weariness when he spoke at last. "I have to find Welo if I can. Raghe says I have to kill him to wash the curse from the Téuta."

"I know," Sntejo said.

"Do you think he's still there, at the old village? I don't know." he watched the river for a very long time. Then he said, "But I will go."

"I know. And I'll go too."

Krepus turned to look at him. "Why? Do you think you can kill Welo better than I can?"

"I don't know how to kill a giant either, Krepus. But I'll go with you. I have reason to cleanse us of this curse too. Not just the cleansing of the Téuta, of course that—but what do I have to stay for? Chaisa is gone, Kaikos has disappeared, so I have nothing here to keep me. And I think Do will go. But, Krepus, I need to be honest with you about this..."

Krepus looked at him, with an odd mix of exhaustion, humility, anger, and fondness. "You are always honest, Sntejo. You never lie to anyone. It makes me glad to talk to you. You're going to tell me about Kaikos, aren't you?"

"Yes. I think she is alive, and I think she has also gone to find Welo."

"Why do you think that?"

"Because of all I know about her. I know she hid with Chaisa. And I think she has learned all that has happened, that Prsedi is dead and Chaisa was in Raghe's hands, and so dead too. She thinks I follow you wherever you lead, which is usually true. She would think that Welo is the only family she has left. She would try to find him."

"Kaikos would face a giant? She has the courage for that?"

"Yes. Yes, she does. Either that or she doesn't understand what danger is. I've hunted with her. She does what she thinks she needs to do, no matter what."

"Well then, Sntejo. Let's test the limits of your honesty. If I need to kill her when we find her, will you follow me then?"

"No. Not in that. I will try to save her. I promised Chaisa I would save her if I could."

"You would stand against me then?"

"I hope I never have to, Krepus. But yes."

"And you would have Do with you."

"I think so, yes."

Krepus smiled for the first time in many days.

"Sntejo, you make me glad to be Téuta. I've never wanted to harm Kaikos. Raghe always says the gods want her death, but when I see her I can't believe it. I can't. Still, if she is with Welo—I don't know. If the giant hasn't already killed her, if they are together—then I don't know what to think."

"Let's not think of that. Let's hope we find her before she finds Welo, and something good can be saved from all of this."

They sat together watching the flood, thinking, or not thinking.

Finally Krepus said, "Good. You will come, then. And Do will come. There will be three, at least, and the right three. Maybe together we can kill this giant."

Krepus considered that. Then he continued, "I was young when we came here, and I never knew Welo, but if there were a giant as big as a mountain at the old Téuta I would remember that. And maybe it isn't Welo who is doing this. Or any god. Maybe Dhegm is simply dying, and we will all die with her. Have you thought about that?"

"Yes, many times," Sntejo replied. "I asked Prsedi once. But Prsedi said Dhegm is well. That all the gods are well. It isn't that."

Krepus stood, shook himself as though he were drying his hair.

"If you will go with me, then we should go. There's no reason to wait, and I don't like being here right now. I don't want to watch Raghe strutting through the street as king of the Téuta."

Sntejo could agree with that. Nothing Raghe did or said was hertus.

But both of them turned to look at the village in ruins again after the river surge. Both would help however they could. They would find time to rest, and prepare, but first they would once again help to right the Téuta.

ꓕꓕ ꓳ ꓩ

Morning came down bright; waves flowed through the grasses that remained after harvest time, and dawn, daughter of the sky and the earth, Dhegm's daughter, showed bare and blushing in the east. Sntejo saw none of it. He stared at the empty space where Raghe's temple had stood. He walked to the place where he had stood with Krepus the night before, but now in a brilliant morning, watching the serenity of the high river. *At least Chaisa has been taken to the sea*, he thought. *I hope she has. I hope she's been taken far, far from Raghe.*

With a grim face he turned, and started to walk away, through the streets of the village toward the gate. No one would stop him, or question him; everyone knew he was mourning, that he had done what had to be done to save the Téuta, and at great cost. And no one did stop him until he walked through the gate. But on the outside, he was stopped. Do stood there.

"Do, please stand aside," he said. "I can't stay in the village right now."

"I'm going with you."

"You can't come with me, Do. I want to be alone for—"

"I'm coming with you."

"No. Stay here. This is a personal journey I must take."

Do stepped aside, and Sntejo walked on. But Do followed. Twice Sntejo turned to tell him to go back, but he knew it was useless. But the third time, when he turned, he finally looked at Do's face and saw no laughter there. There were no jokes coming out, and no jokes held inside. Do stood there watching him.

"Do, I must be alone now."

"And I must be with you now. I know where you're going. Of course I know, Sntejo. What else would Chaisa ever ask of you? You have a task, and it's my task too."

Sntejo looked hard at him, heaved a deep breath, and then he nodded. He turned and walked on and Do caught up with him and walked by his side, both men looking behind them from time to time to see if any others were following. But the Téuta had other things to do that morning than follow Sntejo. Only Krepus would have thought of it, and Krepus was distracted now. He had penance to do of his own, and he had his own grief.

When they arrived at the place where Kaikos had spoken to them, they looked around; they knew where her voice had been, but they could see no place there for her to hide. Sntejo called loudly for her but got no response. They searched for a hiding place, on both sides of the creek. They knew it was here, but it still took a long time for them to find it. Even when they were standing almost on top of it they couldn't see it.

Sntejo was the first to notice the narrow crack behind the brush and rocks, but it seemed impossibly small, impossibly narrow. That couldn't be it, could it? But he stuck his hand and arm into the crack and felt only empty space behind it. He called Do to look at it.

Do was not Sntejo. Do, only seventeen years old, still had the lithe slimness of the young. He looked, and walked to the crack, and with some effort, scraping his chest hard on the rocks, he slid into it. Sntejo watched him simply disappear, as though he had melted into the solid rock wall.

Inside Do could see very little. The darkness was total, except for the weak shaft of light from the small opening to the outer world.

"Sntejo," he called. "Can you make a fire for light? A torch so I can see? It's dark in here."

It took some time, but finally Sntejo passed a makeshift torch through the crack, and Do lifted it. The cave was empty. He was ready to leave, but something puzzled him: he saw no evidence that Kaikos had ever been here, but he could smell long dead fires and some residue of the smell of baked bread. This must not have been the exact place, but this was the cave; he was certain of it. He walked around the edges of the cave looking for an answer to this puzzle. It took some time to find the opening to the inner cave.

Do walked back to Sntejo and told him through the crack that he had to walk further into the cave to find Kaikos' hiding place. "But," he said, "I don't think she's here. She would have noticed this torch. She would have smelled it and heard me scuffing. She would have come to see who it was, and she hasn't."

"Find her, if you can," Sntejo replied. "I'll wait here. She is gone, I think, but I have no reason to run back to the village. Let the Téuta take care of the Téuta right now. I'll wait."

Do walked to the back of the outer cave, and he squeezed through a second small passage to see what was there. He entered a large, high cavern, and here he saw the remains of a makeshift fire pit, ashes cold, but there was wood stacked and dry moss. He took the time, since his flimsy torch was beginning to drop bits of charred wood around him, to pull moss into the fire pit and start the fire. He pulled some wood onto it to keep it burning, then turned to look around the chamber.

A pale body, naked, lay against the wall near the entrance; it startled him because he presumed the worst, presumed this was Kaikos, that she had died here naked and cold, and a terrible cry came out of him. He ran to the whiteness and turned it toward him.

Chaisa, not Kaikos. It was Chaisa! How did she get here? She had survived the flood, somehow, and she had spent the day and the following night walking. Nothing else could explain this. Her skin was very light, very cold, but mottled with enormous bruises. She was barely breathing and did not seem to be aware he was there.

But barely breathing is still breathing. He pulled his fur parka off over his head and lay it across her, picked her up and carried her to the fire. Then he looked hard at her and held her close to give her his heat too. He pulled the fur around both of them, and sat there holding her until slowly her breathing grew, a little.

Sntejo must have heard his cry, because Do could hear pounding through the crack to the outer chamber, which was, which must have been, Sntejo pounding with river rocks against the narrow opening to make it bigger, hammering against it to get inside.

Do held Chaisa as close as he could, willing her to warm, to come back to life. But her skin was very cold. *Very* cold. She felt as cold as the dead. But she was less horribly still than she had been. Her breath was steadier. And finally Do thought he could leave her for a moment. He lay her down again, under his fur but with the side toward the fire open to gather heat. Then he took what was left of his torch and ran to the opening.

"Sntejo!" he called out, but Sntejo took some time to get there to respond. He had been at the creek looking for bigger rocks to pound with.

"Sntejo!" Do called again, and finally Sntejo was there.

"You found her? She's there?"

"Yes! No, I mean Kaikos isn't here. But Chaisa is here, Sntejo, nearly dead from cold and hunger. Stop pounding and get furs and food. I'll keep her alive until you return, if I can."

Sntejo sat suddenly and hard.

"Chaisa?"

"Yes! Chaisa! Stop marveling and help. We can widen the opening later, but right now, get food, wood or dung for fire, so we can make a stew. There is a fire pit and a frame and a leather pot here, but we need water and meat and grain. Get what she will need to stay alive."

Without waiting for an answer, knowing he didn't have to wait for one, Do returned to Chaisa, crawled into the fur with her and held her hard against his own heat. He found two other furs stacked as a bed, and he used those to help make Chaisa warm.

Twice Do left her to build the fire bigger. Slowly, slowly, she began to revive. Do was holding her tight when he felt her push against him.

"Who is it?" she asked. "You're holding me too tight. It hurts."

Of course it hurt. Every part of her was bruised.

She pushed a little harder, but still not hard. She didn't have the strength to push hard, Do thought.

He slid away from her, and she looked, finally, at who was with her. "Do! Why are you here? Where is Kaikos?"

"I don't know. Sntejo and I were trying to find her, and we will try again. But you, Chaisa, are alive, and I need to find food for you. Lie down again. Rest. Take the heat into you."

rt ◖◗ ⱶⱤ

Through the day Do and Sntejo gathered what Chaisa would need here. Do fed her a warm slurry made with what they had with them or what they could find in the cave; at first a barley slurry, but Sntejo left and returned with two rabbits, and the slurry became more substantial. After a day of warmth, of sitting by the fire, and food and water, Chaisa rose, went to the entrance, and slipped through. Sntejo was gone, hunting for other things to bring to help Chaisa survive, but Chaisa and Do waited. When Sntejo returned with furs and grain and more wood for the fire, they were sitting outside the cave.

Sntejo dropped what he held and held Chaisa instead. Chaisa shrank at his touch, because it hurt, but she put her arms around his back and wouldn't let him step away. She had been sure she would never be able to hold him again.

It was a long time before he could speak. But he had to ask them both, and in the end he did ask.

"Kaikos isn't here?"

"No." It was Do who answered. "There was little left here in this cave. Some moss and wood for a fire, some grain, two furs and the leather pot, and that is all."

"I told her before that she should move farther up the mountain. She must have done that," Sntejo said.

Do stayed with Chaisa all that day, and all the next; Sntejo still couldn't get through the opening, but for now that was a good thing. The opening should stay hidden. Sntejo made sure Krepus was busy with projects in the village, and when he could he brought food and other things for Chaisa and searched for Kaikos' second hide.

Krepus, after all the work repairing the village, rested and prepared for a long hunt; he prepared to face a giant. At the end of the third day he was finally ready. Sntejo visited Chaisa that evening. He had not found any sign of Kaikos, and Kaikos had not come back to check this place.

"She would have watched this place. She would have come back. I think she knows what happened in the Téuta. She thinks I'm dead, thinks Prsedi is dead, thinks you are lost to her too in a way, Sntejo. She thinks she's alone in the world. I worry what she might do."

Sntejo sat for a long time thinking. Chaisa didn't need his honesty now, but she deserved it.

"I think you know what she would do," he said, finally.

After a moment's silence she said a single word: "Welo."

"Yes. I think so. That's what I think too. And Krepus is going after Welo. I'm going with him, to find Kaikos if I can."

Chaisa tried to insist that she go too, but Sntejo argued against it. She wasn't strong enough for that yet. And in any case, Krepus would be walking with them, and it was better for now to let Krepus think she was dead. After a long argument, Sntejo convinced her to stay, and to leave the protection of Kaikos to him. Chaisa, wrapped in furs, went back inside the cave to be warm. She went inside to do the hard work: to survive and hope until Sntejo and Kaikos could return to her.

Sntejo and Do went back to the Téuta. They spent the following day bringing supplies to Chaisa. Her hut was gone, and the Téuta thought she was dead. The hidden cave was her home and would be for a very long time.

While the Téuta recovered from the flood no one noticed them. No one followed them. But Krepus was tired of waiting. At the end of that day they left Chaisa well stocked with food and wood and furs; they left her with enough to live through the winter there if she had to. They returned to the village. Krepus was chafing to go now. Time had run out.

In the morning they left the Téuta behind them. As they walked from the Téuta the three friends found a fourth: An was waiting at the gate for them, asked by Raghe to go with them on their journey. And so they went, four hunters: Krepus to hunt a giant, both Sntejo and Do to stay with him, hoping to find Kaikos along the way so they could take her back to Chaisa—and An to watch them. An to make sure they did what Raghe said they should do: kill Welo, and kill or capture Kaikos if they found her.

They were leaving the village's stresses behind them, and they were setting out on a bright day into the open and beautiful world. But it was clear to them: each of them had his own purpose, and his own hope. They had been friends for most of their lives and were friends still at the start of the hunt. But that friendship, they all knew, would not survive at the hunt's end.

PART III

Late Autumn
in the Mountains

CHAPTER TWENTY-THREE

†

The air was fresh and cool, the day just rising, when the four of them started their journey. They had the long walk to the old Téuta ahead of them. Where else would they start to look for Welo? The mood was as cool as the air as they walked from the village walls and turned toward the river. They would follow that into the mountains.

Hills rose around them, and in places the path was steep and the river strong and rough, but they made good progress. And as they left the village behind, left the whole plains behind, the mood rose with their elevation, and with their distance from the troubles in the Téuta. They spoke little, feeling the seamless, endless river beside them, which, except for the occasional turbulence as it dropped over some incline, was quiet and was always full of life.

The first evening they speared fish for their dinner. Then they spread their rolled skins on the ground and settled into the warmth of their cloaks. Sntejo, Do and An slept instantly and soundly, but Krepus lay awake watching the sky and the steep hills around them, listening to the burble of the water. He had a rising, good feeling that at first he couldn't define—and then he could.

I am free now, he thought. *Maybe it's best for me to just keep going, to go far from the village. Best to not return.* And if it were not for Raghe, if he believed Raghe could be trusted to lead the Téuta, he knew he would simply walk up the river. He would join Sntejo's quest to save Kaikos and leave his own quest behind.

In the morning they walked again, still quiet, with the river channel rising around them until the cliffs on each side rose over their heads, then twice that high, and the further up the river they walked the higher and wider the cliffs were on either side. Krepus found that the world around him was good, and that the anger that walked everywhere with him in the village had stayed in the village behind them. The stench of Raghe's rooms, the tumbled huts, the surging water that washed everything away, all were gone, and there was nothing around him but the harsh beauty of the world, the sharp cold morning, the stirring weather above him, and peace.

An had his own thoughts and didn't seem to notice the change in Krepus, but Sntejo and Do watched him, concerned, wondering what he had done with the Krepus they had always known.

ᚻ ᚐ ᚻ

The seventh day after she started walking Kaikos woke to the sound of men somewhere in the distance. She found a quiet place behind some rocks well up the side of the ravine and waited. Soon the group, four men, came close to where she sat. They walked past, a hundred paces away, on the other side of the rocks. One of them was big.

Krepus. It had to be Krepus. The others she couldn't tell; maybe Sntejo was with him. It seemed like Sntejo's bholos. She thought, *they're hunting. But what are they hunting here? The big herds are in the other direction, on the flat ground, not in the hills. Are they hunting for me? No, they wouldn't hunt this far looking for a girl they thought would die on her own.*

And if they had been following her, they would have been spread out, walking more slowly, looking for her trail. They weren't. They were simply walking, watching the cliffs and the sky, not the ground. She was glad she had decided to walk along the edges where her tracks would be less visible, or they would have seen them whether they were looking for them or not. It was odd that Krepus and Sntejo would walk this far up the river unless they were hunting for something they thought would be here.

Then she knew, with no thought at all she knew: they were going to find Welo, as she was, but they were going to try to kill him. Raghe had to have blood. Raghe always wanted blood, it seemed. *Maybe that's right*, she thought. *And maybe that's good.* She had heard her whole life about Welo the terror, the danger, the curse. Maybe ending Welo would end all of it, and the world would be well again.

But what chance did even Krepus have against a giant who, like her, could see the bholos that blew across the world, swirling and mindless, but could also see with his eyes? She had heard the story all her life, and she believed it. Welo would see them coming long before they could see him.

Raghe didn't only want Welo's blood, though. He had taken Chaisa's blood already, and Prsedi's, and he wanted Kaikos' blood to add to that.

And now Welo's.

That's it, Kaikos thought. *That's what it is. These hunters are Raghe's sharp knife against us.* She was sure Krepus had been told to cleanse himself from the death of Prsedi, the friend of gods, by doing what Raghe had always wanted anyway: by taking the lives of all of those Raghe thought were his enemies. Welo the giant who thought he *was* a god. Welo, and any who were his family, until nothing of Welo was left on earth.

She couldn't recognize the fourth man's bholos, although she thought she had seen it before, but the third was familiar.

Do. The third man might be Do, she thought, and hated thinking that. Could it really be Do? Could even *Do* be hunting her?

Kaikos watched them walk, until she could hardly see them, they were so far away. They were little bholos flames the size of mice. Then she shook herself, picked up her bags and she walked after them. She would watch, to see what they would do.

Maybe when Welo was dead they would be satisfied. Maybe the Téuta would take her back, after Welo was dead. Until then, though, she had to be careful. So she didn't just follow the river. She climbed over the rocks to follow from above, to follow from the top of the always rising cliffs, keeping out of the sight of eyes that could not see through rocks or trees.

They would walk through the passes, the easy routes, with their feet in leather shoes and their legs in warm leggings, and with fire and food at night, and she would climb the mountains above them with her grass shoes becoming ragged, with three sacks with a few bits of dried meat left in them, covered only by a woven grass vest, a fur parka, two fur capes and a belt. That was what she would have if she followed them, and it was also all she would have if she stayed here shivering in fear of them.

Of the three people closest to her in her life only Sntejo was left alive, and Sntejo was there, walking with Krepus, walking with Raghe's knife. And Do. She had Do. But Do might be there too, walking with those who hunted her. She couldn't quite believe that Do and Sntejo were her enemies now, but even Sntejo said she should trust no one. Not even him, he had said, with Do sitting beside him. And Kaikos trusted Sntejo always to tell her the truth.

Krepus and Sntejo and the other two walked all day through the pass. Kaikos climbed among the cliffs high above them, staying always on the other side of solid things. It was not difficult to follow them, but she was getting hungry. Her grass shoes had disintegrated on the rocks. Her feet hurt sometimes. The pass was rising, always, climbing the mountainside. In the pass the ground rose slowly but steadily.

The men were hiking to higher ground in the shelter between

high rock walls, and Kaikos had to climb over rocks above them, over a rough mountain with no trails, to keep up with them. It was still only early Autumn so the air was cooler than summer, but in the day she was not cold. At night, though, the mountain air was bitter, and she had no fire to warm her.

When the men camped in the evenings Kaikos wrapped herself in her capes high on the mountain in whatever shelter she could find, and she watched with her othersight as the men made their night fire, took out their food and sat to eat it. She decided the third hunter *must* be Do, because it seemed his bholos quivered often, and that quiver spread to the others. *Do is laughing*, she thought.

Then she thought, *how can it be Do? How can even Do be my enemy now? What has happened? What has made the world so terrible around me?* That the world was terrible now she could not deny. It was evident in everything that happened. If even Do and Sntejo were her enemies what was left for her in the world?

She walked, and followed the men, because she had started and had no reason to stop. But she also had no reason to continue, she thought to herself. What did she want? Just to watch Welo kill them? She didn't want to watch Sntejo die.

But in the morning she followed them again.

Their strange trip continued, until one evening the wind grew blustery, birds flinging themselves across the sky in great flocks, rising and clumping and separating and swirling, flying in one direction and then changing to a different direction to fly. They flew like trees tossing in a storm, like foam on the river rocks. It was enchanting to her, to see this turbulent swirl of bholos organizing itself, and when it was organized suddenly violating its order to reorganize in a different form. She had seen this before, and she had always loved it. It was a game the birds played, she thought. A joyful game.

What it meant, though, was that the wind the birds played in was strong up high in the air, and that the weather was changing. By this time she was so high above the men in the pass that she could barely sense them. When they stopped for the night the sky smelled like storm. It smelled, up so high on the mountain, like snow. Kaikos found a deep rocky overhang, crawled to the back and curled into a ball, still belted inside her cloak with Chaisa's cloak covering her like a blanket. She wasn't sure in this cold whether she would wake here in the morning or in the shadow world. She wasn't sure why she would want to wake here, or why the shadow world made her so afraid.

Maybe it made her afraid because there she would have to face Dhegm and all her savage anger.

⚳ ◖ ⴳ

Sntejo had the feeling he was watched. Krepus did watch him, and so did An, but that wasn't it. He'd been feeling this for days as they followed the river. But yesterday, late, he had decided it wasn't just the strangeness of being so far from the Téuta, so far from home, and for so long.

He was watched. He knew it. And the watcher could be Welo, or it could be a predator. Or—he hoped for this—it might be Kaikos, watching from the cliffs above. He could imagine her cold, probably hungry, hopeful, fearful. But alive. She had no way to know whether the men below her were friends or enemies. She would guess, he thought, that they were enemies, or at least that she would need to be careful about them. *About us*, he thought. *She would be right to think that. But we don't all hate her. She isn't as alone as she might believe.*

What can I do, he wondered? *What can I do to let her know she has defenders here?*

The men walked in the dawn, and as they walked Sntejo's sense of being watched faded.

⚳ ◖ ⴳ

When she woke, late in the morning, the men were gone. She could not othersee them at all. She crept back out of her shelter. The ground was very cold, and very wet. Probably snow, she thought. She should just go back into her shelter; her tattered grass shoes were not well suited to this. Her feet were already cold, and very sore, and she was tired of walking on the mountain.

"It's not the mountain, or my feet," she said, "I'm just tired. What is so wonderful about seeing a giant? Why am I walking in the cold just to die in the end anyway?"

I should stay here in my shelter, she thought. *It's warmer here than in the open. And I can die here as well as anywhere else. Then I can ask Dhegm what I did to anger her.*

The mountain was strangely quiet around her, and cold. Why had she left her warm shelter near the Téuta? This long walk seemed endless, in endless mountains. She would walk forever in the cold unless she chose to stop walking. She would walk *until* she chose to stop.

She had no reason to believe that waiting a day would make this go away. She was not sure whether it wouldn't just get worse, in fact. How could she know? The day smelled of snow, and the air smelled of snow.

"This cold wetness on the ground is snow. It must be snow".

And more snow is on its way, she thought. *Better to get over the top of this mountain, and down into the pass as quickly as I can.*

Or maybe better to stay here, huddled, eat the last of her food and wait. Go or stay? She couldn't decide which was a greater risk, or which she really wanted.

But when she stood up at the edge of her overhang, when she was out far enough to stand up straight and observe the bholos around her she thought, *it won't matter whether I choose to go or stay, because in a moment I will be dead.*

At the edge of the small level space, near her shelter, was a large swirling flame of bholos, too big to be a wolf or a cat, big enough to be a bull, but it didn't seem to be that. *Maybe you are a bear,* she thought. *I have never seen the bholos of a bear before.* Then she said aloud, "Am I in your shelter? I'm sorry, bear. I didn't know it was yours."

CHAPTER TWENTY-FOUR

It seemed to be looking at her, or its bholos seemed to be facing her. She was never really sure, but she thought she could tell that at least.

It stepped toward her. With the rocks beside her and the cliff behind, Kaikos knew there was nothing she could do. She waited for it to come.

The animal stopped with its face nearly touching her, and now that it was close it didn't seem to be a bear either. She knew it couldn't answer, but something in her had to ask.

"What are you?"

A swirl of bholos reached out toward her, and a breath came from it, a breath that nearly smothered her, and she leaned back away from it for a moment, and then stood straight again. She felt her death in front of her and was afraid. But she reached her hand toward the nostrils that breathed against her, and she touched a roughness, and smelled what she was touching.

Kaikos hesitated for a moment, puzzling about what she sensed. But her brain, still groggy from sleep and cold, finally sorted through it. The animal had no way to understand what her face did at that moment. Even Kaikos didn't understand it. She smiled. It was a small, frightened, trembling smile, but a smile nonetheless.

"I know what you are," she said. "You are a pig. A big mountain pig."

She watched the bholos around her, under her feet, and the great swirl of it in front of her. Kaikos had never sensed the bholos of a mountain pig before, but she had heard about them. She knew they were strong, and dangerous. She didn't know what to say to a pig, and she was too frightened to be very clear, so she just said aloud what she was thinking.

"You are going to kill me," she said, "but I know what you are."

She touched its snout, and it backed away one step, then came close again. Her hand felt wet on its nose, then felt the side of its face, and landed on a long, smooth curving thing—*a tusk*, she thought. *That's what it's called. Sntejo told me about these, that wild pigs have teeth that grow long outside their mouths.*

"I think you are beautiful," Kaikos said, her voice shaking only a little. "Your tusk, your prickled skin, your swirling bholos, you are a beautiful thing in the mountains, and since I would die anyway in this cold I'm glad you found me."

Then she thought, *maybe Dhegm sent you to kill me out of anger, but it will be easier to be killed quickly than to walk over the mountain on my hurting feet.*

Kaikos started to kneel and turn her face to the ground to honor this pig, this enormous, beautiful animal, still with her hand holding its tusk.

The pig rocked its huge head to throw her hand off. It was massive, ten times her weight and a hundred times her strength, and Kaikos put her hands against her own face then and crouched, expecting at every instant that the long tusk would tear through her. But the animal only put its snout on her back and pushed her so hard she tumbled over her legs. Sliding hard across the snow disoriented her. She nearly fell off the cliffs into the pass far below, but an outcropping of rock stopped her; her shoulder struck it so hard she was afraid a bone was broken. It made her dizzy, and she struggled to sit up again. She expected, still, to die on the tusks of this wild pig.

When she looked, when her head cleared enough to look with her othersight, the pig was gone.

She sat with her arms wrapped close around her, still trembling, and spent long moments waiting for the dizziness to stop, and for her head to clear. She felt her shoulder. It hurt when she touched it, and it hurt to move it, but she thought no bones were broken. Then she looked around, as far as she could see along the mountainside. The pig was far away because she couldn't find it.

Smiling. and happy to be alive, Kaikos thought to herself: *I'm glad I came here. I'm glad I saw you, huge beautiful pig. I haven't found Welo, but I found a giant on the mountain anyway. I don't think Dhegm sent you to kill me; she sent you to tell me to go on. To keep walking. Maybe to go back, or maybe to go on, but to go. That's why you pushed me so hard.*

That made no sense, when she thought about it, but she was sure of it anyway. She looked below into the pass. The men were gone, but they would follow this, the pass, the river, and so she could find them if she did the same. It would be warmer in the pass, and if the men had gone far enough ahead of her she didn't have to hide from them, so she should look for a way down the cliffs to the river.

She would need to walk through the snow today, though, and maybe for more days. She went back into the shelter of the rock overhang and spent part of the morning taking skins from her cloak, the small animal skins that were sewn together to make it. She used her knife to cut one of these into long leather strings. She wrapped the furs around her feet, and she tied them on. These were not shoes. They slipped a little on her feet, and they wouldn't last forever. They would get wet inside and would be cold. But they were something. They would help.

She walked through snow that day and the next; she had walked almost to what she thought was the highest point of the mountain next to the pass, higher than the highest place she had ever imagined, and then she had finally found a way down almost to the river. She would have descended to the river itself to get water, but she stopped when she saw the men ahead.

She had eaten her last food two days before, on the day she saw her pig. She thought she had lost the men, that they had gone too far ahead for her to find them. Now, though, on the seventh day of following them, the second since she had eaten her last food, she finally sensed them ahead. The men had stopped early to make camp. They too were running low on the food they had brought with them, so they stopped early to replenish their stores. Kaikos saw Krepus, Sntejo and the fourth man leave the campsite for most of the afternoon. They came back with what Kaikos thought might be a deer.

ᚻᛏ ᚺ ᚻᚱ

When they returned with their kill the fire was well established, surrounded by fairly flat rocks, and the area tidy and orderly; Do had prepared well for them. They sat and set to work cleaning the deer next to the river, and then they began to cut meat from the carcass, as much as they could eat and the rest to dry and carry in their back sacks. Before they had finished, though, Sntejo hesitated. Krepus watched him for a moment, then reached a hand out to grip his shoulder.

"Leave that," he said quietly.

Sntejo looked up, surprised. He was silent, and Krepus must have seen his puzzled face.

"She is probably hungry. She will need it," he said, glancing up at the cliffs.

"You feel it too?" Sntejo asked.

Krepus was as relaxed as Sntejo had ever seen him.

"I saw you glancing up to the cliffs and guessed. But yes, after that I felt it. That was days ago, but she might still be there. It's strange, isn't it? If she came down then you would fight to take her home, and An and I would have to fight to keep her. I hope she stays away, because I don't want to fight over something so crazy. But I also don't want her to be cold, or to be hungry. Leave that for her. And leave some embers in the fire for her in case she tries to warm herself. We can hope she finds what we leave and accepts it."

Sntejo smiled to himself about all the contradictions that were Krepus. Then he carried what he had cut back to the fire, and went back to drag his gift for Kaikos closer. The air was cold. It would be colder overnight. The leg and rump he left for her would keep overnight and through the morning too if scavenging animals didn't take it. They laid much of their meat out on rocks near the fire, salted it, and left it to dry as much as it could overnight.

In the morning, as Krepus, An and Do walked ahead leaving him to douse and bury the fire, Sntejo left some salted meat on the rock for Kaikos, in case she came here. If she found that, meat already salted and dried, she would know she had friends on this long walk.

What an astonishing child she is, he thought to himself. Chaisa was right to be confident in her. Right to know she still lived, against every challenge that threatened her.

ᚳ ᚤ ᚻ

The next morning Kaikos let the men walk on until she almost couldn't see them anymore. She knew their direction, and she would follow in time. For this moment she had other plans.

Kaikos removed the coverings she had made for her feet, since they were slippery and would be a hazard for climbing. They were filled with snow and ice by now anyway. They still helped in walking over rough mountain ground, but they did not keep her feet warm anymore. She shook them out and stuffed them into one of her sacks in case she needed them again. Then she made her way slowly down the cliffs to the campsite the men had left.

At the cliff bottom the air was warmer, and the ground was flatter. Kaikos felt for embers in the ashes of their fire, hoping she could rekindle it to warm herself. The ash was very hot. She nearly burned her fingers on some live embers in it. The men had hardly covered it over at all. She went to the woods and found some leaves and bark to put on top of the old fire, and sat blowing on them until, to her surprise, they caught. Then she ran to find some small pieces of wood to put on top of that. A small fire was enough, very small, since if she made a big one the men might smell it even from a distance. The wind was with her, though, the air drifting down the pass instead of up, blowing any smoke away from the men ahead.

When the fire was burning well Kaikos held her feet out to it. They ached badly where the heat warmed them, but she still held them out toward the flame. The warmth of the fire was luxurious, so she sat by the fire and cast her othersight around the ground, looking for the deer carcass. She found a place no more than five paces away where the ground was strangely lumpy, where there seemed to be something lying there. Reluctantly she left the fire to examine what was there. What she found was the remains of the deer with some of the meat still there—they had taken all of the meat from the back, most of the rump and sides, but there was some meat left on three legs—and on the fourth there was more meat, even a bit of the rump on it. And there was a side with some meat on it too. They had also left all the bones. They had left all of that for animals to find.

Why had they left so much?

She didn't have the time or energy to think about that. Hunger drove her. She took out her flint knife again, well wrapped inside her pouches. She cut what meat she could away from the bones, away from the legs of the animal. It took her much of the morning to do this, but she was determined to survive the day. When she was done cutting her meat she added more wood to the fire, pulled the one leg with so much meat left over to it and laid it across the top,

resting the rest of her scraps of meat on top of that. She was driven
on by fear, determination, and hunger. While the meat cooked she
cut more, whatever bits she could find, from the carcass. She scavenged all she could and cooked it over the fire.

Kaikos ate the hot, tough meat, which took a long time to chew
but tasted good. She drank from the river. And she wrapped some of
the cooked meat in leaves she found to take with her. Most important, she put a bundle of twigs and some dry leaves in her pouch and
wrapped some embers in layers of fresh green leaves also, to take
with her to start her next fire.

The dried salted meat Sntejo had left for her remained behind
on the hot rocks, open and obvious to anyone with eyes to see it.
Its bholos, though, was not different from the rock it lay on, and
Kaikos did not have eyes to see it. She never found it.

It was well after noon before she stood, packed her sack with
scavenged meat, and walked on after the hunters, or the war party,
or whatever it was. There was no need for her to climb back up the
hill now, since they were so far ahead of her, so she walked along the
pass, on the softer, more even ground. Her feet hurt badly after the
long walk through the cold rocks above, but she ignored that.

She walked until the night grew cold, but she didn't see them yet.
Then she climbed up the hill some distance to find a sheltered place
behind rocks in case they came back this way. When it was late,
when the night smelled like the sun had been down for a long time,
she decided they were not coming back this evening. She climbed
down a short way to look for wood, and when she had found some
and brought it back, she took her ember out of its pouch of leaves
and put it down with the dry leaves and twigs. She managed to start
her first fire in many nights, a small one, but for once she could
sleep warm in her little shelter.

Kaikos slept until full morning. Then she looked as far as she
could along the river ahead and behind her, and when she was sure
she was alone she climbed back down to walk along the river. She

walked among the trees far to the side of the pass, hoping to sense their bholos ahead along the river before they could see her with their eyes.

Kaikos had not found them by late in the day. She decided to climb into the rocks again. Maybe she could find them from higher up.

When she was at the top of the rocks at the river's side, she did see something. In the far distance, at the limit of her othersight, she sensed tiny bholos-flickers that might be men or might be wolves. She walked toward them while the sun moved down along the sky, while the men, or wolves, seemed to stay where they were.

Then, finally, she could sense the men clearly. She could sense what they were doing: they were poking around in the ruins of old huts, in what must be the old village from thirty years ago. Did they think Welo would just sit here for all this time? Maybe. But why would a giant stay here, or anywhere? Couldn't a giant just step over the mountains and go wherever he liked?

Or maybe this was just the first place to look, and they hoped to find a clue here about where Welo had gone. They wandered back and forth looking, she thought, at the ground. What did they expect to find after so many years?

As she got close to them, though, she knew they were looking in the wrong place. Because she could sense something else, or some-one else, near the top of the cliffs behind the village. Whatever was up there was large. And it was watching the men in the ruined vil-lage below, she thought; she couldn't be sure, but the thing seemed to be watching them.

Then she looked beyond the cliffs, and the thing on the cliffs, and saw that the ground film of bholos seemed to bend up into the sky. It went up, always up, until she could no longer see it.

She sat down and stared at this. *It must be mountains,* she thought. *That must be what a real mountain is.*

Prsedi had said there were mountains behind the mountains she could see. This must be that one, the behind mountain. The last mountain. *It's the end of the earth. Welo, if that's him, lives at the end of the earth.* Kaikos took out a bit of meat to chew on while she thought, and watched the men searching around the ruins.

Was it Welo up in the cliffs? It was large, yes, but not as big as a mountain, not as big as she had imagined a giant would be. It was like a big man or an ox. But it was watching, if that was what it was doing, from hiding, from behind rocks and trees.

It was watching the men below with othersight. Watching with the other sight that she had, and Welo had, and no one else had at all. The thing on the cliffs was not the giant she had imagined, but it was Welo. It had to be Welo.

Kaikos thought about all that had happened, and how much had changed since she was happy in the warm wind tossing the grain to winnow it, since she had visited Prsedi, and the next day Sntejo came to see her and Chaisa. She remembered all the good things, the festival, and knowing Prsedi so closely in a way she had never thought possible. And then she thought about the horrible things. The earthquakes, the death, the anger, and Krepus and Sntejo and Do hunting her as though she were a dangerous animal.

She thought, *it is fear that makes people act this way. Fear of the world, of the gods. And fear of the strangeness that I share with Welo, the sight without eyes.*

That was why Prsedi was dead, and Chaisa was dead, and Sntejo and Do were enemies who would kill her if she didn't starve or freeze first. Her blindness made her a burden, and her othersight made her a stranger in the village, even among the few who were her friends. And then when bholos cracked and the earth shook, they were afraid. They could not see the bholos cracks, but the shaking earth brought down their houses and hurt them. They could not see the bholos steaming from the ground, but they felt the ground shuddering deep under their feet. When they felt that, they were afraid.

But shuddering in the ground was only the last thing that made them afraid. The first thing, the biggest thing, was the bholos they couldn't see. Talk of bholos made them angry from fear. Fear of what, she wondered? Of nothing, of everything, of all the things that a blind child could see that they could not. Afraid because there *were* things they couldn't see.

What danger could a small blind girl possibly be to them, though? She wondered this again and again, as she watched the men searching below her. And the man up there on the hill, the very old man if that truly was Welo, had stayed where they left him so many years ago. He threatened no one. But in resentment against the cracking earth they turned against her, and they turned against him too: *abominations both of us because we can see something they can't.*

But that is how the Téuta are now, she thought with a bitterness that crept into her when she didn't work to keep it out. *They are full of rage and fear.*

Then she thought to herself, *why should I follow these men who want to kill Welo, and to kill me too if they knew I were here? I came to see Welo, and now, maybe, I know where he is.*

Whoever was at the clifftop was on the other side of the village, the other side of the river, on the other side of Krepus and Sntejo and the other two men. She would have to cross the open ground to get to him. Kaikos turned around to go back along the path she had walked. She went to find a way down to the river that was far enough away from Krepus that he wouldn't see her. Back among the trees, in the low ground of the pass, she could cross the river and climb the other side.

With the meat in her bag and some small things to eat she had found along the way, she set out again to achieve her goal: to meet the giant who stamps his feet and shakes the earth.

CHAPTER TWENTY-FIVE

Walking along the river was pleasant enough for the three men, and there was nothing for them to do except hunt, walk, breathe the mountain air, and gather whatever they could find to eat along the way. Their path was sometimes straight, but more often turned back and forth along the turns of the river, along the walls of the canyon, and the canyon grew steep. But even hunting was not necessary now and wouldn't be for many days. Yesterday they had killed a deer. Their packs were full.

There was snow, light in the canyon and heavier up the slopes, but that wasn't a bad thing for them. Krepus, looking toward the sky, watched the snow come down, feeling the cold as it spotted his face. He liked weather, all of it: the fresh winds and rain of spring, the heat of mid-summer, the storms of late summer, the cold of winter. All of that weather had to happen; they were the balance in the world. Their balance was the world's beauty.

Krepus didn't notice when that feeling first trembled and flickered. When he did notice he didn't understand—at first. Then, gradually, understanding came to him. As they walked Krepus began to look around, and he recognized the canyon features. He had been here before, long ago. When he was ten years old he had known this part of the canyon well. He knew where the turns were, where the crevasses in the cliffs beside them were. He knew it with the intimacy that children have with the places near where they live; he knew where there were secret springs, where there were patches of herbs, where to hide from the adults, laughing with your friends about some mischief you had done.

He became more and more somber. There was fear in his stomach and in his legs, and both Sntejo and Do noticed it. An seemed distracted, as though he, too, was mulling some problem. They walked in silence for much of the day.

It wasn't Krepus' old anger returning. This was something different. Krepus stopped them early. He made silent preparations for sleep. When food was hot over the fire Krepus said he felt sick. He couldn't eat. He didn't eat the next morning either when their walk continued.

Their arrival at the old Téuta was expected; they knew they were close. But it was still a surprise to Sntejo when they rounded a curve in the canyon and saw the village in the distance. Their camp the night before had been only a short walk from the curve that opened to the old Téuta; if they had kept walking for one more hour the day before they would have found it then.

Krepus was not surprised. He knew what would be there, and what they would see when the canyon stopped hiding the sight from them.

There were huts, some of them whole but neglected, some fallen inward or outward, with the walls tumbled and the roofs lying down inside them. Then there was a field of tumbled boulders, many as big or bigger than the huts themselves, and several much bigger— the size of two or three huts together. From under the edges of the jumble of rocks and boulders they could see the remains of huts that had been crushed by them. People who had been inside those huts were still there, unseen but inevitable; they too had been crushed by the weights that still rested on top of them.

Behind that, and beside that great pile, was a cliff the height of ten men standing on top of each other, and behind that, fifty or more paces, was the high cliff, as tall as thirty men. The smaller, closer cliff, it was clear from looking at it, was also part of the fallen rocks; the face they could see had once been level ground high above them. A section of the old cliffs had just tilted forward and fallen until it met the ground. It was massive—and it was clear that anything, or anyone, that had been under that when it fell had, in an instant, vanished into the crushed ground beneath it.

Sntejo wanted to ask about what might be under it. A glance at Krepus dissuaded him from any talk. Withdrawn silence was the better choice for now.

It was a strange experience. Their ancestors were buried here, some intentionally and with care, but some just flattened under all the mound of stones, large or small, from the cliffs above them. But no matter how they were buried they were here.

At first Krepus just crouched on the ground and stared at the village that had been his home for the first ten years of his life. He remembered all of it as it had been then. Every inch of the paths, the huts, the cliffs that remained around the village, the mountains behind them. And his mother, his father, his brothers, all now deep under the jumbled rocky mass that was once their sheltering cliffs, the cliffs that had, for hundreds of years, kept the cold north winds away from their huts in the winter.

He remembered the sound of the cracking cliffs, the loudest sound he had heard in his life. He remembered the screams of the people trapped under the fallen rocks, and of those whose huts had collapsed. He remembered the quiet of those quickly dead under the big boulders, and the abrupt silence that followed the impact of the biggest of all, the one that now looked like a cliff itself. Even the injured had stopped making sound for a moment when that struck the ground. That was where his family was. Under that mass.

The Téuta, the old Téuta, or what remained of it, had saved those they could save. But when he had rounded the last turn of the canyon and saw the village there half buried, Krepus also remembered with unexpected clarity all of those they couldn't save. He took time to let his emotions settle before he stood again, and the other men stood silently nearby and watched him. Sntejo was far too young when the cliffs fell to remember much about it and Do had not been born yet. An understood a little; he had been six. They could all see that they needed to wait for Krepus. They could see that accepting this old memory would take some time for him.

Krepus turned his eyes to the ground because he didn't want to see it. He felt something that until now he didn't remember ever feeling before in his life: fear without excitement, anger without joy. Now he remembered feeling exactly these things the day the cliffs fell. He wouldn't accept it, wouldn't let it bully him. He forced his eyes back up, and looked at the great fallen rock that lay exactly over the place where his home had been. If he had been in his home that day he would be there now, under the rocks, with his family. With his family. With his family.

With his family under the rock.

He tried to remain standing, but his fear pushed him back down. His loneliness pushed him down. It was as though the rock was sitting on his shoulders now, pressing him into the ground. He wanted Perkunos, the joy of Perkunos, but Perkunos had deserted him. He was alone.

I don't want it. I don't want any of this; I don't want to do what I have to do to stop it. But this thing I'm looking at, this mass of death and loss, can't happen. I won't permit it to happen again. Whatever I have to do, I won't permit this.

But still his fear kept him crouching in place, unable to approach the old Téuta.

In the late morning Perkunos finally came to him. He remembered a kind of anger that he could use, anger that could do good in the world, the anger of contest, and he pushed aside his fear. This was a contest, against the enemies of the Téuta, not of this Téuta but of the new one, where he lived. Against the gods, perhaps. Against Welo the giant. And most of all against the biggest enemy, to him, the one who swaggered now through streets of the new Téuta as shaman-king.

With Perkunos' help, with Perkunos in him, Krepus finally stood strong again, looking with determination at the ground, and at the sky, and at the cliffs that stood now, the rocky face that had been hidden thirty years ago behind the cliffs that fell. Krepus walked toward them. The other men had to hurry to keep up with him; he walked fast, with a single focus.

The four of them entered the wreckage that was the old Téuta, looking carefully for any sign that could tell them where Welo might be, whether he had stayed or left. There was nothing obvious—it had been so long that nothing really could be expected, but where else were they to look to start a hunt for him?

What was left of the village was rubble and fallen huts, terrible to look at. They walked peering at all the ruin, examining the ground, the interior of the few huts that still stood. There was nothing; one place where some debris seemed to have been disturbed long ago to find whatever was under it, and at first nothing else.

At mid-day, though, they found a pair of huts, connected to each other, that seemed cared for. There was still the smell of old fire and ash in the fire pits of both huts, and both were clean. Both were undamaged; they seem to have been built after the falling cliffs were well settled.

But who had built them? Who had lived in them, and when? And where were the builders now? None of the three had really known what to expect, but from the old hazy legends Welo was a giant, so they had expected to find giant things, giant fire pits, giant walls, giant footprints, if they found anything. But these huts were normal huts, for people of normal size. One of them had a stack of goat skins, and a platform that had been used for sleeping. It was still covered with grasses and skins to make a soft place to lie down, and the bed was sized for a normal man. The man who had slept here was not much larger than Krepus, because when Krepus lay on the sleeping platform he nearly filled it.

They spent the afternoon walking through the village, and then spent some hours making excursions outside the village, searching for signs that anyone had been nearby recently. They searched for likely paths Welo might have followed. Through all this Krepus was all business, all quiet purpose, saying very little.

Evening approached, and arrived. Through the whole area there was no sign they could use. When the light became too slight to help in their search anymore, Krepus walked to the shorter cliff, to a place that seemed to the others to have meaning to him. He placed his hand on it and placed his head against it. He stood like that until the light was gone altogether and night had come.

Do walked to him, intending to suggest they use the two sturdy huts with fire pits to sleep, but as he approached Krepus turned, and all the storms Perkunos had ever made were in him. He said nothing, then or for the rest of the night. He just turned and started walking back toward their last camp. It was clear to both Do and Sntejo that Krepus did not intend to sleep here, in the old village. It was clear that nothing on earth would make him do that. They followed him as he left, and An followed them, his eyes watching Krepus carefully.

So all of them left, walking back along the river. As they walked Krepus seemed calmer, and as they rounded the curve of the canyon that hid the old Téuta from their sight, Krepus stood straighter and taller. But his face never lost its solemn determination. He strode out ahead of the other two, walking fast and hard, even though he had nothing except his old memories to hurry him.

Without a sound, Krepus went to the place where he had slept the night before and lay down. Do and Sntejo started the fire for warmth, and cooked and ate some of their meat. An ate too, with seeming pleasure, carefully smiling as he watched the others. Krepus didn't want to eat, but he ate anyway, without any pleasure or even any sense of eating. He was hungry, but that wasn't what made him eat. He ate from determination to finish his job, to keep his strength for when he would need it. But he didn't sleep. Even when the others slept at last, Krepus simply lay there watching the sky.

"Perkunos," he said at last. "Come here. I need you. I need the courage of the hunt to do what I have to do." It was not a voice lifted to show any love for his god. It was a request for help. It sounded, almost, like a command for help.

CHAPTER TWENTY-SIX

The old man faced her and looked toward her as she walked. She had come all this way to see him, but she realized that she had thought until she first saw his bholos that she would find him already dead. She believed that she, and then the hunters rummaging through the huts in the old village, would find only weathered bones, giant bones, if they found anything still here after all the years since they had left him. Welo, if that was him at the top of the thin, rising trail, was very far from dead. Her othersight was clear.

Now that she was closer she saw his living spirit like a gray bonfire on the hill. Far up the slope—it was an afternoon of walking at least, and her feet hurt, but it was easy walking through the forest after all the days she had traveled over rocks on the mountain— she could see the old man waiting. He knew she was here, she was sure of that, and that she was coming to him. She was too far away and too hidden in the forest for him to see her with his eyes, and besides, he was so old, older than Prsedi, older than anyone she had ever met. By now he was probably almost as blind as she was, but if this was Welo he could still see without eyes.

What the old man might think she meant by finding him she

could not even guess. She wasn't sure herself what she meant, or what future she could hope to achieve here. But to stay behind was almost surely death—death for them both, and for any like them, if she understood what had happened—and not just death, but maybe even death by Sntejo's hand, or Do's, and she wasn't ready for that.

With her othersight she watched the tall glow of trees, and Kaikos looked with her othersight around her in every direction. She was in no danger. She had left the wild mountain pig behind days before; it was no threat to her here. She had sensed some wolves hunting yesterday, but they had been far to her west and north, so the wind carried her scent away from them, and they had showed no interest in her. Today she saw nothing that might harm her on her path. She walked softly, quietly, but quickly, and in the evening she finally approached his cliff-top hut.

When she approached him he was sitting on the ground. He was a big man, taller than Krepus she thought. But not as heavy, not as wide as Krepus. Not big enough to do what they said he did.

She sat on her knees near him and watched her hands, turned her head down to honor him, and to show him she meant no harm. She was a stranger to him.

"May I speak?"

"What would you want to say to an old man?"

"I'm sorry, Grandfather. I mean no harm to you. Are you..." but she faltered when the question was on her tongue.

"Yes, child, you may speak," he said with a gruff, unpracticed voice, quavering with age and disuse, and tight with his ancient grudge. "I want you to speak, to say anything at all. I have been alone for a long time. I'm curious to hear human speech again."

She raised her head, her eyes facing the trees beyond him.

"Are you Welo?" she asked.

His bholos shook and split, formed and reformed like the birds in the storm. He looked at her for some time, and then he looked away.

"I am an old man, alone, and so I have no name at all. What

would I do with one? What use would a name be to me?" He paused, agitated, and then settled. "But long ago when I lived with the Téuta and had a use for names, I was called Welo."

She almost spoke again, but he seemed unfinished. There was some question he meant to ask, but he put that question off for the moment and instead asked a different one: "May I ask, child, what has happened to your eyes? You don't look at me. You don't look at anything."

"I am blind, Grandfather Welo. I was born this way. But I can see anyway, as they say you can see, without eyes. I see the bholos around me with othersight. It is not the same as sight with eyes, I think, but it is a help."

Again his bholos leapt, and then quieted; he still had his grudge against all the world but he was also curious.

"Yes, true, it does help. Bholos? Steam? That's your word for what you see? And you call it othersight—good, good, it's good to have a word for it. I never thought to give it a word, since no one else could sense the things I sensed, so I couldn't talk to them about it."

They were both quiet for several minutes. Then she asked him the question that always lived inside her: "You have both eyes and othersight, Grandfather. Can you tell me, is it better to see with eyes? I think it is. People tell me about things that they see that I don't see at all."

"What do they see?"

"Leaves on trees. Needles. Hair. Color, they tell me, something that can make two things that are the same seem different. And they tell me that colors are sometimes beautiful. That things they see with eyes are beautiful. Mountains, and barley fields in the rain when there are fires in the hills. They say those are beautiful to people with eyes."

The old man paused, watching her. "What is your name?"

Her voice was sad when she responded. "I'm alone now too, Grandfather. When I lived among the Téuta, many days ago, I was called Kaikos, because my eyes don't work. That is the only name I have."

Welo sat quietly. He had learned with age and long solitude to find comfort in quiet, and it was hard for him to speak well since it had been so long since he had found any reason to speak. He was gruff, and held his grudge, but she didn't seem to be its focus anymore.

"For small things, and close things, eyes are better. For things far away, or behind other things, othersight is better. Did they never use your othersight to find things like that for them? For those things othersight is better."

"Oh."

"Well? Did they?"

"Sometimes they did, I think. Or Sntejo did."

"When I was among them, they used my othersight to find game behind the hills and to avoid predators they couldn't see through the hills, or through the trees. What did they ask you to find?"

"Animals under the ground, to hunt them. Groundhogs and sometimes rabbits if they were under the earth. I didn't like to tell them it was othersight, though, unless it was only Sntejo. I pretended I could hear the things under the ground."

"Yes. Othersight makes you different, doesn't it? But everyone hears." He paused. Then: "Who is your mother, Kaikos? What family are you?"

"My mother was Chaisa. I think you are my mother's mother's father, Grandfather Welo."

"Chaisa! *Chaisa?* Really, you are Chaisa's daughter?"

Welo had been sitting, but he stood suddenly when he said that.

Then Welo was quiet, or almost quiet, and seemed to be shaking with some strange emotion that Kaikos had never seen before. He might have been crying. At least his bholos shook like that.

"Yes," he said at last. "You might be. You are the right age." The old man broke his gruffness and almost smiled at some memories that clustered around him.

But Kaikos squirmed and called to him. "You know Chaisa? I mean you knew her, before?"

"I knew her when she was a baby. When she was not much more than a single year old. Before my daughter died, and her father took Chaisa away with the Téuta."

Kaikos was quiet for a moment, but she turned to sense what she could down the hill, then turned back.

"Grandfather, please. I need to speak some things quickly. I'm sorry to be so hurried, but I have something I need to tell you. Will you hear me?"

"Yes. Does it have anything to do with those creatures following behind you? Are they men or animals? I think they are men."

"Behind me?"

"Yes. They were rummaging among the huts below until late today. Then they walked back along the river."

"They are men, Grandfather Welo; they are hunters from the Téuta. You can see them from here? Your othersight must be better than mine."

Welo sat waiting.

"They are coming to kill you, Grandfather Welo. To kill us, I think."

Welo was startled, but he showed little outward sign of it. Until they had left him here, he would not have believed such a thing. He knew that fear could make even friends, even family, act with cruelty, but when he heard they were Téuta he had hoped that they were coming home.

"Why?" he asked, although he thought he knew why.

"Because the ground trembles. They think we cause it, Grandfather. I tell them I don't, but they are grown and won't believe a child."

"Yes. But it's not because of your age. They didn't believe me thirty years ago either, and I was grown then. I was a man with high place among the Téuta. But I'm big, and people said I look like my bones don't fit me, and I have this thing you call othersight, so I always made them uncomfortable."

He waited again, slow to speak after such a long silent time alone here.

"But then they didn't kill me, or even try to kill me. They only left me here to die where they couldn't see it. Who are they? Are there any I might remember?"

"I don't know. The leader is Krepus, a very big man, and very strong. It was Krepus, or the shaman Raghe, who decided we should die. It was Krepus who killed Prsedi and gave Chaisa to Raghe to be sacrificed."

Now Welo stood, and the bholos around him flared in a way that Kaikos knew meant anger.

"Prsedi! He killed Prsedi? And gave Chaisa as sacrifice? Who is this man, this monster? Prsedi never hurt anyone in all her life. When I knew her she was all goodness, far better than I was. And she was a favorite of the gods, always. Does this man have no fear of the gods?"

"I wasn't there in the Téuta when this happened, but I don't think he meant to kill her. I think it was an accident. And I think Chaisa went on her own, gave herself as sacrifice to save me."

Welo stood and paced, his bholos flaring and blowing like a fire in strong wind. His voice was tangled when he spoke again.

"Krepus—his mother is Cenakrot? Yes, a big one. He was about your age when I was left here, and he was already much taller than others his age. He is leader now?"

"Yes. He is the Téuta war leader and hunt leader and work leader."

"But you said another name for the shaman. Krepus is not a shaman? Leader but not a shaman?"

"No, Krepus is not a shaman, which is hard for him, I think. He depends on others to know what the gods want from us. But Krepus organizes things, and settles things, and keeps us safe, and Raghe wouldn't, at least people think he wouldn't. Some don't care about that, though. Maybe they think the gods would keep us safer if a shaman were leader."

Welo looked at the stars and traced the channels between them, the channels in the white path through them. He shook his head and sat in silence.

Kaikos couldn't wait so patiently.

"We must run away from here, Grandfather Welo; they will kill us."

"There's no hurry. Kaikos—your name is Kaikos? They have stopped now and made a fire. But they also have no hurry. You've left a clear trail for them to follow. You came all the way here on injured feet to warn me, Kaikos? That was silly. I'm old. It's not hard for me to die now. I have nothing left to do. But I don't think you want to die."

Kaikos sat for a moment, surprised that the hunters behind her might find her trail so easily. She had tried to stay only on rocks or in the water, so she wouldn't leave prints behind her. But if she left any trail at all then they found it, or soon would.

"I came the last part to warn you. But I started just to *see* you. They say among the Téuta that you are a giant, and I had nothing else left, so I wanted to see a giant."

Welo snorted. *A giant*, he thought. *Of course a giant. I shook the earth, didn't I?*

Kaikos waited, becoming more anxious with each moment.

"I think we must go, Grandfather. We must be far away when they come."

And Welo sat and thought for so long that she was afraid he meant to sit here to be killed. But finally he turned to her, abruptly and with more speed than she expected. Then he stood and walked to her, and he knelt in front of her.

Kaikos bent over as low as she could; she didn't feel comfortable being higher than Welo, who was almost a god, or so she had always been taught. But Welo said, "Calm, Kaikos. We have no time for formality right now. I need to look at your feet for a moment."

Kaikos sat still, confused and reluctant, while Welo picked up one foot and examined it.

"You have walked a long way in the cold without anything to cover your feet. Your hunters behind you are following a blood trail from your feet, as though they followed a wounded animal. Do your feet hurt?"

"Yes. I have walked because I had nothing else I could do, and they do hurt. And my shoulder hurts where I hit it against a rock."

"Good. You can still feel them. Come with me. You won't be able to walk much longer on these. No, just sit, I will move you to where you need to be."

"We don't have time for that, do we?"

"Yes, we do. We don't have time to have you become crippled along the road. We save more time by doing what we can to help your feet now, before that happens. It won't take long to give them a little care. Now be still. Do what I tell you."

Welo picked her up easily and carried her to the edge of a small pond next to his hut, the slow-flowing pond where he got his water. It seemed to be fed by a spring, which sent a trickle of water to join the river below. Kaikos felt strange being carried by Welo, by the almost-god so feared by the Téuta. He sat her on a rock and plunged her feet into the water, which was very cold, so cold she recoiled from it, but he pushed her feet into it again and washed them with his hands. It hurt very much for him to do that, but Kaikos sat as still as she could. When he was finished he put the backs of her heels on the ground in front of her.

"Don't move. At all. Leave your feet where they are."

Kaikos, trembling a little from cold and from confusion and fear, did as she was told, and Welo walked into his hut. She waited a moment, bewildered by him. He was not at all like what she had been told when she was young.

He came out of his hut with a crock, filled it with water from the pond, and went back into the hut.

Welo was gone so long she might have thought he had just left her if she couldn't see his bholos inside the hut. *Maybe he forgot I'm here*, she thought. Twice she started to stand to go to him; one foot moved, but then she remembered his instruction and put it back where he had left it.

He hadn't forgotten her, though. He returned, sat beneath her and lifted her feet one at a time. He spread something on them that felt like clay and smelled like honey, and wrapped them in some kind of leaves, and then wrapped them in grass mat, and then in scraps of leather tied with spun grass cords.

"What is that you put on my feet?" Kaikos asked.

"The first thing was to help your feet heal, and the leaves help keep them warm and take away the pain. I use them for my shoulders. Now that I am old my shoulders hurt very often. I'm not a healer, but a friend taught me some things about healing when I was young."

"Oh. My feet are—my feet don't hurt as much, and the leather makes them warmer, but it is a very strange feeling. It's squishy. Like wading in the river."

"It will sting a little, and feel hot, but that's all good."

"Are we going to wait for Krepus?"

"No, Kaikos. I don't want to die either, even as old as I am. We will leave in a few minutes. But let's talk while the medicine works."

"What will we talk about, Grandfather Welo?"

"Let's see—what does a blind girl do in the village?"

"What do I do?"

"What chores do you do?"

"Oh." She thought for a moment. "I help with the gardens when Chaisa lets me. I thresh and winnow the grain. I can help dry the meat and bake bread. Sometimes I hunt too, with Sntejo, to find rabbits or small animals because I can find them, but Sntejo won't let me kill them."

"Ah. That is why I see in the distance and you don't. You have never practiced using othersight to see things far away. You will have to learn, though, to survive outside the Téuta."

"Can you teach me?"

"I don't know. Maybe. But we will walk together for a while, so there may be time to teach you a few things on our way. My eyes will help you, and perhaps together we can escape them. For me it doesn't matter, really. I don't seek death, but it will arrive soon whether I seek it or not. But you are young. Ten, eleven years?"

"Twelve years."

"Hm. Small for twelve years. But I think you will grow soon. Have you eaten today?"

"Yes, I have some cooked meat. But Grandfather—don't you need to sleep tonight? You are old, Grandfather Welo, very old I think. And—"

Kaikos was not sure how to ask what she needed to ask.

"And what, Kaikos?"

"Can you walk, Grandfather? We might have to walk a long way. They will not give up easily, since they have come as far as this already. And Krepus is stubborn."

Welo laughed at that.

"I'm old, Kaikos, but still strong enough to walk, and to hunt, and as I get older, I need less sleep. But anyway, I slept today after I saw you coming here. I didn't know who you were, and I wanted to be ready."

He rummaged for a few minutes, filled a sack that he carried on his back, and turned to Kaikos with something in his hands.

"Take this." He handed her some bread and five or six nuts. "Your cooked meat will not last, although it will last longer in the cold where we are going. I know a place where we can rest."

"Rest. Will there be a fire? Will it be a warm sleep?"

Welo, still a little gruff, and still wrapped in his ancient grudge, watched her but said nothing.

Then he lifted her again and placed her on something that smelled a little of blood and old meat, and she felt herself lifted to his back in a sling. Her legs were around his waist. She felt uneasy being treated so casually, like a carcass carried home after a hunt. Maybe Welo would eat her after all. But it was not uncomfortable, really. Welo's back was warm, and he didn't seem like a threat.

"We'll eat while we walk," he said. "I will carry you for a time, at least until your poultice dries, and the carrying will be easier if you relax. Settle on my back, Kaikos."

And so they left Welo's hut and walked into the trees, with a long walk ahead of them and hunters behind.

CHAPTER TWENTY-SEVEN

Sleep slipped over her almost as soon as she climbed up to rest on
Welo's back. His strength was a surprise; he carried her, and his
large travel sack filled with skins, with her sacks inside it, and a bow
with a quiver of arrows, all with no visible effort, as though he were
strolling to the river in the morning to get water. Kaikos closed her
eyes with early night smells among the trees, and opened them only
a second later, she thought. But she opened them high on a rocky
slope, with birds wakening around her.

"I can walk, Grandfather," she said, moving in the sling, adjust-
ing her weight ready to take her share of the work, but he wouldn't
let her down.

"Stop squirming," Welo said. His voice was quiet, but still a surprise in the dawn. He was harsh at first. It seemed like a violation
of the peace in the early day. Then he softened, a little. "Let your
feet heal, Kaikos," he said, in a gentler voice. "You walked too far in
the cold. It's only a little farther to go. I can still carry you that far.
Krepus and his hunters are far behind us, searching for our trail.
You are no longer leaving the trail of blood they were following. My
track is less easy, I think. They will find it, if they keep trying, but

I think we have a full day at least, probably many days. Maybe they will give up and go back to the Téuta. We're far beyond their vision, around many turns, and I've been walking on rocks the whole way. I've left little for them to find. We may have some time before they find the right path. Let your feet rest until then."

Now that Welo mentioned them, her feet began to itch inside their dry honey-mud casing.

Welo walked with Kaikos on his back until the sun was well up. Then he slipped through a narrow slit between two high rocks into a long open space with high walls all around. To Kaikos it seemed as though he walked through this canyon with tall cliffs and a tiny sliver of sun for a long time. Then they emerged into a large flat area open to the sky. It was a large round well in the center of a rocky butte, difficult to find, difficult to get to even if you knew it was there. At the back of this space was an overhang of rock, and beneath that overhang was a small hut with a roof.

"Sometimes in the summer I come up here to live," Welo said. "The hunting is good here, and there are few dangers in this hut; few animals ever come in here, and no big ones." He carried her to the hut, put her down just outside it, and put his pack down inside, and hers as well. He had carried all of them through the whole night.

He is a giant, Kaikos thought. *He must be, to carry so much so far with so little effort.*

Welo walked back to the entrance and placed several large rocks in the crack they had come through to get there. It would be very hard to see this place if you didn't know it was here, and there would be no reason for the hunters to think it was important even if they did see it. Welo himself, even with his othersight to help him, had missed it many times before he found it—but he had been wandering this mountain for thirty years and had found many things that were hidden.

When he was finished doing what he could to disguise the entrance, Welo walked back to the hut. "Watch that direction,

Kaikos. When they come, if they come, it will be from there, and if that happens we should leave. There's another path out behind the hut, but it's very tight and ends on a narrow ledge, so they probably won't come that way. They would have to go all the way around this butte to find where the ledge opens to wider ground. You should watch to make sure they never get close to the path we used to get into this place. I'm tired; I must rest. Please, watch while I sleep, and then I will make shoes for you. And leggings. You might need them later, where we may need to go. You would need them even here in the winter."

He spread a thick-furred skin from a stack of them in a corner of the hut on a pile of woven grass mats in the corner, rolled one smaller skin to put under his head, shook another out to put on top to lie under, and he and lay down. He was asleep curled on his side almost before his head found its place.

Kaikos sat alone then, and wondered why this stranger, this ancient Welo, would trust a blind girl to watch, to be his guardian, after he had known her for only a day. For less than a day. But Welo had othersight too. Welo knew she could sense people around her. *And*, she thought, *maybe he trusts me because I am Chaisa's daughter. Because we are family.*

We are family! I have family with me, and I am with family! She was astonished at the thought. Astonished, she said to herself, at the truth. Because it was the truth. She wasn't sure yet but she thought, maybe, she was glad. This trusting old man who healed her feet was the dreaded, hated Welo. There was a great deal to think about in that.

ᚻᚈ ᚉ ᚻᚱ

Krepus slept, at some point, because the sun woke him in the morning. He rose, silent, wordless, rolling his bedding and preparing himself for the day with violent gestures. The others prepared as well, Sntejo and Do watching him with worry, and An with satisfaction:

he could see Krepus was his ally now. The sight of the old Téuta had turned his heart. He would do what must be done.

Krepus started back toward the old Téuta—because where else would they go?—and Do and Sntejo trailed behind him again, and An behind them.

They had walked no more than fifty paces when Krepus stopped and stared at the ground ahead of him. Sntejo, with his sharp eyes, had seen the same thing from a greater distance. There were footprints—small footprints—painted on the ground. They came from the rocks on one side of the river, disappeared into the river, and resumed again on the other side, ascending over the rocks there. On the light colored rocks the prints showed very dark.

"Kaikos," Krepus said.

"Yes."

"She's going to meet Welo. How does she know where he is? They are working together in this."

"I don't know what she's doing, or where she's going," Sntejo said. "But I know she has no part in this, or no part that is a danger to us. To anyone."

Krepus was silent for a long time, simply staring at the footprints.

"You can't know that," he said.

Then he turned and followed the prints, across the river and up the hill to follow Kaikos. He had a direction. He had a real destination at last.

They reached the top of the canyon side, following the footprints back and forth as they picked their way up. At the top he turned to Sntejo, not with anger but with simple, unrelenting purpose. "They are together. Something is not balanced, and I have to balance it. I *will* balance it."

Then he walked on, following the path Kaikos had left the day before. Following up the hill toward Welo.

There was no difficulty in following her trail, and for much of the morning Krepus simply strode on at a good pace. He paused from time to time to find the trail again when something had disturbed the signs, but it was never difficult to find it again. He was following clear footsteps, prints made by bloody sores on Kaikos' feet.

As the day wore on he began to soften. Kaikos, the girl he had seen as an infant, had seen from time to time on festival days, the girl he had watched as she grew year to year, was walking on feet so sore they bled. It wasn't a thought he liked. It was not a thought he wanted.

And yet, he thought, *she is going directly to Welo, or so it seems. Why? And how does she know how to find him when Sntejo, Do and I, three of the best hunters in the Téuta, and An who is determined, did not find him, even after looking for a whole day in the old village?*

Was there a different explanation for this? He wanted to think so. He decided to wait, to see what he saw when he found Kaikos, as now, inevitably, he would.

Following her path was not hard, but it took them most of the day. When they reached the top of the hill it was late. They did find a hut, very like the new huts in the ruins of a village that was now almost directly below them. They saw signs of activity, of preparation, of a lot of walking here and there. It was clear Kaikos had met someone, Welo probably, and the two of them were gone. A great deal had been left behind, but it appeared that a great deal was also packed to take with them; they had packed for a long trip. And there was no very clear single direction to follow them.

The men started a fire in the still-warm fire pit in the hut, and they settled for the night. They would continue their search in the morning.

⊓⊤ ⬭ ⊬⊓

Through the day Kaikos watched. Her feet still itched, so she picked at the mud around them during the day, and gradually it fell off, leaving her feet free. They did feel better. They felt better because the clay was gone, but also they didn't hurt as much as they had on the last walk to meet Welo.

She walked around the hut, touching what she found to figure out what it was. There was a stack of hides, small and large, maybe twenty of them, and some woven grass mats, and in the back of the hut she found a second bow and many arrows, and two spears, and two obsidian knives; she knew that from the smoothness of the bholos that lay over them, and that they had no smell, although she didn't touch them. Where did he get the obsidian, she wondered? The Téuta had to trade for it or send people on very long expeditions into the mountains to get it. But Welo lived in the mountains. Maybe he knew of a source nearby.

Kaikos walked out of the hut and sat on the ground. She watched in the direction Welo had said they would come, but nothing was there. She looked in other directions too, but there were no disturbances in any direction. When the sun was thinning, and the heat was gone, when it almost felt like night because the tall rocks all around them made cool shadows across this small space, she felt Welo's hand on her shoulder. It startled her. She had not heard him approach. She always heard everything around her, and always knew when someone was close to her, but Welo had come suddenly with no warning from any sense.

"Come into the hut, Kaikos. We have some work to do."

She stood to go inside, but Welo went to the rocks in the direction he had told her to watch. He leaned his head against them and closed his eyes. He leaned there for as long as it took her to walk to the door of the hut, then he smiled and came inside with her.

"They've taken a wrong path; they started right but took what seemed like the best direction on the rocks. That will delay them a few days, I think, if they don't give up altogether."

"Krepus will not give up," Kaikos said. "He thinks we are a threat to the Téuta. He will never give up until he thinks we are dead."

He sat for a moment and thought. He said nothing about Krepus, or about threatening the Téuta, or about death.

Instead, he said, "Kaikos, sit here on the hides. I want to look at your feet. I see you kicked off your mud boots. I know they itch, so I understand, but you will need healthy feet soon. Sit here for a few minutes and I'll be right back."

She sat and waited for what seemed like a long time, and then he was back inside. He came to her and knelt in front of her, and she slid off the rugs and to her knees so she would not be above him. It still felt wrong to be higher than Welo, who was an elder and a giant. But he took her shoulders and sat her on the rugs again, and in a stern voice said "Sit still. You can't walk on these feet, not far, and you say with stubborn Krepus following we might have very far to walk, so sit still and let me fix them."

He looked at her feet, then he put his hands on them—his hands were wet, and he had a bowl of water next to him. This felt wrong and awkward; before she found Welo, no one had done anything like this for her for many years, and then it was only her mother, not an elder. But he was determined that her feet should be clean.

"This looks good, Kaikos. I think your feet will heal quickly. But you are young, so everything heals quickly."

He sat back, looking hard at her feet. Then: "We need to make good boots for you in case we have to leave in a hurry. Stand now, for a moment."

Welo took a knife from his pack, again an obsidian knife, and put one of the hides from the stack on the ground.

"Put your foot here," he said, and she did what she was told. He worked, kneeling as she stood, and she felt awkward and odd. She had never felt so awkward in her life. He should not be doing this, kneeling at her feet. She fidgeted until he told her to stand still.

"Stand away for a moment," and he moved the skin to the side.

"Now put your other foot here." He worked for a few more minutes before he leaned back and seemed to be finished with what he was doing.

"Now you can go sit outside if you like, Kaikos, and let me work."

I wish I could stay here to watch you with eyes, Kaikos thought, *so I could learn how to do this.*

Welo sat quietly on the bed to work with the hides to make her boots. But when Kaikos stood he said, "Sit, remember that. Or lie still. Don't walk around, as you have been doing since you kicked off the mud that protected your feet."

So Kaikos walked outside again and lay on the ground, feeling the shadows move across her body. The parts of her in shadow were cold, and the rest was warm from the sun. It felt like she was very slowly sinking into the river. But she just lay there, still, as Welo had told her to do.

When almost all of her was cold, covered in her imaginary river, Welo came out with honey-smelling mud and covered her feet again with it, pressed grasses into it to make it dry harder, and then wrapped her foot in something that smelled like very old leather.

"Sit here until that dries," Welo said. "It would be good for you to just sleep."

He went inside. When he returned the rustling of a grass mat kicked air onto one side of her. Then Welo lifted her, put her down on the mat of grass, and put a fur cloak over her with her mudded feet sticking out the bottom.

For some time she waited, but he said nothing more to her. She felt the closeness of the rocks around her. She felt the hardness of the ground under the mat. She felt warm, but with cold, uncomfortable feet. She settled into a silent sleep, hearing Welo bustling about all around her. She dreamt about Chaisa, about her songs, dreams of the bholos-swoops of flying hawks, and of the slow evening stealth of hunting foxes.

CHAPTER TWENTY-EIGHT

XXXX

The sun warmed her for only a few hours every day. Welo said that was because of shadows from the walls on every side of them. Nights were cool, but the hut had a firepit that gave them warmth when they needed it, there was food Welo found or hunted or had stored away, and Kaikos didn't have to start the fires.

Life was peaceful in this hidden place. For Kaikos, it was her first peace in many weeks. It was her first real chance to sit still, leaving the first shock behind her; her first chance to mourn the loss of Chaisa, and the loss of Prsedi. And, in a different way, the loss of Sntejo and Do.

She did mourn them, and the loss of all the life she had ever led, and all the life she had wanted. But she knew that under the peace that gave her the freedom to mourn, there was the threat. Welo seemed at ease here, but Welo didn't know Krepus. Kaikos did. She knew Krepus would not give up. He would never give up. She would take it while it was here, but this peace was temporary.

During the days Welo watched Krepus and his group wandering across the land below, through the forest around Welo's hill-hut, trying to find the right path toward them and making little progress.

They started out several times, walked along a track that Welo may have left in his wanderings in the days before Kaikos found him, and returned to their starting place. On the trip up here Welo had tried to take more than his usual care to walk where he would leave no prints, up on the rocks, always up; in this he must have been successful if even Sntejo could find no trail.

If rain came, all traces would be washed away. Kaikos started to hope for rain, although she wondered what would happen in this rock hole if it rained. Would it fill up with water to drown them? But Welo's hut here had been dry and had survived with many things inside it even though he wasn't here in it. The rain would drain out through that long entrance. So she wished for rain, or that winter would come and drive Krepus away, and that somehow Welo would know how to survive here. He must know. He had survived here for thirty years. But he had didn't have a blind girl to care for during those years.

She was sure she could help, though, so she would not be a burden for him. She began to hope she and Welo could just stay, and live here in a secret space, a safe space. Each day her feet felt less sore, and her shoulder felt less sore. Each day everything felt less sore, except missing Chaisa and Prsedi. And Sntejo. She missed Sntejo in a special way. Sntejo was her grown-up friend to play with through her whole childhood. Sntejo was the one who seemed like her father.

She missed Do. She missed laughing with him.

During the nights, when she was awake, Kaikos watched Welo as he slept. She had been lost, had accepted and expected death, before she found him. In a way she had even wanted to have death, to live in the land of the dead, but without having to die to go there. That was one of the many things that made no sense to her now, but it was true. Because she had been alone. Because Prsedi and Chaisa were dead. Because nothing was left of any life she had thought would happen for her, or around her.

Now there was Welo, her great-grandfather the giant, and she wasn't alone. The giant, the fearsome giant. Sometimes Kaikos lay awake, bewildered that the Téuta could tremble in fear of this old man who knelt to make boots for her while she stood, this man who healed her. This man who saved her and who fed her.

For some time every day they were both awake, and they talked. He told her about her grandmother, and about the old Téuta village beside the cliffs. He told her about where her grandmother was now, beneath the hut he had built for her, buried with all she needed to take with her to the land of the dead.

"Welo," Kaikos said one day, "I'm sorry I brought Krepus to hunt you."

"You didn't bring him, did you? You followed him."

"But he didn't find you until I left a trail for him."

He was quiet for a moment, taciturn as he usually was.

"The big one, Krepus, is always moving, Kaikos. He paces. He was reluctant to leave the village below because he saw all the traces I had left there when I visited your grandmother less than a month ago, I think. He scouted around the village. He would have found the trail up to the cliff tops, and he would have followed it whether you came that way or not. You just left a clearer trail for them than they would have had. And if you hadn't come, I would probably have waited for them. I waited for you, and I might have waited even for them, even though there are four of them and only one of you. They would have come, and I would not have had the strength to fight all of them."

The day passed, with Welo working and Kaikos mostly sitting, which he said she had to do to let her feet heal. At the end of one day, before Welo went inside to sleep, before he left the watching to her, she spoke again. She asked about what was worrying her.

"Welo, I don't do anything now. I don't do chores."

"You can't do chores. Your chore is to make your feet well. You will need them."

"But you work all the time. You make things all the time. You will be tired soon of having me to feed."

Welo stopped. He turned to look at her. Kaikos had trouble understanding what his bholos was doing.

"I won't be tired, Kaikos. Not tired of that. You are Chaisa's daughter. My daughter's granddaughter," and he paused, absorbing those words. "My daughter's granddaughter! Chaisa's daughter! I won't be tired of you that easily. And I haven't had anyone to talk to for thirty years. I've saved a lot of words to use."

Kaikos felt lighter after that. Even though Chaisa, Do, Sntejo, Prsedi, all were lost to her, she still had family. Strange family, but family. She liked him. He was grumpy, and bitter sometimes from habit, but not angry like Krepus and not cruel like Raghe.

This is Welo, she thought, often. *Welo the giant, who curses the Téuta. Like I curse the Téuta, which means not at all. This giant Welo couldn't make the earth shake. He's big, but not bigger than Krepus. His feet aren't big enough to shake the ground like that. This Welo isn't the giant the Téuta have been talking about for all these years.*

Welo worked, and prepared. Kaikos began to forget that Krepus was coming, determined to erase the curse that lay over the Téuta, to redeem himself to Dhegm or Dyeus Pter or whoever it was who was cursing the earth.

But Welo didn't forget. He prepared for what he knew was going to come for them.

Welo made her strong boots that were secure and warm around her feet and stretched high on her legs, and long leggings from goat skins that covered the tops of her boots and were held up with leather strings tied to a belt. They were very uncomfortable. She had never worn leggings before. Even when she was walking on the open ground they brushed against her thighs as though she were walking through tall, dense grass. He said she needed them. The mountains where they were going would be cold, he said, and she would need the leggings there, and she should get used to wearing them.

Summer was over now, and days were colder everywhere. A ripening autumn troubled her: they had few reserves here, little saved for winter. No rain came, but winter was closer than it seemed from the mild weather during their stay in Welo's little fortress. Kaikos had faith, though, that Welo knew how to survive.

Then early one afternoon, as Welo watched and Kaikos slept, one of the hunters came far in the right direction, actually came close enough that he might have seen them in the distance if there had been no rocks between. But then whoever it was turned and left.

For ten days they had lived safe in Welo's hidden hut, with Welo watching during the day and Kaikos watching at night. Krepus and the others with him had seemed to be sending single scouts out in all directions searching for a hint of where Welo had gone. But now, on the eleventh evening, Welo knew one of them had come close enough that even Kaikos would have seen him with her othersight. He hoped whoever came so close would have nothing to report when he returned to the others. He wasn't sure of that, though. They might have found a direction, and if they had, then tomorrow they would be coming up the mountain. Since it was no more than a day of walking to get to this place it was possible they would be here soon.

Welo sat waiting by the bed until Kaikos woke. He said nothing. But he was there. Kaikos understood.

She and Welo began to gather their belongings, to pack what they thought they might need. They stuffed skins and clothing into a backpack and food and water into a shoulder sack. Then, since Welo said it would be at least a day before the hunters came, he set her as watchman and slept.

In the dark of the early morning he woke. Kaikos was still awake, and still fresh enough to walk. Welo said it was time; he saw with his other sense, his far-sense, that the hunters were awake and on the way.

Welo spent the morning packing another backpack for each of

them to carry; they would need food, and in the mountains they would need warm clothes. By the time he was finished, he said the hunters were close. They would probably stop for the night now, since light was almost gone. But tomorrow, Welo said, they would explore, and might find their way here. When they explored, they would approach on the entrance side, not on the hut side, he said.

So Kaikos and Welo left by the other passage to leave no trail for the hunters, the one behind the hut, which was longer and went through the rocks, with no sky above them. Sometimes, when they had to crawl and pull their backpacks behind them, Kaikos was afraid in the tight space with so much rock above her. She didn't like to be so closed in. But they went. What was the point of this, she wondered? Death was coming close behind them.

Welo exited first, with Kaikos only moments behind. They stood then on a narrow ledge, with a cliff up on one side that they had just crawled through, and a cliff down on the other side. Welo pushed Kaikos in front of him; there was only one way to go. They moved quickly along the ledge and then over some rocks. After that they were on open ground, with the butte behind them.

When Welo had last looked back the hunters were making camp for the night on the other side of the butte, ready to conduct a search in the morning, so Welo and Kaikos were well ahead of them. They might be a day, or two days, looking for the path around the butte; the front entrance path became a difficult climb only a few hundred paces past the hidden break in the cliff that led to their hideaway, and the back passage, the one they had just used, was impossible to get to from the other side of the butte. So Kaikos, by now accustomed to being hunted, simply lived in the evening, felt the cool wind against her cheek, and swayed as she walked, dancing to birds, to the sound of the wind, to the eternal music of the world.

They were turning past an outcrop that would hide them when Welo cursed softly and fell. He kicked his way around the turn, and stood, unsteady at first. He was quick to recover, but he still cursed softly. Then he put his pack on the ground, rummaged for a moment, and handed Kaikos a small grass mat. Then he turned and said, "Press this against it."

Kaikos didn't have to ask what he meant. She could smell it. There was an oddness in the bholos on his back; it was wet when she touched it. A steady stream of blood flowed from a long slice across his upper back, near his shoulder. Blood had soaked into the pack he had worn, but the pack had helped put pressure on the wound. But whatever had cut him had also cut through one of the straps that held the pack up. That would make it harder to carry.

The mat Welo had given her was too small, but Kaikos pressed it hard against the wound for several minutes. Blood seeped through the mat and across her hand, but she kept pressing. It seemed to take a long time to slow, but it did slow, finally. Welo told her to bind the mat in place with cords he gave her from his pack.

Then they moved on. Krepus would be behind them, Welo said. The wound was from an arrow that had skittered past him down the rocks but had come close enough to cut him. The four behind them knew where they were. Welo said it would take some time for them to find this path, though; it wasn't possible to get here from the top of the butte, where the arrow had come from, or from the entrance they had used to get into the center of it. The hunters would need to find the entrance and then find the exit behind the hut, or go around by a longer route that took them backward toward the old Téuta before turning back toward the path Welo and Kaikos followed. That would take time, probably many hours and possibly days, since the hunters didn't know even where the entrance was.

But they knew it had to be there. Whoever was on the top of the butte must have seen the well in its center and must have seen the hut. They would find the entrance. Kaikos tried to sense them, but she couldn't. She knew they would be coming, though. And now Welo was wounded, and that brought the reality of being prey back to weigh on her.

Escape. Escape, again. It seemed to Kaikos that her life had turned into escape, escape, escape; she had almost forgotten all of that while she lived in Welo's hidden hut. Now it was back. Now it seemed impossible. Escape, she knew, couldn't go on forever. Not with Krepus behind them, now that he knew where to start his hunt.

They walked for the rest of the day, higher into the mountains, into the cold. When evening came Welo turned to look. He said that even he couldn't see them. But he was sure they would find something that would draw them in the right direction.

"I'm not sure, Kaikos, whether this is all wasted. They will find us."

Kaikos looked at him closely. He seemed so much older now than he had when they met. She bent her head to honor him and took his hand.

"Maybe. Probably. Krepus is determined, and he's a great hunter, and there is no better hunter than Sntejo, unless it is Do. I've been hunting with Sntejo many times, and Do is alert. He doesn't miss anything. I think those are three of the four we've seen behind us. But we still will do what we need to do. We will keep doing it until we can't."

They rested in the night, one sleeping while the other watched.

CHAPTER TWENTY-NINE

K repus, Do and Sntejo used Welo's clifftop hut as a center and a storage space, as a shelter sometimes. He had built it well. There was a comfortable bed in it; there was no reason not to use it. But the hut, and the scene, troubled Krepus and again made him wonder; the bed was large, but not so large that a true giant could use it. That Kaikos had come this way there was no doubt, and it seemed probable that she had left with whoever lived here. But was it Welo? That didn't make sense, with a hut and a bed this size. But nothing else made sense either.

Whoever it was, they would find him, and find Kaikos.

Day after day they searched in all directions, but found little to guide them. Krepus would not give up. He believed he was all there was on the earth that could stop the destruction; what had happened to his family in the village below could happen again if he didn't find a way to stop it. He had to protect the new Téuta, from raiders, from rivers, from gods. And from Raghe, who thought both the gods and the Téuta were his possessions. Krepus had to cleanse the earth, and he himself had to be cleansed when he returned to the Téuta so that he could return as king.

He would find Welo and Kaikos. He would cleanse himself or he would not return.

Each day they split up and walked in different directions. Each evening when they returned Krepus asked if anyone had seen any sign, anything that would tell them which direction to go. And each evening the men told each other that they had seen nothing. They decided that they would need to look farther; they would leave one morning and return the following evening to talk. Each time they met they reported that they had seen nothing, and it began to seem that they would need to stay on the clifftop for the rest of time.

Until the evening when Do replied that he still had not *seen* anything, but he had smelled smoke. Distant smoke, and faint. But it was there.

"Up the mountain," he said, and he pointed toward where he had been.

In the morning they set off again to hunt. They left the comfort of Welo's hut behind them. It took most of the day to get to the place, and when they got there they smelled nothing, and it was time to rest. They found a place to sleep but chose not to have a fire of their own, thinking their fire would mask any smoke that might be in the air when they woke.

But Krepus was restless. They were close. He wanted a last walk around the area before they slept. He found nothing, but he saw that the cliffs were curving and always the same height. He returned to the others.

"We won't find them sitting here with the cliff so high above us," Krepus said. "The area at the top of the cliff is flat ground, I think. I'm going to climb these rocks to see if I can see them." He didn't wait; this was his decision. He dropped his pack but kept his bow and quiver with him as he climbed up in the dim evening, sometimes groping for places to put his hands and his feet. It didn't take long. He was at the top well before sunset.

Krepus walked carefully across the top of the butte. It wasn't long before he found an empty space, large and deep—and here he smelled the smoke. Here he smelled it strongly. In the dim light he looked down into the chasm and saw a large rock overhang. It was well hidden, but he could just see the edge of a small hut built at one side. He also saw what seemed to be the only exit, and he thought, *if we can get to the end of that, we can trap them. Unless they have already left.*

Carefully he made his way around the well to its other side. The sun was almost blinding as it set. He walked toward the end of the cliffs, where he could look down at all the land around this place. And on that wrinkled, rocky land below him he saw two figures, small at this distance, but one was very tall and one was not.

He had his bow and quiver with him. He had little chance to hit them, but being high above them he might at least reach them with an arrow. He fired three arrows toward them, then he moved back to get the others without waiting to see if any of his arrows hit their mark. To get to the two they would need to backtrack a short distance, then find their way around these cliffs.

When he got back to the others, he told them what he had seen: Welo was there—it must have been Welo, because Kaikos was with him. But he wasn't a giant, not a giant of the kind they had feared. He was just a big man, and only one, and there were four of them.

An looked excited by this news. He looked eager but said nothing. Do and Sntejo watched him, and watched Krepus, and wondered what they could do to save Kaikos. If Krepus were their ally they might find a way, but since their time at the old Téuta he seemed to be driven by terrible visions. They couldn't win in a fight against both Krepus and An.

But they had to stay with the group or Kaikos would have no friends among them, and no chance at all to survive.

Through a long, late evening they searched for a way around the rocks. But the sun was down and night was here. They found no easy way to get to the path where Krepus had seen Welo and Kaikos.

They were tired when they had arrived, and they were more tired now, so they decided to rest for the night. They knew, once they were past the rocks, where the two had been when Krepus loosed his arrows. They could find the trail. These two, blind Kaikos and old Welo, could not escape them now that the hunters knew where to start their search.

†† ⬭ ⊢𝒜

Winds came from everywhere, cold from the north, pushing the leaves ahead of them along the ground. Kaikos and Welo walked, and sometimes ran. Her feet were still a little sore, but she could use them, and in the fur boots they stayed warm.

Every day they walked until the hunters behind them made camp for the day; then they would walk for another hour before they stopped. Welo didn't want to build fires, which only left a clearer trail for those who followed, but sometimes he had to. The cold was becoming hard for them. Sometimes, when they were near despair, Welo would make a fire, make a stew with grain and dried meat they mixed with water from the stream. Each time they did that they knew they were marking their path for the hunters behind them.

The way was up, always, higher onto the mountain. Warming their bodies and their spirits with stew mattered. It nourished them, yes, but also lifted them so they could walk again the next morning. They had to wake early every day to move on. Their journey was constant. They had to move, though; they couldn't rest.

Krepus and his hunters behind them had to search the ground, always, to track them, so they were slowed by that. But they were relentless. And they both knew the truth: Kaikos was still a child, a blind child, and Welo himself was old and wounded. They had taken time late on the first day to make a mud poultice to keep the grass mat in place, and the bleeding had stopped for now, but the wound was still there. The hunters behind them were strong men, and great hunters in the prime of their strength. Sooner or later the hunt would end. The hunters behind were against them, and the mountain was against them, and the winter cold would overtake them no matter how fast they ran. But Kaikos had decided, and Welo had agreed, that while they lived, they would run.

Days passed, each morning a little colder, and a little higher on the mountain. And each day the hunters behind them were there, sometimes closer, sometimes farther, but always there. The two of them, the hunted, were tiring day by day. They slept when the hunters slept and tried to rise before them. They tried to walk on the tops of rocks to leave less trail for the hunters to follow. One day at the top of a steep rocky slope, with trees around them stretching into the distance, Welo nearly fell. *His age is finally showing,* Kaikos thought. *He seems strong, but he is very old.* He was old in his body as well as in years, as he had known from the start, and Kaikos was learning.

Welo could see far into the distance with his othersight, far beyond anything Kaikos could see. He had said he would show her how to do that if they lived long enough to find a place that was safe. Now neither of them expected that would happen. But as he tired his distance vision faltered. It was hard to do, he said. It tired him even more than the walking. He tried not to use it, or use his othersight at all; he wanted to preserve the energy he had left.

But that left him unprotected, in a way. He had to use his other senses, the ones he had in common with everyone, to know what was around him, and that was unusual for him and made him jumpy. He was out of practice at using only eyes and ears out in the world, out among the trees where there were dangers to avoid. When a noise sounded close in the forest as they walked in the morning along a scarp over a stream that was a major tributary to the river that ran near Chaisa's hut, Welo was startled. He stepped, one small step, away from the forest—and then his foot slipped on the scarp edge, and he couldn't stop himself. Kaikos watched his bholos flame disappear over the edge.

The climb down the slope was long, and Kaikos was careful, so the sun was nearing the middle of the sky when she reached him. He was sitting in the water, holding his shoulder with one hand and his ribs with his other, his arms wrapped close around his body.

"Can you stand? Walk?"

"I don't know, Kaikos. You should go."

"Stand up Welo. Walk with me. They won't expect us to be down here. This will slow them a little, because of that, but they will figure it out."

Welo stood, slowly.

"The fall opened my wound, Kaikos. I may not be able to walk far."

"Just walk. We'll figure it out. But we will have to walk along the river. We can't climb up the cliff again."

Welo began to walk, but quickly sat again.

"I can't walk, Kaikos. You should go."

"No," she said. She was firm, and he saw it and heard it.

They sat together in the stream for what remained of the morning. Then Welo stood. They walked, but very slowly, and by the day's end they could sense Krepus and the others behind them, high above them. The hunters probably couldn't see the two fugitives since they had only their eyes to see with, but they were there.

There was something else happening too, and whether it was good or bad for them Kaikos couldn't guess, because the two fleeing ahead of them wasn't all the hunters couldn't see with their eyes. The bholos was rising again from the earth all around her. It wasn't tall shafts like she had seen in the fields; instead it looked as though the whole world was roiling like the surface of the river.

CHAPTER THIRTY

xxl

Krepus, Sntejo, Do and An settled into the long hunt, each for his own reason, and walking in that order: Krepus ahead, Sntejo and Do behind him, and An following. Krepus walked forward, toward the fugitives, and would walk until he died if he had to. He believed the safety of the world, or at least of his world, depended on finding them. Sntejo was seeking the girl who in his heart felt like his daughter, and he was keeping his promise to Chaisa, for whom he would promise to cut his heart out if she asked. Do, for some reason of his own, felt that Kaikos' safety was his personal responsibility too. And An was a believer, on a quest from Raghe. The two who were their prey on this hunt were smart and had grit beyond anything they had ever hunted before. But their prey was tiring. That was the nature of hunting the wounded. Follow until they tired. Follow until the prey decided that living mattered less than resting.

This prey was not giving up. Night after night they would find a campsite that Welo and Kaikos had used, and in the morning they would find a track to follow, or at least a trace that gave them reason to know they had not gone far astray. Night after night they slept, often in the same place their quarry had slept the night before, and woke in the morning to hunt again.

Do tried to lighten the mood, to create laughter, but neither Sntejo nor Krepus rose to his temptations, and An barely heard them. Krepus followed Welo like a big cat hunting, and Sntejo followed Krepus closely. He followed so he could defend Kaikos against his lifelong friend with all the strength he could gather, if it came to that. But Krepus alone, focused and strong and energized by fixed determination to end this threat to all the earth, was probably a match for both of them together, and Welo and Kaikos at the same time. With An on Krepus' side to help him in the fight, the task seemed impossible.

There were mitigations, flickers of hope that kept Sntejo moving. He knew Krepus had always had a kind of affection for Kaikos. As leader he had never wanted to do what Raghe asked. But Krepus was changed. The single mountainous trauma of his early life propelled him now, as he climbed a physical mountain to find relief. Sntejo watched him. Krepus seemed to link Kaikos and Welo now; he seemed to feel now that the two who ran ahead of them were everything that kept him from the end of trauma, and no distant affection for Kaikos would deter him from that prize.

His prey was tiring. He would pursue, and he would find them. What he would do then was not clear, but it was hard for Sntejo to imagine that the outcome would be good. It would not even be good for Krepus. Nothing could lift the memory of that day thirty years ago. Whatever he did now would be a new memory that Krepus would carry forever.

A day came when the trail seemed to disappear. Nothing around them showed them where Welo and Kaikos had gone. Krepus backtracked, walked the trail back to the last track they had, and walked forward from there. He did this three times before he understood.

"Welo went over the cliff here," he said. "It looks like he fell here. I don't know why. Kaikos must have followed, more carefully."

Krepus, with Sntejo close behind and Do behind Sntejo and An last, climbed slowly down the rocks to the stream below, and stood looking upstream and downstream to decide where to go.

"If it were me," Krepus said, "I'd go downstream to create confusion. But they've walked up the mountain day after day. I'm going to head upstream to find them."

Even the hunters were exhausted. The prey must be dropping to the ground by now. What kept them standing? Krepus had never hunted a prey so determined to live.

He walked through the water when he had to, and along the dry edge when he could, and where he went the others followed. A full day, and then a search for a dry place to make camp for the night. The next morning they went on. They passed rills that entered the stream, that augmented it here and there. Sometimes the tributary stream followed its own channel that presented a different path the fugitives could take. Each time the hunters had to choose which path to take, the main stream or the new entry. But they went on, for a long day, before Krepus said he sensed nothing around him, and he must have missed them. He turned, walked downstream for a hundred steps, and stopped. There was a tributary to his right, a modest flow of water but with canyon walls five times as high as he was, with a narrow slit at the top that showed a splinter of sky, and no more. He didn't speak, didn't ask, he just turned and walked into it.

Turn, then turn, then turn. And then a long straight section, where the sky was wider above them and the banks were dry. Turn again. And at the end of one turn, around the edge of rock, far down a straight section, he saw them, far ahead. Far ahead, but within sight. He was too tired to pick up his speed, but where could they go now? They were trapped. There was no need to hurry toward them. They would be his soon enough.

On and on, and the sliver of sky seemed to narrow to nearly nothing high above. Now they walked always in the water; it was to their knees sometimes and had a good current to trip those who were too tired to resist it. On he went, until he came to a waterfall, a cascade of water down from above, and a dry gully to the left. Of course they had taken that; they could hardly have climbed up the falls. On a good day, a fresh day, well fed and rested, they might have tried it. But no, they couldn't do it now. *He* couldn't do it now.

He followed the dry gulch, the course of a stream in some long past time. He walked through the slit of dry ground and watched the sky diminish above him. Once he thought he felt the ground tremble, a small shiver, and he stopped to look up, to see all the rock above him ready to fall. Sntejo and Do behind him paused and whispered to each other. An, behind them, only watched. The others had stopped talking to Krepus several days before; now they simply followed. They were disturbed, clearly, by the shaking ground. But the cliffs didn't fall. They seemed oblivious to any trembling.

Krepus dismissed it. He thought it must have been the falling water hitting the rocks, as it had for hundreds of years.

Or maybe not. I'm following Welo and Kaikos. They are sending the tremors to warn us. They are sending them to tell us they will bury us if we follow. It was a thought, and not really a thought. He was too tired to have thoughts he understood. It was the thought that was in his bones.

The other thought in his bones was this: *I have no choice. I must follow, or we are all lost. These cliffs will fall, all cliffs will fall, all houses will fall, and all people will die under them.*

So he followed, and the others followed behind him. There was another long straight section, and he watched Kaikos and Welo turn at the end of it. When he reached that turn, he paused. A long way ahead the cliffs closed above them, closed completely. The dry stream bed led into the mountain, where Kaikos and Welo could trap them by shaking the canyon down behind them, or kill them by bringing the mountain down on top of them.

No matter, Krepus thought. *The world is ending. The Téuta is ending. Everything is ending unless I end this.*

Krepus could feel his own fear, and the fear of the three behind him. But he understood them. He knew that if he went, they would come, because Sntejo and Do meant to save Kaikos. Deep inside he wanted to be with them, to join their goal, because he wished for that goal too. If An were not behind he might have been tempted to relent. But An was there, Raghe's eyes, and they had been to the old village and seen what angry gods did to those who defied them. And so he walked ahead, even when the canyon closed above them.

Almost immediately, his fears, his predictions, came to life: the earth shook hard under them, and the canyon walls came down. Sntejo and Krepus were in the caves, but Do was outside the cave mouth, and An well behind him in the canyon. Krepus and Sntejo both turned to look. The tumble of rock was huge; it closed the cave completely. Long thin shafts of light shone through high above them, but their path back was blocked by huge stones from the canyon sides.

Do could not have survived that. What remained of Do must be under the crush of rock. An, farther back, might have escaped the falling rocks. But maybe not. Maybe the whole canyon fell in, and Krepus and Sntejo were saved only because they were already inside the caves.

Do was dead. Do, so devoted to Kaikos, was dead. Sntejo grieved for him. But Krepus was simply angry, as angry as he had been in his life. He had no need for Perkunos; he had no desire for him. Anger consumed Krepus whole at this event, anger at the earth, and at the two ahead of him who controlled it. This was their doing. His bones had predicted it, and now it was here.

CHAPTER THIRTY-ONE

"Kaikos had been walking through water between cliffs, and Welo with her, hour after hour, for so long she had lost a sense of when she entered them. Bholos spouted up higher now, always higher. But still she heard the hunters behind her; their sound echoed along the walls and came to her.

Kaikos walked on, unsure of what to do."

The canyons widened until there were wide banks on both sides of the water. There was a smaller stream flowing from a side canyon and she guided Welo to that, hoping the hunters would miss the turn and just keep following the main channels. She and Welo walked on. Welo was tired, and hurt, but he walked upright. He was grim, and his bholos flagged and fluttered, a guttering gray flame, but he would not stumble, and he would not bend. Gradually the canyon widened around her. The cliffs were high, and for a time widely separated. But the bholos spouted higher each minute.

The canyons didn't last forever open to the sky; gradually the walls narrowed again, and the gap of sky over them became steadily smaller. She came to a place with water falling from the top of one cliff, and another canyon, dry ground, went to the left. She followed that, and she and Welo walked on.

Turn after turn, and then after a last turn, with her othersight, she could see that not far ahead the canyons narrowed, narrowed, and somewhere ahead the film of bholos closed up high. *Caves* she thought. *Somewhere ahead are caves that just go into the mountain.*

She had felt the ground shake twice, only very small shakes but big enough to ruffle the waters around them, with the walls of rock rising on both sides ready to fall and bury them both. She did not want to enter caves with the ground unsteady under their feet. She didn't want to enter them at all; caves seemed like death to her. But she didn't want to be here either, between the canyon walls so close against them. She felt the earth breathing and blowing, and the bholos spouted out of it higher than the top of the cliffs, and so she knew that soon it would shake again, hard this time.

If she had to enter the caves, she would, she decided. It was a terrible thought, but there was some hope in this: it wasn't terrible only for her. Krepus would never follow her into a cave as long and tangled as the web of caverns ahead of them with the earth preparing to shake. Surely they could feel the trembling earth now, could feel the coming cracks in the earth rising beneath them. And even if they couldn't, Krepus believed that she, Kaikos, and Welo too, could create this shaking. Even Krepus would not be determined enough to follow into caves if he thought the two he chased could bring the cave down on top of him.

In the afternoon she felt Welo pause, and she knew they had found the mouth of the cave. She could almost hear his thoughts: *the cave is danger, but scaling a wall as steep as these is impossible for a damaged old man and a blind girl, and staying here is certain death.* So they went on.

The caves were wide at the entrance then became tighter. Kaikos felt warmth, and moist air, and she smelled the damp rock walls. She felt the lost sun behind her. Strangely the enclosing tunnels were almost a comfort to her, because she was sure the dark inside would be far more frightening for those who were used to sight. Surely Krepus would stop.

They walked for only a short time in the caves before she knew that he would not. Krepus and the others were following through the canyon, continuing even when the cliffs narrowed above. They were approaching the cave entrance. Krepus walked with determination. He followed them wherever they went, Sntejo and Do followed him, and the other man was farther back but still with them.

Welo walked slowly now, and it took Kaikos some time to realize why; he, too, was used to sight, and here, so far from the entrance, it was black. That would slow the hunters behind them too. That was good. There was hope in that. Now that she knew the hunters were following them into the caves, though, Kaikos felt confined. She felt the walls closing around her in the caves. They walked on, with Kaikos pulling Welo's hand to hurry him. She wanted to reach the end of this cave-walk as quickly as she could.

"Welo," she said, "stop using your eyes. Stop using your sight. Use your othersight to know what is around us and where we are going."

She waited for a minute while Welo tried this. It was hard for him. It was hard to relinquish a sense he had always relied on. She could feel him relax, slowly, as he realized that he didn't need eyes to see the path out.

"Yes," he said to her. "Thank you. That is much better."

After standing for a few moments finding his bearings with his othersight, Welo stood straighter very suddenly. He said he could sense a path; there were some narrow places and some climbs, and many wrong turns that would take them deep into the ground, but if they kept to the right path then far ahead, a day of walking ahead of them he thought, the sky would open again over them. They would be in canyons again, and then finally on open ground.

These tunnels were made by streams long ago. The old stream had cut this rock and had cut the old river canyon they had followed to get here. And the stream that had exited the mountain here had entered it far ahead. If Dhegm let them get that far, if the earth didn't fall on them or block them before they got out, there was a path.

Kaikos was hungry, and thirsty too, but at least it seemed warmer in the caves, without the cold winds. Welo was thirsty too, and he was growing weaker. His wounds exhausted him.

They kept on.

Then the earth rumbled and creaked under their feet. In the caves they could hear it long before they felt it, but it rumbled and moved, and it lurched violently.

The two of them stopped and crouched, wondering if they were about to be buried, and behind them the voices of the hunters rose to shouts for a moment, sounds that were small because of the distance, but clearly shouts echoing in the tunnels. Then they were quiet. Kaikos looked behind with her othersight and could see only two of them inside the cave, and there was chaos and tumble around them. The tunnels had held, but the canyon cliffs had not. Welo paused, too, sensing back through the caves with othersight.

He spoke, softly. "They are trapped now," he said. "Two of them are. The smallest one, the young one, is not there. I can't see him, or the man who followed. There is too much chaos there to sense what is behind the fallen rocks. But these two are trapped with us. More rocks tipped and fell across the opening, and more are falling still. They are trying to move them, but they can't."

Kaikos wanted to sink into the rocks beneath her. Do was trapped outside, maybe injured. She refused to think more than that. She couldn't quite accept it. She didn't quite believe it. Then she was aware again of Welo beside her, waiting for her response.

"I know," Kaikos said. "I see them, just barely, but I do see. What should we do?"

Welo thought for a few minutes. He sat and rested. Krepus was trying to move the new rocks, and would keep trying to do that for

a while. *These hunters are tired too, and they are now close to panic,*
he thought.

"We keep going. They may sit there until they die, because there
is light there, and they don't know there is a path out at the end."

"I think Krepus will find a way. He's very strong. He finds ways
to safety. He always does. Krepus will find a way to save them."

Kaikos spoke with confidence, but she wondered. She couldn't
see a way for Krepus to succeed now. But she didn't know anything
to do to help them, so Kaikos and Welo walked on in the dark, making their way through the tunnels with their othersight.

⊓⊤ ⓪ �

Krepus had never had any problem in his adult life that he couldn't
just push through with his big muscles, so he pushed hard, and at
first Sntejo pushed with him. Kaikos could barely sense them as she
walked. But nothing budged, and Sntejo stopped trying. Krepus
paused, and seemed to turn to Sntejo, and then Sntejo went back to
push at the rock, and Kaikos thought maybe the rock would move
with both of them pushing.

Kaikos and Welo kept walking, and she lost sight of the men
behind them. They were too far away. But after a time she could
hear Sntejo's voice echoing through the caves, shouting, shouting,
saying what? Saying *stop, stop, stop,* and then another crash.

"Ahhh. Now they may follow," Welo said. "What else can they
do? They will be afraid, and angry, and we can't help that."

Krepus and Sntejo were far behind them, in a maze of black tunnels; there was no real possibility that they could follow here, find
this place, except by sheer luck. Welo sat for a while, to rest, and
Kaikos sat with him. Welo closed his eyes, which were useless here,
and both sat feeling only the rocky ground and the walls around
them. Eventually they heard voices moving, still far behind them,
but here the voices carried through the channels of the cave.

So Kaikos and Welo got up and walked. The hunters were slow

and hesitant, Welo said; the hunters were blinded by darkness and their prey ahead of them walked free with othersight to guide them. Kaikos smiled at that. *Now, here in the caves, their eyes are blind too,* she thought. Krepus and Sntejo were blind here, and she could see.

The hunters seemed to walk with their hands on the wall to find their way, although Kaikos couldn't be sure of that. However they were trying to find their way, Welo could see that it was useless for them. They had no guide, and no sense of where they were, and they had taken wrong turns more than once and were moving deeper into the mountain. Twice the hunters turned around to try to find their way back to the blocked entrance, hoping that somehow they could get through the debris, or just breathe fresh air and see light. But they had switched hands too often, taken the wrong turn too often, and they were just as lost going back as going forward.

Kaikos could almost feel them lose hope in the blackness around them. Even Krepus had lost his swaggering bluster. She couldn't see them, but Welo said Krepus seemed too slow. Sntejo went back to him to bring him along more than once. But he seemed to slump, again and again. They were beaten. They were beaten, and they knew they were beaten. Even Krepus knew.

Finally, Kaikos felt them stop moving. She felt the quiet behind her.

"Welo," she said, "look. Look at them. I think they have stopped; they no longer chase us. If we can find our way through these caves we can live, we can do as we like. So much is lost—Prsedi, Chaisa, Do—but I will have you. I will have Welo."

"I don't know whether I will live or not, Kaikos. There is a path, I can see it; this cave is a long tunnel made by the water we can hear flowing somewhere. I wish we could find it. I'm thirsty."

Kaikos helped Welo stand, and they walked on. Welo tried to describe to her the directions among all the turns and splits of the tunnels ahead, but it was a very long list of turns, and he sometimes became confused about where he was in his explanation. He tried, over and over. And Kaikos tried to learn the long list of turnings by heart.

In the end Welo said to her, "I'm an old man, Kaikos, and you are young. If I fail, go on. I'm satisfied."

She didn't respond for a while. They walked together along the damp tunnel floor, until Kaikos broke the silence.

"I need you, Welo," she said. "How can I live even if I get through this mountain? How can I hunt, with no weapons, a girl who can't see? I need your help outside, if we find the outside."

She walked along the caverns in silence for a few moments.

"And if you die, I will have no family left, Welo. Please. Don't give up here under the mountain. Don't die here."

They walked on for an hour in silence, the path before them clear in their othersight. The tunnels sometimes widened, or narrowed, sometimes they had to stoop to get through, and sometimes the rocks over them were so far away they couldn't touch them. Once Kaikos tried to throw a rock up to the ceiling over them, and the rock hit nothing and came back down.

But Kaikos was troubled. She walked sadly, and Welo saw that, somehow.

"What is it, Kaikos?"

"I played with Sntejo all my life. I hate that he will die here, so far from the Téuta. That he will die so afraid."

Welo was silent for long minutes. Then: "Is it so important that they are in the dark? They have travelled all these weeks to kill us, Kaikos. To kill you. And you still worry about them?"

Welo had been stumbling for some time, walking without his usual steadiness. He said, "Let's rest for a few minutes." They sat, and she watched with her othersight as Welo leaned over and curled on his side, and in a moment he went to sleep.

Kaikos, alone in the darkness, waited and leaned back against the wall. She thought about Sntejo, about how it was for him, for someone who was accustomed to sight and had no access to othersight.

Sntejo would never show terror. But she knew he had to feel it.

She didn't want to spend the rest of her life thinking she might have saved him. But Welo was right; it was foolish to worry about people who were chasing them.

She looked back and could not see the hunters. They were too far behind.

CHAPTER THIRTY-TWO

"We are lost," Krepus said, and the sound echoed through the caves. He sensed defeat, something he had rarely tasted in his life before. His voice was as dark as the cave around him, thick with hopelessness. The falling rocks at the entrance had bent his foot hard. Something inside was badly damaged. Broken, he thought. Walking hurt, and not walking hurt almost as much.

"We should try to get back to the entrance. At least there is light there, a little, and we can plan."

"Can you find your way back there? I don't know in this tangled cave one direction from another. I see nothing at all; I know you are there only because you speak. I don't even know where *you* are Sntejo; the caves make sounds come from everywhere. Do you say you can find your way back there?"

"No."

"Then we are dead. This is not just! Not balanced, not hertus! It is not hertus that we will die and Welo the monster lives. It is not hertus that Raghe will lead the Téuta. If we are not there, nothing stops him. *Raghe!*"

Sntejo tried to lighten the mood; he made jokes, although Krepus never really liked jokes.

"All my life I have been inspired by Perkunos," Krepus said finally, "but what good is his fierceness here? What can be accomplished by the angry joy he shows all around him? Perkunos is not here under the earth with us, and I can't light the caves as Perkunos lights the skies. What good is the beauty of Perkunos in this place?"

The two sat silent, ready to die. They didn't know how long they sat. They may have slept, one or the other or both. Sntejo began to wonder if this were death, this darkness. He slept again. He dreamt about his childhood, about the barley fields, about the stream where he could hear Chaisa when she sang. He wondered what would happen to Chaisa now that he and Kaikos were gone. He dreamt about rebuilding the Téuta in some lost future. From time to time they spoke, although there was nothing to say.

Krepus found the silence hard. He found the blackness hard. His ankle hurt more with every minute. It was swollen so thick now that he couldn't move his foot. He wanted the entrance, the light again. The conversation was always the same. Until the last, which was not the same.

"Sntejo, are you still here? Answer."

"I am still here."

"We should talk," Krepus said, hoping that just hearing sounds would help keep him from the terror of the silent dark. "I think you are right that it would be better to die at the entrance, with some light there to help us."

"Yes. But you're right too. We have no way to find the entrance again."

They spoke these words, these same words, again and again. But the last time they said these things a voice from everywhere, a voice from the walls on every side of them, a voice from gods or demons said,

"I can guide you there if that's where you want to go."

Krepus shouted as he stood, cringed at the pain in his leg, and grunted as his head hit the rock above him. He had no idea what direction to look, or whether to look near or far, even if there were light to see her.

"Kaikos!" he said, and all his fear, all his disgust, all his sense of injustice was carried in that sound.

"I can guide you to the place that used to be the entrance, Krepus, if you want to die there," Kaikos said.

"Where are you? Where is Welo; is he dead?"

"Welo is alive, I think, maybe a quarter of a day of walking away. It's difficult to know how much time passes here. There is no wind and the smells never change."

"You have killed us, Kaikos! You killed Do when you crumbled the side of the cliffs, and you lured us into these caves to die. But there is some justice, Kaikos; you are trapped here too, unless you think you can lift a thousand rocks bigger than I am. You killed all of us and you killed yourself!"

Kaikos' anger struck fire through her like Perkunos' storm across the hills. She couldn't ignore it now. Do was dead. Krepus said so. Prsedi, Chaisa, both dead, and now *Do was dead too??* Her scream of grief swept like a flood across everything under the mountain. Maybe even Welo could hear it, so far away. When the echoes died, she spoke to them in a voice filled with an anger she rarely felt, not even thinking about the words, but letting them spill out.

"I did *not bring the wall down*, Krepus; I can't control the earth! I only ran for my own life when you meant to take it away from me. *Lured you?? Lured you! Lured you Krepus??*" And she felt tears spring from her eyes. "Krepus, *you* decided to do that, *you, you, you* wanted to take my life from me. And *you* decided to chase after me when I ran away from you. I am blind, and young, and small, and not strong, and *I can do almost nothing Krepus! I can do almost nothing!* I can't even grind grain by myself because I spill too much! I surely can't bring down walls or make the earth shake. The only thing I can do is see the bholos jump from the ground, *just see it.* Nothing more.

But *yes, yes, yes, I see it without eyes*, and that frightens huge Krepus!
Doesn't it? Doesn't it Krepus? Tell us how frightened you are, Krepus,
of the dark that does nothing to you and of a little blind girl who
also *does nothing to you!* And huge strong Krepus will crush and kill
anything that frightens him!"

Kaikos had shouted that, and her small voice roared in the caves
so much that Krepus ducked, wondering if the mountain would
collapse on them. When the echoes of her voice finally stilled the
silence collapsed on them instead. Had she gone? Had she left
them here?

"You killed Do," he said, but he didn't shout it. Noise now frightened him as much as the quiet did.

"*I???* I killed him? I did not kill anyone, Krepus. *You* killed him
by making him chase me across the shaking ground, and you kill
yourself if you choose to die here. I don't want to be here either,
but I was chased here by you and Do and Sntejo and whoever else
was with you. You chose to follow. You all chose to follow me so *you
could kill me!*"

She sat quietly for a moment.

"And Welo too. You want to kill Welo, who is just an old man
who accepted what you did to him, who lived alone for so many
years, and who did nothing to you either. All right, then, Krepus,
Sntejo. I offered to guide you to the entrance, and you still only
want to attack me. Sit here then. You can sit here to die. I came to
help you, but you don't want help from me so I will go."

They could hear her feet scrape on the rocks somewhere as she
rose to leave them.

"Kaikos!" It was Sntejo calling her.

"What?"

"How can you know where the entrance is? Here, under the
ground in the darkness there is no direction."

Kaikos turned toward the misty flame of them. She tried to speak
calmly, but her voice was louder than she meant it to be; it carried

her fear and the terrible sadness of being thrust out of her village, and about her mother, who she would never see again, and Prsedi, and Do, and even Sntejo and Krepus trapped here in the blackness; it carried her isolation, her hunger and her weariness, and all of that echoed down the caves. She watched the two men's glow become smaller as they flinched.

"What darkness, Sntejo?" She asked. *"What darkness are you talking about?* For me there is no difference here, except that it smells damp everywhere, and it's warm here. I don't know what this *darkness* thing is. Here and everywhere I see bholos steaming around me, as I always have in every place, and that is what I see, and that is *everything I see*. Outside it is better to have eyes, to see the eyes of other people, or their breath—do you see that? Their breath? Sometimes people have told me that on some days, on cold days or something, they can see that. Or the hair on arms. I never see those things; I can feel them with my hands, but I will never see them. I only see bholos. But here that is enough for me to see the paths that lead back to the entrance, and the paths that lead into the mountain. It's like when we hunted rabbits, but we are the rabbits now. The bholos flows like a river through all these paths."

"You could really find the entrance?"

"Yes, Sntejo. And I can find the path out, too, or Welo can. He can see much farther than I can. He can see the path through the whole mountain. He could, at least, before he became so tired that othersight is too hard for him. I came to help you when he looked back with his far-othersight and said you had stopped, and I thought of you here sitting alone and lost.

"We used to play together, Sntejo, and now you want to kill me. No, I don't think you want to. I don't think you could really want to. But you will. You will because Raghe stews in his hatred and fear, and Krepus follows Raghe and you follow Krepus. The bunch of you are like a centipede crawling on my arm, one pair of legs following another. Raghe can see nothing even on the open ground, even on the brightest day he sees nothing, or he sees things that aren't there. You come with me if you like, Sntejo. Let Krepus stay here, if he loves Raghe so much. Let him stay and shout to the walls about how little Kaikos, the blind girl child, can shake the whole earth."

She sat again on her heels, listening to the hiss of their whispers scurrying like mice feet through the tunnels.

"No," she said. "I've changed my mind. I won't show you the way to the entrance. You would only die there. You can follow me out, a long walk through the caves, or stay here. Or you can try to find your own way. That is your choice."

Sntejo called out to her, "Kaikos you won't let us see the light one more time before we follow you? It will make us stronger for the journey."

"No. The trip is long enough without having to go all the way back to the start and then back here. I'm tired. I'm tired after weeks of running from you. And I'm hungry, and thirsty. But also, to lead you I have to be close to you, or to stay ahead of you, and if I am ahead I am trapped and you will kill me. If I am close you still might catch me and kill me. I don't want to be killed today, Sntejo."

Again she heard them hissing together. Finally Sntejo spoke.

"Kaikos, how will you lead us out if you won't come close to us?"

"I will tell you how to find your way out, as far as I know, and I will stay close enough to sense your bholos, and come close enough to call to you when you stop, or when you take the wrong path. I can tell you which paths to choose, or leave a sign to show you."

"What sign?"

"Maybe a rock in the wrong path. Most of the way through is like these tunnels we are in, long, and sometimes you have to bend down to get through. Krepus will have to squeeze, but I haven't found a place yet that even Krepus could not get through. Welo says there is one place at the end where you will not think you understand. In one place you must turn off from the tunnels and squeeze through a space that is small. It will be hard for Krepus. You won't want to go through there, but it is the only way out that Welo can see. But when you get through that you are almost out; it is not far from there. When you get through that there might be light."

And again the two men hissed to each other in sibilant whispers. She could not hear what they were saying, but she could guess.

"Sntejo, Krepus. I am going now. But I will tell you how to find your way back to the right path."

She sat for a few seconds to think.

"Walk a little ways in the direction you think is right."

She watched the two bholos flames for a few minutes while they decided, and then saw the smaller one move.

"Yes, that is right, that is the right direction. Now Sntejo, put your hand on the wall, your strong hand, the one you throw with. Keep your hand on that wall as you walk. You will come to a place where it turns very sharply and there are tunnels in two directions. You must still follow it after that, keep your hand on the wall and go around that sharp turn and continue that new direction. That is a good direction. Do you understand what I am saying?"

"Yes, I understand."

"Then keep following that wall. Walk until you come to a place where you can stand very tall, where you can reach as high as you can into the air and you will not touch the rocks over your head. When you get there, put out your other hand and move to the other side of the tunnel, and follow that wall. Soon it will turn again and narrow again. Then move back across the tunnel and use your strong hand again to follow the wall. Can you remember that much?"

"Yes."

"After that there are three big places where the path splits and one path is right but you will be walking into the mountain on the other. These are places where there are two big channels that lead away. When there is only one small channel and one big one, always take the big one. For two of those where there are big paths you can keep following the wall with your strong hand. For the other one,

I will put a pile of rocks in the wrong path, so you will know you must find a different tunnel to follow. When you have found it, do as you are doing now—yes, I see you moving, Sntejo. Put that strong hand against the wall again and keep going like that. Do you understand?"

"Yes, so far I understand. I can remember that. Kaikos, Krepus says we should not trust you, that you are trying to make us lost."

"Why would I come all the way here to *make* you lost when you are already lost? I am trying to make you *not* lost. And if Krepus doesn't want to trust me, that is his choice. But I am going now, before you get to where I am."

And so she stood and walked away. She walked easily as though she were walking in the fields, and behind her Sntejo and Krepus stumbled through the rocky blackness with their hands on the wall to find their way.

CHAPTER THIRTY-THREE

Kaikos moved quickly along the tunnels, and Krepus and Sntejo followed slowly. *To them,* she thought again, *this is very hard; they don't have the senses they know, the sight they know. They don't have any sight. Everything is dark around them, and no smell or touch or taste in the deep caves can help them choose which path to follow.*

She slowed sometimes so she didn't lose sight of them completely, and also because what she had told them was true: she was very tired, and very hungry. Once she had to go back to tell them they had taken a wrong turn. She repeated the instructions from that point, and then moved on again.

It seemed like a very long time walking to her, but to her this was less strange than it was to them. To Krepus and Sntejo it seemed like days, days of walking with no direction to go and no sun to tell them when days ended or began, and no sense of where they were. They had no way back and no way forward except following the instructions Kaikos had left them, and they were not sure those directions were good. Kaikos said she got the directions from Welo, and Welo was an angry giant who shook the earth and killed the Téuta people. They lost hope many times. More than once Kaikos saw Krepus simply stop and she saw Sntejo move back to him. When that happened they would sit for some time where they were before they stood again. Then they went on together.

When Kaikos reached the place where she had left Welo, he was limp, but the bholos around him still showed strong enough. He was alive. But he didn't respond when she rocked him.

Kaikos stopped to think. What could she do? She tried to lift him. He was too heavy for her to carry, but when she pulled hard on his hand to try to get him up, he did respond. Her hand was wet from touching his shoulder. She smelled her hand. Welo was bleeding again. Not heavily, but the blood was there.

"Leave me here, Kaikos," he said.

"No. I won't. And anyway, I can't; you are the only one who can see through to the end. You must get up."

And so Welo got up, and with Kaikos under one arm to hold him he limped along the passages with his eyes closed, since they were still useless in the dark. They walked, and they walked; they walked through the flow of bholos until every step was hard for her. She was tired from long before they entered the caves, and they had come so far. She didn't want to give up. But she had to carry her weight and half of Welo's weight too. She was tiring quickly, and sometimes stumbling under the weight she carried, until she knew she had to stop. She had to rest. She wasn't sure where they were, and she wasn't sure Welo was awake enough to guide them. They might be as lost as Sntejo and Krepus. She saw the long streams of bholos ahead, and where the streams split ahead of her, but she no longer knew which branch to take. Welo was walking asleep; he could not really wake up anymore to guide her, and she was too tired to remember.

When she looked back, she no longer knew where Krepus and Sntejo were. She couldn't sense them.

She sat and let Welo sit beside her. He was so exhausted that he was doing whatever she told him to do, and so when she said to sit, he sat beside her without a word. Then he leaned to the side and fell, and he slept.

Kaikos listened to Welo breathing and put a hand on his shoulder so she wouldn't feel alone. But Welo was no longer really with her. He was too tired, too old now, too wounded, to help her through. *I don't think I can do this*, she thought, *and I've lost Sntejo and Krepus. I don't know where they are.*

Kaikos was more tired than she had ever been in her life. The bholos flowed slowly past her, in eddies and whorls. She started to sense dots and jagged shapes, and she seemed to sense them with her eyes. She had never sensed anything with her eyes before. She wasn't sure whether she was awake. Maybe she was sleeping, like Welo beside her.

Her head nodded forward, and she watched the jagged shapes, and she seemed to be moving with them through a tunnel, not the cave tunnels but a tunnel in her mind, and the bholos whirled around her faster. She was only half aware of it, but it seemed big; it seemed to be forming into a giant flame around her, and her head nodded again. The flame of bholos was too big for the caves. It reached far down into the earth below them and up through the ceiling of the caves above them.

Something was strange. She sat up, abruptly awake, and looked around with her othersight; she thought maybe Krepus and Sntejo had found them, but the two lost hunters were far, far behind them. But something was different. A giant flame of bholos, bigger than anything she had ever seen, bigger than the storms Perkunos sent, bigger than flocks of birds in the sky, bigger than the caves or the mountain the caves were in, a huge bholos storm was in front of her, and it was behind her, and stampedes of animals were swirling past her. Bholos was flaring around her like a storm of fires.

The ground will shake again. The cave will fall and bury us here, she thought. But no, it didn't feel like that. She felt no tension in the ground.

Then Kaikos understood, and she threw herself to her knees and bowed forward until her face was touching the rocky cave floor. Dhegm was with her; she was sure of it. She could sense Dhegm's bholos spread through the mountain in every direction, and she could feel Dhegm's hand on her head.

She heard an empty voice say her name from every direction.

"Kaikos..."

"Mother Dhegm, I'm sorry to be so long in your caves," and she flattened herself to the ground. She would have been crying if she had not been so empty of water that she couldn't.

"Kaikos, sit up. You need to walk."

"I don't know where to walk, Mother Dhegm. I'm sorry. I'm so sorry. I'm so sorry! I don't know what I did to anger you, but I'm sorry for it."

"I'm not angry with you, Kaikos. What have I done to make you think so?"

"Everyone says so. And you shook the ground in the Téuta."

Kaikos felt something that could have been confusion or laughter, even though gods would not be confused and probably also didn't laugh.

"I didn't shake the ground, Kaikos. Sometimes the ground shrugs around us to be more comfortable, just as you do sometimes. It doesn't mean to harm the Téuta. It doesn't know about the Téuta."

Kaikos flattened herself even harder against the ground. This bholos flame was too big. "Why does the ground shake without you saying so?"

"The ground is the ground, and I am Dhegm. That is all."

"Oh. I—Mother Dhegm, I'm sorry. I'm sorry to be afraid here, and I don't understand what you've told me."

A voice spoke then that was familiar to her. It spoke softly, from just in front of her.

"Kaikos, sit up now. No ceremony. We are friends."

This startled Kaikos and she raised her head.

"Prsedi?"

Then Prsedi's voice said, "Prsedi is here, Kaikos. She is with us."

Still Kaikos could not bring herself to sit up in the presence of the mother of the earth. But she felt Dhegm's hand on her back, or Prsedi's, she wasn't sure.

"Kaikos, you can't go to sleep here. You must sit up."

So Kaikos sat, still on her knees with her head bowed.

"Stand, Kaikos. You must walk, the end of the tunnels is not far from here. I'll show you the way."

"Mother Dhegm, I will follow you, but I can't lift Welo anymore. He is too heavy, and I am too tired," although she realized suddenly that she wasn't quite as tired as she had been when she sat down.

"We will carry him together then. You take one side, and I will take the other, and together we will carry him to the end of the tunnels."

Kaikos tried to think for a moment. It was very hard. But she was being told by Dhegm, or by Prsedi, she was not sure which one was there; she was being told what she must do, so she did it. Then she felt Welo's arm on her shoulder, leaning on her for support, but he was not heavy anymore, or not as heavy as he had been. It did seem as though someone else was helping him. Someone else was holding him up. Kaikos' arm was around Welo's back. And against her arm she felt another arm, Prsedi's arm, Dhegm's arm, carrying him from the other side.

They went on, with Kaikos putting one foot in front of the other, walking in the swirling bholos, walking when she knew she couldn't walk, but walking with the energy the earth's mother was giving her.

As they walked Dhegm-Prsedi talked to her, and she talked back, about threshing and winnowing, about gardens, about the shaking ground, the cooling years. Once the awe of the moment had receded, Kaikos asked questions that only a child would ask. She asked about Dyeus Pter, father of the shining sky, and about Perkunos, the god of stormy skies, of war, of rich and beautiful anger. She asked if Dhegm was with the men gods as Chaisa was with Sntejo sometimes. And again the mother of the earth seemed confused and possibly amused.

Dhegm didn't seem to understand. "What does this mean?" she asked.

And Kaikos told her about lovers and children, and that this was how life continued.

Dhegm thought a moment. She spoke half in Prsedi's voice and half in her own. "Each day we have a daughter," she said. "Each day the dawn comes, and the dawn is a child made by the sky and me; is that like what you mean? And sometimes the dawn is a shining dawn, and sometimes she is stormy. Each day there is evening when the sky and the earth meet closely. Sometimes the evenings are shining, and sometimes storms are in them. And each day the light must end so that the next day can be born. Do you feel that too?"

Kaikos found herself again so close to tears that she would have shed them if she could. When she found water, she would drink, and then she could cry as much as she wanted. She understood what Dhegm had told her. It was more beauty than she could hold inside.

They walked on, talking of many things. Sometimes they talked of the affairs of gods that Kaikos could not understand. Sometimes they talked of human things that Dhegm tried to understand. She had heard them before, and knew them, but still she was curious and still a little confused about them.

They came finally to a crack in the wall that was thin, that Kaikos needed to turn sideways to go through, and it led down a long way.

"I can't go much further with you," Prsedi said. "But you are strong, and you will find a way. And at the end of this narrow space there is water that you can drink. Fresh water."

Kaikos thought of something then.

"Prsedi-Dhegm, is Chaisa here? Can I talk with her too?"

"Chaisa is not with us yet, Kaikos."

"Is Do here with us?"

"Do is not here with us yet."

She didn't question it. She was too tired, and too hungry to think of how to question it.

"Prsedi, Dhegm, can you show the men how to get out? Sntejo and Krepus? I can't find them now. I don't know where they are."

Prsedi thought about that. She wasn't sure that was the right thing to do. But it was Kaikos asking.

"Are you sure?"

"I don't want them to chase us anymore. But I don't want Sntejo to die so afraid. Or Krepus either."

"I will show them the way," Prsedi said. "Or Dhegm will. If I tried, they wouldn't hear me. Not everyone hears the dead. I don't know how to keep them from chasing you. Dhegm may think of something. She has lived since the earth began and has learned many things."

Kaikos paused for a moment, troubled, and thinking.

"Okay," she said finally. Then: "You can't come with me, Prsedi? I think I will need you."

"I can't, Kaikos. I can't come with you to the outside. Maybe if you build a hut near the cave, or near the mountain anywhere, I can visit you in the shadows. But you must go the last part of this journey with Dhegm only. She can go where she likes; she is always where she likes to be. Don't be afraid. You will feel stronger when you have had water. Welo will too. But don't stop there; you must get out of the cave altogether. Trust me, Kaikos, and trust Dhegm. There will be a climb, and you will find it hard, but you must keep going until you are out."

Then Prsedi was gone. But Kaikos wasn't alone. The giant storm of bholos that was Dhegm rose up around her like a hurricane.

CHAPTER THIRTY-FOUR

Kaikos pulled Welo to the crack in the rocks, and into it. They slipped slowly along it. Welo was still stumbling, following her instructions, and Kaikos was somehow dragging him with her, her arm around him and Dhegm's arm linked with hers. The narrow space seemed longer than she had expected. But it was not so tight that she couldn't scoot herself through it, and Welo was old and thin, and he could get through too. Krepus would have trouble, she thought, and so would Sntejo. That would slow them down. Maybe Krepus couldn't get through at all. But she thought Sntejo, at least, would be able to do it.

At the end of the crack she dropped a foot to the ground, and had to step down again three times, long steps where she had to lie down and put her legs out over the edge and drop, before she could walk upright. Welo fell down the steps.

But then there was water, a great pool of fresh water. Kaikos drank and lifted water in her hands for Welo. She pulled him into the pool, into the shallows where they both could stand. They drank, and washed, and drank again. The water was good, and she felt restored by it, and Welo also seemed to be more alert, and to have more strength. He could stand by himself, and he could walk a little.

Kaikos stretched her othersight out. The last tunnel opened in front of her, and she wanted to run through it, but although the water had helped she was still hungry, and still tired.

Welo could take some of the burden himself, but Kaikos still held him up on one side, and something, Dhegm or something, seemed to hold him on the other. She no longer felt Prsedi's arm, but something lifted Welo.

The path was steep in places. In some places they had to climb. At the end there was a very steep climb, almost a cliff, and there was a trickle of water over the rocks, so she moved carefully. Welo, still stumbling, complained that there was too much light; it hurt his eyes, but Kaikos saw only what she always saw, the bholos sifting through the tunnels and clustering here and there.

"Close your eyes, Welo," she said to him. "Keep them closed. If you are too tired to use your othersight, I will help you find your way."

She stopped before the cliff; it went straight up for too far. But she felt Dhegm near her, and Dhegm spoke without sound to tell her she could climb this cliff, and that together they would carry Welo.

Kaikos couldn't tell how long she clung to the cliff. It was a long time. But then she was at the top, and pulled Welo over onto the ground above, and after a rest they went on.

As they walked the trickle of water under their feet became a flow, so although the ground was finally more level they had to wade for some time because the flow of water filled the bottom of the tunnel. It seemed so long only because she was tired, but at last she felt the ground really flat under her feet. She and Welo walked on for a short time.

Then the walls were suddenly open above her, and she felt rain fall on her hair, and Kaikos put her face up to the glorious rain to be washed. She held her mouth open to catch rain in it, held her hands out to catch it and bring it to her mouth. Nothing had ever tasted so good or felt so good to her. Even the bread that Prsedi made was not as good as this.

All around her she smelled the open world, the rocks washed with rain, and growing plants between the rocks. She found it hard to understand that the caves were behind her, and the sky over her. Welo seemed still dazed, but his eyes opened and he watched the rain, and saw the water running in trickles down the cliffs on both sides of them. They both sat down on the ground in the water that was slowly rising and breathed the cool air. The creek they sat in seemed to be new, fed by the new rain; possibly it was dry when there was no rain. But the rain had fed it enough so that there was a flow, from the mouth of the ravine and also cascading down the sides.

When she was ready, when she believed she really was in the open world again, she saw that the flow of water was increasing and the water rising. The rain was feeding the creek they sat in, and she wasn't sure whether it would rise enough to wash them back into the caves.

Kaikos stood, feeling strong again and alive, and she lifted Welo from the water where he was sitting. She helped Welo walk along the stream, around a corner in the stream's canyon, until they found a place where there was wide dry ground on the sides of the flow of water, and there she sat again, because Welo could not go on. She let him lie down near the cliffs, far enough from the stream that she didn't think it could rise enough to take him.

For the first moments she was still afraid Krepus and Sntejo would leap from the cave to kill her, but she stretched her othersight as far as she could and she couldn't find them. She thought if the rain continued, the stream flowing down into the caves would gradually become bigger because the rain would keep feeding it. Soon it would be a river into the caves. She realized that even if they got to the cavern it would be hard for them to walk upstream toward her. They might have to wait at the bottom of the last climb for the rains to stop.

That was good, she thought, good for them; they could rest in the light at the mouth of the caves, rest at the bottom of that last cliff, and they could breathe the freshness, and drink the water. And it would slow them. She probably had at least a day, she thought, before they got to the big cavern, and then they would have to wait until the rains left and the water drained away before they could continue. A few minutes resting here would not hurt her.

In a few places in the stream she could put her face completely under the water now. There were small pools collecting on the side of the ravine where the water found a basin, and she could climb into these places and feel the cool water all around her. The water seemed luxurious, and it was not too cold where it collected near the cliffs. She found such a place partway up the rocks, beneath a flow down the side of the cliffs, and drank deep from it, and settled next to it. She was tired after weeks of flight, after many days walking and running through forests and across the fields and what seemed like days inside the mountain. So she lay back in the fresh sweet-smelling water, and let it flow slowly past her, and she closed her eyes.

When they opened again the rain had stopped, and Sntejo was sitting below her.

Kaikos dropped her head. How could she have slept? How long had she been here? She waited, not sure whether Sntejo could see her or not, but she thought he could. Then he spoke her name, "Kaikos."

Tears flowed down her face.

"I fell asleep Sntejo, so now you have caught me. I don't want to be killed. I don't want to be killed Sntejo, it will hurt and I don't want to do it but Welo is weak and I can't run from you."

"Kaikos, thank you for guiding us."

"Where is Krepus? Why is he not here crushing me with rocks? Sntejo, Sntejo, I don't want you to kill me. Let Krepus kill me."

"Kaikos! Don't say such things to me! I won't kill you. Do you really think that? No. I couldn't do that even if I thought it was right, and I don't think it is right."

The girl hardly knew what she was hearing at first. It wasn't a thing she could understand after all the weeks of running. She still buried her face in her hands, and now, after the whole day of rain, the evening seemed cold, so she shivered. But finally she heard and lifted her face.

"You are not going to kill me? But where is Krepus! He will do it."

"Krepus thinks you are still inside. We thought we heard you calling to us, but we couldn't know where your voice came from, it sounded so far. It must have been wind, but where would the wind come from in the caves? We thought it was you. And also, he is injured and can't climb up from the cavern below us. He was injured the whole walk. When he tried to clear the entrance the rocks fell on his leg and broke it hard. We had no way out then, so we followed, and were lost as you know.

"Krepus—sometimes he did not want to continue through the blackness inside the mountain. It felt like a whole season inside the mountain, although it was probably not more than a day, or two days. He fell sometimes, back in the darkness. He was sure you were leading him to death. And then you were gone, and we were lost again. We wandered, lost completely, until suddenly we weren't lost; we found the small crack you told us about, and we could see very dim light in it."

Dhegm showed them the way, Kaikos thought. But Sntejo continued to talk.

"To get through your little crack to get to that last cavern Krepus had to scrape hard, he had to force past some sharpness, which cut deep into his chest. But he is strong-willed, as you know. He is stubborn. And when he saw the light through the crack, nothing could keep him from it."

"Yes. Once he sets his mind, he doesn't change it."

"I am not Krepus, Kaikos. I am Sntejo. I thank you, and I would lift you to my shoulders and carry you home if I could do that. I think Krepus is grateful too. I know he is happy to be alive and to feel the water and see the light and breathe the cool air. But his leg is bent and broken, and he is bleeding. He is holding his chest to stop the blood. I don't know if he will live, and he will not be able to climb out of the cave while he holds his blood inside. He probably will not be able to climb the last cliff for weeks. His mind is not on you. For now you are safe. But be quiet. Let him still think you are lost inside the mountain."

"If he can't climb, why should I fear him?"

"*I* fear him. He sent me up to find food so he can regain his strength. And I came also to make torches to look for you in the caves! But I've found you here, and I need no torches. Krepus is still injured. So I will go back and try to heal him enough to get him home.

"But I don't want him to know that I spoke to you. I don't want to remind him of his goals, or let him know you have escaped. After we found the old Téuta he went a little crazy for a while, but I think he's found some balance again. I don't think he wants to hurt you either; in his way I think he loves you. But it's hard to be Krepus. He wants, more than anything else, to save the Téuta. I'm not sure what he thinks he needs to do to save them."

"*Krepus* loves me??"

"In his way. The first time we ever saw you, you were a baby covered in barley flour. It was hard not to love you."

Kaikos wasn't sure what that meant, so she stored it away in her mind to think about later. But she thought about Krepus holding her up at the festival.

"You really won't kill me if I come down? You will let me pass?"

"Yes, Kaikos. I always thought it was crazy to say you were shaking the earth. This has all been crazy, this whole hunt, and it's not justice, and I'm sorry."

"Why did you chase me then?"

"Krepus chased Welo to cleanse himself from killing Prsedi, which he never meant to do. I followed because I promised Chaisa I would try to find you and try to protect you. I hoped that Krepus would be satisfied with Welo and would leave you alone after Welo was found. Welo, a giant, who would probably have killed us, and then you would be safe. Then maybe someday you could return to live with Chaisa. That was what I thought then."

Kaikos sat up. "Chaisa is alive. I know that. I should know that. When I heard she was gone to Raghe and couldn't return, I thought she was dead. Prsedi is dead, I know; I spoke to her. But Chaisa is not dead, and Do is not dead."

"What did you say about Prsedi? When did you speak to her?"

Kaikos hesitated, still not sure she should say these things aloud. But she found she couldn't keep herself from trusting Sntejo. She had trusted him since her birth. So finally she said, "I spoke to her. I spoke to her in the caves. Dhegm was with her."

She told Sntejo all that had happened in the caves, and how she had found her way out, and how Dhegm had helped her to carry Welo at the end when he couldn't walk. And she told him how she had asked Dhegm to guide everyone out.

Sntejo smiled. He wasn't certain he believed it. She might have been dreaming. He couldn't explain how he and Krepus had found their way out of the caves, though. He said nothing to Kaikos about his doubts, and to himself he thought, *if Dhegm would speak to any-one living on the earth she would speak to Kaikos, and Prsedi, alive or dead, would speak to Kaikos if she could.*

Then he turned and looked at the thin old man sleeping nearby. "This is Welo? He does not seem to be a giant. I don't think he could eat us whole. And I don't think he shakes the ground, or makes the years grow colder. But Kaikos, you say that Do is not dead? We saw the walls of the canyon collapse, and he was under them. He must be dead."

"But he is not with Dhegm, Sntejo. Prsedi is there, but Chaisa and Do are not there yet."

"Kaikos—the canyon collapsed on top of him. If he wasn't with Dhegm when you spoke to her, he may be with her now."

"Oh."

Kaikos' grief rose up again. It hurt. *It will always hurt*, she thought. She had a new grief for Do, but she also had an old grief lifted. She turned to Sntejo and spoke, "Where is Chaisa?"

"Chaisa is in the hills above the Téuta, in the place you found to hide her, where Krepus won't find her and Raghe *can't* find her, and none of the people around either of them will ever even try to find her because they think she was washed to the sea."

Kaikos thought of Chaisa alive, Chaisa in their safe space where they had held each other in their sleep, and she felt better. Then she thought of something that soothed her deepest heart.

"Raghe lied, Sntejo. He lied to everyone." The words sounded harsh, but Kaikos' face was full of joy when she said them. "Dhegm was never angry with me, or with Chaisa. Or Welo. She told me she was never angry with us. My whole life I've been worried, and all the Téuta stared at me, because Raghe said I was hated by the gods. But he lied. He speaks to the gods all the time. He must have known that wasn't true."

"Kaikos, I never thought it was true. Prsedi never thought so. But Raghe is Raghe."

They sat together quietly for some time.

"And now," Kaikos said. "What will happen now? What will happen with the Téuta?"

"Now I think Krepus will not be able to walk anymore, Kaikos, not really walk. His leg is bent. If we had straightened it at the entrance, if we had been able to let him heal then—but we couldn't. We walked for so long through the mountain. His leg is bent and will stay bent. Someone else will lead us now. But not Raghe; we should go back, Krepus and I, to make sure of that."

"You are finding food to take to him so he can recover enough to go home."

"Yes."

"If he is not leader can I go home?"

"He is not leader, and he knows it, but he is still strong, and still big, and he still listens to the only god-speaker left at the Téuta. And Raghe is stronger now than he ever was, and he has always wanted your death, Kaikos. He says it's because it's part of the curse that you were born blind. Even if he's lying he still says it, and people still believe it. With Prsedi dead, and Do dead, and Krepus no longer king, what would stop him? I would try. But I'm only one person, against all of Raghe's believers. It would not be good for you to go back openly to the village for now. You still will need to hide. But you can hide with Chaisa, and I will visit sometimes."

"But not Do."

Kaikos felt for a moment that the world was an ugly place. But she remembered Dhegm, and Prsedi, and thought that Do could tease Prsedi and help her laugh in the land of the dead.

"I am hungry too, Sntejo," she said. "Welo is hungry, and he's wounded. We had water from this stream, but we have not eaten for a long time."

He stood back and thought a moment.

"I will carry Welo. I will leave you both somewhere far from here, and then I will hunt in this place. When I've found something to eat I will cook it out here in the open. You and Welo and I will eat up here, and I'll bring some of what is cooked back to Krepus. But I think you should hide from Krepus for now. I don't know what to do, Kaikos. I don't know how you can live after I go back with Krepus unless you come with me. And I must go back."

Kaikos jumped down from her canyon-side pool as quietly as she was able, so quietly that Krepus wouldn't hear, and smiled, her eyes seemingly focused on the far side of the canyon.

"I am a little blind girl wandering on the earth, Sntejo, but I am not helpless. I can see the bholos all around me, and that helps me see the nuts and fruit hidden in the trees and the vegetables hidden under the ground. I have Welo with me, and we can help each other. I will live, since you have decided to let me. And now, Sntejo, I know! I know Dhegm is not angry with me, was never angry! And Chaisa is alive, and you are alive and are still my friend, and Prsedi can visit me sometimes in the shadows. And I have Welo, family, with me. And if Krepus goes back to the Téuta, if Raghe doesn't know I'm here, I am safe. What else do I need, what can I need more than that?"

Sntejo sat quietly. He watched Kaikos, and although she couldn't know it, although he was hungry and tired, watching her buried any hunger or fear. He was smiling. To him the world became an open flower; it became beauty, and good. All the world was hertus. Then he stood, lifted Welo like a new lamb, and walked out of the canyon, out of the course of the creek, and onto the open plains around them.

Kaikos looked back. She felt Krepus down in the cavern. She would follow Sntejo, but she had something she wanted to say first. She turned toward Krepus and knelt and put her face to the ground. She spoke softly. She wanted to say this to Krepus even if he would never hear it.

"I'm sorry about what I said in the cave," she said, "and about what I said just now to Sntejo. I don't really want you to kill me. If I have to be killed let Raghe come here himself to do it. That wouldn't matter so much. I mean, it would; I don't want anyone to kill me, but it wouldn't be as terrible if it were Raghe, because he is a liar, and he doesn't matter. But I would be sad to be killed by Sntejo, or by you, Krepus."

She thought for a moment. Then she said: "Or by my giant mountain-pig, because he is beautiful."

She stood then, and turned away, and followed Sntejo onto a wide, flat mountain valley filled with trees and grass and birds and life, and surrounded on all sides by cliffs.

CHAPTER THIRTY-FIVE

Sntejo hunted that evening and cooked his kill, and Kaikos, tired and hungry but also hungry to do her part after so long without any chores, hunted ground creatures and brought a groundhog for Sntejo to cook. They had a feast that night before Sntejo went back to care for Krepus in the cave.

Every day for almost a month Sntejo came out to explore the valley, looking for an easy way out of it that didn't lead through the caves. Once, while talking to Kaikos and Welo when the old man felt strong enough for conversation, he said there were cliffs or steep slopes above his head around the valley everywhere he had been, and Welo suggested that the valley might once have been filled with water, that it might have been a lake before the water found out how to drain away through the mountain.

Every five or six days Sntejo hunted, made a fire and shared his kill. With Welo's instructions, he found honey and clean mud, the right mud, and medicinal herbs to make a poultice both for Welo and to take to the cave to treat Krepus. Krepus' cuts mended quickly, and Kaikos watched old Welo's wound heal more slowly. In this, Welo showed his age.

And if Krepus noticed that Sntejo showed knowledge of healing that he never had before, and that he always left much of his kill out in the valley, he said nothing about it to Sntejo.

On a late, cool autumn day, Sntejo told the two fugitives that Krepus was restless, and almost well enough to be able to climb the last steep rocks, that he would be able to escape the cave soon.

"Kaikos," he said to her, "Krepus can't know where you are. He might guess, but we can't let him be sure that you and Welo still live. You both must hide now," and he paused and frowned. "You should follow us back," he said finally. "You could live in the hills above the village, with Chaisa. You could be with her again."

Kaikos' sightless green eyes seemed to gaze across the valley in the direction of the Téuta village, and she wanted to go. She wanted so much to be with her mother, and with Sntejo, and even with Krepus. She wanted to be Téuta again. She was quiet for a long time.

"I can't, Sntejo," she said. "Welo is wounded, and old. I don't think he can make the long walk down the mountain. Tell Chaisa I'm here, that I'm alive, and that I will come when I can, when Welo is whole, or—" she paused only slightly— "or when he dies. But for now I need to take care of him. He's not strong anymore, not for now, and he has nothing else now but me."

Sntejo was quiet for a very long time, and Kaikos watched him. She knew what he was thinking.

"I'll be alright, Sntejo," she said. "Welo will heal before winter, and we will live. I walked here, didn't I? I walked alone and in snow for the first part, and now I have someone to help me. I won't die. Tell Chaisa I will come back. I will. But you must promise that you will never tell anyone else except Chaisa that you saw me here, or Raghe might send another expedition. Next time he might send one that really wants to kill us."

Sntejo made his promise to Kaikos, and kept it, as he had kept his promise to her mother.

The next morning Welo and Kaikos began to walk across the

wide valley. They walked for days, slowly because Welo was still weak, until they found shelter near some solid rocks, all the way across the valley as far from the caves—as far from Krepus— as they could get.

It was a good place. There was a stream through the center of the valley, a stream of water from the top of the mountain above the trees where the ground was covered all the time with snow. The stream flowed across the whole plain until it disappeared into caves on the other side, near where they had arrived here. In a wide area in the center of the plain there was a deep lake full of fish and frogs. When he was well, and had the time and strength to do it, Welo could hunt the mountain goats who tasted wonderful and had skins with long hair, and Kaikos could gather nuts and fruit and roots and hunt for animals under the ground.

That first year Welo gathered wood and stone and mud and built a small, makeshift hut for them. They did whatever they could to make the work faster, since they had little time before hard winter arrived. They used a natural formation, an overhang of rock, and built mud brick walls around that extended slightly out from the cliffs. They covered the extended part with dirt and straw, and built a crude fire pit oven in it with a hole in the roof above the oven to let the smoke out.

The first winter was hard for them. Building the hut left them little time to hunt, and little time once they had hunted to dry meat for the winter, and they had no time or place to store grain. That winter they were often cold in their little hut, and often hungry. Through the whole winter there was deep snow on the mountain plain, and neither of them was used to so much snow. Sometimes Kaikos lay awake while Welo slept. She sensed him lying on his side with his knees partly bent, and she wished Chaisa and Sntejo were with them.

In the spring Kaikos moved some of the valley plants closer to the hut, so they had a garden of sorts, but it was only wild plants.

She had no seeds to plant peas or lentils. They spent the spring making crocks to hold grain, and making the hut bigger and better, and making the garden better. When Welo was finished they had a hut with two rooms, one small and makeshift and the other very large. In the small hut they had their old fire pit and their sleeping space, and in the larger hut they had a grinding stone, and a storage space, and another oven—a better oven. Kaikos had never been allowed to go inside the Téuta village wall, so she had never seen a hut so big.

Welo was very good at making pots. He was almost as good as Chaisa had been. He spent many hours instructing Kaikos in that art. By making gruff demands of her while claiming weakness from his old wounds, he trained her in every art. Kaikos noticed that, in spite of his weakness from old wounds, he had strength to hunt and to carry his kill home alone, scrambling down the mountain rocks with a goat over his back.

All summer Welo made Kaikos do things: he made her fish and hunt on her own and showed her how to scrape and treat the skins of the goats and other animals that they killed. He explained that she should save her urine to cure the skins and how to work them to make them soft. He made her learn to grind grain, explaining that his back wound hurt if he did that task—but his back had enough strength to make a grinding stone, and to make large wood basins to put on each side of it so she could let the unseen flour fall off the edges and then lift the basins and pour it back on the stone. He made her light fires with sparks and moss, light them alone while he watched silently. He would not let her escape the work or the lessons simply because of her blindness. He told her gruffly to use her othersight and learn to work on her own.

The whole of the valley filled with wild grasses in the spring, and in the late summer they both worked to harvest them to fill their little makeshift granary, and worked to dry meat and fish. When the second winter came they had their shelter and their food, and they could live through it gladly. Welo spent all the winter hours telling Kaikos stories of past times, and training her to othersee distant things, to see as he did, linking the bholos near her to what the bholos itself saw, and what the bholos that the bholos sensed saw, in a chain into the distance. It was difficult and made her stomach upset to do it at first. After the first time Welo made her practice outside the doorway until she could do it without throwing up. But she tried, and kept trying.

The winter passed, and then spring came again. By spring she could othersee across the whole valley, or through the high rocks behind their hut to watch the goats jumping across the mountain.

The two alone on the mountain built a third hut linked to the first two, but this time Welo made Kaikos make bricks with grass and mud and dry them in the sun, and carry them to the place where the hut was built. He made her bring mud, made her put the bricks and mud together to make the walls, showed her how to lay beams across the center and branches across the top, and then cover it all with mudded grass, and then thatch thick enough to keep the water out.

They built a double wall around the outside of the cluster of huts together so they were protected and hard and had some insulation against the winter cold. And he kept teaching her to fish, which she liked to do, and to use weapons other than her little knife to hunt bigger game, which she did not like to do. She was never very good at hunting larger animals. With only othersight she couldn't aim a bow, or hit a target with an arrow.

In the third winter they learned, both of them, to make wide stiff shoes that were better for walking on the snow. They learned to carry things on the snow on platforms with sticks under them, and they learned many other lessons about living through the winter in the mountains.

In the next spring, the third spring of their life there, Welo fell sick. He was old, old, old, by his count he had lived through seventy-two winters at the start of that year. He had suffered from his wounds, and suffered walking through the mountain, and suffered again from the cold over the first winter. He tried, but he could not live through his sickness.

He deserved to be buried under the hut he had built, but the ground under the hut was rocky and hard and she was not Welo, not a giant. She knew she had to take him to another place and build a burial hut for him there. Kaikos couldn't carry Welo when he was dead. She could pull him, but even that was hard after the spring thaw.

It was not the honor he deserved. Welo would forgive her, she thought. He knew she loved him and honored him, and that this was all she could do for him. She laid Welo on the surface on a level spot near the cliffs, where the ground was softer than inside the huts he had built. She laid him in the position he used to sleep, since in the early year with the ground still cold she couldn't dig into even the softer ground for him.

She covered him with one of the mountain goat skins to keep him warm, and put his bow and knife beside him, and a bowl of grain and some dried meat so he wouldn't be hungry on his journey. She also placed in Welo's hand a round of bread soaked in honey and wrapped in leaves as a payment for his passage across the water to the land of the dead. When she thought she had given him all he might need, she covered him with grass mats and worked for a week to build a simple cairn over him.

Then Kaikos the blind child was alone in the high valley.

If Welo had died three years earlier, she thought, and she was left alone then, with no Welo and no Téuta to build a hut for her or to hunt the big animals for meat and skins to keep the cold out—if that had happened, then when the deep winter came on the high valley, when the snow came, Kaikos would have had nothing to keep her from the cold. She would have frozen on the mountains when the long, cold winds of winter came over the peaks.

But Welo had lived through his wounds that first year, and

through the winter that followed, and in the years that followed that he had built for her and made her learn. So now Kaikos had her hut, and her garden, and she could hunt for the animals that burrowed in the ground and fish in the lake, and dry the meat, and gather and clean grain in the summer, and grind the grain into flour to make bread. She could make pots, and she could make blankets and shawls from the skins of the animals she killed. She could start her own fires. Welo had taught her to do all these things on her own.

It turned out that Kaikos the little blind girl *could* survive alone in the world, even without the help of a village. She loved him. She mourned his death. But through their three years together he had made sure she could live without him.

CHAPTER THIRTY-SIX

Kaikos sat grieving near Welo's cairn for four days, leaving only to bathe and drink, and in the evening to eat. She slept overnight beside him. In the hut she felt the awful absence of him. She felt alone.

When she recovered from grief enough to think, she was afraid. She was afraid to stay where she was, but also afraid to strike out blind to find a distant village with no direction, no knowledge of how to find it, and no knowledge of what she would find if she ever got there. But Welo had died because he was old, and she thought if she didn't go, she might grow old herself there alone on the side of the valley and die alone in her hut that her great grandfather had built for her.

Going was dangerous and hard. Staying was giving herself to death. She had been in this place before.

But she was Kaikos, and she remembered Dhegm, and Prsedi, and her big mountain pig. So she stood, after her days of mourning, and began to prepare for her long uncertain journey back to see her mother.

One day in her preparations, before she could start her journey, she saw with her othersight, with her far sight, a group of people walking toward her from across the valley. She was concerned, and wondered if she should hide, until she saw flames of bholos among them that were familiar.

Sntejo had come back. He had come to find *her*, and he had brought her mother Chaisa with him and thirty-seven others, including sixteen grown men. They carried seeds for peas and lentils and wheat and barley, and they had twenty-six sheep with them. There was an almost new baby who walked and ran after Chaisa. Sntejo brought news of a split in the Téuta, created by meanness. Created at its root by Raghe, but he was not alone in creating it.

After Sntejo and Krepus had found their way back to the Téuta village, Raghe could have welcomed them as valued members of the Téuta people. Instead he had been angry and arrogant, and had wanted to continue as shaman-king. Some supported him in that.

But some, having lived under him for many months, did not.

Krepus didn't want to be king again. He had tasted freedom. But he had looked at the disarray in the Téuta, and solved the issue as he often did when confronting Raghe: with his size and strength. He had insisted that he was still the leader even with a bent foot. And he was accepted as leader even if could not completely cleanse himself by reporting that he had seen the deaths of Welo and Kaikos, because he had always been leader and the Téuta knew him.

Raghe took note of that failure and wanted to send Krepus out again to hunt down the two who he claimed had made the ground shake and the years colder. But the ground was quiet, and neither Krepus nor anyone else, except Sntejo, had any idea where Kaikos and Welo were—and Sntejo was silent about it. Krepus, with his bent foot, couldn't lead a long, aimless expedition to find Kaikos and Welo, and the rest of the village had no interest in an expedition like that anyway. Most were glad to have Krepus and Sntejo back. Even most of those who wanted Raghe as shaman-king were glad.

Krepus had tried to restrain Sntejo from telling the truth about how Kaikos had come to rescue them in the caves, guiding them through with her othersight. Krepus might have wanted to tell the truth too, but politics and the struggle for kingship intervened. Raghe said he thought it was shameful for a leader to be saved by a child, and a blind child, and a girl child. Worse even than that, Raghe said, was to be saved by a *cursed* child. No one, Raghe said, who had been so feeble that they had to be saved by a child like that could be a king in the Téuta.

So Krepus told a story of how they had never seen either Kaikos or Welo, but he alone mastered the caves and found his way through the black underworld with a broken foot, and how he alone had led a *terrified* Sntejo to safety. Most of the village had sided with their leaders Krepus and Raghe, and only a few sided with Sntejo, even though the whole village knew, really, that Sntejo told the truth. The village had broken into enemies, with neighbors turning against each other.

Krepus' foot festered. In the third winter he died, although no one knew why or how. One moment he was walking, lumping along on his twisted foot, towering over everyone with his wide shoulders, and then his face twisted strangely, and he just fell forward over his bad foot and was dead. It happened so suddenly that he might have been dead before he fell.

The Téuta had still been split. In the spring the biggest faction, led by Raghe, had told Sntejo and those who believed him to leave and to "go find the bones of your lost friends and live with them."

So they did leave. And they did find Welo dead, and found that his bones were buried in a cairn. But they found Kaikos' bones still well fastened inside her living body. Her mother was astonished and shouted her name when she saw Kaikos standing next to her hut waiting for them. Chaisa dropped what she was carrying and ran to Kaikos and held her. Kaikos realized that she and her mother were the same height now, and she felt her mother's tears on her own face where their cheeks were pressed together.

Chaisa spoke with a thick voice and said "Kaikos! Kaikos, you are a woman now, look at you, look at you!" and held her out to look at her and then held her close again. Kaikos put her arms around her mother. *How familiar*, she thought. *How comfortable, how ordinary it seems to be held by Chaisa. How ordinary it seems to want the sweetness of this moment to last, always, always to last.*

They spent the whole afternoon exchanging stories about the three years they had been apart, while the rest of the women and the children listened, a little surprised at many new details of Chaisa's life in the hills above the village, and astonished at Kaikos' travels, her life with Welo (and the news that Welo was not much bigger than other men), and her life alone after Welo died. The men explored the area, looking for the best place to build a longhouse where they, and their sheep, could live through this year. Smaller huts would wait until that was completed.

In her talk with the women Kaikos didn't mention Dhegm, but on the long trip from the Téuta village Sntejo had told all of them again and again about how she found her way out of the caves, and who had helped her do it, and that Kaikos had met Prsedi in the caves, and that she had met the mother of the earth face to face and spoken with her as a friend. Many of the women treated Kaikos with deference, even with awe.

Chaisa's new child, whose name was Dhewo because he ran so much, saw how the grownups treated Kaikos, so he hid from her behind Chaisa. When Kaikos learned his name and called him he came to her, and knelt with his face down, as he had been taught to behave with honored grownups. Kaikos was startled, at first, but then she laughed at that, found his hair, then his shoulder, and followed his arm down to its end, and took his hand.

"No ceremony with me, Dhewo," she said. "You are my brother. We are friends."

And after that it was hard to keep him from running everywhere while they talked. Often the conversation had to wait for Chaisa to run after him and bring him back.

Kaikos noticed, after a time, the laughter of the men at work, and thought that it was a rich and wonderful sound. It sounded like running herds of cattle, like thunder in a far place. It reminded her of the thick warm fur of mountain goats. But what she noticed even more was that the laughter was frequent. She turned to look at Chaisa, who shrugged with a resigned smile. "It is Do. Even injured he laughs and makes everyone laugh."

The surprise and then concern Kaikos showed in her face made Chaisa realize that Do's story was new to Kaikos.

"Somewhere here the cliffs fell down on him, I think you know more than I about that. It didn't kill him, though. It took him a long time to move the rocks off his leg and his arm, and much longer than that to come back to the Téuta. He told us he was found nearly dead by some people from another village. They gave him shelter for the winter and straightened the broken places, and he healed as well as he could. He thought you and Sntejo and Krepus were all lost in the caves, or dead, which he thought must be the same thing."

"When did he return, then?"

"He came back just last winter. Three years ago after you all left An came back first—"

"An? Oh."

"Yes, and I'm glad I was hiding in the hills where I never heard the story he told. I don't know what I would have done if I had heard and believed it. An told the village you were all dead, you and Welo and Krepus and Sntejo and Do.

"But then Krepus and Sntejo came, about a month later, with Krepus hurt, and Sntejo came to see me as soon as he could. He thought Do was dead but explained about you and Welo—and about Prsedi and Dhegm too. I was giddy; I spent days laughing and crying, days of joy that you were alive and sadness that I would not see you, that you were so far away. And then last winter, two years after he had left, Do returned alive. He came back, he said, to see if I was alright. Walking was slow and hard for him. His arm and leg were bent on one side. They have broken places. But his good side is still strong. He does good work with the good arm and leg he has left."

Kaikos felt like she was floating, for a moment. Chaisa was here, in front of her, and Sntejo was here. *And Do was here!* All were here with her.

Why didn't Do come to see her?

Well, why didn't she go to see him? Chaisa was telling her she should, saying he was still a good man even with his injured arm, that he had talked about her often. Kaikos did want to go to him. She did, but she felt a strange emotion, an inexplicable emotion, one she had never felt in her life before, at least not since she was very young.

She felt shy.

When the men's work was done for that day, Do did come to see her. They sat together, traded stories, and talked. Do didn't know what to say at first, so he just said, "The moon is bright tonight."

"What does it look like?" Kaikos asked.

She has never seen the moon, Do thought. *Of course she hasn't. Sometimes it's easy to forget her blindness.*

He tried to describe the moon to her and she thanked him. She told him she knew about the sun, she could feel it on her skin when the sun was up in the day. But she could neither see nor feel the moon, and it seemed to have no bholos around it.

"It must be very far away," Kaikos said, "if I can't see its bholos even with far othersight."

The arm he had toward her, his right, was good and whole, and very strong. She wondered what the other arm was like and asked him. He got up and moved to her other side so she could touch it. The muscles were good there too, but smaller, and it was bent a little bit. The bones were bigger and twisted in two places. She could feel Do's anxiety about her touch. He thought his injured arm might be ugly to her.

"Do, I'm glad you're here, with broken arms or whole arms or any arms. I've missed you, and your laughing, and all of you."

She wanted to tell him she thought his injured arm was beautiful, but she found, to her surprise, that she was shy about saying such things to him. Maybe tomorrow, or the next day, she would find the courage to tell him.

They were quiet in the night, feeling the air around them and listening to the night sounds. All around her there were people who talked easily, even with Kaikos there. The people all simply did what they were doing. They didn't stare at her with fear, or with anger, or hatred, and she realized that she felt another thing she had never felt before. She was not the cursed girl anymore. She was not the refugee, running. She was not thrust out to live far away. She belonged here, in this place, with these people. They had come, all of them, to her hut to be with her.

Kaikos chose to sleep in the first hut, the small hut under the rocks, and left the other huts for Chaisa and Sntejo and Dhewo.

That evening when they were settling in to sleep, Kaikos heard a sound she had not heard for three years: she heard Chaisa singing. She sang with a joy she hadn't felt for a long time. She sang, Kaikos thought, like a cooling breeze from the mountains. She sang like a trout swimming in the lake, or like a young goat leaping across the rocks. She sang like grain in the air when Kaikos tossed it to make it clean, like the chaff drifting in the air smelling like winter bread.

And when she slept that night she dreamt of arms, and of hands. She dreamt of all the arms that had hurt or helped her, of Krepus, when his hand kept her from falling at the festival, and also when his arm struck Prsedi. She dreamt of Welo's hands as they spread honey-mud on her feet, of Chaisa's arms when she held her in the night. She dreamt of Prsedi's arm when Kaikos leaned against it at the festival, and again as Prsedi's arm—or Dhegm's arm—helped carry Welo from the caves. She felt Dhegm's hand on her head in the caves, and heard Dhegm saying she wasn't angry, that she had never been angry with Kaikos.

And she dreamt a long dream about Do's good arm, and about Do's bent arm, which—in her dream—was warmer than the late summer sun on the bare of her back and legs.

EPILOGUE: LIFE IN THE MOUNTAINS

What happened to them on the long fertile plain in the mountains? The archaeological record is unclear, so we can believe what we want to believe. We can tell the story we find most likely, or the one we like best. Sometimes those are the same story.

That Kaikos and the others made a new village is nearly certain. And it's likely that they found, in the mountains, good sources for some of the resources that are scarce on the plain: obsidian and salt. With these they established a trading relationship with towns down the mountain in all directions.

At first they may have avoided the new Téuta village; Raghe and his adherents would have been difficult to deal with. But eventually, when the world warmed again and crops were plentiful both in the mountain and on the plain, they may have found a vibrant and useful trade relationship with their old home.

It is no more than a speculation on my part that, at some later time, in some later year, Kaikos played a beautiful bone flute.

"Where did you get it?" someone may have asked her, perhaps Sntejo or Chaisa, or someone else.

"I made it."

And the asker looked at the flute, at the perfection of its sound, and asked another question:

"Where did you learn to make such a perfect flute?"

"Prsedi showed me how."

And the questioner accepted that without thought; whoever it was thought Prsedi had shown her how long ago, in the Téuta, while she was still living. But we know that's not true. Prsedi had no time while she was still alive to show Kaikos how to make flutes. The living Prsedi never saw Kaikos again after making that promise at the festival.

That's a fun story, and I'll believe it, although I have no evidence that it really happened.

Do and Kaikos became a marriage, a household, and lived in the huts that Kaikos and Welo had built. Chaisa and Sntejo made a hut a short distance away. The main village started near there but spread slowly toward the lake that remained, the lake that was the last and lasting remnant of the big lake that had once filled the valley before the water found out how to drain away through the rocks. So again, Kaikos lived a little outside the main town. She didn't mind that. It was what she was used to. But she and Chaisa still ran to the lake each morning to bathe and swim in the cold water.

Chaisa had two more children, mountain children in this new place. In time Kaikos had seven children of her own. Some chose to see only with eyes, and some with both eyes and othersight. And those children grew to be adults, and they too had children of their own, and their children had children, and they again had children— and so on and on, down through the long millennia.

And if that last version of the story is what you choose to believe, then you must see the implication of that. You see, don't you? That after so many thousands of years it's not impossible that *you and I* are at the end of the long chain of Kaikos' children. Just the opposite. It's very *likely* that we are.

Try to calculate how many ancestors you must have that far back into prehistory, at a time when there were only a few million people in the whole world. Somewhere in the great multiplying array of your ancestors—if you could trace your whole family back through time, past the rise of modern nations, past the crusades, past the temples of ancient Greece and the pyramids of Egypt, if you could trace your whole ancestry back *that* far, and then back that far again—then maybe you would find among that multitude of your ancestors the blind woman Kaikos, who, when she was a child, walked alone over a mountain in the snow, and carried a giant under another mountain in the dark, who once spoke with Dhegm, the mother of the earth, as easily as you would speak to me, and who made her own place and her own people when the Téuta wouldn't have her. It's possible, isn't it? That you are Kaikos' great, great, many-times great grandchild? Really, it's the most likely thing. It *is*.

Do the math, and you'll see.

ARCHEOLOGICAL AFTERWORD

First—absolutely first, before anything else—I have to remind anyone who dives into this afterword that the book is fiction. Although I did research the time period while writing about it, I am not an archeologist, and the Téuta villages, the new and the old and final village in the mountains, are all fictions based on no specific archeological site or discovery. I did try to at least be reasonable about the structures, the culture, the gods and the habits of Kaikos and Chaisa and the Téuta people, but I decided early on that anything that happened within a thousand years or a thousand miles of the story setting was fair game. So here I will only point out some of my excuses for the story as it's told and describe the village as I imagine it. Fortunately, while a good deal *is* known about the people who lived on earth 8200 years ago, there is also a good deal that we still guess at, and that leaves an ample space for our imaginations to comfortably expand and settle in.

Let's look first at the big issue, on which Kaikos' story is based: assigning blame. Scapegoating is an ancient human habit. It's probably been practiced since long before modern humans evolved, and it is still practiced now, in every country and with many names. It's always easy to blame whatever misfortunes arise in your life on someone else, or some other group, and, as we read in newspapers all over the world, sometimes this blaming becomes lethal. Blaming is both ancient and modern. Human sacrifice by one name or another is probably equally ancient, and equally modern.

The climate crisis described in the book, and for which Kaikos,

Chaisa and Welo were blamed, is now called the 8.2k event. It really did happen, apparently affecting climate all over the world (but particularly in the areas near the north Atlantic). It has been measured in Greenland ice cores and in many other ways. The name derives from the timing of the event. The central event began around 8,200 years BP-Before the Present. But BP is an odd way to measure time elapsed from any historical event, because "the present" is a moving target. To help resolve the confusion, "the present" in the archeological discussions is fixed at 1950 (implying, clearly, that archeologists are living in the past). 8200 BP is 8272 years before the date at the top of my computer screen as I write this. So, in this case, 8200 BP would be 6250 BCE. In the story I used 6262 BCE as the start of the temperature decline, and 6189 BCE as the end, which is probably off by a year or two at either end. But it's not important to debate the dates. The exact timing is not critical to the story.

The 8.2k event was not the ice age, and it also was not the deepest climate collapse after the ice age ended and the glaciers retreated. The Younger Dryas was much deeper. But the Younger Dryas also happened much earlier (12,900 to 11,700 BP) when humanity was more mobile; we were hunter-gatherers, and when the world turned colder, we could move south without too much drama. When the 8.2k event happened we had settled into more permanent communities, villages or towns that had been our homes for hundreds of years, with long-tended fields around us where we grew our crops. We were strongly invested in where we lived. Moving south to avoid the cold had a much bigger cost.

Named gods in the story are based on the Proto-Indo-European (PIE) pantheon, even though this is a people who probably didn't exist until well after Kaikos, Chaisa and Welo were gone. We have to surmise their existence from clues in the modern world; they left us no texts since they had no written language, and there is no specific archeological site that is known to be left by them. But their spoken language is the root for languages spoken from India through the

Middle East and all of Europe. It is the common linguistic ancestor of languages as distant as Sanskrit and Gaelic, German and Kurdish, Greek and Ukrainian.

One (sometime contested) view is that the Proto-Indo-Europeans lived somewhere in the steppes north of the Caspian Sea in the fourth or fifth millennium BCE. I didn't want to make up gods out of thin air to impose on a real historical time, so I used the gods the PIE are thought to have had in their beliefs about the world a thousand years or more after the time of the Téuta. Maybe the Téuta were *proto*-Proto-Indo-Europeans.

Only a few of the PIE gods are mentioned in this story. The most relevant, and the only one who becomes a character here, is called Dhegm in the story because I needed a short name for her, but she would have been called Dheghom Matr, mother earth or mother of the earth, by the Proto-Indo-Europeans. Dyeus Pter, the father of the shining sky, and Perkunos, the god of storm and weather, are drawn directly from the PIE pantheon; there was also Hewsos, the goddess of dawn, mentioned but not named in the story, and many others.

I should also mention that most of the names of characters are actually slightly mangled words from PIE. To create a new name, I just used the first characteristic that came to my mind about the new character and looked up that characteristic in PIE. For example, "beautiful" in PIE is "chaisos". And so Kaikos' mother, who is supposed to be quite attractive, is Chaisa. Kaikos, with no changes, means "blind". Sntejo means "think", because Sntejo was intended to be a thinker. Krepus is PIE for "strong". Prsedi's name came from prosedjom, which is PIE for "kindness". The name of the village, Téuta, is from the PIE word for "people"-so when they say they are the téuta they are simply saying they are the people, and the title of this book could mean The People's Child.

The Téuta clearly did some farming, but they also did some hunting and gathering in the open world around them, they kept sheep and they also fished in the river. This is not unrealistic; while agriculture had been emerging already for thousands of years, there was no strong reason for them to abandon all the other known ways to feed and clothe themselves. Peas and lentils were among the earliest garden crops, and early grains in Europe and the Middle East (including the area where the PIE are thought to have lived) were wheat and barley.

The Téuta houses and walls would most probably have been built of bricks formed with straw and mud, dried in the sun. Walls and structures built of rock are possible, and I did refer to Chaisa's hut in Chapter Three as having portions built from rocks. Maybe when Chaisa and Sntejo first found the spot where she and Kaikos would settle they built a simple shelter from the winds with whatever materials were at hand, and then spent the next weeks making mud bricks for the rest of the hut.

The huts would have been single rooms, basically, about twenty feet on a side, but with some internal dividing wall-sections to designate an area for food storage, for example, or for some other purpose. The interior walls would probably have been plastered to make them smooth and could have had artistic paintings on their surface. The floor, too, may have been plastered.

In my imagined version, the huts have no windows and very short doors that you would have to duck low to get through. There would be a hole in the roof to allow smoke to escape. That might sound like a very dark place, and it would be. But it's also a reasonable idea: the dwellings in Catalhoyuk, an excavation site in Turkey which was inhabited through the time of this story, had no windows, *and also had no doors*. The only opening into their houses was the smoke-hole in the ceiling, and there are sometimes clear markings of steps or ladders that led down from that hole into the room. People entered and left the huts through their chimneys.

(In the first chapter I refer to Prsedi as looking so fierce that a leopard would have been frightened—this was a very tiny nod to Catalhoyuk, where there were so many images of leopards that Ian Hodder, the head archeologist there, wrote a book about the site called *The Leopard's Tale*. A famous figurine of a woman was also found there, seated, naked and very fat with deep, drooping breasts, but her arms were resting on the backs of large cats, possibly leopards. Who was she? No one knows, really; many people see her as a mother goddess. Some even claim that a bulge at the base of her chair is a new child, and that she is in the act of giving birth, although to me that seems to be a strange thing to do while sitting comfortably upright and casually resting your arms on the backs of leopards. I don't want to dismiss it as impossible; a goddess can do whatever she wants. But when I look at pictures of this figurine, my own imagination sees her as real, as a very powerful and very respected living woman.)

Raghe's tall monolith outside his temple was prompted by descriptions of stones at Goblekli Tepe, another ancient site in Turkey.

The old Téuta, the village that was crushed under falling cliffs, was a community of about a thousand people, and the new Téuta—the survivors of that catastrophe—was reduced to about 300 to 400 people. This would have been a goodly cluster of humanity for the time, but not at all out of reason. Catalhoyuk, at its peak, is estimated to have had a population of between 3500 and 8000 people.

I often refer to Krepus as the Téuta's king, but with a lower-case k. He wasn't a head of state. Eight thousand years ago there were no states. But a village or town of any size does need some way to organize labor for public tasks, and it needs to have some way to settle disputes without bloodshed. In this story I imagine Krepus as having some worldly authority to do those things. His authority was no more than public habit, though. People just expected him to be in charge, partly because he was big, partly because he was known to be dedicated to the welfare of the Téuta and willing to be responsible for figuring out how to get things done, and also partly because, when he organized people to work on public tasks, he worked with them, as one of them, and did far more than his share of the work. He was king or leader because people knew, respected and trusted him.

One of the many cultural habits that we moderns might find discomfiting is the burial of the dead under the huts they lived in. But this was a common practice at that time. It wasn't the only place burials occurred, as is more or less implied in the story here; in fact, most people probably were buried outside settlements, and many were buried elsewhere in the settlement area. Some were interred inside walls, in fill areas for structures, and so on.

There were burials under doorways, too, as described in Chapter Four, and those burials were most often infants or young children. Not all infants were buried in doorways though; most of the discovered infant burials were elsewhere, either inside the huts, sometimes near the household chore area near the ovens, or in pits by the walls. But sometimes infants or young children (but rarely adults) were buried under a doorway.

Why mostly infants? I don't know. Maybe because infants were the only ones who would fit there, or maybe because they were valued but not yet part of the household, so burying them at the threshold of the house made sense. But it would be a clumsy place to bury someone, a clumsy place to try to dig if the doorway already existed, or if it did not then placing a door over an existing interment would require significant planning. We might speculate that only a special circumstance or a special purpose would justify that kind of effort. I took the easy way out in Chapter Four and treated it as a kind of ritualistic protection magic, setting the infants up as door guardians. But that was a description that fit the fiction, nothing more. There is no reason to believe that was really why a few infants and children were buried under doorways.

Chaisa and Welo made excellent *and beautiful* clay pottery. Most of the earliest pottery was functional, not decorative; early pots were plain and sturdy. But I said at the outset that, since this is a book of fiction, I thought anything that happened within a thousand years or a thousand miles of the story setting was fair game. Decorated pottery was not far off from the time of the Téuta. The Hassuna and later the Halaf cultures in Iraq, for example, made high quality and highly decorated pottery at about the time of this story or within a thousand years after it. Allowing Chaisa to be an accomplished potter, allowing her to be known to make high quality and beautifully decorated pottery, is well within the limits of my fair game.

Finally, since we've returned to my distance-from-time-and-place condition for fair game, and since I have specified a time for this story, we might ask *where* the story happened? What was the place?

I don't know. I didn't decide the Téuta's location before I wrote, and while I was writing I didn't think very much about it. But after the story was written, I've had a few discussions with people trying to locate the Téuta, and you are welcome to join the conversation with your own guess.

We know a few things. The Téuta lived near mountains and near a river. The names of the characters and the names of the gods are Proto-Indo-European, a group which may have lived in the steppes north of the Caspian Sea. Some of the physical structures, and the farming, the pottery and other characteristics of the Téuta, while entirely made up, were prompted, at least, by things I read about villages or towns like Catalhoyuk in Turkey, or by other towns scattered across the Middle East. Where is the Téuta then? I still don't know. Wendy, who is one of my beta readers and also my older sister, thinks it is somewhere near the northernmost Zagros mountains, a chain of mountains which runs down through western Iran starting from a point near the Black Sea. I want to argue for the area with the Black Sea on the west and the Caspian Sea on the east, the Greater Caucasus mountains to the north and the Lesser Caucasus mountains to the south—in other words, I would place them somewhere in modern day Georgia or Azerbaijan. But I'm not fixed on those as the only possible locations. Maybe the mountains Kaikos fled into were the Urals, or the Pyrenees, or the Alps. I'm open to any reasonable suggestion.

ACKNOWLEDGMENTS

Like anything humans are involved in, writers heatedly debate the craft with each other: plot vs. character, point of view, physical vs. psychological, how much show vs. how much tell. One of the most contentious differences among fiction writers is the cleavage between plotters, who like to organize the story first and then write it, and pantsers, who just sit down and write, hoping that whatever comes out has a plot (writing by just putting your pants on the chair). I'm a pantser, and I'll tell you up front that I hate plotting. I tell everyone that. And I tell everyone that writing a novel is hard work.

But I'm lying about both of those things. I do hate plotting the way all the how-to-write-a-novel books say it should be done, by making outlines or lists, or writing events on index cards and organizing them scene by scene into a sensible, well-planned order. If plotting had to be done that way, I would never have written this book, or any book. Still, what I did was at some level plotting, wasn't it? It must have been. The book does have a plot. Here's how I did that: I wrote whatever came out, and then beat it into submission through each long day, and then, that evening at dinner, as I sipped my wine, I revisited it, and thought about what could come next.

I wasn't eating alone, though. Night after night, I dragged my wife 8000 years into the past to discuss what Kaikos or Chaisa or Sntejo had done or what they would do next, or how to get them to do what I knew they had to do, or about whatever book I was reading about Neolithic lives or minds. And night after night, she responded with both patience and curiosity, and sometimes with disputes about whether the characters would have done what I had made them do or could ever do the things I thought they needed to do. That's how I plotted this book, and that's how I wrote it.

In the end I did organize things, of course, but by then the book was more than half finished. By then I *knew* what was happening, and I knew where the plot was going. The plot had emerged organically, and I was "plotting" in the ordinary sense only to make sure events had the time they needed to unfold, or that they didn't occur before all the other events that caused them. And guess what? That was *fun*. Every part of it was fun. Hard work? It was hard, that part is true, and it took time, but hard *work?* Not really. The old adage is that if you're having fun, it isn't really work.

So the first person I should recognize in this acknowledgement section has to be my wife Barbara for making that whole process fun. I probably *could* have written this in isolation. But it wouldn't have been nearly as much fun, and so it wouldn't have been nearly as good.

The next stage in evolving a book is revision; nothing is good as a first draft. Revision *is* work. Real work. Hard work. Ugly, dispiriting work.

The first revisions can be done by the writer, but a writer is far too close to the words to see all their flaws. It has to be read by others, first by beta readers (friends, associates, family, who agree to read through the book and tell you what they think), and then by professional editors.

So thanks to all my beta readers (Wendy, Jadis, Polly, Dan, Katy and Gage). And finally, thanks to Kathryn Johnson, who gave me a "critical read" from a professional novelist and made significant suggestions, and to Anna Bierhaus, who provided a strong, professional developmental edit to the final work. These two women pushed me to create chapters that did not exist when they read the book, and to accept some of the hardest and best revisions in the long process of creating Kaikos' world and telling her story.